A Cruising Affair

by

Mandy Lee Sim

The right of Mandy Lee Sim to be identified as the author of this
work has been asserted by her in accordance with Section 78
of the Copyright, Designs and Patents Act 1988

The book cover picture is copyright to Gino Santa Maria

This book is published by
Grosvenor House Publishing Ltd
28-30 High Street, Guildford, Surrey, GU1 3EL.
www.grosvenorhousepublishing.co.uk

A CIP record for this book
is available from the British Library

ISBN 978-1-78148-436-4

In honour of my father Mr George Alexander Sim who took his own life aged 52.

I will be donating a percentage of all royalties received from the sales of my book to a children's charity very close to his heart.

Dad you are always in my thoughts.

Chapter 1

'For God's sake, wake up!' Ben's voice ripped through the silence of Sasha's sleep, shattering the peacefulness of her bed. He whipped off the duvet and shook it to within an inch of its life. 'We're going to miss the bloody flight!'

It was just after 5.00am and the alarm hadn't gone off. As if to emphasise that, a series of long and strident blasts from a car horn outside told them that the pre-ordered taxi was already at the door, the driver was becoming increasingly impatient.

Half-dressed, Ben rushed to the window. He leaned dangerously out. 'All right, just a minute!'

'Okay, okay. You take your time, mate,' was the helpful response from the balding, overweight fifty-something year old taxi driver. 'It's not me who needs to catch a flight.'

Ben rushed back to the bed. 'Sasha. C'mon. Get up.'

'Okay, okay. You don't have to shout. I heard you all the way to Heathrow.'

'Gatwick.'

'Whatever.'

'Well move it then!'

Half asleep, she sprang from her bed and tried to go two ways at once, mouth agape, uncoordinated limbs; a picture of human confusion. Eventually, when it was clear that that wasn't getting her anywhere, she peeled off left and headed full-tilt for the bathroom debating if there was still time to wash her hair, with Ben's voice booming out in the background as he repeatedly cursed the over-packed suitcases at his feet. There was panic in their voices.

1

The house was freezing. The timer for the heating didn't come on until six. It had been a reasonably mild winter, but the heavy frost on the car windows outside was a strong indication that the weather was starting to change for the worse.

They had allowed two and a half hours for the check-in at the airport terminal instead of the recommended three, so Sasha was probably being hopefully irrational by suggesting a shower before racing like a lunatic to catch their flight to Barbados. But within ten minutes, the hurricane in their apartment had died to little more than a whirlwind. They were washed, dressed and almost respectable looking.

'Passports?' said Ben. 'Where are the passports?'

'Here, I've got them.'

'Tickets?'

'In my bag. Look, stop panicking. We're good to go.'

'I'm not panicking!' he screamed. Then looked round with fresh alarm. 'My wallet! Damn, where did I put my wallet?'

'Over there, on the table,' said Sasha, forcing herself to stay calm. 'Beside your keys.'

'Okay, I've got them. Now let's go. Pass me the cases.'

Sasha grabbed one, and then the other. Ben reached out and got a purchase on one.

'Jesus, Sasha, what have you got in here? They weigh a tonne!'

'No they don't. I've already weighed them, and they're fine. Just keep calm.'

'We're already over an hour late,' said Ben, his eyes roving around the room for anything else they might have forgotten, such as mobile phones, foreign currency, and their sense of humour.

'And whose fault is that?'

Ben said nothing and simply headed for the door, his keys rattling between his teeth. Two minutes later they were sitting in the back of the Mercedes cab.

Without further ado, the taxi driver stamped on the accelerator and launched them off down the road. Sasha took the hint and motioned to Ben to put on a seatbelt. It looked like it was going to be one hell of a ride.

As they hurtled along, the atmosphere between them in the car was hostile. But Ben decided to forgo any further conversation until he was safely inside the airport and standing in front of the check-in desk, bags loaded onto the carousel with his boarding card safely in his hand.

* * *

Thirty minutes later the dark blue Mercedes cab screeched to a halt outside the departure hall at Gatwick airport. Ben threw the luggage onto an abandoned trolley, set it rolling and raced through the rotating door.

Back in the cab, Sasha was opening her purse.

'Just call it seventy love,' said the driver, smirking. 'Need a receipt?'

'No. And you obviously don't need a tip.'

With no time to argue over the extortionate charge, and Ben nowhere in sight to back her up, Sasha reluctantly handed over the fare.

'Good luck,' said the driver. 'Better hope you catch your flight. The weather's due to change by the weekend. Snow forecast, I believe.'

'Really, I thought we were in for a heat wave,' Sasha replied, now exiting the vehicle and eagerly warming her ice-cold hands inside her long leather coat.

The airport was packed. Travellers were hurrying in all directions between the check-in desks and the departure gates, the car hire desks and the coffee bars and restaurants. The queue at security was overflowing into the departures hall. If they were going to make this flight, things were going to have to move a little more quickly.

As the revolving door spun continuously behind her, Sasha saw in the distance Ben's distinctive blue puffa jacket and faded blue jeans. The jacket wasn't going to be much use in the baking hot Caribbean sunshine, but was essential for surviving these bitterly cold winter mornings. As she approached, Ben was slouched over the trolley staring at the departures screen. Closer still, she could see their flight at the top of the list.

BA 2155 06.40 Barbados Gate 34C Now Boarding – Check In Closed.

'Oh, that's fantastic! Absolutely bloody great!' Sasha could feel the tension as she looked round at Ben. His teeth were gritted in anger. His well-defined jaw line was quivering like a lion about to strike its prey. The look he gave her was one of pure anger and hatred, and it was obvious that there was no doubt in his mind who he blamed for this terrible situation.

'If you hadn't stayed up so late packing, we wouldn't have overslept,' he said. 'You should have been more organised, Sasha. I can't bloody well believe this.'

You can't believe this? Nothing to do with the fact that the alarm clock you apparently set didn't go off and that's why we slept in! Thought Sasha.

'Marvellous,' continued Ben, 'there goes our cruise. Honestly, Sasha, how many times do I need to tell you that leaving things to the last minute always results in chaos? This is all your fault.'

Mortified by her fiancé's outburst, Sasha stood silent hoping any minute now he would calm down and stop yelling. But he didn't calm down, not even slightly. He went on and on about the thirty minutes they should have allowed for bad traffic, for breaking down, for punctures, or – God forbid – an earthquake to tear up the M23 during their fifty minute journey to the airport.

Thinking about it now, they really should have allowed an extra hour in case the weather turned unexpectedly nasty during the night, Sasha decided. But it was definitely too late for recriminations. The argument was very one-sided, but the situation was bad enough. There wasn't any point in adding fuel to the fire.

This really was a dreadful predicament to be in at the best of times, least of all at six o'clock on a cold, dark January morning without so much as a cup of coffee in sight.

The crazy thing was, Sasha never really wanted to go, anyway. Well, that wasn't exactly true. She had wanted to go on the Caribbean cruise that they had booked two years earlier, but just not with Ben.

As she stood in the departures hall, blinking hard to stop the tears from streaming down her face, she tried to devise an alternate plan. She knew British Airways had two flights leaving for Barbados that morning. All they had to do was get hold of a member of check-in staff and ask if there was any room on the later one. Two last minute flights to the Caribbean wouldn't be cheap, but they would be nothing compared to what they were about to throw away if they didn't join the ship.

Anyway, they were here now, packed and ready to leave. The ship was due to remain berthed at the port in Barbados until 8.30pm. It would undoubtedly be a tight connection, but there was still time to get there, time to salvage the cruise.

Unwilling to let Sasha try and resolve the terrible mess they had got themselves into, Ben picked up his brown leather hand baggage, threw it over his shoulder, took hold of his suitcase and, without speaking a word, disappeared into the crowd.

＊　＊　＊

Penny hated flying and hadn't realized how much her job would involve travelling when, one month earlier, she accepted it. But there was something about travelling business class that made the experience a whole lot more enjoyable. So far, during the flight, Nadia, the very attractive flight attendant, had offered everyone a glass of champagne while they made themselves comfortable in their exceptionally large, fully reclining chairs. The legroom was hugely impressive compared to the normally cramped economy experience. Nadia then continued to serve a selection of drinks from the bar, while the passengers browsed over the menu deciding what they would like for lunch.

To start, Penny opted for the antipasti, followed by the fillet steak with porcini mushrooms and red wine jus. The meal was accompanied by a selection of fine wines from the bar. Nadia then offered a choice of crème brûlée, or cheese and biscuits to finish, accompanied by coffee and liquors.

The meal was fantastic. It lasted almost two hours, which perfectly suited Penny. After lunch, she lay back in her chair reclining it ninety degrees to a comfortable position before dozing off for a good hour and a half. The timing was perfect. She woke just in time to catch the start of *The Departed*, a movie she had been looking forward to watching since it was released last summer. With Leonardo Di Caprio and Matt Damon to keep her entertained, it couldn't be a bad choice.

As the movie concluded, Nadia began preparing the cabin for afternoon tea. Penny was surprised how keen most passengers were, eagerly participating even after such a large lunch, but it seemed that most of them were prepared to have a go anyway.

The last two hours of the flight passed relatively quickly, and the plane landed on schedule at Barbados airport. As the cabin doors opened and the crew secured the stairs for the passengers to disembark the aircraft, the initial blast of heat that filled the plane was exhilarating. Penny, who was definitely more prepared than some of the other passengers, removed her cashmere pullover, rolled up the sleeves of her blouse and unbuttoned the top few buttons. She then placed her sunglasses over her eyes in preparation for the strong sunlight that she was about to encounter.

After a short bus ride to the terminal, she passed through passport control without too much of a wait, collected her baggage from the carousel and left the airport in the direction of the taxi rank.

* * *

'Welcome to Barbados,' said the first in a large group of taxi drivers. 'Where would you like to go, gorgeous?'

'Ocean Magic, please,' Penny replied, feeling a little self conscious as several of the taxi drivers, who you would think had never set eyes on a female before, pointed and sniggered at her while she made her way into the first in a long line of taxis.

'No problem. You want a tour of the island first? Bridge Town? Christ Church? St Lawrence Gap? You name it, I'll take you there, lovely.'

'No, thanks. Maybe another time, huh?'

'All right. Ocean Magic it is.'

Sam, possibly the friendliest taxi driver Penny had ever come across, interrogated her all the way to the cruise terminal. With her shoulder length layered blonde hair and piercing blue eyes, Penny had a strong resemblance to Sienna Miller.

Sam was convinced that he had picked up the genuine article. Rarely a month would pass without someone staring, or even stopping her in the street to tell her how much she resembled the talented actress.

Airports were the worst place. That was where people expected to see celebrities passing through, and exotic locations like the Caribbean – especially at this time of year – were the sort of locales you would read in *Hello* and *People* magazine about holidaying Hollywood stars such as Sienna.

'That's twenty-five dollars,' said Sam, when they arrived, 'and here's my card in case you change your mind about that tour.'

'Thanks,' replied Penny as she handed over two twenty-dollar notes.

The money was difficult to make out. The notes were all the same size and colour. She remembered that she had thought the same thing a few years ago when she had spent the summer working in New York as an au pair.

Outside, the pink-coloured L-shaped cruise terminal oozed Caribbean charm. Several small beach huts were offering Carib lager for two dollars a bottle, or ten dollars for a bucket of six, while others were standing by hoping to sell some last minute beachwear and loud Caribbean shirts to unprepared passengers before they set sail for their first port of call.

Inside, the terminal was decorated from top to bottom with Christmas trees and various yuletide decorations while the resident quayside band were playing 'We wish you a merry Christmas' on steel drums – which felt a little strange considering the clear blue sky and the soaring temperature outside. Apart from that, Christmas and New Year were well and truly over with for another year, but the locals were obviously determined to keep the celebrations going for as long as possible.

Penny made her way past the first stage of security and stood in a long queue at the other side of the cruise terminal waiting patiently to go through the grey metal detector archway before boarding the ship.

Sam, the taxi driver, had taken charge of handing over her luggage to a member of the ship's company who, in turn, instructed a colleague to label and deliver the case to the allocated cabin. This enabled Penny to walk a great deal more freely, unencumbered by the thirty kilos of clothes, shoes, and other items she deemed essential for her two weeks onboard.

Most of the other passengers had flown out on a charter flight from one of the nominated airports. London, Manchester, Birmingham and Glasgow were among the choices available. The flights, should one wish to accept them, were included as part of the cruise package. Having got to know each other during the flight, the group members were all chatting away. On her flight, Penny had spoken briefly to a couple from Dublin. They were going to Sandy Lane on their honeymoon. The other two couples that sat within earshot were also staying in Barbados on holiday.

The three hundred metre long cruise ship stood nineteen decks tall, a colossal vessel berthed at the dockside. Penny stood patiently trying to work out where her cabin would be. The cabin number was C16, so she knew it was on the starboard side of Deck 9 near the front of the ship. She counted up the decks, and was fairly certain she could locate it. The queue moved a little faster than she had anticipated and, before she knew it, she was standing in the grand atrium on Deck 5.

'Welcome onboard, madam.' A trim-looking officer placed colourful lei over her head and smiled. 'I hope you enjoy your time with us onboard Ocean Magic.'

Penny smiled back. 'Thank you.'

For the next fifteen minutes, she stood motionless, carefully surveying the eight large glass lifts, each moving and stopping at different levels. The mammoth waterfall fountain was the centrepiece of this astounding atrium. Adjacent to it were four sets of winding stairs leading up over four or five levels of shops, bars, restaurants, cafes and various other public rooms. It was breath – taking.

Deck 6 hosted the main reception, the tours and excursions desk, and the internet café. Deck 7 boasted a large shopping arcade complete with its own champagne bar, cocktail lounge and several other casual dinning outlets, including a speciality tapas bar and exclusive sushi lounge to give one the impression of shopping on Rodeo Drive in Beverly Hills, California.

Throughout, the décor was contemporary with a fantastic combination of neutral and dark furnishings to give a relaxed and tranquil feel to the endless selection of rooms. Penny, a little overwhelmed at the sheer size and presence of the mighty vessel, followed a group of excited passengers into one of the lifts.

'Wow! It's the size of New York,' a fair haired little boy said to his sister as he pressed his face against the front of the glass lift.

When the lift stopped at Deck 9, Penny excused herself and made her way down the long, narrow corridor towards her cabin.

The cabin key worked first time, which was an added bonus. Penny smiled as she opened the door. She couldn't remember the last time she had stayed in a hotel where she didn't have to about-turn and go back to reception to get the card reprogrammed.

She spent the first twenty minutes exploring her home for the next two weeks. Impressed by the beautiful floral display and the bottle of champagne she found waiting by the bed, she opened the card and read:

Dear Penny, We hope the flight went well. Enjoy the rest of your day. Looking forward to seeing you tomorrow.
Danny, Josh and Katie x

* * *

There was a loud knock on the cabin door. Sasha's heart skipped a beat. For a second she thought it might have been Ben. Catching her breath, she cautiously opened the door and was greeted by a rather friendly and immaculately presented member of the ship's crew.

'Good Afternoon, Ms Carter. I'm Joe, your cabin steward and I'll be looking after you for the duration of the cruise.'

'Oh. Hi, Joe. Nice to meet you.'

Joe smiled. He had perfect teeth and clearly knew it. 'Your suitcase has arrived.'

'Great. Can I have it?'

'Yes madam, it's right here'

'That's fantastic, thanks'

'Would you like me to get you anything else?'

'Such as?'

'More tea or coffee, perhaps? Or maybe a different brand?'

'No, I... I don't think so,' said Sasha, gently attempting to close the door.

'And your companion, madam?' Joe called out. 'Mr Benjamin. Will he be arriving shortly?'

She stopped closing the door and gazed thoughtfully at those perfect teeth.

'Uhm, no. I'm afraid there has been a change of plan. It's just going to be me.'

'Very well, madam. Enjoy your stay onboard Ocean Magic. And remember, if you need anything at all, please don't hesitate to ask. And if I'm not around, you can page me. My number is beside the phone.'

Sasha nodded and gently closed the door and stood for a moment composing herself. The flight had gone well, all things considered. It hadn't been as luxurious as she had hoped, but she knew she was lucky to get any seat at all on the later flight, let alone one with extra legroom as she had originally booked. The two glasses of wine she had enjoyed during the flight, coupled with the four-hour time difference, were helping make light of what was far from an ideal situation. But she had to know if Ben was regretting his decision to leave her alone at the airport. What had he expected? That she would follow him home, apologise profusely, begging him to forgive her for something she hadn't done?

Well that was never going to happen. He probably just needed a little time to cool off, and then he could join the ship in another port of call. Once again, this was far from ideal, but he could make it possibly to St Lucia tomorrow, or Mayreau on Monday.

After making a second cup of strong black coffee, Sasha unpacked her laptop and organised it. Sitting back in her chair, she logged on to her email on the off-chance Ben had made contact.

* * *

At dinner that night, it was made quite apparent that someone was missing from the already prepared table for eight. While the group introduced themselves, the restaurant manager cleared the spare table setting and apologised for the mistake. Edna and William Cockburn, a couple of senior citizens from cabin A180 began the introductions. This was their eighteenth cruise together. They had sampled the fleet several times, and were classed as 'Gold Club Cruisers' – which basically meant they got invited to lots of cocktail parties and enjoyed a special lunch, which was laid on for them to meet their fellow regular cruisers.

'Nice to meet you,' Sasha replied, keen to move on and meet the second couple. This was Kris and his partner Megan, and it was their first cruise, which drew a rather frosty reception from Mrs Cockburn.

'How could they possibly put first time cruisers on our table?' she said, then glanced at her husband. 'William, did you hear me?'

'I heard you Edna,' he replied, 'and so did everyone else. Now please just be quiet.'

Mrs Cockburn winced at the thought, while William tried hard to ignore his wife.

'Kris is in the police service,' Megan continued, 'and I'm a teacher.'

This, however, did seem to meet Mrs Cockburn's approval. Kris and Megan also lived relatively close to the Cockburn's, which drew a second nod of approval from the old lady.

Sasha was quite excited to meet the third couple, which were Richard and his wife Lucy. They had a surreal but somewhat understated aura about them. They just seemed so happy and perfectly suited to one another. Sasha looked at them a little longer than she had realized, thinking about Ben, and how much they used to be like Richard and Lucy. Now she was here alone, sitting at a table of strangers while her fiancé was back home in bitterly cold England.

'Sasha, isn't it?' Richard said, interrupting her thoughts.

'Yes, sorry. Sasha Carter.'

Richard smiled.

'So what brings you to the Caribbean on your own?' Mrs Cockburn asked wasting no time in butting into the conversation.

'I quite often holiday alone,' Sasha said, blushing ever so slightly at the little white lie she wasn't remotely prepared for telling. It had come out so unexpectedly.

Richards's wife Lucy, however, was extremely quick off the mark and rushed in to help her dining partner by raising her glass to toast the holiday. As the others joined her, Sasha felt the intensity of the intended interrogation dissolve. Lucy flashed Sasha a friendly smile.

'Thanks,' she whispered, as she sat back in her chair and began to relax.

Dinner passed off relatively peacefully, certainly better than she had anticipated. There was, of course, the odd remark here and there about single women holidaying alone, and the image it portrayed. These comments came from Edna Cockburn, actually, but no one encouraged the shallow remarks, and at every opportunity ignored the old woman.

After dinner, Sasha excused herself from the table and returned to her generously sized cabin. She had received a free upgrade at the time of booking an 'early bird booking bonus'. That was what the girl at the travel agency had told her. Not that she needed half the space. The huge double bed and the three-piece suite only emphasised the fact she was here on her own.

Alone.

Dinner had been a confusing mix of pleasure and grief. She simply needed a little time on her own now. Out on her balcony, Sasha sat wrapped in her fluffy white bathrobe sipping a Bombay sapphire with slim line tonic. Once he realized she would be travelling alone, Joe, her cabin steward, had left a small selection of drinks for her as a welcome-on-board gesture. As she watched the waves cascading against the side of the 106,000 tonne cruise ship, she desperately wanted to call Ben. It had just gone 11.00pm, local time, which meant it was 3.00am back home.

She decided against calling, and opened her laptop instead. There was a slight chance he might have emailed her while she was at dinner. She keyed in her password, and froze for a second not knowing what she wanted the email to say.

The thought of leaving Ben behind earlier made her stomach churn. She began to feel a little sick at the thought of how callous she had been. How would anyone ever understand what she had done? And had she just made the biggest mistake of her life?

Maybe Edna Cockburn had been right after all. What possible good could come from a single woman cruising the Caribbean on her own? No good, that's what.

No good at all.

Chapter 2

St Lucia 08:00 Arrival 17:30 Departure

By seven the following morning Penny was up and about. Josh had been awake since six. Keen to explore the ship, and not realizing the time, he had picked up the phone and called Penny. He wanted to arrange for her to join Katie and himself at nine o'clock and take a tour of the ship.

Three days earlier, Danny and the kids had flown out allowing them to spend some time together in Barbados before joining Ocean Magic. The arrangement for the cruise was a little different from the contract Danny had drawn up one month earlier when he agreed to take Penny on as his full time nanny.

Penny lived with the family when they were at home, and was provided with her own accommodation when the family were on holiday. The hours were a lot more flexible too, as Danny was keen to spend some quality time with his children while he wasn't working.

'Hurry up Katie, will you stop playing with your food and just eat it,' Josh snapped at his little sister.

'Leave your sister alone to finish her breakfast,' said Danny.

'But in less than five minutes we're meant to be meeting Penny. She might think we're not coming.'

'I'm sure she will wait Josh. Anyway you have two weeks to explore the ship.'

'Fine,' Josh agreed hastily, signalling to his sister to finish eating. And behind Danny's back; *'Penny's waiting for us, you idiot.'*

'Finished,' Katie announced as she enthusiastically left the table.

'Okay. Have fun kids.' Danny winked at Josh then kissed Katie on the cheek.

'We will, dad,' they replied.

'And Josh, you are in charge of Katie until you meet Penny. Do you understand?'

Josh made a face. 'Yes. Okay. I understand.'

'Oh, and Josh...'

'Yes, dad.' Josh turned once more in the direction of his father. 'What is it?'

'It's that way, son,' Danny laughed as he pointed in the opposite direction to where they were heading.

'Right. Of course, I knew that!' Josh took his little sister by the hand and led her out of the dinning room.

'Are you our new mummy,' Katie squinted at Penny, her little forehead creased as she looked up and waited in anticipation for Penny to answer.

'Don't be stupid, Katie,' said Josh. 'Penny's our new nanny. You know that.'

'That's enough, Josh,' said Penny. 'Apologise to your sister, please.'

'Sorry, stupid,' Josh sniggered to himself as he sprinted up the stairs two steps at a time.

Katie shook her head in dismay as her brother pushed open the door onto the open deck.

The warm Caribbean breeze was exceptionally inviting compared to the frigid draft from the air conditioning inside. It tasted fresh and salty and hopeful. Penny placed Katie's sunglasses over her eyes and suggested Josh did the same. Reluctantly he agreed. He removed them from his head where he had been wearing them all morning, perfectly placed, to allow his blonde hair to peak in the middle.

'But I want to tell you a secret about mummy, is that ok?' said Katie.

'Of course it is, sweetheart.'

Katie signalled for Penny to crouch down to her level and reached out to cover her ear with her tiny hands.

'I miss her,' she whispered. 'Is she dead?'

Penny, who had only been briefly informed about Danny's separation from his wife, was taken aback by Katie's question. She realized for the first time how confused the break-up had become in the four-year-old's head.

'No, darling. She's not dead. She's just gone away for a while, but if you miss her, I'm sure we can arrange for you to call and speak to her.'

'Daddy said mummy's not coming back, so I think she must be dead.'

The poor child had convinced herself her mother was dead and everyone else was carrying on as normal as if nothing had changed. Danny obviously has no idea what his daughter had been going through.

Josh was a keen swimmer. He was standing by the family pool wearing a pair of loud Quicksilver shorts; a pair of flip-flops, and a blue and white striped Ralph Lauren t-shirt. He was pretending to be swimming breaststroke and making exaggerated movements with his arms as he hopped between his feet.

'Come on, Josh, let's explore the children's area before we get changed for a swim.'

'I love swimming,' called a little voice, as Katie started swinging her arms about like her brother.

'But I don't have any wings with me.'

'That's okay, darling. I was thinking that I might teach you to swim during the cruise. What do you think?'

Katie could barely contain herself as Penny marched them along the deck towards the children's department.

'I'd love to swim like Josh can,' she squealed with enthusiasm, thrilled at the prospect of being able to swim like her brother.

The onboard children's facilities were fantastic. There was a team of eighteen youth leaders employed to look after the children 24/7. The parents brought their children along and signed them into the care of the department and, after that, rarely saw them during the cruise. Penny had wondered why Danny had gone to the expense of flying her business class to Barbados; then providing her with her own cabin, the cost of which was in excess of four thousand pounds. Yet she knew the children would most likely choose to be in the care of the youth leaders, instead of their nanny.

Katie looked pleasantly surprised when she stepped inside The Play House, a room designed specifically for two to five year olds. It was bright and airy, with an endless supply of toys, books, arts and craft paraphernalia and musical instruments. There was also a large soft play area with a slide that led down to a huge colourful ball pool, all specifically designed for the children to tire themselves out in.

'I won't need to wear my wings in there,' Katie giggled with excitement as a slightly smaller child with messy blonde hair walked towards her with a wet paintbrush. Stacy, the youth leader, was straight on to him and prised the brush out of the child's hand before the little boy painted Katie and her beautiful new yellow summer dress she was wearing for the first time.

Next-door was the Hide Away for the six to nine-year-olds. Josh had asked if it would be possible to go into the next age group. He was nine and a half and felt the eight and nine year olds in the Hide Away were too immature for him. His dad had very kindly left it up to Penny to make the decision. The only concern with allowing him to hang out in The Club was the fact that there was no signing-in policy. That would make it difficult to keep track of his whereabouts during the cruise, and that in turn meant the parents needed to directly monitor their children's comings and goings from the department.

'Oh please can I go to The Club, Penny?' said Josh. 'I'll behave, I promise.'

Penny looked at him sceptically.

'Okay, but on one condition, Josh.'

'What is it? I'll do anything.'

'You must be back in your cabin every night by ten o'clock. That's an absolute deadline, and if for any reason you're late, you'll be demoted to the Hide Away where your father and I can keep track of you. Do you understand?'

'What's demoted?' said Katie.

'Sent back,' said Penny.

'It's a deal,' said Josh. Excited by his negotiating skills, he squeezed Penny's hand.

'Thanks. I won't let you down. I promise.'

Josh and Katie collected their welcome packs from the officer in charge of the department, and eagerly began studying the programme of activities scheduled for the cruise. They had read about so many games, sports, music activities and events in the brochure. They had to make sure that some of them were going to take place during their cruise.

Meanwhile, Penny encouraged them to leave the children's department and get ready for a swim.

By eleven o'clock, Danny had found himself a sun lounger by the family pool. He topped up his sun cream and sat back to watch the children enjoy themselves.

Danny was an incredibly talented travel writer and dedicated father, not to mention somewhat good-looking with his slightly long, dark brown hair, brown eyes and year round tan. Although he had never set foot inside a gym in his life, he was also blessed with a lean and perfectly toned physique; a body most men would give their right arm for.

When Danny wasn't locked away in his office writing, he would spend a lot of time away from home travelling and researching his next book. He did his best to limit the travelling to Europe, but on rare occasions, his work took him slightly further afield.

Danny's work routine, although far from ideal being married with two young children, had been working reasonably well. He would generally spend two to three weeks away, then a month to six weeks at home. Writing about his latest experience. He tried his best to stick to this routine allowing him to spend as much time as possible with his family. He was also fairly flexible when it came to Josh's school and Katie's kindergarten holidays. If he had to go away unexpectedly, he would always try to fly his wife Victoria, and the children, out for a long weekend to spend time with him.

Although far from ideal, Danny's wife also worked full time as a personal assistant for a very highbrow advertising company.

But a few months ago, and completely out of the blue, Victoria admitted to having an affair with her much older but nevertheless charming boss. She had also, much to her surprise, fallen pregnant with his child.

Victoria had worked with Parker for the past eight years. Danny had always known they had an unusually close working and personal relationship, but had never felt threatened. He had often encouraged Victoria to accompany Parker to various business dinners, and even on numerous last minute business trips abroad. Because he was away from home so often, he felt it only fair his wife had the opportunity to attend foreign business trips whenever the opportunity arose.

Parker's wife, Angela, was clearly as oblivious to the affair as Danny. She frequently turned up unexpectedly with a steak pie or chicken casserole for Danny and the kid's expressing guilt that her husband had once again dragged Victoria away from her family for a couple of days.

Danny had taken the news of the affair badly. Well aware that he was away from home a lot, but only ever due to work commitments, it had come as one hell of a shock. He didn't have the slightest inclination his wife would contemplate having an affair, and quite often listened to her passing remarks about the neighbours, or people at work, who were rumoured to be playing away from home.

Victoria had practically floored Danny with the news. After spending two and a half weeks in Rome working on his latest book, he had returned home late one evening. The trip had gone well, and he arrived armed with a bouquet of flowers and a bottle of champagne. He had bought these for his wife at the airport; only to get home and find Victoria waiting for him at the front door with her suitcases packed and mind made up she was leaving. Confused and distressed by what was happening, Danny literally begged his wife to stay. But Victoria wouldn't even entertain a conversation. She was sorry for what she had done. But it was over. She was leaving. Goodbye.

It wasn't until three weeks later when Danny bumped into Victoria at the Health Centre that he came to realize the whole sordid truth. Outraged by the discovery that his wife was pregnant with another man's child, Danny filed immediately for divorce. At the same time, he applied for custody of Josh and Katie.

Victoria didn't stand in his way. She didn't put up a fight. She was quite prepared to let him proceed; convinced he would struggle to look after a nine-year-old boy and a four-year-old girl.

Josh and Katie, although not fully understanding why their parents were no longer living together, knew that if their mother was prepared to just walk away from them, then they were almost certainly better off with their father. Josh understood it wasn't that his mother didn't love him any more, but that she had fallen out of love with his father. At least that's what he told Jack, his best friend at Tae Kwon Do class, the night after his mother left.

Danny did his best to be honest with the children, but at the same time wanted to protect them from the complicated divorce that was sure to follow. Thankfully, Josh had shown a great deal of maturity dealing with the separation, which in turn rubbed off on Katie. Obviously, they had their moments, but Danny seemed to manage to keep them under control.

To enable him to continue working, Danny immediately hired a nanny. He had hoped to prevent the children's routine from being disrupted any more than it had to be, but the arrangement between him and Josephina, their first nanny, really hadn't worked out. She was completely wrong. Danny had hired her based upon her looks rather than qualifications. It was a feeble attempt to make himself feel better, and hopefully get back at his wife believing she would inevitably change her mind and want him and the children back. It was something he longed to hear her say, but would take ultimate satisfaction in declining.

He knew Josh and Katie would automatically be drawn to Josephina because of her long dark hair, ocean blue eyes and model like figure. He hoped in turn they would prefer to be with her, rather than running back to their mother. Josephina, however, proved to be a complete liability, and on several occasions acted totally irresponsibly, often punishing Josh and Katie for petty crimes as an excuse to send them to bed early and get them out of the way.

Danny knew things weren't going as well as he had hoped, and deep down he knew he had to get rid of Josephina. But he struggled to find sufficient evidence to justify sacking her. One Thursday afternoon, however, when he came home early from a short trip to Venice, he found her drunk and entertaining a feisty young man on the sofa. They had just enjoyed a candle lit dinner of Greek salad, and one of Jamie Oliver's prime aged rib eye steaks. Danny had bought the steak in Sainsbury's earlier that week. He had planned to cook it on Saturday night, and then kick back with a movie and a glass of red wine while Josh and Katie were at their grandparents for a sleepover.

To once again accommodate Josephina's private life, Josh and Katie had been sent to bed with a bag of tortilla chips for dinner. This really was all the justification Danny needed to instantly dismiss her. Unwilling to even listen to Josephina's slurred excuses and feeble attempt to keep her job, he had thrown her and her latest conquest out into the street before unwinding for the evening with what was left of his two hundred and fifty pound bottle of XO brandy.

The little bitch had gone too far this time, he told himself as he picked up the paper and began looking for a replacement nanny.

Thankfully, Penny was proving to be a Godsend compared to Josephina. Just watching her with his children proved he really had made the right decision.

Josh swam up and down the pool like a fish, while Katie screamed every time someone splashed water at her face. These swimming lessons were going to be harder than she thought; Penny contemplated as she wiped the water from Katie's sunglasses. The pool was reasonably quiet, as almost everyone had gone ashore for the day. Danny had promised Penny the afternoon off so she had a chance to see the island. He had made plans to take Josh and Katie to the beach.

* * *

Sasha awoke to the sound of Steel drums on the quayside of St Lucia. With the sun beaming through the gap in the brightly coloured curtains, the guilt that had sat heavily in her stomach the night before lifted. Her mood changed completely. She realized that her hasty decision to leave Ben behind yesterday was a strong indication of her feelings towards him. Yes, their relationship had been on the rocks for a long time. Nevertheless, it was as if a voice had entered her head while she was sleeping.

If he hadn't been so quick to walk away, he could have had the last seat on the later flight and maybe then things would have been different. As it was, Sasha had been left with an awkward choice. Anyway, fate had told her it was the right thing to do, so she did it. So get over it.

There was a knock on the cabin door. Sasha presumed it would be Joe, her steward, coming to service the cabin. It was only nine thirty. She would have to negotiate a more suitable time. She wasn't a particularly early riser, but neither did she like being rushed, especially when on holiday.

'Just a second,' she called as she wrapped her bathrobe around her slender frame.

Sasha opened the door, startled.

'Oh. Mrs Cockburn.'

What the hell is she doing here?

'Hi, Dear,' said her unwelcome visitor. 'I just wanted to let you know that William and I won't be down to dinner tonight. We're trying one of the alternative dining venues. Jasmines, I think you call it. The Thai restaurant on Deck 16.'

'No problem,' Sasha replied, puzzled by why Edna Cockburn thought she would be in the least bit interested in knowing about their dinning arrangements for the evening. 'I'll pass it on.'

'Yes, some of our friends who were on here for the Christmas cruise – or was it New Year, I can't remember. Well, anyway. Yes it was Christmas, I remember now. They told us you must book early to avoid disappointment. Apparently it gets very busy towards the end of the cruise.'

'I'm sure it does. I will let the rest of the table know you won't be down tonight. Thank you for calling.'

Not meaning a word of it, Sasha stood patiently listening to Mrs Cockburn as she went on to say she thought it best to call in past Sasha, as she was on her own. The others were couples, after all, and it wasn't fair to disturb them. Sasha struggled to contain herself. She didn't even know this woman, and yet she had come to her cabin at a ridiculously early hour to insult her yet again.

'Okay. Goodbye then,' Sasha replied, closing the door on the old woman's face.

'Oh, I've not finished dear,' called a muffled voice.

Oh great, what was coming now, she thought? Another insult about travelling alone? Or perhaps she was going to vent her opinion on why all women over the age of eighteen should be married and settled down with a family just like it was three hundred years ago when she was young.

Sasha gently opened the door again and put her foot behind it.

'I was also wondering if you would like to come ashore for lunch with me and William today.'

Good God, no! I couldn't think of anything worse. I'd rather stay here and pluck out all of my eyelashes.

'Seeing that you are on your own and all...' continued Mrs Cockburn, unperturbed.

There she goes again! Hell, would the woman please just stop. She really knows how to ruin someone's day before it even begins. Sasha tried to remain calm but she was beginning to loose patience with the old dear. Although, it was probably actually quite a nice gesture really – but not so nice that she couldn't turn it down.

'That's very kind of you, Mrs Cockburn,' Sasha replied, forcing a smile, 'but I've got a few things planned for my day.'

'No problem, dear. In that case we will see you tomorrow night at dinner. You will be there, won't you?'

'Yes, I'll be there.' Sasha flashed the old woman a second smile as she closed the door, a little slower this time.

She had, however, no plans past making a cup of strong black coffee and vegetating on the balcony. Everything else would just have to wait.

Sitting out on the balcony, admiring the perfect china blue sky and turquoise sea watching everyone else rush ashore was one of the things Sasha enjoyed most about cruising. The tours all-congregating by the buses as they were sent off one by one to explore the island. Couples armed with their beach bags and matching white towels with Ocean Magic embroidered in blue and red across them heading off to find a quiet spot to sunbathe, and the groups of young guys and girls, probably ship's crew with a little time off rushing ashore to get away from the passengers for a couple of hours.

They all seemed in such a hurry. It was exciting.

The hours ticked by. The sun climbed the sky. Presently, glancing at her watch, Sasha realized it was 4.00pm back home, which meant that now would be a good time to get in touch with Ben. Slightly less keen than the night before, she knew she couldn't relax and enjoy herself if she didn't know where she stood with him. She collected her laptop, plugged in the charger, and opened her email account; then started typing.

Ben. Can we talk?

Okay, not a brilliant start, but a start all the same. She lay on the end of her king-sized bed wondering if emailing actually was the right thing to do. Then again, what choice did she have while he refused to answer the phone? She had tried to call him on his mobile several times yesterday. She'd wanted let him know that she had managed to get a later flight. But Ben had obviously turned off his phone and answering service.

She sent the email and waited, breathing slowly and tapping a finger. Five minutes later, her heart rate quickened as Ben's email address flashed up on the screen. He was online and communicating at last.

I have nothing to say to you.

Okay, not exactly the response she was hoping for. But it was a response. A reply. A reaction.

She tried another message. *We need to talk. Why won't you answer the phone?*

The reply came a little faster. *We need some time apart. I think we should call off the engagement.*

Ben it was all a misunderstanding. We need to sort things out. Let me get you a flight to join the ship in Curacao. We'll be there in a couple of days. There's an officer onboard who can make all the arrangements for us.

Don't bother Sasha, I'm over it. The ship, the Caribbean, and you!

Ben. Please can we at least talk about this?

Like I said, I've got nothing to say to you. Enjoy your cruise.

Ben, don't leave things like this. We need to talk this through. Ben, please call me. Ben…

* * *

Josh and Katie were in their element as they ran up and down the white sandy beach throwing buckets of water over each other. Danny had bought three passes for them to use the facilities at the Rex St Lucian Hotel. Katie was losing terribly on every attempt to splash her brother as Josh ran away from her every time she got remotely close. Leaving the water to go all over her again – and on one occasion over an old man who was sitting on a sun lounger reading his newspaper – Josh panicked at the thought of getting told off, and went over and apologised profusely to the man hoping his dad hadn't noticed.

As he walked away from the not very amused old man and his less than impressed wife, he decided it was safer to spend the rest of the afternoon splashing about in the clear green blue sea catching small fish with his hands as they swam around his feet. Anyway, it was fun to watch Katie squeal as he chased her with them and threatening to put them down her bathing suit.

Danny found himself a quiet little table in Nelson's beach bar where he sat with an ice-cold bottle of Banks beer watching Josh and Katie play while he read the odd chapter of his book.

'Can I have my camera, dad? I want to film Katie.'

'Be careful with it, Josh. If you get sand in it, it'll be ruined.'

'I will, dad. Don't worry. Come on Katie. Smile!'

Josh had asked for a digital video camera for Christmas. Danny was surprised at the interest his son had shown so far, making short documentaries everywhere they went. The excitement would surely wear off. But for now, whatever kept him happy was fine by his father. Danny's face dropped when he looked up to see that Josh had trusted Katie to film him splashing about by the waters edge. Thankfully, Josh had had the sense to put the strap around his little sister's neck, in case she dropped it into the sea.

'Smile, Josh. Come on, do something funny' Katie giggled to herself as Josh posed happily for the camera.

The afternoon had been wonderful. Danny felt completely relaxed while Josh and Katie had exhausted themselves endlessly running around. Danny finished his second beer and looked up from his book to see Josh wandering casually off up the beach with Katie trailing on behind him. He quickly turned to the table beside him where an attractive middle-aged woman was engrossed in her book.

'Excuse me,' he said. 'Will you watch my bag for a second? My kids have just wandered off and I've not paid the bill. Would you mind?'

'No problem,' the woman replied as Danny leapt out of his chair and ran off up the beach after Josh. On closer inspection, he realized his inclination was right. Josh's incentive for being so trigger happy with the camera was a beautiful, tanned blonde haired girl topless sunbathing a little further up the beach.

'Josh! Katie! Come back here this minute.'

Katie's eyes lit up as she spotted her father. She came skipping back down the beach straight into his arms.

'Hi, dad. Josh is taking lots of film for his holiday video.'

'Is he really darling? Come on, give me your hand.'

'Yes, his teacher said he had to keep a video diary of our holiday. He has to do a presentation to the class when he gets back, telling them about everything he does and what he sees on his holiday.'

'Okay, Katie, but not now. Josh, come on. We're going back to the ship, now please.'

'Now please!' Katie copied her father's harsh tone finding it very amusing.

'Okay, dad. Smile!'

Danny looked rather unimpressed as Josh turned and flashed the camera in his face.

'I've just discovered how to take still shots; you should see some of the photos I've taken. They are so cool. Look dad, check these out!'

Josh turned the camera screen towards his father and thumbed through a number of images. In the brilliant sunlight, it was difficult to see clearly. But Danny got the general idea.

'Yes, very good, Josh. But I think we should save them for later when we have a little chat about your choice of subject! Come on, let's get our things and go back to the ship.'

Later, while Josh sang away to himself in the shower, obviously rather pleased with his day's achievements; Danny deleted the images of the topless girl. What was he thinking about, Danny wondered? I hope this isn't an indication of Josh's chosen career path, he mused. Mind you, he did have a good eye for the camera. Try as he might, Danny couldn't deny that. But picking the good-looking blonde with a body builder for a boyfriend probably wasn't the smartest thing Josh had ever done.

Little did Danny and the kids realize, Penny had been sunbathing only a few hundred metres away at the next stretch of beach; Spinnakers beach resort. She had arrived just after two o'clock and found the only spare sun lounger on the beach. It had been a beautiful afternoon, with clear blue skies. The temperature had probably reached the high thirties.

St Lucia was one of the islands Penny had been most keen to visit. The buzz she felt when she stepped ashore was exciting. Not really knowing where to go or what to expect, she felt she had done quite well in sounding as if she knew the beach that she had read about in the tour guide just minutes earlier. It was a tip Danny had mentioned to her before he had gone ashore.

'If you sound like you know where you want to go, the taxi drivers will be less inclined to whisk you off on a tour of the island. Not that I want to worry you or anything. St Lucia is perfectly safe. It's just that you're a single woman.'

The conversation hadn't quite come out the way he had intended it, and it had made Penny feel a little apprehensive about getting into a taxi on her own in unfamiliar surroundings.

Danny had offered Penny the opportunity to go ashore with him and the kids, but she felt they wouldn't want her tagging along with them in every port, so it was probably best to get used to going ashore on her own.

After negotiating a set fare with the taxi driver, she arrived at the beach feeling pleased with herself. Her afternoon had been wonderful, lying in the sun reading her book and enjoying the odd virgin cocktail. All that splashing around in the pool with Katie earlier had completely worn her out, but she didn't care if swimming was all Josh and Katie wanted to do all day and every day. That was fine by her. She still couldn't quite believe she was on a Caribbean cruise just one month after she'd started her new job. It really was a dream come true. She was getting paid to lie here on the beach soaking up the rays. It was amazing.

Later that afternoon, Penny ordered herself a strawberry daiquiri from the beach bar. There was certainly no shortage of rum in it she confirmed as she took another sip and sat up in her lounger to do some people watching. She couldn't take her eyes off one family; a thirty-something year old lady and two small children splashing about in the sea together as if they didn't have a care in the world. They looked so happy, but Penny couldn't help but wonder if there was a father figure in the children's lives.

It couldn't be easy bringing up a family single-handed. Danny was doing such a good job with Josh and Katie. But it was early days, and their mother hadn't been back in their lives since she walked out on them six months ago. Penny wondered how she was going to tell Danny about the way Katie had been dealing with things, and decided it was probably for the best to leave it for a while. She had cleared things up in the meantime, and she didn't want Danny to think she was interfering with the way he was bringing up his children.

At three o'clock, the bar staff turned up the music and announced the start of happy hour. Within minutes, the beach bar was in full swing, and everyone seemed determined to let their hair down and enjoy themselves.

Penny was definitely one of the more attractive looking females on the beach that afternoon. Her shoulder length blonde hair was tied back with a pink bandana, that matched the shade of her bikini, and her golden skin glowed in the sun. The night before she left for Barbados, she had applied a Saint Tropez 'all over' body tan. She had everything going for her, but still didn't have the confidence to join in the fun.

Penny's looks, along with her perfectly toned slim figure, had attracted a reasonable amount of attention, and unknown to her she had become the subject of a bet. By late afternoon, she found herself in a rather embarrassing position when approached by three good-looking guys in their early twenties.

'Sorry to bother you,' the youngest of the three began. 'It's just that we were wondering...'

'Yes?' Penny raised her Gucci sunglasses and looked him in the eye.

'You're not an actress are you?'

Penny laughed as the three men took a step back.

'You see, my friends think you might be famous. But I disagree, and so we were just wondering if you could clear things up for us.'

'Well who do your friends think I look like?' Penny replied teasing the young man.

'Oliver here thinks you're an actress, but he can't name a movie you've been in, and Liam thinks you're a singer. But like I said, I think you're just here on holiday.'

'And you are?' Penny waited for the young man to introduce himself.

'Sorry, I'm Cameron.'

'Well Cameron, you'll be pleased to know your friends are wrong. I'm not an actress or a singer; I'm just here on holiday.'

'But you would say that,' said the one named Oliver. 'I mean, if you were a famous actress, for example.'

'You're probably right,' Penny replied. 'So if you don't believe me, I guess you'll never know.'

'What do you say we buy you a drink and we can figure you out for ourselves,' Cameron said.

'That's very kind of you, but I'm afraid I have to get going.'

'Is that because you've been spotted, or because you have a magazine shoot to get ready for?' said Oliver.

'Neither' Penny replied, dressing quickly before packing her beach bag and towel.

'You would say that too if you were famous,' Oliver persisted.

'See you tomorrow?' said Cameron.

'You never know,' Penny replied, smiling to herself as she walked back along the beach.

From the chair on her balcony, Sasha watched the sun go down. She had been sitting there all afternoon thinking about Ben and his proposal to call off their engagement.

What on earth would she tell her family? If she and Ben split up – which at this point in time was looking increasingly likely – she would undoubtedly never hear the end of it. Her mother would quite possibly never forgive her.

Elizabeth Carter, a wonderful lady in all respects, worshiped the ground Ben walked on and was waiting patiently for the announcement of the big day.

It will be any day now, she religiously told her friends. I would imagine a winter wedding, and definitely somewhere exotic, if Ben has his way.

Mrs Carter had a heart of gold, but continuously blamed her husband's death for Sasha's fear of commitment.

The announcement for 'first sitting passengers to make their way down to the restaurant' interrupted Sasha's thoughts. A quarter to seven already, she thought as she dragged herself out of her deck chair.

The second Captain's Welcome Onboard cocktail party started at eight. She remembered Lucy getting rather excited about it at dinner the previous night. Lucy had talked Sasha and Megan to death with a description of everything in her wardrobe, uncertain which evening dresses to bring on the cruise. In the end, and much to her husband Richard's disapproval, she had brought seven different outfits to wear over the three formal nights onboard. How she didn't get charged an extra fare for her excess baggage was a miracle.

There wasn't much else for it, Sasha decided. Either she motivated herself enough to get ready and join her table for dinner, or she was facing a rather depressing night in on her own, and after the day she had had, she was utterly sick of her own company.

On a good note, she reminded herself that the Cockburn's wouldn't be down to the table tonight, so they would probably have quite a nice time. The priority now was getting in the shower. The dress she had in mind was compatible only with silky smooth legs.

She turned on the shower, and found the remote control for the television. She was just in time for the evening radio show hosted by the ship's DJ. Meatloaf's, *Like A Bat Out Of Hell* wasn't necessarily her music preference, but at least it was something uncomplicated to listen to. The shower helped to wash away the negative thoughts of her tarnished relationship, and the large glass of Chablis she had poured herself, accompanied by the Scissor Sisters, was all she needed to get herself into the mood for a night out.

Chablis was one of Sasha's favourite white wines. She had ordered a bottle that afternoon through Joe, unsure at the time if she was going to lock herself away in her cabin, and drown her sorrows, or use it as a pick-me-up to get ready for a night out. A few moments later she felt a slightly dizzy sensation while she appreciated the rich oak flavour of the wine going straight to her head. Remembering that she hadn't had anything to eat since dinner the previous night, she decided to take it easy with the wine and confirmed that a night out with some nice food, a little wine, and good company was exactly what she needed.

The cocktail party was full. On all tiers of the atrium, people had congregated, each dressed in their formal attire and eagerly waiting to set eyes on the captain. There was an abundance of officers. They were spread evenly through the public rooms. Every one of them was looking very smart in their well-presented black and white mess kits, all displaying a different number of gold or sliver stripes indicating their rank onboard. One or two were looking rather dishy thought Sasha as she stood next to a lovely Irish couple who were travelling with their two young children.

The little boy was no more than six-years-old. He was kitted out from head to toe in the cutest little tuxedo, his short brown hair styled to perfection. His sister, about four-years-old and standing at his side, was looking very glamorous in her gorgeous little pink party dress with matching patent shoes. You could tell she was excited to be wearing that ensemble.

For a little over a minute, the children distracted Sasha's attention. Then, with something of a bump, she realized that if she was going to have a family of her own while she was still young, she would have to get her act together – either with Ben, or meet someone new in the next couple of years. She wasn't getting any younger, she reminded herself.

Ben had always wanted a big family. Both of his brothers were married. His older brother, Nathan, had five children; three boys and two girls. His younger brother, Jamie, had three children; two boys and, recently, a new baby girl. Ben loved being an uncle and spent as much time as he could with the children, mostly playing sports with the boys, or taking them on long walks in the park, or swimming, and quite often ten pin bowling at the weekends. Occasionally he would volunteer himself and Sasha to baby-sit so as to allow his brothers and sisters-in-law a night out without the children.

Ben would usually tire the children out playing in the garden, and then tuck them up in bed by seven or eight o'clock. Then he would order a takeaway, and together with Sasha, would unwind for the evening in front of the television.

Sasha hadn't been as keen on the idea of a big family. One or maybe two children at the most she had agreed. No more than that. That's what she had said the last time they were round at Jamie's babysitting. It was usually after they had spent the night with Ben's nieces and nephews that he would again raise the thorny subject of children.

Sasha paused for a second on that thought, and then diverted her attention to another couple who seemed to be disagreeing over something. The very attractive looking lady stood tall and slim in her elegant figure-hugging red cocktail dress. She had obviously been to the salon to get her long golden hair done as each strand was perfectly placed, therefore definitely professionally put up. She seemed to have quite a fiery personality, shooting icy glares at her husband every time he spoke.

They weren't arguing aloud, or anything too obvious. But it was clear something wasn't pleasing her. He seemed a little embarrassed by his wife's behaviour, and he was doing his best to placate her. But it was almost as if nothing he could do or say was right.

Sasha knew exactly how he felt.

Across the corridor, next to the Piano Bar, Sasha's dinner companions – Megan and Kris – were enjoying a glass of champagne. They seemed to be having a nice time. When Sasha looked over again, Kris caught her eye and called her over to join them. Not wishing to intrude, but glad of the company, she walked over to meet them.

'Sasha, how has your day been? Did you go ashore in St Lucia?' Megan asked, keen to know what she had done with her day. Sasha felt herself wanting to lie, but realizing she could really get herself into a lot of trouble if she kept this behaviour up all cruise. She smiled at the couple.

'No, I just had a relaxing day by the pool.'

It was out before she could stop herself, another white lie Sasha thought, but what else was she meant to say? No my fiancé broke off our engagement this morning, so I spent an extremely depressing day crying my eyes out alone in my cabin.

'I hope you haven't been working too hard,' Kris remarked.' You're a journalist aren't you?'

'Yes, but I'm not working at the minute. I've left my pen and pad at home so I can enjoy my holiday.'

'Oh, I see.' Kris looked perplexed. 'We thought you might be doing an undercover article on passenger service or something. That would explain why you're...'

'On my own,' Sasha interrupted.

'No, no, of course not.' Kris blushed, somewhat embarrassed by what he had said.

'We went down to Marigot Bay, just along the coast from Castries,' Megan began. The expression on Sasha's face had suggested the conversation needed to be turned around. 'We shared the most wonderful seafood grill for lunch. It was enormous, enough for a family of six, at a gorgeous little restaurant next to the marina.'

'Sounds lovely,' Sasha replied, obviously still unimpressed at Kris's remark.

'Oh it was. Then we came back and sunbathed on Deck 15 all afternoon. It was nice and quiet. I think most people were still ashore.' Realizing Megan was about to ask where she had been sunbathing, and considering Sasha hadn't taken the time to venture out of the cabin and had no idea where the pools were located, she decided to change the subject.

'Have you seen Richard and Lucy today?'

'No. They were going on one of the tours. Not sure where, but I don't think they were getting back until late,' Megan replied. 'They won't miss this party though. They'll be here somewhere.'

'Oh, the Cockburn's won't be down to dinner tonight,' Sasha informed the couple.

'Nothing we've done I hope,' Megan remarked.

'No, I think they just want to have dinner on their own, that's all. They've booked a table in the Thai restaurant, Jasmines.

'I don't know why they didn't book a table for two in the restaurant. They don't seem very happy sitting with us,' Megan replied.

'Oh well, if they're not happy, I'm sure they'll request a move.'

'Chance would be a fine thing. Maybe we could arrange it for them. You know, as a little surprise,' Kris remarked, smiling cunningly at Sasha.

'Kris you're terrible,' Megan giggled, shaking her head.

'At least we won't feel like naughty school children at dinner tonight,' Sasha said.

'I know,' Megan replied. 'What was all that about last night? I bet you felt like you were on trial?'

'Oh, nothing better to talk about I guess. She had to pick on someone, and I suppose that was me. At least she's got it out of her system. It'll be your turn tomorrow night, just wait and see,' Sasha laughed. 'We should think ourselves lucky we don't have to dine with her every night. It's William I feel sorry for, poor man. Must be at his wits end.'

'I know, can you imagine putting up with that twenty-four hours a day. I'd have buried her under the patio years ago,' Kris joked. 'You might think I'm kidding, but don't be fooled. This is a warning, my dear Megan. Start behaving like Edna Cockburn and it will be goodnight Vienna.' Megan and Sasha laughed hard while Kris tried his best to look like he meant it. 'Seriously, don't be fooled by my good looks, charm and charisma, its all part of the act.'

'Sure darling, whatever you say.' Megan smiled sweetly at her partner. He really was quite entertaining.

'I hope you don't think I'm being nosey, Sasha, but if you're not working, where is your fiancé?'

'Megan,' Kris snapped. 'You are being nosey.'

'It's just that last night I noticed you were wearing an engagement ring,' Megan continued.

Her heart was in the right place, but with her inquisitive mind, she was about as subtle as a bull in a china shop. She had also decided to ignore Sasha's dry response to Kris's suggestion that she was working incognito. The poor girl just couldn't control her curiosity.

'Megan.' Kris looked at her as if to say she was as bad as Mrs Cockburn and one step closer to being buried under the patio.

'No, it's okay,' Sasha replied. 'We are separated. I just haven't had time to get used to it yet, that's all.' Little did Kris and Megan know that her long term relationship and three-year engagement had only just turned into a temporary separation a few hours ago.

'I'm sorry, Sasha. I didn't mean to upset you.'

Wiping away a tear, Sasha smiled to suggest it was okay.

'Well, you've come to the right place, haven't you? Have you seen how many men have looked your way tonight? It must be that dress. It looks fantastic on you.'

'Really, Megan.' Kris shook his head putting Megan back in her place once more.

At that moment, Sasha, Kris and Megan noticed that there was something going on around them. They looked round and saw that the captain had taken centre stage in the atrium. Everyone was silent and listened as he made a very pleasant speech introducing himself and one or two of the senior officers, before naming all the wonderful ports they were going to visit during the cruise. He then continued to talk about the highlight of the cruise; The Transit of the Panama Canal.

Megan said, 'Kris is so excited about the Panama he even hired that DVD. You know, the one with Pierce Brosnan in it. *The Tailor of Panama*. He watched it three times before he gave it back.'

Sasha laughed as Kris squirmed in his tuxedo once more; there was nothing he could say to defend himself.

Sasha began to remember all the things she had planned for her holiday. It seemed like a lifetime ago, the notion of lazy days lying on the beach, feeding the sharks and swimming with the stingrays in Curacao. Watching the cliff divers, and of course, shopping in Acapulco.

'A glass of champagne, madam,' said a very pleasant South African voice from behind. Sasha turned to face a good-looking dark haired young man dressed immaculately in a perfectly pressed pair of black trousers, a crisp white long sleeve shirt complete with a black silk bow tie and matching cummerbund. The white shirt emphasised his dark tan.

'Yes, please. I'd love one, thank you.' Sasha caught Megan's eye as she lifted the purposely-overfilled glass off the tray blushing ever so slightly.

'See what I mean, Sasha. This could be your best holiday ever.'

After the cocktail party, Sasha made her way down to dinner with Kris and Megan by her side. The glass of champagne and interesting conversation was exactly what she needed to lift her spirits. She had also managed to clear up any untrue rumours that had obviously been the topic of conversation after she left the table the previous night.

Tonight she actually felt quite good about herself.

The Four Seasons restaurant, one of the two main dinning rooms, was exquisite.

Sasha hadn't noticed the sheer volume of tables spread over two levels, each holding up to five hundred covers. The previous night she had only concentrated on not falling head over heels down the marble spiral staircase as she had made her entrance into the dinning room. Tonight, the restaurant looked sensational. The various sized tables were all dressed with matching cream tablecloths, each with brown silk trim. The chairs were mahogany with cream cushions individually tied to them. The table was set with the finest silverware and luxury china. The large balloon-shaped crystal glasses sparkled with the light from the chandeliers. Sasha's table was set for five. The Cockburn's must have informed the restaurant manager they would be dining elsewhere after all.

'Good evening everyone. Welcome to the Captain's Welcome Onboard dinner.'

'Thank you,' Sasha and Megan smiled as they accepted their menus from the waiter. The menu choice was a difficult one. For the first time in days Sasha actually felt hungry. As she contemplated the smoked salmon with dill dressing, or the terrine of smoked duck for a starter followed by fillet steak tournedos, or grilled lobster tail as a main course. That's what she had narrowed it down to so far. The wine steward appeared by her side. She could feel his presence but was too busy deciding what she wanted to eat and didn't want to waste a second looking up in case the waiter came to take her food order.

'Hello again,' called the familiar tone of the South African accent she had heard only moments earlier.

'Hello again, indeed.' Megan smirked as she nodded approvingly at Sasha.

'I'm Tom, and I will be your wine steward for the cruise.'

'Hi, Tom. Very nice to meet you,' Megan replied, unable to control herself.

Kris quickly diverted Tom's attention to him. As he was the only man at the table, he felt it only right he should take charge and order the wine. Kris chatted away to Tom as they went through a choice of recommendations together.

'I think we'll have one white, the Sancerre, and one red, the Châteauneuf-du-Pape. That should keep us going for now. Tom complimented Kris on his choice, and promptly went off to fetch the wines.

Richard and Lucy appeared at the table just in time for their order to be taken. Lucy was looking very glamorous, in a slightly revealing low cut silver evening dress complete with a beautiful matching silk scarf wrapped around her shoulders. Certainly not one of the numerous choices she had mentioned the previous night. Her long brown hair was put up in a bun worn to the side. She really did look very dashing.

As the white wine was offered round the table, Lucy stole a quick look at Tom as he filled her glass. The girls' eyes met across the table. Megan gave a little giggle indicating her approval. Tom smiled at the ladies, obviously used to all this attention Thankfully, Kris and Richard were too engrossed in conversation to notice what the ladies were up to.

The atmosphere at the table was affable compared to the previous evening when the Cockburn's had accompanied the group. Sasha, Megan and Lucy really connected and chatted away continuously, stopping only to draw breath and enjoy the odd mouthful of food. They all felt as though they hadn't had the chance to talk properly while Mrs Cockburn was there scrutinising their every word, and so were certainly making up for it tonight.

Kris and Richard were as bad as the women, chatting away about work, sport, cars and the rather attractive female string quartet that had played in the atrium during the Captain's Welcome Onboard cocktail party. The pair were getting along very well, and continued making conversation through coffees and liquors.

The girls were more than happy to have their own conversation, Tom being the main topic of the evening. When the last drop of wine was finished, the group thanked the waiters and Tom for the excellent service and set off for the casino. Sasha welcomed the way the couples just presumed she would be joining them. It made her feel very much included and was just what she needed at the moment. Kris and Richard disappeared towards the roulette table at the back of the casino while Sasha, Megan and Lucy scanned the room for something easy to play together. It was just going to be a bit of fun after all.

After twenty minutes playing the slot machines with no luck, Sasha remembered she had played blackjack once before while on holiday in Spain with Ben. Lucy and Megan openly admitted they had no idea how to play, encouraging Sasha to explain the rules. Sasha quite happily did the honours, and cajoled her friends into taking a seat.

The first two rounds were hopeless. Megan and Lucy couldn't make head nor tail of the game. Believing that luck simply wasn't on their side, they gave up and decided it was more fun to order a couple of martini cocktails and watch Sasha play.

Things were looking a little more hopeful for Sasha, and she continued placing reasonably sized bets on the table. Before long she had a crowd of ten or so gathered round watching her play. She had trebled her chips, and was having the best fun she'd had in ages. When Kris and Richard joined them wondering what all the fuss was about at their table, the two couples watched in amazement as Sasha calmly placed all her chips on one game. The dealer gave himself the ten of hearts and the nine of diamonds, and Sasha the queen of spades and the king of clubs. The group was silent as Sasha asked for another card. With five hundred pounds pending on the outcome, she received the ace of spades beating the dealers twenty-three.

'That was amazing! Where did you learn to play like that?' Lucy asked excitedly.

'I can't believe I won. It was just luck, really it was.'

'Well lady luck is certainly on your side tonight, well done.'

'Yes, well done indeed,' Lucy joined Megan in congratulating their new friend, while Richard and Kris walked off stunned by Sasha's cool response to her big win.

'One for the road,' Kris suggested as they walked past the nightclub. 'Come on; let's check it out. I've got moves like you wouldn't believe, and it's open until four, apparently.'

The girls laughed nervously as Kris and Richard led the way into Barbican.

'Mojitos all round.' Kris had caught the bartender's eye and had ordered before anyone had a chance to say anything.

'Okay, but only if I can get them,' Sasha offered. 'It's only fair. I didn't pay for the wine at dinner, after all.'

'Just because you're flush from your big win, show off!' Kris remarked in a very amusing camp voice. He often put it on after a few drinks. But before Sasha got the chance to pay the bill, Kris had her up on the dance floor impressing her with his unruly dance moves.

'She's only just separated from her fiancé, you know.'

Lucy looked at Megan in surprise. 'Who has?'

'Sasha. She told me tonight, that's why she's here on her own.'

'Oh that's terrible. I hope she's okay.'

'God, yeah. She's fine. Look at her. I mean she doesn't look too bothered to me. Better keep an eye on our other halves, you know, just in case. She's not the worst looking woman around.'

'I don't think we have anything to worry about there, Megan. I'm sure the boys are quite safe.'

'I'm not so sure about that,' Megan grunted as she watched Kris escort Sasha back to the bar.

An hour later, Sasha was the first to call it a night.

'I'll walk you home, Sash,' Kris volunteered. 'We don't want any young men following you back to your cabin now, do we?'

'Don't be silly. I'll be fine, honestly.'

'If you're sure,' Kris offered again.

'Yes, positive.' Sasha smiled as she wished them all a good night.

Well at least I've got nothing to worry about, Lucy thought to herself.

Chapter 3

Mayreau 08:00 Arrival 16:00 Departure

It was Monday morning, although remembering which day of the week it was was becoming increasingly difficult. Onboard Ocean Magic, every day was like a Sunday – for everyone except Edna Cockburn that is.

It didn't seem to matter to her that William was still curled up fast asleep in the single bed next to hers after a restless night tossing and turning. As soon as that old brass alarm clock of hers went off, the ever-familiar ringing noise filled the cabin for what felt like eternity. And from her bedside, without any effort at all, she lit the cabin up like the Blackpool Illuminations.

The bright lights and constant ringing were shortly followed by the Good Morning Ocean Magic breakfast show blaring from the small plasma screen television in the far corner of the room just above William's bed.

'Morning, William. Rise and shine.' Edna's high-pitched tone echoed across the room. 'William, come on, dear. It's gone five. If you lie there much longer, we'll miss our tour.'

'Chance would be a fine thing,' William mumbled into his pillow.

'Sorry dear, I didn't quite catch that. What did you say?'

'Nothing. I didn't say a word,' he mumbled again, pulling the duvet cover up over his head in an attempt to drown out the voice of his wife and the extremely enthusiastic entertainment officers who looked like they were actually enjoying being up in the middle of the night to present the breakfast show.

'Nonsense, William. I can hear you complaining. You're on holiday, for goodness sake. You should be happy.'

'I am happy. In fact, I'm over the moon. The only thing that could possibly make me happier is if I could have a lie-in for once. But quite honestly, there's probably a greater chance of winning the lottery.'

'Really, William. There is no need to take that tone, dear. You know that if we don't stick to a routine, our sleeping pattern will be disrupted. Then heaven knows! We won't know if we're coming or going. Now are you going to make the tea, or will I have to do it myself?'

'Goodness no, Edna. You sit there and I'll do it,' as always he thought to himself as he pushed back the covers and climbed slowly out of bed.

William spent a few minutes dealing with that, and a few minutes later, the welcoming brew was ready.

'Sugar?' he said as he handed his wife a cup and saucer and a handful of Demerara sachets.

'Don't be silly, William. You know I only take sugar in my cocoa before I go to sleep.'

'Yes, of course. How silly of me,' William replied, opening four sugars and stirring them into his tea. Yawning uncontrollably for extra measure, he sat down on the edge of his duvet.

'Sounds like someone got out of the wrong side of bed this morning,' Edna chuckled to herself, knowing full well William had never been a 'morning person'.

'Very funny,' William replied, turning to his wife who was now perched on the chaise longue as if she were the Queen of England. Checking her watch for the third time in five minutes, she started waving her arms about signalling to her husband.

'Chop-chop, dear. You're first in the shower,' she instructed William, taking his cup of tea from him before he could finish it. 'Like I said, we don't want to keep the tour waiting.'

With at least three hours until we are due to be at the pontoon, that's highly unlikely thought William as he closed the bathroom door, glad of the peace and quiet on the other side.

By eight o'clock, the couple had finished their breakfast and returned to the cabin. Edna impatiently paced the floor while William completed his crossword, patiently waiting for the announcement that their Mayreau tour party was ready to leave.

Edna had decided that a tour was the best way to see the small island. She felt they had wasted their day in St Lucia. Trying to be independent was no good for an old couple like them, or so she told the officer on the gangway when she boarded the ship the previous afternoon.

Nevertheless, the day had been a huge success, and it left very little room for criticism.

William had taken charge of the arrangements and had organised a taxi to take them to the historic Pigeon Point and Pigeon Island National Park on the north west side of the island. On arrival, a very pleasant tour guide who talked knowledgeably about the history of Pigeon Point met them. With great enthusiasm, she explained how it had at one time been an island attached to the mainland by a long narrow passageway, which was used as an observation-point when England and France took to war against St Lucia.

William listened intently to the guide's detailed lecture, but Edna had already switched off. Always one step ahead, and more interested in where she was going to have her morning coffee, she quite blatantly ignored the cheerful young woman.

After a short coffee break, the elderly couple spent an hour strolling around three or four of the forty odd acres of desolate fortresses, caves and ruins taking photos as they went. They then continued to explore the historic walls and barracks of Fort Rodney. After convincing his wife to smile for the camera William had taken an impressive photograph of Edna resting against one of the abandoned cannons, with the clear blue sky and deep blue sea as a back drop to the photograph. William was clearly elated with his work.

'Apparently, it's named after Admiral George Rodney the Englishman whose troops won the Battle of the Saints right here in 1784, sorry 82,' immediately correcting himself, William enthusiastically reiterated to Edna.

'Really? How interesting, dear,' had been her aloof response. William might as well have saved his breath. The couple continued on into Pigeon Island Museum. William was keen to explore more of the museum and learn the full story behind the war but Edna had other plans, and after five minutes promptly marched him off on a walk along the beach.

The beach was truly beautiful. The couple very much enjoyed their stroll, stopping occasionally to cool their hot tired feet in the sea. At one point, Edna even looked like she was enjoying herself. At 2.00pm, the taxi was waiting as arranged to take them to The Lime restaurant at Rodney Bay. William had asked the tour manager onboard for a recommendation, and as a surprise for Edna had then booked a table. Although impressed by her husband's gesture, it didn't stop her complaining that it was far too late to eat lunch.

'It was almost time for afternoon tea, for heaven's sake!' had been her initial response. It had been an eventful day, which, in the end, ended with a very enjoyable lunch. By 4.00 o'clock, the elderly couple were tired out and happily returned to the ship for an afternoon nap.

Today their tour was going to Saltwhistle Bay in the northern part of Mayreau. It had been described by the girl at the tours desk as an experience they would never forget.

At last, and right on time, the tour was announced. The couple happily made their way down to the pontoon where they were instructed to take a short boat ride to the shore where the buses and the guides would be waiting.

'Look, William. There's the captain and his wife. Well, I *hope* it's his wife. You know what these sailors are like...'

'Don't be silly, Edna. Of course it's his wife – and can you please make it less obvious that you're talking about them.'

'Don't worry William they *want* to be noticed. I mean, look at them. If they wanted some privacy, don't you think he would have arranged for a private boat to take them across the water?'

'He's the captain of Ocean Magic, for heaven's sake, Edna. He's not James Bond. He doesn't have an endless supply of private speed boats, helicopters and cars with wings on them at his disposal.'

'Oh, William. You really do have a vivid imagination,' she chuckled. 'You must cut down on the amount of television you watch.'

As the tender boat pulled up alongside the ship, Edna edged her way forward in the queue taking William with her.'

'Excuse me. Out of the way. Move please,' she repeated, pushing everyone else aside. William, unable to stop his wife, followed behind apologising to everyone in his path.

'We're with the captain,' she whispered to a young couple who were obviously extremely unimpressed at her pushing to the front of the queue. The man who wasn't prepared to stand for such blatant rudeness was stopped from speaking his mind by his wife, who suggested it really wasn't worth it.'

'Old people can be so rude,' he added for good measure, much to his wife's disapproval. The comment however went straight over Edna's head.

'Terribly sorry,' William apologised to a middle aged man as he brushed past trying his best to keep up with his wife who looked as if she had been in training for the Olympics.

'You will be if your wife hits my daughter again with that stupid handbag of hers. Old bat!' he cursed before turning to console his six year old daughter who was leaning over holding her head.

'Edna, you really need to be more patient and wait your turn. Do you realize that you practically knocked a child out back there.'

'Nonsense, William. Anyway, a cruise ship is no place for children. They just take away from the enjoyment of the other passengers. Anyone who pays to bring their children on a cruise must have more money than sense. Honestly!'

'Regardless, Edna, there really is no excuse for that type of behaviour.'

'Yes, yes, dear. Whatever you say. You know, William, you really do need to try and relax more. In fact, I think I'll book you in for one of those massage things when we get back. Yes, that should do the trick.'

Unable to make his wife see sense, William shook his head in disgust. No matter how often she was told, Edna Cockburn couldn't control her inexcusable behaviour, and more often lately her wicked tongue.

Relieved to have reached the shore and finally get free of the old woman who had sat as close to the captain and his wife as possible without actually sitting on top of them during the quick run ashore. Alex took his wife by the hand and led her out of the tender boat onto the key side, where he had arranged for an air-conditioned limousine transfer to take them to the island's most exquisite restaurant.

'Look, William, they've got a private car laid on. Most likely at the company's expense I shouldn't wonder! Hmm, where do you think they are going?'

'I honestly have no idea, Edna, and quite frankly I don't care! But if you'd prefer, we can ditch the tour and follow them around all day.'

'William, there really is no need for you to take that tone, dear. Now come along or we'll miss the bus.'

Feeling like he couldn't win, and exasperated by his wife's behaviour, William shook his head once more and led Edna towards the group of tour guides who were waiting for them to join them.

* * *

After a short drive up the hill, Alex and Sally arrived at The Edge, an exclusive restaurant named appropriately after the cliff top upon which it sat. Unsure of where her husband was taking her, Sally looked suitably impressed as she took in the ambience of this elite venue.

The twelve dinning tables were dressed in cream satin with the most amazing tropical flower arrangements centred in the middle, the scented tea light candles gave a relaxing romantic feel, and the exclusive glassware sparkled in the sunlight. The dinning area was open plan, and each table was allocated an outdoor kitchen with a private chef so you could watch your food being prepared in front of you if you so desired. Guests were also offered the opportunity of increased privacy as the tables were at least five metres apart and could be segregated by beautifully hand crafted wooden screens.

A very friendly young man welcomed the couple by placing a beautiful orchid lei over their heads. 'Welcome to The Edge. Do you have a reservation sir?'

'Yes. The name is Taylor. I booked a table for 1.00pm. Is it okay if we just have a drink for now?'

'Of course, sir. Please take your time. I will get Todd to take your order at the bar, and I will come and advise you of when your chef is ready to start cooking.'

'Come on, I want to show you the best bit,' Alex grinned excitedly as he put his arm around his wife's waist and walked her across a small bridge into what felt like another restaurant altogether.

'Gosh, Alex. This is truly amazing.' Sally gasped as she took in the striking scenery. If she and Alex weren't already married, she would have been certain he was about to pop the question. She hadn't experienced anywhere like this in her life.

To match the restaurant, there were twelve identical little thatched huts, each with two bar stools, a very comfortable looking arrangement of outdoor lounge furniture, and a small garden featuring its own fish pond.

Their own private bar; the ultimately exclusive dining and personal chef. It was almost too much to take in, Sally concluded.

Along with a tempting assortment of canopies to wet the appetite, each bar offered a vast selection of champagne, cocktails, wines spirits and soft drinks. While Sally tried hard to study the drinks menu, there was so much going on it was hard to concentrate. The sommelier arrived at Alex's side with a well-chilled bottle of Dom Perignon and two champagne glasses.

'Mr Taylor.'

'Yes.' Alex looked at him in surprise.

'This is for you.' He gestured to the bottle of champagne while signalling to the bar steward to bring an ice bucket.

'From a Mr Nelson. I believe he is the ship's agent here in Mayreau.'

'That'll be Mario.' Alex looked bewildered. 'He really didn't have to do this.'

'Oh, I assure you, Mr Taylor, he did. He was very precise with his instruction and insisted lunch is also on him. Now, Mrs Taylor can I interest you in a glass of champagne?'

'I was going to order a sparkling water, but why not.' Sally smiled, accepting a glass from the – dare she think it – extremely handsome young man.

'Meantime, I'll leave the bottle here if that's okay, sir?' Giles asked.

Alex smiled to suggest that was more than fine with him.

'Well cheers, Sally. Here's to us and to your cruise, of course.'

'Cheers.' Sally joined in lifting her glass to meet Alex's.

'So was it Mario who told you about this place?' Sally asked, keen to find out how Alex had discovered what she thought was the most amazing restaurant in the world.

'Yes. He's mentioned it to me almost every time we've been here, but I wanted to wait until you were with me before I booked a table. Apparently it's a very well kept secret.'

'You can see why,' Sally agreed, taking another sip of champagne.

'Some caviar, madam?' Another adorable young man offered, putting the selection in front of Sally.

'They compliment the champagne,' he continued before walking away, not wishing to intrude.

'This just gets better and better,' Sally smiled, taking a small portion of caviar from the tray.

'So what do you fancy for lunch?' Alex asked, engrossed in the menu. 'It all sounds so nice.'

'I'm not sure really. I was thinking about the lobster, but now that I know Mario is paying, I don't think it would be very fair to order it. Have you seen how much it costs?'

'Nonsense, Sally, you must have what you want. If Mario was here, we would be eating lobster and drinking champagne all afternoon. Just as well he's not really, as I've got a ship to sail this evening. Mustn't forget about that.'

'At least it won't go without us,' Sally joked.

'You would think not. But I've got a third mate on at the minute who thinks he should be next in line for promotion to captain. Let's just hope he doesn't decide to take her out.'

'Really?' Sally giggled.

'Seriously, I've never worked with anyone so confident. Anyway, that's enough about work and me. Tell me what you've been up to. I've really missed you the last few weeks.'

'I know. I've missed you too.' Sally looked longingly at her husband and smiled. 'Where will I start?'

'Well how's work? You've not said much about it lately. Have you sold many pieces?'

'No, nothing much at all. Things are really quiet at the minute. Just after Christmas, it's always the same. Art is not a priority. Everyone is too busy paying off credit card bills from overspending. You know how it is.'

'So there's nothing for you to rush back for then? You could stay on for another cruise.'

'Let's just wait and see how this cruise goes shall we?' Pretending he hadn't asked the question, Alex glanced at the menu again.

'Are you sure you don't want a starter?'

'No, thanks. I'm saving room for dessert. The tropical fruit Pavlova sounds delicious.'

'Might have guessed.' Alex took hold of his wife's hand while he topped up her glass of champagne and waited for their order to be taken.

After lunch the couple walked hand in hand along the magnetic, golden sandy beach. From above, they had been admiring the view for the last three hours. Handsomely dressed with coconut trees it really was a beautiful sight. Alex couldn't help but be impressed by the large display of luxury yachts anchoring side by side with numerous tourists onboard, all eager to set sight on the stunning island. He wanted nothing more than to take early retirement, sell up at home, and live on a yacht. Sadly he knew it was the last thing Sally would want.

'If you're ready, we should make our way back to the ship. You'd be surprised how just a few hours out of the office will see my inbox filled. I really must try and clear it before I take the ship out.'

'Yes, of course. I'm ready when you are. Thanks again for such a wonderful lunch. It was such a lovely surprise.'

'I think Mario deserves the credit for that one. I'll thank him later when he comes up to the bridge for departure. And just so you know, there are plenty more surprises up my sleeve, especially if you give my offer some thought. I promise you won't be disappointed.'

'I'll definitely think about it,' Sally replied.

* * *

'What should I wear tonight?' Sally called from the shower.

'The dress code is smart-casual, so whatever you think,' Alex replied as he quickly changed into his uniform and hunted for his pager.

'What are the couples at our table like?' Sally asked.

'They're really nice. I'm sure you'll like them. There's James and Cathleen, an older couple from Kent, Steven and Jennifer – they're from Belfast, although I think they only moved there a few years ago. He's a lawyer, and she has her own beauty salon. The third couple, Lewis and Diane, have recently relocated to Alicante in Spain. They've opened a restaurant or café or something. You'll get on well with them. They're an interesting couple. And then there's ourselves, of course, making up a table of eight. I've told them you'll be joining us tonight, and they're all looking forward to meeting you.'

Wrapped in her bathrobe, Sally searched in her wardrobe for something to wear. She pulled out a light coloured beige trouser-suit, a similar coloured vest top, and a pair of light brown Nine West high heels with a clutch bag to match.

Once she was dressed, with her hair and makeup done, she walked out onto the outsized balcony to watch Alex sail the ship.

The captain's suite was huge. It was by far the biggest on the ship with a large day room complete with a corner suite that comfortably sat twelve adults; a dining room table with chairs that also accommodated twelve; a vast desk work area with a flat screen computer for Alex to get easy access to his emails; and a 52-inch plasma screen TV complete with home entertainment system, to name but a few of the furnishings.

Separate to this was Alex's office and bathroom and, of course, the bedroom. The balcony was an added bonus. None of the other ships offered this feature, allowing the captain and his wife ultimate privacy when they wanted to sunbathe.

Sally loved sitting out on the balcony watching Alex take the ship in and out of port. Because she didn't travel as much as she used to, she liked to watch as many arrivals and departures as possible. Tonight, being a tender port, departure was reasonably straightforward. Sally watched as Alex took control of the ship turning it through 180-degrees preparatory to setting off again for the next port of call, Isla Margarita.

He really does look very handsome in that uniform, Sally thought as she admired Alex from afar.

* * *

'Do you think we've done the right thing?' Charlie asked as she chose a low-fat option from the dinner menu. She was watching her weight carefully now. The wedding dress she had bought two months earlier was still a little tight. She had bought it this way on purpose, promising herself it would be loose by the big day.

Charlie and Mike had come on the cruise to get married. Charlie had dreamed of the traditional big white wedding, while Mike was more of a realist and promptly brought her back down to earth reminding her that it wouldn't work because of their family's complicated backgrounds. In the end, Charlie had given in and acknowledged her fiancé was right. Her parents had recently divorced after her father was caught having an affair. The break up had been a messy one. Charlie's father remarried as soon as the divorce papers came through and started another family with his new wife, while Amelia, Charlie's mum, was still on her own and devastated by the effects of the break up.

Mike's family weren't much better. His parents were still together, but he had never seen eye to eye with his father. He kept his distance where he could, and only made contact on special occasions, like Christmas and Birthdays, and even then it was only because he felt guilty for neglecting his mother. His parents weren't even aware he was engaged, let alone about to be married.

This was Charlie and Mike's first cruise. A few months earlier, they had watched a holiday programme together, and the following day Mike had made a trip to the travel agents to get more details about getting married at sea. The girl at the travel agents had got so carried away with the idea that the excitement began to rub off on Mike. Seven and a half thousand pounds later, he and Charlie were booked on a holiday of a lifetime, and the wedding was scheduled for the twenty third of January. The reality of what he had done hit him like a wet fish across the face when he approached Charlie's front door to tell her the news.

It was a Friday, and they had planned a quiet night-in with a take away and a movie. But when he put the key in the lock, he suddenly felt a little sick. What if Charlie had different plans for their big day? Christ had he just wasted a huge amount of the wedding fund.

As he opened the front door, the excitement rapidly wore off. He realized quickly that he needed to approach the conversation with caution. After sharing a bottle of wine with his fiancé, most of which he poured into Charlie's glass, he decided this was the best time to break the news. The plan he decided, apart from getting her a bit tipsy, was to act so excited that she couldn't possibly say no. And the plan worked perfectly – until the next morning when doubt started creeping into Charlie's mind.

'So it will just be you and me? That's all?' she asked over breakfast in bed.

Mike's next best attempt was to keep the excitement going.

'Well, you me and the captain. Can you believe that the captain of Ocean Magic will be marrying us?'

'Right so it will just be you, me and the captain. And I always thought three was a crowd,' Charlie replied.

That was the point when Mike seriously doubted his impulsive decision. He realized very quickly that he really should have talked to Charlie first.

* * *

'Good evening madam are you ready to order?' the waiter interrupted.

'Yes, please. I'll have the green salad to start, and the salmon with cherry tomato relish as a main course. Is it possible to have it poached rather than fried?'

'Yes, of course, madam. No problem at all.'

'With steamed vegetables and no dressing on the salad, thanks.'

'The shrimp cocktail and the lamb for me please,' Mike requested. 'With French fries.'

'Certainly, sir. Excellent choice.'

The waiter left, and Mike looked across the table at Charlie.

'Look, there is no other way for us to do this.'

'But don't you think we should have told them we were planning to get married during the cruise? They deserve that much, surely?'

'I know. I feel as guilty as you. But what option do we have?'

'A glass of wine, madam?'

'Yes, please,' Charlie replied, taking a large sip as soon as it was poured.

'Cheers. Here's to us.' Mike raised his glass.

'Cheers.' Charlie took another large sip. Mike forced a smile while they looked at each other sympathetically wishing they didn't feel so guilty. After all, their wedding day was meant to be the happiest day of their lives.

* * *

Just after eleven, Penny walked back towards her cabin. As she made her way down the long corridor, she saw a figure enter the cabin next door that was being used by Danny and the kids. It was a little darker than normal, and the cabin steward's trolley was for some reason parked just outside the room, so she couldn't make out who it was. She just knew it was too early for Danny to be calling it a night. Wasting no time, she sprinted along the corridor to investigate.

She had a spare key for the cabin and didn't hesitate to use it. If she had known how to get hold of Danny immediately, she might have waited for him to arrive. But Josh and Katie were in the cabin fast asleep. She couldn't afford to waste any time.

She opened the door to the family sized room, which was in complete darkness, then as she moved towards the light switch, the bathroom door flung open and Josh ran fully clothed straight under the covers of his single bed.

'Josh! Christ! You scared the life out of me, where have you been?'

Josh's expression was blank.

'Did you sneak out again after you told me you were going to bed?'

Not only that, but he had made it sound a whole lot more convincing coming back at half past eight telling Penny he had eaten too much at the pizza party and needed to go to bed and sleep it off.

'I did warn you, Josh, that if you're not to be trusted, then you'll have to be with the younger boys and girls.'

'No, Penny. You can't do that. I'm sorry. I won't do it again, I promise.'

He had been so careful not to get caught out. He knew Penny's routine like the back of his hand. After he checked in with her, she would go out to watch a show or get something to eat, but she never normally came back until after midnight. It was now only ten minutes past eleven, and she had well and truly caught him out.

'Give me one good reason why I shouldn't tell your father?'

'Because he'll kill me,' Josh replied.

'Seriously, Josh. I'm this close.'

'Okay, okay,' he answered, and then added in a squeaky, embarrassed tone. 'There's this girl, and she's allowed to stay out until The Club closes at midnight, and I think she likes me. But if she knew I had to be home by ten, she wouldn't be interested.'

Interested in what? Was Penny's next question. But that, she decided, was a conversation for Josh and his father.

Penny had known Josh for only a little over a month, but the impression he had given her was that he was tremendously shy when it came to girls. If he was volunteering this much information, he obviously really liked this one.

'Okay, Josh. You've won me over. But this is a very rare occurrence. Don't think I'll be so lenient in the future. So this is the deal, and listen carefully. You have my permission to stay out until midnight, but not one minute past. But if I'm going to help you, you need to help me – and if your father finds out, it's the first time you've done it ok?'

'Okay,' he replied, thinking that was easier than he thought it might be.

'And I will come past The Club every night to check you are alright. Now get some sleep, and don't forget to get undressed.'

'Okay,' he said, smiling cunningly at Penny as he pulled his t-shirt over his head.

Penny closed the cabin door taking care not to wake Katie, and went next door to her cabin. Realizing she would probably lose her job if Danny found out she had faltered so easily in her first confrontation with his son. She knew also that if she didn't give Josh permission to stay out, he would continue to sneak off after hours regardless. No, it was much better that she knew where he was than discover he wasn't in his bed one night. At least now she could keep a closer eye on him.

* * *

It might have been approaching midnight, but Sasha was sitting out on her balcony enjoying the warm Caribbean breeze blowing through her hair. Today had been the best so far. She hadn't ventured too far from the ship; just far enough to get away from the crowds of passengers who seemed to be invading the small island and setting up deck chairs and laying down beach towels as soon as they found a bear patch of sand, thereby marking their territory for the day. She had been looking forward to snorkelling for so long. She had even taken her own snorkel and mask that she had bought the last time she was on holiday.

The sea was emerald green. She had walked towards it enticed by the gentle ripple of waves calling out to her. The lukewarm temperature was irresistibly inviting, and without realizing it she had spent three hours looking through her mask at the multitude of beautiful multi-coloured fish. The underwater camera she had bought in the ship's gift shop captured some fantastic images.

The ship had sailed hours ago, and she had sat out on the balcony for the last two and a half. She decided to pass on dinner, and instead ordered a salad from room service. The night before had been very enjoyable, not to mention eventful, but she couldn't help but think the other couples on her table, as nice as they were, wouldn't want her tagging along with them every night.

She had also lost her appetite again, which made going down to dinner even more of a pointless exercise.

Maybe her mother had a point. Sasha considered that notion as she picked at the chef's salad that she hadn't made any effort to eat. Her father's betrayal had caused an unbelievable amount of pain and heartache. Maybe it had caused her to push Ben away. Yes, maybe he felt that he was left with no option but to call off the engagement.

The break-up would have been bad enough normally, but at least she would have been at home where she and Ben would have had a chance to talk. Cruising around the Caribbean onboard the ship of her dreams made it all feel so surreal.

Sasha and Ben had got engaged five weeks before Adam Carter's death. The engagement was meant to a short one; six months ideally, or a year at the absolute most. Or so Ben had insisted. But the unexpected news of her father's death had resulted in the wedding being put on hold indefinitely.

Sasha and Ben continued to be engaged, but a wedding date was never set. Now, three and a half years later, the only one who continuously reminded them that they couldn't stay engaged forever was Sasha's mother.

Sasha had been working abroad. She had volunteered to write a freelance article about underprivileged children in the Far East. Visiting Orphanages and doing various charity work along the way. It was something she felt very passionate about and when the opportunity arose she grabbed it with both hands. She had just returned home from a three-month trip when her life changed forever.

It was a Saturday morning, and she was keen to spend as much time as possible with her family, filling them in on where she had been and what she had experienced during her trip to Asia. Adam, Sasha's father, was in the kitchen preparing a fantastic Spanish feast for all the family as a way of marking his daughters return. Mr Carter loved Spain. He spoke fluent Spanish and he and his wife holidayed there all the time.

Sasha was looking forward to her dad's homemade gazpacho soup, array of tapas and paella valencia. This was to be washed down with a jug of his own special recipe sangria.

As the dishes were prepared one by one and the table set as if they were having important guests join them for dinner that evening, Adam announced that he was going to the corner shop to get some fresh fruit for the sangria. After lunch Elizabeth insisted on pouring herself and Sasha a glass of ice cold Sancerre to celebrate her daughter's safe return, and congratulate her on her successful trip.

Sasha and Mrs Carter sat gossiping and flicking through photographs of Thailand, Cambodia and Malaysia. Elizabeth was wishing that one day she could convince Adam to take her there instead of Spain, just for a change. Not that she didn't enjoy Spain, she just fanaticised about experiencing a different culture, embracing a different way of life. Little more than an hour passed when Elizabeth remarked on how long it was taking Adam to get the fruit. Sasha dismissed the comment thinking her father had got caught up in conversation with someone at Lenny's store. But as it approached three o'clock, Sasha poured them both a second glass of wine, and as she did she could see her mother getting more and more anxious.

'It's not a problem,' Sasha claimed. 'I'll give him a ring on his mobile'.

As she finished dialling, her fathers mobile rang out somewhere in the room. *Oh that's strange* she thought. *He hasn't taken it with him.*

'Call Kyle and ask if he's with him,' Mrs Carter suggested.

Sasha did and scrolled down the phone's address book until she found what she wanted. Soon the phone was ringing.

'Is everything okay?' said Kyle, evidently sensing something was wrong.

'Yes, fine.' Sasha reminded him to be home by seven o'clock as dad was cooking a special meal. 'But just before you go, you haven't seen him today have you?'

'No,' Kyle replied. 'I've been working non-stop. I was meant to finish by lunch time, but I'm too far behind.'

With that, Mrs Carter remembered Adam mentioning something about popping round to Neive's to finish her kitchen that he was tiling for her. So Sasha picked up the phone to check if he was there.

'No,' Neive replied. 'I haven't seen him since Tuesday night. Is everything okay?'

'Yes, fine I think. Dad popped out a couple of hours ago and hasn't come home yet. I just wondered if he was with you, that's all. Just give me a ring if he stops by.'

'Okay, I will. See you at seven.' Neive confirmed the dinner arrangements.

'Yes, see you then,' Sasha replied, disconnecting.

Lenny's shop was only two hundred yards from the house on the corner of Richmond Street where they lived, so Sasha decided to go and investigate where her father had got to. By now she was also starting to worry; a concept, which seemed a little strange that at 3.30pm in the afternoon, on a relatively pleasant autumn day, caused any concern whatsoever. After all, he was a 56-year-old man who was more than capable of looking after himself. *Why was mother so anxious,* she thought? He could have popped round to see one of his friends, such as Jim or Clive. Or he might have stopped off at the local for a quiet beer, none of which were likely options as he never went off on his own without telling someone where he was going.

When Sasha arrived at Lenny's and asked after her father, the vacant look on the face of Lindsay Gould, the shop assistant, made the hairs on the back of her neck stand up. Lindsey knew the family quite well and was positive he hadn't been in at all that day. Three and a half hours had now passed, and Mr Carter hadn't been where he said he was going. On opening the kitchen door, Sasha had expected to see him standing there wondering what all the fuss was about. Or, at the very least, expecting her mother to say she knew where he was.

Just then, the phone rang and Sasha rushed to answer it.

'It's Neive here,' said a voice. 'Have you heard from dad yet?'

'No, I think you'd best come over – and don't bring the kids. Mum is acting very strange. It's almost as if she knows something is wrong.'

Sasha spoke in a whisper so her mother couldn't hear.

Afterwards, she picked up the phone again and made a quick call to Kyle asking him to come home early. Before Neive and Kyle arrived, Sasha had noticed her father's car was missing, which was unexpected as Adam was meant to be walking to the shop. This gave Sasha the feeling that everything was okay again. Maybe he had just gone for a drive. It was a beautiful day, after all.

When Kyle arrived, there was only one thing for it. He and mum would go and look for dad while Neive and Sasha would wait for any phone calls. Bridgewater wasn't a big town. It would only take them twenty maybe thirty minutes to drive round and see Adam's car.

One and a half hours later, Elizabeth walked in the front door. It seemed a little irrational, but she wanted to call the police straight away. While she was dialling, Kyle explained to his sisters that they had been out in the car and heard sirens heading towards the Castle. They followed two police cars and an ambulance, but they quickly blocked the road leading up to the Castle before they got there. Mum and Kyle had got out to investigate and saw the taillights of Adam's black Saab 93. The strange thing was, the number plate had been covered up. Mum had tried to get through the roadblock shouting at the officers on duty that that was her husband's car and that she needed to see him. But she was told they must leave the scene immediately and return to the house where someone would come and talk to them.

Elizabeth wasn't willing to wait until it was convenient for them to call past. She wanted to know right there and then where her husband was and when she could see him. Obviously there had been some sort of incident. But what was with all the secrecy surrounding it?

Twenty minutes later there was a knock on the door. During all the earlier shouting at the Castle, one of the police officers had managed to make contact with Kyle and told him to call a close friend and have him or her wait with his mother in case there was any bad news. Kyle knew there and then, the few words spoken were confirmation his father was dead.

Fiona appeared at the door of the sitting room armed with a bottle of brandy in case Kyle's suspicion was right.

'Can I come in?'

'Come in, come in,' Elizabeth cried. 'Something bad has happened to Adam, and I don't know where he is.'

Five minutes later, the doorbell rang. They answered it quickly, and two very young looking police officers asked if they could come in.

'I have some very bad news,' the youngest of the two announced. He was trembling slightly at the thought of what he next had to say. 'Adam Carter had a heart attack at 3.15pm this afternoon. He lost control of his car and crashed it. The emergency team were quick on the scene, and they did their best to save him, but failed. He was pronounced dead at 3.35pm. I'm terribly, terribly sorry.'

He paused for breath, and then continued.

'Miss Jolly, his secretary, however, survived. She escaped the crash with only minor cuts and bruises.'

'Miss Jolly?' Elizabeth screamed. 'Who the hell is Miss Jolly?'

'Oh shit,' the young policeman swore. 'I presumed you knew he had company.'

'God, Kyle. What now?' Sasha remarked. 'This is a real live nightmare.'

Thinking back to the horrific phone call she had to make to Joe her youngest brother who was at university in Edinburgh at the time, it had truly been the worst day of her life. But still even now, it was the betrayal that hurt more than anything. That feeling would stay with her forever.

After months of mourning her husband's death, along with his betrayal, Elizabeth Carter became obsessed with the idea of finding another man to keep her in the style that she had been become accustomed to. Neive, Kyle and Joe, however, knew that no man would be a patch on their father, and they preferred to keep their distance as much as was acceptable under the circumstances. He had betrayed them all, but he was still their father, and until this day they hadn't said a word against him.

Sasha, on the other hand, was of a very different opinion. Elizabeth Carter had been on several dates since her husband died. She was absolutely devastated at the time, and looking back, Sasha much preferred the way she was now compared to the wreck she was three nearly four years ago. It was, after all, thanks to her that her mother was back up and about after months of trying to steer her off antidepressants and arranging hours and hours of counselling. She had hoped her mother would get back to having some sort of life again, but hadn't expected the change to be quite as dramatic.

Sasha didn't get on with her older sister. Or, more to the point, Neive didn't get on with her. Their parents, and even Neive's husband on at least one occasion, admitted that Neive was jealous of her sister's good looks and trim figure. And then there was the successful career that Sasha had made for herself as a journalist, not to forget that she was soon to be married to an extremely handsome and enormously successful businessman, or so they thought.

Neive was quite different to Sasha. She had the same straight dark brown hair and green-blue eyes, but was a lot plainer in looks; she didn't have the same attractive features as her sister. And to add insult to injury, Neive struggled with her size 14/16 figure where Sasha was a perfect ten.

Although, having two children in two years probably had something to do with it. Neive had also experienced a terrible long run of bad luck in miscarrying twins two days before her father's funeral. For months afterwards, she suffered very badly with depression, cutting off her friends and family and refusing help from anyone.

Sasha did her best to support her sister, but Neive always misconstrued Sasha's good intentions as gloating at her misfortune.

Sasha could never understand this, and worried now that Neive would use the news of her break-up with Ben as an opportunity to gloat back at her.

Kyle and Joe wouldn't be particularly bothered if she and Ben were to split up. They got on okay with Ben, but didn't think the sun shone out of him the way their mother did. It upset Kyle that his mother never worshiped him or Joe like she worshiped Ben.

If it had been anyone else apart from Ben, Mrs Carter would probably be more understanding, or so Sasha thought. Unfortunately for her, the nightmare hadn't even begun.

After re-living the horrific events of that day once more, it became blatantly clear to Sasha that her mother was right. Her fear of commitment was undoubtedly down to the fact she didn't know why her father felt he needed a secret life. If she didn't know and understand her father, who had brought her up and been around her whole life, how was she ever meant to trust another man, someone she had only known for a few years?

Ouch, Sasha thought. *The truth really does hurt.*

Chapter 4

Isle Margarita 08:00 Arrival 16:00 Departure

'Happy birthday gorgeous!' Alex announced as he came bouncing into the cabin. 'Now, I've got two presents for you, but unfortunately I only have time to give you one at the minute.' With a cheeky smirk on his face, he continued. 'The other I was hoping we will have time for this afternoon!'

Taking Sally in his arms, Alex ran his fingers through her shoulder length blonde hair and kissed her passionately.

'Now that's just an appetiser, and no matter how hard you beg you're just going to have to wait till later. Okay?'

'Okay.'

Pouring a glass of iced water to cool himself, Alex smiled at his wife.

'Seriously though, I have got a meeting with some of the seniors in five minutes, so I've only got time to give you this.'

Checking his watch once more Alex walked over to his desk drawer and produced a birthday card along with a very neatly wrapped gift. Inside the card he had written the words: *To My Darling Wife. You mean the world to me. Have a wonderful birthday and enjoy your cruise. All my Love Alex, xx* And in small print at the bottom he added; *Dinner tonight 9pm. Just us.*

Sally's face lit up as she accepted the small parcel. She gasped as she opened the dark blue leather box to reveal the most fabulous diamond encrusted Bulgari necklace.

'Thank you, Alex. It's gorgeous. But seriously, darling, it's too much. It must have cost a small fortune.'

'Don't be silly. You're worth every penny. Try it on. Here, let me help.'

Taking hold of both ends, he looped the necklace around Sally's neck, carefully securing the double catch at the back.

'There. Turn around and let's see what it looks like.' Smiling shyly, Sally did as he suggested. 'Wow, it looks great.'

'It *feels* great. Now I just have to decide which dress goes best with it.'

Still not quite able to believe her luck, Sally thought back to last summer, the first time she had seen and fallen in love with the necklace. She and Alex were in Nice for a long weekend. After a long lunch in the old town they had spent the afternoon window-shopping. Sally had noticed the necklace in the window of a jeweller's shop on Rue de la Buffa; just a few streets back from the famous Promenade des Anglaise. She even tried dropping a few subtle hints, hoping the bottle of wine they had shared over lunch would be enough to make Alex buy it for her. But unfortunately, it failed to have the desired effect.

Alex, however, managed to get free for an hour later that afternoon. Sending Sally to La Gallerie Lafayette to do some shopping, he had returned to the jewellers to inspect the necklace. But as a spur of the moment gift, the price seemed a little excessive, so he bought the necklace for Sally's next birthday, and also bought matching earrings. It was intended as a special surprise to be presented at dinner that evening.

Cheeky, Sally thought. *I knew he couldn't have missed my subtle hints – or, more like it, my stare-you-in-the-face blatantly obvious demands. Thinking back on it now, he sent me off shopping so he could do a little sly purchasing of his own. Well I call that a win-win situation.*

Sally kissed and thanked Alex once more. The fact that he had reacted scored almost as many points as the necklace itself.

'God, is that the time?' said Alex. 'I really must go. Meeting to host and I'm now officially late. See you at one, don't forget!' he called back to his wife as he grabbed his folder and rushed out of the door.

'I won't. Looking forward to it,' Sally shouted after him grinning uncontrollably, unable to wipe the smile off her face.

A few minutes later there was a knock on the door and Jay, the captain's steward, walked in with a beautiful bouquet of flowers accompanied by a bottle of vintage pink Moet.

'Good morning, madam. These are for you. Where would you like them?'

'Wow, they're lovely! Just put them on the table over there. Yes, that's wonderful. Thank you, Jay.'

'And the champagne?'

'Hmm. I think we'll put it in the fridge for now.' Sally smiled.

'Very well, madam, and happy birthday.'

A little overwhelmed by all the attention she was receiving, Sally walked over to the table and opened the small white envelope. She took out the card which read; *Happy Birthday Sally. Have a wonderful day onboard Ocean Magic, from James and the Hotel Team.*

James was the hotel director onboard. He was in charge of the entire hotel operation. He was remarkably friendly, and whenever she travelled he always treated Sally with a huge amount of reverence.

Relaxing back in her chair with a cup of green tea and still wrapped in her white Ocean Magic embroidered bathrobe, she thought her day couldn't possibly get any better. Birthdays were never this good at home.

After the initial excitement wore off, she realized Alex wouldn't be back for a couple of hours when they had arranged to have a long lunch on the balcony. Alex had pulled out all the stops and arranged for the executive chef to cook the lunch personally. He knew it would be an extra special affair.

Unsure what to do with her morning, Sally decided to phone the spa and book herself a full body massage and possibly even a manicure, if they could fit it in. Most of the 3200 passengers had gone ashore, so the very pleasant receptionist confirmed both appointments straight away.

As she walked across the open deck to get to the health spa, the ship was very quiet. She watched a couple of children splash about in the family pool, enjoying the freedom whilst almost everyone else was taking advantage of the port of call.

When she arrived, she was presented with a bathrobe and slippers and asked to change and wait in the relaxation room where Maria would come and get her.

Maria had for several years worked at sea. Sally recognised her immediately from having worked on the last ship Alex was captain of. The massage was wonderful, and lasted a whole hour and a half. During the treatment, Sally had dozed off several times and felt more relaxed than she had done in weeks.

The manicure had done wonders for her hands, and Maria even threw in a quick pedicure.

'After all,' she remarked, 'if you can't spoil yourself on your birthday, then when can you?'

Sally concluded her visit with an unexpected thirty-minute facial. She had been on her way out of the spa when one of the girls offered her the chance to try the new oxy jet luxury system. They had just introduced the programme onboard, and the beautician was keen to try it out. The relaxation and pampering session had really done the trick.

By 12.00pm she left the spa feeling like a million dollars. Arriving back at her cabin, she passed through Alex's office and found three more birthday cards awaiting her. She had only looked in his inbox tray hoping to find the ship's daily newspaper. She thought it a little strange at first that having joined the ship only two days ago in St Lucia, how did so many people know it was her birthday?

She thought about saving the cards for later, then curiosity got the better of her and she decided; *What the heck?* She would open them now.

The first card read; *Lunch tomorrow in Curacao—my treat. I'll call you later to arrange a time. Happy birthday, love Joyce.* Joyce was the chief engineer's wife. Sally and her got on really well, and always looked forward to cruises together. But it was a rare occurrence nowadays, as Sally was cruising less and less. They didn't get the chance to catch up as much as they used to.

The second card made her laugh. The writing on the front read; *Feliz Cumpleaños* Inside it read; *Birthday wishes from James and Cathleen, Steven, and Jennifer and Lewis and Diane,* along with an apology for not finding anywhere during the cruise selling birthday cards in English.

Sally appreciated the kind gesture. As she slid her thumb under the seal of the third envelope, puzzled by who it could be from, she opened it slowly and read the very neat and stylish handwriting.

Suddenly her breath quickened and her hands started to shake as she read the words. *Alex is having an affair.* Instantly, her legs felt loose and disconnected, and her heart started beating so hard she felt it was going to explode. She fell back onto the sofa, the card held tight in her hand as the envelope fell to the floor.

The bellboy had delivered it through reception, and all three cards had arrived at the same time. How would she ever know who had sent this particular card? Was it a joke? A very sick joke nevertheless. It had to be, hadn't it? Alex wouldn't cheat on me. Would he?

The facial had put a bit of colour in her cheeks, but now she looked as if she had seen a ghost. *What if it was true*, she thought? This mysterious person knew it was my birthday today. Did Alex tell her? Surely that's the only explanation, and in that case, it had to be true. Sally's imagination was beginning to run riot. Or was it just someone trying to cause trouble?

Alex was in a very high-powered and high profile job. Maybe someone has a grudge against him. *But how did they know it was my birthday today?* Sally considered all the facts, but no matter which way she looked at it, she couldn't come up with a reasonable explanation.

It was approaching half past twelve, and the steward was already out on the balcony setting up the table for lunch. Sally was trying hard to stop shaking, and trying to put the thought of her husband having an affair out of her head. For the time being at least, she decided to hide the card.

She had only accompanied Alex on two cruises in the last seven months. There could be a very good chance he was having an affair. *But why does he keep asking me to travel more, and stay on longer every time I come away?* Sally thought. Maybe he's playing games with me. That would give him very good grounds to dismiss any rumour that may arise. *Well I'm not going to say anything*, Sally decided as she poured a white wine spritzer for herself and a sparkling water for Alex, taking a few large sips she tried to calm herself down.

Lunch passed a little quicker than Alex had planned. He had taken an extended lunch break to celebrate his wife's birthday and enjoy some quality time with her as they saw so little of each other while he was away. Sally struggled to eat, but did her best to force down some salad whilst trying hard not to let Alex know that anything was wrong.

The array of salads was accompanied by the most magnificent display of fresh lobster. Knowing that it was Sally's favourite dish, Alex had requested this specially.

'Thank you,' she smiled as Alex placed half a lobster on her plate.

'Is everything okay, sweetheart?' he said. 'You seem a little distracted. Is there something on your mind?'

'No, I'm fine really. I just can't believe you have gone to so much trouble for me.'

'Nonsense, Sally. You're totally worth it. How many times do I need to tell you? I'm so proud to have you as my wife.'

Sally forced a second smile, and accepted a kiss from her husband.

She waited as long as she could before excusing herself. As soon as she felt it was acceptable, she left the table and went into the bedroom and lay down on the king sized bed. With a slightly different idea in mind, Alex picked up their glasses and followed his wife into the bedroom. But Sally subtly brushed him off claiming she hadn't slept well the night before. Alex, whose ego was slightly bruised by his wife's rejection, was starting to become a little concerned. He decided it was probably best to leave her to sleep and placed a blanket over her to keep her warm. Then he kissed her forehead and turned out the light.

* * *

Charlie and Mike had waited until after lunch to go ashore. Isla Margarita was another anchor port, so there was always a bit of a queue to go ashore first thing in the morning. Porlamar is one of Margarita's larger towns, with plenty of tourist attractions to enjoy. Charlie and Mike hadn't planned anything hard and fast for their afternoon ashore. They had hoped to pay a visit to one of the churches not far from the Plaza Bolivar.

Mike had watched the port presentation, and decided it might be worth a visit. Charlie wasn't interested in churches, museums, or anything along those lines, and had other plans; to go to the beach and work on her tan, for instance. The couple struck a compromise and, after Mike's agreed half hour visit to the church, they got in a taxi and went to Playa El Agua.

Playa El Agua was a fourteen-mile taxi ride from Porlamar, but it has a lot more to offer in the way of, cafes, restaurants and water sports and general entertainment compared to La Caracola beach, a short journey from the ship's designated tender point. The couple arrived at the beach, where Mike arranged a couple of sun beds and placed the beach towels on top of them, while Charlie topped up her sun cream before relaxing into her chair with a bridal magazine she had brought from home.

As she browsed the pictures of the beautiful brides in their gorgeous gowns, she couldn't help but notice all the things she didn't even have to think about when planning for her wedding. Arranging a gift for the bridesmaid and best man, a bouquet of flowers for the mother of the bride, fun cameras and favours to put on the tables for the guests' amusement during the reception, the name cards and table seating plans. The list went on and on. All of a sudden she felt her eyes fill up at the thought of her walking down the aisle, with no one to tell her how beautiful she was and how well she had done losing sixteen pounds for her big day.

No one but Mike, of course.

Mike appeared by her side with two bottles of coke. 'Here you go.'

'Thanks.' Charlie forced a smile as she looked up to take the bottle from Mike.

'Hey, what's wrong?' he said. 'We are meant to be having fun, remember. It's a beautiful day, and we're surrounded by sun, sea and surf. We're on the holiday of a lifetime.'

'I know. It's just...' but before Charlie could stop herself, tears started streaming down her face.

'Hey, come here, it's all right.'

Mike took the bottle of coke from her hand and placed it in the sand. He sat beside her and wrapped his arms around her shoulders, holding her tight while she sobbed for a few minutes.

'I'm sorry Mike. I'm just not finding this as easy as you.'

'I know darling, but if we are going to do this, we have to be happy about it. If not, we might as well call the wedding off and get married when we return home.'

'No, it's fine, honestly. I just wish it wasn't just us, that's all.'

Mike picked up the wedding magazine and put it back in Charlie's bag, then handed her back her coke.

'Come on, let's finish these. Then I'm taking you for some delicious seafood. I know just the place.'

Charlie looked up and managed a smile, and not forced this time.

'Okay,' she replied.

'Oh no.' Mike sat upright in his sun lounger. 'I've just remembered. We've got to get back to the ship. We've got a meeting with the wedding coordinator at three o'clock. It completely slipped my mind.'

Charlie looked puzzled. 'I thought it wasn't until Thursday.'

'It was meant to be, but Angela phoned last night while you were in the shower. There are eight weddings this cruise, and she's finding it difficult to accommodate everyone, what with dates, rehearsals and everything. So I agreed to change the meeting to today. I'm so sorry.'

'So much for a nice seafood lunch!' Charlie replied. 'Oh well, at least I don't need to worry about putting on any more weight.'

'I'll make it up to you, I promise.' Mike looked abashed as he hurriedly put his book and beach towel into Charlie's bag.

After a quick dash in the taxi, followed by a short boat ride to the ship, they arrived back onboard by a quarter to three. Mike had arranged for them to meet the wedding coordinator in Café Rouge, a coffee shop in the main atrium, to confirm the last minute arrangements for the wedding.

They were due to be married at 2.00pm the day after Puerto Quetzal. Mike was excited about the wedding, but no matter what he did to try and make things easier for Charlie, he couldn't seem to get her in the same positive frame of mind.

'What about asking Connor and Tina along to the ceremony?' Mike suggested as they sat waiting for Angela to turn up.

Connor and Tina were a lovely couple. They had met them in Vineyards, the wine bar, on the second night of the cruise. They had begun chatting while Charlie and Mike sampled several tasters of red wine, before choosing a bottle to enjoy that evening. The two couples got on really well, and had even gone ashore for lunch together in Mayreau.

'We hardly know them Mike. We can't invite two people we don't know to our wedding. It's worse than having nobody there at all!'

'Okay, Charlie. Fine. But I have to say I'm beginning to get a little concerned about the way you are acting. Are you having second thoughts?'

Angela arrived a couple of minutes early – and just in time to break up the conversation. When the waitress passed, Angela ordered them all a coffee. She then began to explain the details of the wedding. Charlie perked up a little when she once again saw the ship's wedding brochure. All of the images were of the bride and groom. They both looked so happy, posing in various locations around the ship with the clear blue sky and jade green Caribbean sea behind them. It really did look very exotic.

Angela went on to explain where and when the service would take place. She talked about the order of the ceremony and confirmed their booking in Shu, their chosen restaurant for that evening. Just over an hour later, they left the meeting and made their way back to their cabin.

'You see, it's going to be perfect.' Mike put his arm round Charlie's shoulder to reassure her.

She smiled back at him. 'I know.'

'I was thinking about going to the gym for an hour, if that's ok?' Mike asked. 'The food on here is so nice, and I don't want to look fat in our wedding photos.'

'Of course. On you go.'

Mike changed quickly and kissed his fiancée gently on the lips.

'Are you sure you will be okay?'

'Absolutely,' Charlie insisted as she closed the door behind him.

Glad to be left alone at last, she lay down on the bed and grabbed hold of Mike's pillow. It was all such a mess. For them to have a family wedding, surely it couldn't be as bad as Mike was making out. But the biggest problem of all, Charlie felt, was the fact that her mother would never forgive her if she got married without her being present.

Half an hour later, her mind was made up. All she had to do now was find a way to tell Mike that she couldn't go through with the wedding.

She would tell him tonight, she decided.

* * *

Alex was giving the final instructions to the hotel team for the surprise party he had planned for Sally that evening. Sally had presumed they would be going out for a pre-dinner drink; probably to the Ocean View bar on Deck 15. That was her favourite of the public rooms. But Alex had made other arrangements.

He had invited forty of their close friends, a mixture of passengers, officers and crew to join them in his cabin for champagne and canapés before taking his wife to The Green Room where they could enjoy dinner by themselves for a change, rather than hosting a table as normal.

Sally awoke to the sound of the phone ringing next to the bed. Still half asleep, she sat up and reached for the receiver.

'Happy birthday, Sally!'

She recognised the voice immediately. It was her old friend Joyce. The pair chatted away for a good fifteen minutes before arranging to meet at the Deck 6 gangway at 12 o'clock the following day where they would get a taxi to take them off for lunch.

'Looking forward to catching up,' said Joyce.

'Me too. See you tomorrow,' Sally replied before hanging up.

She hadn't intended to doze off and was glad of the phone ringing to awaken her. As she reached for the alarm clock at the far side of the bed, she realized she had been asleep for three and a half hours. She quickly climbed out of bed and suddenly remembered about the card. She wished it had been a bad dream, but just to confirm it was real, she opened her bedside drawer and there it was.

The bright red envelope.

Sally had planned to stay out of Alex's way for the rest of the afternoon. She found it difficult to hide anything from him, and she didn't want to say something she would regret should the card turn out to be some kind of sick joke. Sally and Alex had a very open and honest relationship. She had never kept anything this big to herself before.

Moments later, when she had finished reapplying her make-up, she suddenly became concerned by the noise and flurry of activity in the day room next door. Cautiously opening the bedroom door, she popped her head round to witness a team of seven or eight bar staff, waiters and other crew members she didn't recognise rearranging the cabin furniture. The waiters were setting up tables, while the bar staff was shipping in crates of champagne, soft drinks and glassware. Alex, who was obviously quite excited by the amount of activity, was standing-by instructing individuals on how he wanted the room set up. Dino, the head waiter from Nachos the Mexican restaurant, was in charge of setting up the bar, while Jay, Alex's steward, appeared along with three others carrying an incredible selection of canapés.

Alex had gone to the trouble of ordering all of Sally's favourites. Anderson, the Maître d', was solely in charge of the champagne waterfall, and was busy arranging flutes one on top of the other. Alex had chosen this to be the centrepiece of the room and, as if there wasn't enough going on, the florist appeared with several flower arrangements.

'There you are sweetheart. I knew you would come out sooner or later.'

'What's going on, Alex?'

'Oh, nothing special, darling!' Alex put his arms around his wife's waist. 'Just a small gathering of some of our close friends to help you celebrate your birthday.'

'Haven't you planned enough surprises today?'

'No, not even close.' He looked into Sally's eyes. 'Is everything okay, Sally? You look a little pale.'

'Yes, of course. I'm fine. Just a little shocked by all this. It all looks fantastic.'

'Sorry I didn't tell you, but it wouldn't have been a surprise if I had, now would it? Why don't you pick out something nice to wear and we'll get this party underway. The guests should be arriving any minute.'

Sally and Alex's dinner table companions were the first to arrive followed by another thirty or so guests, everyone presenting Sally with various cards and gifts. Seriously overwhelmed by all the attention she was receiving, this was the best surprise party she could have hoped for. She continued chatting away to a few friends before spotting Martin, the chief engineer, and his wife Joyce enter the room.

'You really are mischievous keeping this surprise from me,' Sally said to Joyce.

'It wasn't easy, you know. I had to hold myself back from saying see you tonight, when we were on the phone earlier,' replied Joyce.

Martin winked, admiring the beautiful necklace Sally was wearing. 'Alex has certainly done you proud,' he said. 'From what I've heard, you've been spoiled rotten.'

'He's not made it easy for me, you know. It's a certain someone's fortieth next month. How am I going to compete with all of this?' Sally and Joyce giggled as Martin shrugged his shoulders.

The champagne was flowing, and the party was in full swing. Sally glanced round the room. She recognised all of the men, and most of the women, but there were one or two faces she couldn't place.

There was also an extremely attractive lady who stood out from the rest. She appeared to be on her own and was standing by the door wearing a perfectly tailored dark silk trouser suit. Her long blonde hair was put up. She really was quite striking. Must be a passenger, Sally thought. The woman wasn't wearing a uniform or a name badge, so she could be a guest entertainer or someone, Sally mused, perplexed by her presence. But how did she know Alex?

'Senior doctor's new girlfriend,' Joyce whispered in her ear.

'Oh right, of course.' Sally looked away quickly realizing she had been caught staring.

'He's done well for himself there.'

'His poor wife hasn't,' Joyce replied. 'She's been left with a broken marriage and two kids. Worst of all, she only found out about the affair when she was on here with the family for the Christmas cruise.'

'What, seriously?' Sally looked stunned.

'No one knows how she found out. But there was an incident one night in one of the bars where she poured a glass of wine over him went back to the cabin, packed her things, and disembarked the ship the next day. Worse still, it was Christmas Eve.'

'That's obscene.'

'Maybe, but it's true.'

'That poor woman,' Sally sympathised. 'What a jerk. I always thought he was really nice.'

'Just goes to show, you never can tell.'

'You're not kidding!' Sally agreed, pulling a face before taking another sip of champagne.

She had never been the jealous type, and trusted Alex implicitly, but receiving the card and hearing the story of the doctor and his mistress all on the same day was turning her into a green-eyed lunatic. She was going to have to try harder to hide her envious thoughts.

After drinks, canopies and a very enjoyable party, everyone thanked Sally and Alex for the invitation and went their separate ways down to dinner. Sally and Alex stayed behind and chatted over a second glass of champagne before going to The Green Room. As they browsed over the menu, they noticed a couple a few feet away becoming rather affectionate over their meal.

The young man, feeling like he had to explain, turned to Alex and held his glass in the air.

'She said yes! She said yes!' he shouted.

Delighted for the young couple, Alex and Sally stood up with the rest of the restaurant and congratulated them on their engagement.

'How about we send them a bottle of bubbly to help them celebrate?' Alex suggested.

'Great idea' Sally replied, wishing the couple the best of luck.

* * *

Charlie and Mike finished dinner and made their way down to the sports bar for a post dinner drink. Charlie was preparing to tell Mike that she wanted to postpone the wedding; she just hadn't mastered exactly what to say yet. As they arrived at the bar, Mike disappeared to the bathroom leaving Charlie to order the drinks. So far, she hadn't even caught the bar tender's attention and was staring blankly into space wondering how to approach the subject.

'Charlie? I thought it was you,' a voice interrupted her thoughts.

'Maddy? Oh my goodness. What a surprise. You look fantastic!'

'So do you. You've lost so much weight.'

Charlie looked perplexed giving off an almost uncomfortable vibe in her old friend's presence.

'Oh, I didn't mean it how it sounded. Sorry, I meant... God you look great!'

Relaxing a little, Charlie smiled.

'That's okay, Maddy. Seriously though, what a coincidence. Of all the cruise ships to choose from, who would have thought we would have ended up on the same one at the same time? Who are you here with?'

'My husband, Kim, and four other couples,' Maddy replied. 'Do you remember Laura, Sarah, Kay and Joy from school? They're all over there.' Maddy pointed to a group in the far corner of the room.

'I remember Sarah, Joy and Kay, but I'm not sure I know Laura.'

This wasn't exactly true. Charlie had chosen not to keep Laura's company after she stole her first high school boyfriend from her during a school trip to France. James Marshall had left as Charlie's boyfriend and returned two weeks later as Laura's. Charlie had felt particularly cheated by this. Her parents couldn't afford to pay for her to go on the trip, so she wasn't there to personally extinguish the flames between Laura and James.

'Sarah and Kay are here with their husbands. Joy is engaged, and Laura is still Laura. Keeping her options open as usual. She's here with her current boyfriend, Scott.'

'So what about you, Charlie? I've spotted the ring on your finger, but who – and more importantly, where – is the lucky man?'

'That must be me.'

Maddy looked up to see a tall good-looking guy with dark brown hair and a gorgeous smile appear by Charlie's side. Maddy smiled at her friend, indicating her approval.

Charlie introduced Mike to her old friend, and Maddy insisted the couple join the group for drinks.

'Listen everyone, this is Charlie and Mike. Charlie's an old school friend of mine.'

The group got chatting straight away, and Charlie and Mike were made to feel extremely welcome. Mike took to Lee, Sarah's husband, straight away, chatting amiably as if they also were old school buddies.

'So when's the big day, Charlie?' Maddy asked.

'Not long now. We're getting married during the cruise. It's the sea day after Porto Quetzal.'

'Wow, that sounds dreamy. Getting married on a cruise ship. You must be so excited.'

Excited wasn't quite how Charlie would have put it, but she hadn't seen her friends for so long she wasn't about to tell them how she was really feeling.

'So are your families onboard? Or are they joining you later on? I'd love to meet your mum again after all these years.'

'No, it's going to be a quiet affair. Just us, I'm afraid.'

'Oh, that's a shame,' said Laura. 'Was it last minute or something?'

'No, no nothing like that. We just thought we'd get away from all the usual hustle and bustle surrounding a wedding and make it as hassle-free as possible.'

'Well, it's just as well we're here then, isn't it? You'll need a bridesmaid and a best man to start, and what a fantastic location for a bachelorette party. You didn't think you were going to escape that did you?'

'I'm not sure that's necessary, Maddy.'

'Necessary and essential, my friend,' Maddy replied, eagerly trying to get the bar stewards attention.

'So, who is it going to be then,' said Maddy. 'Come on, spill?

'Who is what going to be?' said Charlie.

'Your bridesmaid silly, don't keep us waiting.'

Chapter 5

Curacao 08:00 Arrival 18:00 Departure

'Come on Josh! We haven't got all day.'
'Josh! Not all day,' Katie imitated her father's instruction while she danced round the cabin with her Little Mermaid backpack strapped to her tiny frame. Danny had bought it for her to use as hand luggage on the flight, and she had hardly taken it off since. Finally Josh came out of the bathroom having spent a good half an hour styling his hair and admiring his work in the mirror. Once more, he was now ready to go ashore.

'About time Josh,' Danny called from the balcony. Katie giggled as Josh stole another glance in the mirror.

'You look funny,' she squealed.

'And you're just stupid,' Josh replied.

'That's enough from both of you. We need to get going if we're going to see the sharks.'

'Will they bite me daddy? I don't want to go if they are going to bite me,' asked Katie, a worried expression on her face.

'No, sweetheart. We're only going to look at them through the glass. They won't bite, I promise.'

Katie breathed a sigh of relief, satisfied that her father wasn't going to throw her into a tank full of hungry sharks.

'I want to see the Turtle Pool,' Josh began. 'James told me about it. It's meant to be really cool. He went there last year with his mum and dad.'

'I'm sure we can fit it in Josh, but we really do need to get going. Don't forget your bag.'

Thankful of the reminder, Josh picked up his backpack and closed the cabin door behind him.

'He's going again this year, but only with his mum this time,' Josh continued as they walked along the corridor.

'Who is?' asked Danny.

'James.'

'Oh right. Why? What's his father doing today?'

'Oh, he can't go. He died in a car crash just after they got home from the cruise last year.'

Stopping in his tracks, and shocked by what Josh had just told him, Danny looked stunned.

'That's terrible, son. Did he tell you all this himself?'

'Well sort of,' Josh continued. 'We were playing a game in The Club, and this older boy shouted at him 'your dad's just plain stupid' and he just started crying. So I told the boy to shut up and went over to James to see what was wrong. He told me what happened and I looked after him for the rest of the day. I guess because I know it's not very nice to only have one parent to look after you.'

Danny nodded thoughtfully, impressed with his son's wisdom and sensitivity.

Spotting Penny at the bottom of the gangway, Katie was off like a shot. Her little pink backpack bobbing up and down as she ran.

Dismissing the morbid conversation as if it was everyday small talk, Josh shouted after her.

'Wait for me!'

He overtook both his sister and the queue of passengers who were patiently waiting to disembark the ship. The two children raced ahead barely allowing the security staff a two second window to swipe their cruise cards at the podium, officially signing them off the ship.

Danny, slightly further behind, and not about to jump the queue like his children, was choked by his son's kind gesture. Suddenly he realized that Josh must be missing his mother more than he had realized.

'The sharks won't bite us.' Katie announced to Penny as they climbed into a taxi.

'So long as we behave ourselves,' Penny humoured the four-year-old.

Josh and Katie loved the Sea Aquarium. They stood for over an hour, happily watching over four hundred species of marine life swim around in front of them. The vast assortment of bright colours was amazing to watch. The smaller brightly coloured fish dashed back and forward, while the larger plane looking fish passed ever so slowly in front of them. As a surprise, Danny had booked four seats in the Dolphin Academy for the twelve o'clock show. Katie could hardly contain herself. She laughed and giggled her way through the event, standing up and clapping every time a dolphin jumped out of the water. At the end of the performance, the dolphin keeper asked if anyone would like to come down to the front to feed the dolphins.

Katie had volunteered before anyone knew what was going on, and along with two other children more than twice her age; she made her way down the four flights of steps. As she approached the front of the auditorium, the instructor handed her a small bucket of fish. Katie looked disgusted as she put her hand in and pulled one out. Before she could control it, it slipped through her fingers and landed on her foot. Finding it all a little overwhelming, she screamed and lost her nerve, unwilling to have another go. Penny immediately rushed to her aid, taking the bucket from her and started feeding the dolphins on her behalf. Danny and Josh found the whole thing hilarious to watch, and sat back in their chairs laughing hysterically at Katie's performance.

By lunchtime, the children were beginning to get a bit hot and bothered. The temperature was reaching the mid-thirties. For something to eat, Penny recommended they tried Fort Nassau. The restaurant was built into the fort and had a stunning view of the city. She thought it might appeal to Josh and Katie.

'A table for four please,' Josh requested as they arrived at the restaurant.

'Certainly, sir, right this way,' the waiter replied good humouredly as he escorted them to a table.

'Is this table satisfactory?'

'I think so,' Josh replied with a big grin across his face as he took in the view of the city. 'This really is something!'

Danny looked at Penny. 'How did you know about this place?'

'I read about it in the port guide and I just thought it sounded really nice. I'm glad you approve.'

Danny nodded, impressed for the second time that day. 'Would you care for a glass of wine? I was thinking we could order a bottle.'

'Mm,' Penny agreed. 'Sounds lovely.'

'May I take your drinks order?' said the waiter.

'Yes, we'll have two cokes, a bottle of water with four glasses, and a bottle of Nobilo. The New Zealand Sauvignon Blanc.'

'And a straw please,' Katie added from under the table.

'Very good, sir.'

Danny flashed a smile at Penny. 'I think we deserve it.'

'I've had the best day, daddy.' Katie grinned at her father from across the table having decided that it wasn't much fun sitting on the floor. She was also the first to spot the waiter, or, at least, a pair of shiny black shoes approaching the table to take the drinks order.

'This is a bit like a real family,' remarked Josh, out of the blue. He took a long slurp of his coke to punctuate the comment. 'No one would know Penny wasn't our real mum. Would they Katie?'

Katie smiled at her big brother. 'I won't tell anyone if you don't.'

'Apart from the fact Penny is only twenty-six, and you are nine Josh. That means Penny would have had you when she was how old?'

'Nineteen, no seventeen' he replied a little too quickly, almost as if he had already worked it out.

'Yeah, but no one knows how old she is. People always think girls are younger than they really are.'

'What are you trying to say Josh?' said Penny. 'That I look older than twenty six?'

She gave him a nudge to let him know she was joking.

'No, I didn't mean that,' he replied, blushing ever so slightly.

Josh ran back into The Club. It was four o'clock and he hadn't seen Carly since the day before yesterday. In the afternoon, she was normally by the pool where the older kids would play games with the youth leaders. By studying her cruise card the first time he set eyes on her, Josh had divined her cabin number. But they were only 'just friends'; so to call at her cabin might seem a little forward.

'If you're looking for Carly, she's not well,' a quiet voice called from the far corner of The Club. Josh looked up and acknowledged the curly haired plump girl sitting alone on a large leather beanbag.

'She's got a stomach bug. Her brother told me this morning. Apparently she was up all night, in which case she probably won't be back to The Club for a couple of days.'

'Oh, I see,' said Josh, sitting down in front of the enormous plasma screen TV.

For a few minutes he tried to watch it, but he couldn't concentrate on the movie that was showing.

'Look, why don't you take her a bunch of grapes or something?' the curly haired girl suggested.

'Don't be stupid,' Josh replied, shaking his head. 'Why would I do that?'

The girl smiled mischievously. 'Because that's what you do if someone you know is not well. And let's face it, from what I've heard, she's someone you'd like to know better.'

'Yeah, right,' Josh barked, and found himself blushing for the second time today.

Grapes. That just sounds so weird. But flowers might do the trick he thought to himself. *Absolutely. Girls love flowers.*

Josh got to his feet and headed for the door.

'See you later, lover boy,' the girl waved after him.

'Yeah, much later,' he called back.

Presently, Josh found himself standing in line at the reception desk. He felt very important as he waited to be served.

'Next please,' called one of the hotel officers, an attractive woman in her early thirties. 'How can I help?'

Barely tall enough to see over the desk, Josh approached the woman. 'Where can I order flowers to be delivered to a cabin?'

Deck 6. If you go up those stairs,' she pointed to the steps behind him, 'and turn right at the top, there's a florist shop next to Flutes champagne bar.'

'Thank you,' Josh grinned as he made for the stairs, his heart beginning to thump.

Sheepishly, he approached the florist's desk and was relieved that there was no queue.

There was a rather cheerful man behind the counter. He looked down at Josh.

'Yes? How can I help you?'

'I'd like to order some flowers please, to be delivered if possible.'

'Certainly, sir. Do you have an idea of what you'd like to send?'

Josh pointed to a beautiful bouquet of twenty-four red roses. 'Well, something like that.'

'Yes. Those are very nice, although a little expensive, perhaps. How about I make you up a special bouquet? Something that won't blow all your holiday money in one go?'

'Yes, please.' Grateful for the gesture, Josh stood patiently watching the man arrange a special bouquet for him.

'There we are,' the florist asked as, with a flourish, he tied the bow. 'What do you think?'

Not knowing anything about flowers, Josh felt a little lost for words. 'They're erm, nice...'

'That will be thirty-five pounds then, sir.'

Thirty-five pounds? You're kidding, right? Josh thought to himself.

Handing over his cruise card, he wondered if he should have gone with the bunch of grapes after all.

'Is it for someone special?' said the florist.

'No, no, not really. It's... it's... for my sister. She's not feeling very well.'

'Oh, that's a shame.' The florist took down the card's details and charged Josh's account.

From the glint in his eye, Josh knew that the man was perfectly aware that the flowers weren't for his sister.

'And what would you like the message to read?'

'I don't know. Just 'Get well soon', and her name.'

'I see. And what *is* your sister's name?'

'It's Carly. Yes, Carly Richardson. She's my half-sister.' Josh smirked confidently at the man, now quite honestly believing he had convinced him he was telling the truth.

'Well I hope your sister is feeling better soon,' the florist replied, putting an unusual emphasis on the word 'sister'. 'Enjoy your day.'

'Thanks.' Josh stuffed his cruise card into the pocket of his shorts and walked away from the desk with a huge sense of relief.

There was a knock at the door of cabin G311. Carly's father opened it and let his cabin steward come in. The man was holding a very impressive bouquet of flowers.

'Oh, they're lovely,' Carly remarked from her bed. 'Mummy will love them.'

Reading the card, her father said, 'they're not for mummy, darling. It seems that they're actually for you.'

'Wow!' Carly propped herself up in bed and gazed at the bouquet.

Her father was surprised at her response, witnessing the most enthusiasm she had shown all day.

'Who are they from?' he asked.

As she read the card again, Carly looked puzzled. 'I don't know. All it says is; 'Get well soon, Carly.'

'Hmm. I think someone's got a secret admirer,' said her father.

He took the bouquet, which Carly was now struggling to hold up, and arranged the display for her in a tall glass vase next to the television.

'They look really nice,' she said, 'but I'm tired now. I think I'm just going to have another rest.'

Still gazing at the flowers, she slid back under the duvet.

Her father pulled the covers up to her chin. 'Okay, sweetheart. I'll be here when you wake up.'

* * *

As planned, Sally and Joyce had met at the gangway. Joyce was nicely tanned, and was wearing a white short-sleeved blouse with a high collar and a pair of cream three quarter length trousers with matching coloured sandals. She had been onboard Ocean Magic for thirteen weeks, since the start of her husband's trip, and was due home at the end of this cruise. She liked to return home early to get things in order for her husband's leave. Joyce and Sally were of similar height and build. With the same shoulder length blonde-brown hair and similar features, the pair were quite often mistaken for sisters. Today, Sally felt rather dishevelled next to Joyce. Last night, she hadn't slept for more than two hours. She was worrying about the anonymous card she had received. The long nap yesterday probably hadn't helped, and now she was all out of sorts.

Since the phone rang at five o'clock for Alex's wake up call from the bridge, she had been awake, and by six o'clock she was up and about. With the whole morning to fill, she paid a visit to the salon and managed to get an appointment for a quick wash and blow dry, but this had little effect on improving her self-esteem.

Sally was dressed in a long floating white skirt with small black shells printed on the right side. She wore a matching white vest top. She had fallen in love with the outfit when she saw it in the window of Armani during the sales last summer, and she loved the way it made her feel. But today nothing was working for her. She was glad to be going ashore with Joyce; a bit of time away from Alex was exactly what she needed. She was also beginning to feel resentful for the way she was starting to look at him.

'When I worked at sea, this used to be my favourite place to come scuba diving,' Joyce remarked. 'The clear blue green sea, amazing diving sites, and striking coral reefs. It's heaven on earth. It's a shame those days are behind me.'

'Why do you say that?' said Sally.

'Why do you think? I'm heading for the big four-oh. I can't be seen squashing myself into a wet suit and hanging around with groups of twenty-one year olds,' Joyce said, with an air of regret.

'Well I don't think you're past it. But I see where you're coming from,' said Sally, wondering if Alex thought that *she* was well and truly past it.

86

'Hey, I didn't expect you to agree so quickly. Are you sure you don't want time to think about it.'

'Sorry, I didn't mean you.'

'Well, surely you're not talking about yourself? You've got years on me.'

* * *

Joyce had booked a table at Bistro Le Clochard. The restaurant was situated on the harbour side near the ship terminal. The menu offered a combination of French and Swiss cuisine. It was also relatively expensive, which meant it was a little bit more exclusive than some of the other eateries. Joyce studied the drinks menu while Sally browsed the chef's recommendations. The restaurant was exactly what Joyce had expected. It was also relatively quiet which suited her perfectly, giving her and Sally the chance to properly catch up.

The waiter opened the bottle of ice-cold sparkling water, and poured two glasses before adding the lime while Sally sat back in her chair and began to relax into her old self. The pair talked enthusiastically about family and friends, filling each other in on all the gossip they had missed since they last saw each other. They both enjoyed a starter of deep fried calamari, followed by the most delicious bouillabaisse. They had also allowed Marco, the waiter, to talk them into ordering a second glass of wine, which, over the course of the afternoon, they sipped slowly. Sally had known Joyce for a number of years, and trusted her implicitly. She wondered what her friend would say if she told her about the anonymous birthday card.

She contemplated the idea of telling Joyce over and over in her head and then, without warning, she opened her Chloe hand bag and produced the item in question.

'Well it's nonsense,' Joyce said immediately after reading it. 'A sick joke of some kind, I shouldn't wonder. You don't believe it do you?'

Sally shrugged.

'Alex is a very successful, not to mention an incredibly good-looking man.' Joyce continued. 'He has obviously upset someone.

A member of crew most likely, and they're seeking revenge. It's blatantly obvious.'

'Mmm,' Sally said, not convinced.

'Have you told him about the card?'

'No,' said Sally 'and I'm not going to speak to him about it until I'm sure there is nothing going on. And you mustn't mention it to anyone either, not even Martin. I'm very embarrassed about it.'

'Oh, Sally. Come on, you don't really think Alex is capable of cheating on you, do you? He worships the ground you walk on, for heaven's sake.'

'To be honest, I just don't know what to think. You said yourself that no one knew how the doctor's wife came to learn of her husband's affair.'

'That's different, Sally'

'Oh? How is it different? She came onboard for a cruise and found out the unthinkable. And look at her now, left at home to bring up two young children on her own while he swans off around the world with his new floozy in tow. It does happen.'

'But not to you and Alex.'

'God, I hope not. I couldn't bear to think of Alex leaving me for someone else.'

'Come on, Sally. You need to get this in perspective. Here, have some more wine.'

'Thanks. Maybe it will help me forget about it. Actually I do feel a little better talking about it.'

'I'm not surprised, silly. You should have told me about it sooner.'

'I know. It just came as such a shock, and then with everything else yesterday, I didn't have time to turn around.'

'So what are you going to do? If there is someone onboard sending out poisonous letters to senior officers cabins, they need to be stopped. Alex, as captain, really needs to be informed.'

'I know, but not yet. I want to wait until I know for sure. I will tell him by the end of the cruise, I promise.'

'Well you know what I think, but it's up to you.'

'Anything else, ladies?' said Marco having returned to their table.

Glad of the interruption in the hope of changing the subject, Sally perked up.

'Just two espressos please. Actually, after all that wine you'd better make mine a dopio.'

'Good idea,' said Joyce. 'Same for me, thanks.'

'Coming right up.'

'I'll recommend this restaur—'

Sally stopped mid-sentence and smiled to herself as she remembered Alex's comment from lunch the other day. Rule number one, he had said, was that if you find a good restaurant, never ever recommend it to anyone, otherwise the next time the ship is in port you won't get a table. It's a fact, he had continued with a 'what? I'm being serious' look on his face.

Returning promptly with two double espressos and two shots of the local liquor, Marco flashed the women one of his famous smiles. 'These are on me. Enjoy ladies.'

'Think he's missed the point about the purpose of the coffees?' Joyce joked as she took a sip of the lemon-flavoured liquor.

As the ship prepared to leave Curacao that night, leaving behind the brightly coloured Dutch-style houses, the 'Sail away party' was in full swing. The entertainments officers, and most of the ships passengers, congregated on Deck 12 by the Wave Pool dancing away to Robbie Williams' *Let Me Entertain You*. The bar stewards, dressed in their Hawaiian shirts and combat shorts, were in great demand as they milled around with trays of rum punch. Everyone looked to be having a great time. The atmosphere was electric.

The captain made his departure speech, informing the passengers that his safety checks had been satisfactorily completed and that the ship was about to set sail for Colon; approaching the highlight of the cruise, the transit of the Panama Canal.

'Enjoy your evening onboard, and have an enjoyable day at sea tomorrow,' he announced before the ship's line's were let go and he took the ship out of port.

Some of the passengers had obviously sampled the rum cocktails while ashore, and one or two were looking a little the worse for wear. Charlie hadn't been ashore. She had spent the morning with Mike drinking coffee and talking about the wedding. Now her old school friends were to be attending, she was the most excited she had been since the night Mike proposed.

Mike was thoroughly enjoying the drastic transformation. For the last few weeks he had missed Charlie's beautiful smile and infectious laughter and was excited to have the old happy, carefree, Charlie back. The weather had been fantastic, and Charlie had suggested spending the afternoon relaxing by the pool. They had managed two hours together before Maddy and the girls tracked them down and insisted it was happy hour.

Not wishing to ruin the girls' fun Mike encouraged Charlie to go along. It wasn't exactly what he had had in mind for their afternoon together, but he wasn't about to say anything in front of the girls. After kissing Charlie on the cheek, and watching her glide off along the deck, he attracted the eye of a passing waitress. He decided to order a cold soda and enjoy the sunshine. After all, that's what being on holiday is all about, isn't it?

Three hours had now passed and Charlie was actually making the rumrunners look good! Perched on a stool at the end of the Wave Pool bar, she was doing her best to stay awake. There were only four girls attending the wedding. So why did it look like there were eight or even ten? Wow, this is going to be some wedding, she sniggered to herself.

'Come on, Charlie. Drink up. This is your last week of freedom, remember?' said Laura as she pushed Charlie's drink towards her. 'Well done, girl. Now for a kamikaze.'

'Only if everyone else is having one too,' Charlie giggled. 'Come on, I'm getting married. Let's go crazy!'

'I don't think that's such a good idea, Charlie. You've had more than enough,' said Mike as he approached the group.

'Nonsense. Who asked you anyway?' said Laura, edging her drink closer to Charlie.

Ignoring Laura, Charlie's new best friend, Mike persisted with his fiancée.

'Okay, Charlie. Let's get you back to the cabin. You've had enough, sweetheart. You don't normally drink spirits, and the rum they put in those things can be forty percent proof.'

'Tell me, Mike,' said Laura. 'You're not going to be one of those nagging husbands are you? Like; come on Charlie, eat your dinner. Or Charlie, it's time for bed, be sure to clean your teeth.'

Mike glared at her with his big brown eyes, biting his tongue to hold back what he really wanted to say.

'Fine,' he replied simply. 'You get my fiancée back to the cabin then – once you've finished filling her full of drink, that is.'

'Don't worry, Mike, she's safe with us,' Maddy insisted. 'I'll make sure she gets back okay.'

' Oops,' Charlie giggled as her foot slipped from the stool.

Maddy looked at Laura. 'Mike's got a point. I think she's had enough. We've still got the hen night to go, remember?'

'Jeez, lighten up, Maddy,' said Laura. 'You're as bad as him. We're only having a bit of harmless fun.'

'I'm fine. I'm all right, see? I'm sitting up again.' Charlie propped herself up on the stool. 'I'm okay, look. So what's everyone having?'

The other girls continued to sip their cocktails, while Laura lined up the next concoction for Charlie to drink.

'I'm fine, Mike. You go on. I know you want to go to the gym. I'll see you back in the cabin later.'

Leaning forward, he gave Charlie a kiss on the lips. He loved her dearly, but couldn't help thinking her friends were seriously taking advantage.

Returning from the gym at half past seven, Charlie was nowhere to be seen. Mike had booked a table for dinner that evening in Nachos, the Mexican restaurant, but hadn't told Charlie. It was meant to be a surprise after all. The booking was for 8.30pm, but as Charlie was still out with her friends, he decided to phone and cancel. There was no way she would be in any fit state to go out that evening, he decided.

As it approached nine o'clock, Mike was finding it increasingly difficult to stay calm. He had warned Laura and Maddy that Charlie had had enough to drink and had expected to come back from the gym to find Charlie tucked up in bed fast asleep. He contemplated getting dressed and going back to the bar to find her, but he didn't want to be seen as someone who bossed his wife around as Laura had so blatantly pointed out might be the case.

The attire for the evening was formal, and Mike hated not abiding by the ship's dress code. Twenty minutes later, he threw his tuxedo on the bed and searched for a shirt and bow tie. He realized he had to at least go and talk to Charlie. After all, she was also out in the wrong dress code.

Once he had fixed his hair and laced his shoes, he took the lift to Deck 12 and walked back towards the bar where he had earlier left the group. The deck was deserted, and the bar that had been overrun with passengers a few hours earlier was now closed. Slightly more concerned than before, he picked up his pace and scanned the deck, looking for any sign of his fiancée. Not having shown very much interest in Charlie's friends, he had no idea of their cabin numbers or where they might have taken Charlie back to. As he climbed the wooden steps to Deck 14, he followed what sounded like a group of kids messing about in the adult's only pool. He walked passed the metal rails at the forward end of the deck and saw Charlie, Maddy and Laura fully dressed, drinking champagne from a bottle while dancing around in the Jacuzzi.

On closer inspection, he noticed another empty bottle of Moet lying next to the pool.

'Mike!' Laura shouted. 'Come and join us. It's lovely in here.'

'No, thanks. I'll pass,' Mike replied as he gazed on in amazement.

'Oh, come on. Don't be sluch a spoilsplort,' Charlie slurred.

'Looks like you've had fun, Charlie. Are you ready to come back to the cabin yet? I thought we might order a pizza and watch a movie, or we can go out if you like.' He had no intention whatsoever of taking his extremely drunk fiancée out in public, but knowing this was his only bargaining tool, he was happy to let her believe he would.

'Can we go to Snachos, I sluve Mexican.'

'Sure, Nachos it is. If that's what you want.' Mike picked up an abandoned towel and wrapped it round his fiancée as he helped her out of the Jacuzzi. 'Come on darling. Let's get you back to the cabin.'

'Yeah, good idea,' Charlie replied. 'Then we can go to Snachos?'

* * *

Richard and Lucy had insisted Sasha join them, along with Kris and Megan, for dinner in Jasmines restaurant that evening. But Sasha had thanked them for their kind invitation and declined the offer. She knew it was going to be like a moth to a flame going down to dinner with only the Cockburn's for company, but she was hungry and didn't want to let Edna Cockburn get in the way of a nice meal. Anyway, she quite liked William; it was just unfortunate he was married to the equivalent of Hyacinth Bouquet on speed.

Sasha had managed to survive the last couple of days without being too hard on herself and was beginning to feel the benefit of the holiday. She had thoroughly enjoyed her day in Curacao and was beginning to get used to doing things on her own again.

This morning she had gone on one of the ship's tours, to the Sea Aquarium. She knew it would have been straightforward enough to go by herself, but she felt that the tour would be a good way of meeting people. It had been a wonderful experience. On arrival, the tour split into three separate groups. Sasha had chosen to go with the group to feed the sharks. This was something she had always longed to do, but never thought she would have the courage to go through with it. The group was made up mainly of young couples in their late twenties early thirties, with a few single people amongst them, which made Sasha feel quite relaxed.

The instructor had issued them all with a wetsuit, a mask and an oxygen tank. In the beginner pool, he had instructed them through a thirty minute PADI approved immersion course where they learned how to use the equipment and got to grips with the basics of scuba diving. Being Sasha's first time, she was a little nervous, but she soon got the hang of it.

Once the group were all-competent enough, the instructor took them underwater in pairs to the glass wall behind which were the sharks. There, through the holes in the transparent partition, they fed the creatures one by one. Being so close to such incredible marine wildlife was a wonderful experience. They really were breath taking to look at.

When she surfaced, along with her partner, the instructor informed them they had free access to the snorkelling pool where they were welcome to stay for up to an hour before exploring the rest of the facilities. Sasha had taken some wonderful photos of the sea life, enjoying every second of her morning. Afterwards, she bought various souvenirs from the Aquarium's gift shop, including the DVD and a photo of her feeding the sharks.

But having seen enough sea life for one day, she parted from the tour and went off on her own to explore the rest of the island.

When booking the cruise, Curacao was one of the main places that had appealed to her. With its powder white beaches and stunning rocky bays, perfectly protected along the western coast, there was so much to see and do on the island. Some locations were totally secluded, while others were over run with visiting tourists eagerly taking part in water sports and various other pursuits on offer.

For those who were less keen to spend the day at the beach and more interested in exploring the Island there was the Otrabada Section where you could visit the square and statue of Pedro Luis Brion, Curacao's most famous son. Or the shops and restaurants at Rif Fort, there was also the Water Fort, which also boasts numerous shops, restaurants and cafes on the south side of Fort Amsterdam. To name but a few of the tourist attractions.

Sasha decided to explore the main town where, half an hour later, she found a lovely little restaurant within which she sampled for the first time Rijstaffell, an Indonesian smorgasbord. She had thoroughly enjoyed every mouthful, and finished it off no problem at all, in fact she seriously considered ordering a second but decided against it in the end. After indulging in a bit of shopping, she walked back to the ship where, with her book, she relaxed on deck for an hour and a half before getting ready for dinner.

Unfortunately she hadn't bargained on no one at all showing up for dinner, and felt rather embarrassed sitting at the large table all on her own while the tables round about her looked on.

Thankfully, she realized she was a little early and breathed a sigh of relief when the Cockburn's finally entered the restaurant.

'They didn't ask you to join them for dinner?' Edna began as soon as she sat down. And before Sasha had a chance to answer, she added, 'That's so awful dear.'

'Actually, Lucy and Richard did ask me to dinner,' Sasha replied, not mixing her words and putting Edna back in her place. 'But I declined their kind offer.'

'Oh, I see.' Edna nodded as she took her menu, not believing a word of it.

'That was nice of them to include you in their plans,' William said, smiling at Sasha. 'Now what would you like dear? Red or white? I shouldn't think we will need more than one bottle of wine between us. Although, you never can tell!' William added knowing fine well it would wind up his wife.

'We certainly will not!' said Edna, taking the bait, while Sasha and William exchanged glances both chuckling inside.

Chapter 6

At Sea

'Look Kris, there's a wedding,' said Megan speaking in a slightly choked up, tears-in-her-eyes, emotional fashion.

'So there is.'

Half-heartedly looking up from his book, Kris watched the young couple make their way across the deck to a beautiful floral archway where they were about to be married by the captain of the ship.

In her strapless white gown, which was blowing gently in the warm Caribbean breeze, the bride looked striking. Her long blonde hair was put up and held in place with a silver tiara that sparked in the sunshine. The groom was an extremely handsome fair haired man. He wore a light coloured linen suit and an open necked white shirt. They both had perfect golden tans from the incessant Caribbean sunshine.

'Yes, I thought there was something going on,' Megan remarked as she stood to get a closer look at the bride. 'Earlier this morning, I saw the deck attendants clearing the sun loungers and setting up chairs. Gosh the setting looks so romantic.'

'The guys must be roasting in those suits,' Kris remarked as he watched the groom and the best man take a step back into the shade.

The chairs accommodated twenty guests. They were made up of close friends and family who had all come on the cruise especially to attend the wedding.

Desperately hoping this might be a reminder to Kris that he had not yet popped the big question, Megan's eyes filled up when she watched the captain pronounce the couple husband and wife.

Kris and Megan had been together four and a half years, but Kris didn't see the point in getting married. Every time the subject was raised, usually by Megan or by one or another of their parents, he dismissed it promptly saying he didn't need a piece of paper to confirm he was committed to Megan. Megan on the other hand had all her life fantasised about her wedding day, and wanted nothing more than to be married to Kris. She had every last detail of the big event planned in her head, right down to the meal that would be served at the reception. Catching a glimpse of Megan brushing away a tear, Kris gave her a firm nudge on the shoulder.

'Don't be so soft, Megan.' He laughed as Megan let another tear escape. 'It won't last. I'll give them a year, two at the most.'

'You're rotten, Kris. Don't you have a heart?' Megan said, as if she was a barrister questioning the accused in a murder trial.

'You're right. Pass the tissues. I think I'm going to well up watching two people I don't know get married.'

'Don't be so mean.'

'I'm sorry, okay?' Kris put his hand on Megan's shoulder 'I've just never understood the appeal of, you know, tying yourself down.'

'Tying yourself down? Is that what you're afraid of? Being committed to one person for the rest of your life?'

'Calm down, babe. I'm just saying.'

'Saying what exactly? That you don't want to be tied down to me? That us being together doesn't hold any kind of commitment whatsoever?'

'No, I never said that. Of *course* we are committed to each other. We live together, don't we?'

'I guess so.' Wiping her nose with a tissue, Megan nodded her head.

'There you go then. Let's not rush into anything. One thing at a time, and all that.'

'Fine. One thing at a time,' Megan agreed, but only to put an end to the conversation.

Over on the port side of the ship, by the family pool, the executive chef was instructing his team how he wanted today's special barbecue to be set up. The table, which was the length of two sides of the swimming pool, was beautifully decorated with several large carvings made from various fruits and vegetables. The vast selection of food looked wonderful, and the mouth-watering smell as it cooked was a torment for the senses. As it approached one o'clock, Simply Classical, the ships resident band, warmed up by the poolside. More and more passengers arrived on deck to join in the fun.

* * *

Danny and Penny had today agreed to share responsibility of the children. It was meant to be Penny's day off, but she much preferred to be around the kids, especially when they were at sea.

'There's only so much time you can spend on your own doing nothing,' she told Danny when he insisted she should have some time to herself.

'Josh, Katie,' said Danny. 'Can you come here for a minute? Penny and I would like to speak to you.'

Katie appeared within seconds – and wearing more of her hot dog than she had eaten. Penny reached for a handful of napkins and wiped the spare hotdog from her little pink t-shirt and the escaped ketchup from her chin.

'How would you like to get dressed up tonight and come to dinner with Penny and me?' said Danny. 'You can wear your new party dress, and Penny has agreed to put your hair in ribbons.'

'No, daddy. I want to go to the chocolate party in The Play House with Rosie and Tina and Jenny and–'

'Yeah, and we've got a pool party tonight,' Josh grumbled, appearing from nowhere, and jumping straight in to back up his little sister. If they both refused to do something it usually meant they would get their own way.

The pool party was the highlight of Josh's cruise. He had searched The Club's activity schedule on his first day onboard, and was relieved to see the pool party programmed for the night of the first sea day. Especially for the occasion, he had bought a new pair of Calvin Klein swimming shorts, so nothing was going to stop him going. Penny turned to Danny and they exchanged glances, agreeing that if the kids were happy, it was probably best to leave them to it. The children's facilities were fantastic, and once again Penny wondered why Danny had brought her along at all. The children were looked after from morning to night, and the parents usually had to bribe their children to get them to themselves for half an hour. Meal times were also catered for. The department even had its own children's restaurant where kids tea was served daily between half past five and half past seven. It wasn't just the usual fish fingers and chips either. They had their own extensive menu from which to choose, complete with waiter service or a buffet selection, depending what they were in the mood for.

'Well that just leaves us, Penny. Do you fancy going out for a drink tonight? Or are you going to desert me as well?' said Danny, fingers crossed behind his back.

'That sounds good.'

She was trying not to sound too keen, but her mind was already wandering off, thinking about what she was going to wear.

'Once I drop Katie off at The Play House, I was thinking we could meet around seven in the Piano Bar,' said Danny, interrupting her thoughts.

Josh grinned at his father. 'Sounds like a date. What do you reckon, Katie? Sound like a date to you?'

'Sounds like a date,' Katie added, giggling behind her brother's back.

'Never you mind what it is. You have your pool party to go to, remember?'

Penny knew Danny's invite was just a polite gesture to get her out and about, and not a date as Josh had so tactlessly blurted out, although her heart did skip a beat when Danny had asked.

* * *

'Let me guess. Chicken nuggets, soft but, of course perfectly cooked in the middle, crispy on the outside and a glass of ribena for madam; and a ham and cheese pizza with extra cheese and a chocolate milkshake for sir.'

Katie covered her mouth with both hands and giggled playfully as Wilson, the head waiter, once again predicted what she and Josh would choose for their dinner. Josh, even more amazed than his sister, wondered how Wilson had managed to guess what they wanted to eat every night of the cruise so far. The night before last, Josh had tried to trick Wilson by ordering a burger and fries when he really wanted his all time favourite meal, lasagne. Wilson had brought the burger and fries to the table and swapped them in front of him for a large plate of lasagne with extra garlic bread.

'You should be on the stage,' Josh had told him.

'I'd like to see you finish your dinner before you even think about dessert tonight,' Danny insisted.

'I don't want dessert,' Katie mumbled through a mouth full of chicken nuggets. 'I'm going to a chocolate party, remember? Josh can have mine 'cause he's going swimming and he needs energy to make him go fast.'

'Oh, do I have to dad? I don't want to be too full for the pool party.'

Danny looked astonished. This was the first time he had heard both his children refuse dessert. This also meant he could take Katie to The Play House earlier than planned, thereby allowing him more time to get ready for his date with Penny.

'Are you going to kiss her tonight, dad?' Josh asked as they walked towards the kids club. Katie, amused at the thought of her dad kissing Penny, started blowing kisses at him.

'Knock it off, you two. Penny is your nanny, not my girlfriend.'

'Girlfriend now, is she?' Josh mimicked his father, while Katie continued blowing kisses at everyone who went past.

Danny signed Katie into The Play House for the evening, and arranged with the youth leader to pick her up later from the Sleep Over Den next door. He left a bag with a blanket, some juice and Katie's favourite teddy to help her get off to sleep, and for his own peace of mind collected a pager.

By ten to seven, Danny was sitting in the Piano Bar waiting patiently for Penny to join him. Although he hadn't asked what her plans were for dinner, he had booked a table in the Sea Breeze restaurant thinking it would make a nice change from his regular dinner table, and it was also a way of thanking Penny for all her hard work.

Danny's dinner table was pleasant enough, but two of the couples were related, so they basically just talked to each other, ignoring everyone else around them which made him feel uncomfortable, especially considering that he was on his own. The third couple were older than his parents, so he had very little in common with them. He basically just smiled at them when he sat down, and wished them a pleasant evening when he left. James, the hotel director, was hosting the table making it up to an even eight. James was very pleasant, and did his best to keep the conversation flowing, but the group just weren't compatible.

Penny had decided not to join a table in the main restaurant. She had initially presumed she would be looking after the children most nights, the same, as she would have done were they at home. She was pleasantly surprised when Josh and Katie had other plans for their evenings, mainly participating in the youth activities on offer.

Penny arrived just after seven and straight away spotted Danny. He was now chatting, and possibly even flirting, with two blonde haired girls at the end of the bar.

'Penny. What can I get you to drink?' He asked after kissing her on the cheek. The kiss came as quite a surprise, and got a serious look of disapproval from the tallest of the blonde's.

'A glass of white wine would be wonderful,' she replied, feeling rather self-conscious, as the girls looked her up and down. Suddenly, sensing the tension, Danny excused them both and pulled out a chair for Penny at a table next to the bar.

'You look lovely,' he commented, studying her choice of outfit.

She wore a tight-fitting black and white corset partnered with an equally tight-fitting pair of dark coloured jeans and some rather sexy, strappy high heels. It was clear by the effort made and the ever so slight nerviness between them, the pair were both out to impress one another.

* * *

Kris and Megan weren't having the best day so far. After earlier watching the wedding, there was definite tension in the air. Megan decided Kris must have been joking about getting tied down. He probably said it to throw her off track, she decided. With the wedding fresh in his mind, now would be as good a time as any to have a conversation about their future. Getting a little too carried away with the idea and not thinking about what she was saying, she suggested they should look into the option of getting married at sea.

'There might be a huge waiting list,' she had continued. 'You might have to book years in advance.'

'Perfect.' Kris had agreed. 'Maybe in the year never,' he had said, annoyed by the pressure Megan was putting on him.

'Well that suits me fine. I wouldn't want to waste my life with a loser like you anyway!'

'Loser?'

'Yes, loser!' Megan shouted after him as he stood up from his lounger and made his way to the poolside bar.

Realizing she had attracted a little too much attention on the open deck, Megan plugged in her MP3 player and turned over on her sun lounger to tan her back.

Kris had well and truly lost his patience with her, and was pleased when Richard and Lucy had turned up at the bar. *Great, some normal conversation,* he had thought to himself.

An hour later, when Sasha appeared by the pool bar, Kris called over to her and asked if she wanted to join them for drinks. Megan, pretending she hadn't noticed, had been consumed with jealousy. Just look at her, she thought to herself. All skinny and tanned. *Who does she think she is parading herself in front of my partner like that?* 'Disgusting, that's what it is,' she cursed under her breath.

Richard and Lucy were having a wonderful afternoon, and Kris was determined not to let Megan's obsession with marriage get to him any more than it had done so already. *She'll get over it,* he told himself as he got stuck into another beer.

Richard had checked his emails before venturing out on deck. He had received a three-page message from his brother filled with jokes and funny stories. After a couple of beers, he decided he was in good company and thought he'd share a few of them with Lucy, Kris and Sasha. The third joke made Sasha laugh so hard she dropped her bottle of beer, spilling most of it on the deck. Diving to her aid, Kris had picked up the empty bottle and put it back on the bar before ordering her another one. Sasha had been extremely grateful, mostly because no one had laughed at her and made her feel uncomfortable. To thank Kris, she leaned forward and gave him a kiss on the cheek.

From at least twenty metres away on the other side of the pool Megan had witnessed Kris's reaction, and to say the least she wasn't impressed.

Giving the men time to talk, Sasha and Lucy had ventured over to the barbecue where they chose a selection of chicken wings, lamb skewers, hot dogs burgers and salad for them all to enjoy. Sasha, being the type of person she was, went over to Megan and offered her something to eat, but Megan had smiled dryly and made some comment about Sasha putting on weight if she ate that sort of food.

Not giving Megan's unfriendly manner a second thought, Sasha returned to the bar where Richard and Kris straight away got stuck into the food.

As it approached five o'clock, Kris left the other three at the bar to finish their drinks. In a slightly better mood than before, and feeling a little guilty for leaving Megan, he spent some time making light-hearted conversation before suggesting they went back to the cabin to shower and dress for dinner.

'Sasha's great fun, don't you think?' Kris asked, as he got undressed. 'You should have seen her face when the bottle of beer went flying out of her hand. It was a picture.'

'Hmm,' Megan huffed under her breath. 'Yes, she's nice,' she admitted, reluctantly, the words sticking in her throat as, with dagger eyes, she glared across at her partner.

'She's got a great personality, and by the sound of it has a successful career. Did I mention that Richard thinks she's hot? Can you believe it? With a wife like Lucy! It's not as if he's done badly himself.'

'Richard thinks she's hot! So that's what the two of you have been talking about all this time. Giggling over your beers like two little schoolboys who have just discovered girls,' Megan seethed to herself.

'Did she ever tell you what went wrong between her and her fiancé?'

Why the hell is he so interested? Megan thought. *As if I don't know. He sure as hell isn't asking for Richard, that's for certain.*

'No, she didn't,' said Megan. 'But when I find out, I'll be sure to tell you. You'll be the first to know, I promise!'

'Jesus, calm down, babe. I was only making conversation. What's the problem? Have you two fallen out or something?'

'No, we haven't fallen out. I just don't think she's the amazing Amazon Goddess that everyone is making her out to be.'

'Fair enough, you don't have to like everyone all the time, Meg.'

'It's not that I don't like her. I never said that.'

'All right. Time out. Peace.' Kris realized he'd hit a nerve and decided to change the subject completely rather than risk upsetting Megan any further. 'So how about that pre-dinner drink we talked about?' *And help put some of this day behind us.* 'I thought we would try Flutes, the other champagne bar on Deck 8. Apparently they do a wicked selection of champagne cocktails. Richard recommended it.'

'Fine,' Megan agreed, as she applied her eyeliner. 'Maybe we could go to dinner on our own one night, Kris. Try one of the other restaurants for a change.'

'Sure. I'll make a reservation for tomorrow night if you like.'

* * *

Katie tugged at the youth leader's shorts, but the small window of opportunity for her to tell Zoe that she wasn't feeling well had passed. It was a common occurrence for the children to eat too much chocolate during the ever-popular chocolate party. Now she was lying on the floor, semi-conscious and gazing up with glazed eyes and a sickly pallor.

'Oh my God! Suzy, get in here!' Zoe yelled to her colleague in the next room.

Suzy, one of the other youth leaders who worked in The Play House had gone next door to get the chocolate donuts for the 'Hook a Donut' game, which was next on the programme. As she entered the room, the tray of donuts she was carrying fell to the floor. The group of children, most of whom had chocolate all over their faces, were standing silent and motionless against the soft play area watching anxiously as Zoe tried desperately to revive the limp-bodied four-year-old who was lying on the floor.

'I've called the doctor. He's on his way.' She pointed to the signing-in book on the table beside the door and signalled for Suzy to page Katie's father.

'Is Katie going to die?' Tina, Katie's new best friend, asked with a look of concern.

'No, darling. Katie is going to be fine. She just ate to much chocolate, that's all.'

Trying not to alarm the children, but never the less scared senseless herself, Zoe leaned across Katie's body that was turning a forbidding blue-grey, her eyes now closed. One minute she was laughing and carrying on with the other children, her little cheeks red from running around, and then she was lying flat out on the floor of The Play House, motionless and turning a light shade of grey. It seemed to happen in an instant.

The Play House door flung open. Rebecca, the officer in charge of the children's department, burst through with the doctor and several nurses hard at her heels.

'Is she still breathing?' said the doctor as he placed an oxygen mask over her face. At his instruction, Katie, the senior nurse, pulled out a large syringe and filled it with a clear liquid. Zoe couldn't bear to look as the syringe was placed against Katie's thigh. A second later, the clear liquid was injected into her tiny body.

This looked to be the only action needed, as they all watched in anticipation, expecting Katie to suddenly be okay again. But as the seconds passed – seconds that felt like minutes – she continued to lie there. The tension grew. Someone started crying.

Then Katie's blue lips started to change back to their normal shade of pink, and slowly she regained consciousness. The nurses, who were used to dealing with older passengers having strokes and heart attacks, stood over the child with tears in their eyes.

'Come on, Katie, we've still got the donut game to play.'

Tina really did pick her moments, but just as she spoke Katie opened her eyes. A little confused at first, wondering why she was lying on the floor with so many people around her. She looked up and caught a glimpse of the nurse's name badge. She looked at her in amazement and said; 'Katie. That's my name too.'

* * *

When Danny's pager sounded an alert, he and Penny were chatting away, mostly about Josh and Katie.

'Excuse me a minute, Penny. Let me get this, and then we really should head to the restaurant. Okay?'

Restaurant? Penny thought they were only meant to be meeting for a quick drink. Instantly, she regretted not making more effort with her choice of attire. A summer dress or even a trouser suit would have been more appropriate.

'Yes, it's Mr Harper,' said Danny, speaking from a nearby courtesy phone. 'Josh and Katie's father. You just paged me.'

'Mr Harper, you're speaking to Zoe from The Play House. I'm ringing to tell you that... well, that Katie has been taken to the medical centre.'

'What? Oh my God! What happened? Is she okay?'

'I'm sure she'll be fine,' Zoe replied, but her shaky tone of voice was far from convincing. 'But she seems to have had some kind of reaction to the chocolate she was eating at the party. We think it may have contained traces of nuts.'

'But Katie doesn't have a nut allergy.'

'I realize that, Mr Harper. I have her registration details in front of me, but she certainly took a reaction to something. The doctor is looking into it now.'

'Okay. I'll be right there. Deck 6 forward?'

'That's it. On the port side. I'll meet you there.'

'Katie lay still,' a tiny body in what looked like an enormous bed. 'My little princess, what happened to you?'

'I don't like chocolate any more, daddy,' Katie replied from the hospital bed.

That's hardly surprising, Danny thought to himself.

'Everything is okay now. You try to get some sleep, I'll be right here for you when you wake up.'

'Okay, daddy,' Katie replied before closing her eyes.

Penny appeared in the reception area with Josh at her side. She was just in time for the doctor to explain how lucky Katie had been. Had the youth leaders not acted as quickly in calling him, it would have been a very different story.

Josh was straight from the pool, dripping wet and wrapped in a beach towel. He was completely unaware of what had happened. Thinking the worst, he burst into tears. Overcome by all the excitement surrounding his little sister's accident, he couldn't control his emotions and started lashing out at Katie.

'You stupid girl! What were you thinking? You could have died, for God sake!'

'It's okay, Josh. Your sister is going to be fine. It was an accident, that's all. It wasn't Katie's fault.' Penny held him tight, his hands wrapped tightly around her waist while she stroked his hair, allowing him to sob quietly into her chest. A couple of minutes later he looked up. 'It's okay, darling. You're bound to be angry.'

'Hey, watch the hair,' he joked, when he realized that he had just made a complete fool of himself shouting at his sister and crying in front of Penny and his dad.

Danny and Penny walked Josh back to the cabin and waited until he was asleep. Only then did they go next door and into Penny's room. Penny made some tea and added a couple of sugars to Danny's to help calm his nerves.

'So much for the quiet night,' Danny remarked. 'I can't believe she has a nut allergy. God, I should know these things. I'm her father, for crying out loud.'

'You can't blame yourself, Danny. These things happen. You weren't to know.'

'These things can't afford to happen. Katie almost died tonight. You heard it yourself from the doctor.'

'I know, Danny. It's okay. Really.'

But now it was Danny's turn to let his feelings out. Penny held him close, his head resting against her stomach as she stood beside him. Danny was slumped over the armchair, his eyes full of remorse, blaming himself for not knowing his daughter as well as he should have. The tea wasn't going down too well either. So Penny decided to take control and ordered a couple of large brandy's from room service. Danny, like Josh had done earlier, felt the need to defend his moment of weakness and joked about Katie's run through of events.

'Christ, in the future she'll probably think she's going to keel over every time she looks at chocolate.'

It had been one hell of an eye opener, Danny realized, and without Penny's support he would probably have lost the plot completely.

Shortly after three o'clock, the couple decided to call it a night. As usual, Josh would be up at seven, and they had to go and collect Katie from the medical centre. The doctor had agreed to keep her in for observation purely based on the fact she had asked. She had made a full recovery, and an hour after the attack was back to her normal self. But the nurses had made such a fuss of her she decided she should stay the night, just to be on the safe side.

Chapter 7

Colon 08:00. Arrival and overnight stay

Geoff sat on his balcony with a mug of strong black coffee watching the ship arrive in Colon, a seaport on the eastern coast of the Panama Canal. He was an early riser and rarely slept more than three or four hours a night.

He had come on the cruise with his best friend, Rick, and Rick's girlfriend, Christina. The couple had really looked after him since his fiancée Molly passed away eight months ago, and had insisted he accompanied them on the cruise.

Geoff had initially declined the offer, but Christina had persisted until he finally gave in.

Molly, Geoff's ex fiancée, was Christina's best friend. They had grown up together, attending the same school as Geoff and Rick. The two couples had hung out together all through high school, and were inseparable thereafter. Molly was twenty-nine when she was diagnosed with a brain tumour. She and Geoff had been engaged only a matter of weeks before she was told the dreadful news of her condition. Geoff had been devastated by the confirmation of her illness, and even more so by the time scale of how long she had left to live. It would be anything up to a year; the specialist had told them just after breaking the news of the tumour.

Immediately, Geoff gave up work to spend, as fate would have it, the last four months of Molly's life nursing her full time. Molly loved cruising. When she was a child, she regularly cruised with her family. There were very few parts of the world she hadn't seen.

This was Geoff's first cruise since Molly had died, and he was finding it harder to cope than he had originally expected.

The A Deck outside balcony cabin that Molly had always insisted on booking only emphasized the fact that she wasn't there. The normally over-packed wardrobes looked hollow and bare, and the cabin was so big he felt lost rattling about in it on his own.

Geoff had an unusual fear of heights. He was a fireman, and climbing up ladders and wandering blindly through tall buildings didn't bother him in the least. But when faced with an outdoor balcony cabin onboard a cruise ship, he was overcome by a strange vertiginous sensation that made him feel like he was going to fall overboard. Over the last three years, it had taken him two cruises annually to overcome his fear. Molly had insisted he faced his phobia, repeatedly booking a balcony cabin on Deck 12 telling him it was all the travel agent had to offer. Upon hearing this, he always refused to go, suggesting that they should simply wait until an indoor cabin became available. But Molly, always one step ahead, predicted his response, and on many occasions let him believe they had an indoor cabin only to announce a last minute change of plan or that an unexpected upgrade had been made available.

Geoff, who didn't want to make a big deal out of his weakness, always backed down and accepted the outboard cabin, usually ignoring the problem and telling himself that he would just stay inside where he felt comfortable. Over the years, Molly had been extremely supportive and helped him to get past his fear. She had been thrilled the first time he had, on own free will, walked out onto the balcony. Unfortunately, this was during their last cruise together.

Persistence was one of her main attributes, he reminded himself as he stood confidently against the railings watching the ship dock along side.

He had planned to go ashore early this morning, thereby giving Rick and Christina a little time on their own. As the linesman tied the ship up for the overnight stay in Colon, he made himself another coffee and waited patiently for the captain to give clearance to go ashore. At last it came, and without stopping for breakfast, he picked up his ship's pass, his sunglasses, and a small backpack, and proceeded ashore.

It was an incredibly hot day. The temperature was already in the late twenties and was forecast to reach thirty-five degrees by midday. Geoff approached a taxi and negotiated a price for a half day tour, including a commentary about the building of the canal, and finishing off at Playa Lagosta beach approximately forty-five minutes from the ship where he planned to spend the rest of the day reading his book and working on his tan.

* * *

Sasha woke just after 9.00am determined to do something more productive with her day than on the previous two. She showered immediately before allowing herself to relax into a vegetating state on the balcony.

Without giving her attire a second thought, she collected a jade green bikini, a denim mini skirt and a colourful green and blue striped vest top from her wardrobe, and dressed with a sense of urgency.

Most people had already had their breakfast, so the buffet area in the Sea View restaurant was reasonably quiet. She selected the things that took her fancy and carried her tray outside and browsed over the ship's daily newspaper while she enjoyed a continental breakfast in the sun.

For five days now she hadn't talked to Ben, and being several thousand miles apart, with the four-hour time difference, it seemed to be making things a little easier to cope with. The cruise was everything she'd expected it to be. Deciding what to do with her day was the most difficult part, and with so much on offer onboard it was tempting to not even venture ashore. Most days, she had split her time between relaxing on deck, and going ashore for a couple of hours in each port of call. Her dinner companions had made the biggest difference to her holiday, including her in every way possible. They were great company and lots of fun – with the notable exception of Megan's occasional mood swings. And in a funny sort of way, she was even warming to Mrs Cockburn.

Sasha had made no definite plans for her day ashore. But she had however made some enquiries through the tours department earlier in the week. The girl on duty had talked her through the most popular places to visit during the overnight stay in Colon. She obeyed the tour girl's advice to negotiate a fare before getting into a taxi, and was happy to spend the day on a private tour sightseeing with Lu, the taxi driver. She mentioned one or two of the sights she would like to visit, and left it up to Lu to decide in which order he took her to them.

First of all was The Hotel Washington, a beautiful pink and white coloured colonial-style building. The historic design was hugely impressive, quite literally breath taking to look at. Lu waited patiently while Sasha surveyed the building before exploring inside at her leisure. Before leaving, she stopped to enjoy a glass of fruit juice on the terrace at the back of the hotel while watching the cruise ships patiently queue to enter the canal.

To the far left hand side of the building she carefully studied the house that Ferdinand de Lesseps occupied whilst he overlooked the construction of the famous Panama Canal. From there, Lu took her to the Gatun locks where she managed to catch the tail end of a talk by one of the ship's tour guides on the building and workings of the canal.

Originally, she had planned to book an organized tour thinking it might have appealed to Ben. But touring independently was proving to be much more fun. After that, Lu took her to the Museo del Canal Interoceanico de Panama. The Panama Canal Museum. Constructed in 1875 it was one of the first buildings in the city, it had a somewhat stunning design, which oozed French authority. The most impressive part was of the Panama Railway, which was built before the canal itself.

'So what do you think so far?' Lu asked as they left the Museum.

'It's fascinating. I'm really enjoying myself, thanks.'

'No problem. So where to now? I can take you to El Catedral, or the Palacio Municipal y el Museo de Historia de Panama if you like. Then, that would normally be about it for a half day tour.'

'No, that's fine really. It's been great, but I think I've seen enough. I was wondering if you could recommend somewhere for lunch. With a beach would be ideal so I can have a swim afterwards.'

'Sure, I know just the place. In fact, my cousin owns a place called Coco's. It's a beach bar and restaurant, and is probably twenty maybe thirty minutes from here, if that's okay?'

'That sounds perfect. I'll give it a try.'

'It's easy to get back to the ship once you've finished. My cousin normally puts on mini buses from about 2.00pm. It's something like four dollars per person if the bus is full.'

'Even better!' Sasha agreed.

Coco's beach bar and restaurant looked perfect. It was just what she had in mind. After receiving a warm welcome from Johnson, Lu's incredibly friendly cousin, Sasha sat down at one of the smaller tables at the back of the restaurant and browsed the menu.

'Today's specials are grilled swordfish with garlic potatoes or a mixed seafood salad with mango salsa dressing,' the cheerful young waitress informed her.

'The salad sounds good. I think I'll have that, please.'

'Anything to drink?'

'Yes, a glass of iced water please that will be all for now'

'No problem. The salad will be about twenty minutes. Is that okay?'

'Yes, fine.'

The waitress left, and Sasha took out her camera and flicked through the photos she had taken that morning. She was extremely happy with what she had achieved during her four-hour tour. Then, all of a sudden, it started to rain.

'It'll pass. It's only a quick shower,' said the returning waitress, smiling. She placed a bottle of sparking water and a glass of ice on the table.

'Thanks. That's just what I needed.'

The waitress nodded and left to fetch the salad. Sasha sipped her drink and gazed out at the white sandy beach and the clear turquoise sea. The rain certainly did look like it would pass, and the odd shower at this time of year wasn't uncommon. But the sun worshippers weren't convinced. They hurriedly gathered their belongings and made their way towards the bar, one or two of them taking advantage of the shower to get something to eat.

The bar and restaurant filled up quickly. Sasha watched the mixture of people buying drinks and ordering lunch. Some were locals. Others were holidaymakers, and amongst them some passengers from the ship. Sasha continued eating her salad. The seafood was extra fresh. It was obvious that it had been caught that morning. When she looked up again, she noticed an incredibly tanned rather good-looking man purposefully walking towards her. She had deliberately taken a table in the corner, out of the way, as she hated eating alone. It just seemed like such a sad thing to do.

Unwilling to make eye contact with the man, in case he was about to walk straight past her, Sasha looked away. Aware that he had stopped, and was now standing right next to her, she looked up to see Tom, her wine waiter.

'Hi, Sasha. How are you?'

'Oh, hi, Tom. I didn't recognize you.'

'No, I don't suppose you would. I sometimes forget I'm not in uniform. Listen, can I get you a drink?' he asked, rather sheepishly.

'Thanks, that's really kind. But I've just got one. Anyway you're off duty. You should have people running around fetching drinks for you for a change.'

'Force of habit I guess. Look, can you excuse me a second? I've just spotted a friend of mine?'

'Sure,' Sasha replied, not wishing to hold him back.

'Geoff over here,' Tom called from the table.

Curious to see who Tom was talking to, Sasha looked up to see a very attractive man, in his early thirties with short dark hair and a perfectly toned body. He was walking over to them.

Goodness, Sasha thought to herself. *This really is the place to come,* Her imagination running away with her, Sasha wondered if it was inappropriate to think of Tom, her wine steward, as attractive.

'Geoff, this is Sasha. She's dining on my table this cruise.'

'Hi, nice to meet you,' Geoff replied.

Now rather embarrassed, being caught by two handsome men and having lunch on her own, Sasha discarded her plate and took a large sip of water. There was an uncomfortable pause.

'Do you work onboard as well?' Sasha asked in an attempt to break the silence, still a little overwhelmed at all the attention she seemed to be receiving. They were just standing there saying nothing.

'No, I'm on holiday with two of my friends,' Geoff replied. He looked at Tom. 'I didn't know you would be here. I thought you said you were working this afternoon. If I'd known you were free, I would have given you a call.'

'I was meant to be working, but one of the stewards asked me to change shifts so he could go ashore with his girlfriend. I swapped with him at the last minute. It worked better for me anyway,' Tom continued. 'I prefer to go ashore in the afternoon. It breaks the day up a bit more. Right, I'm going to do what I do best and fight my way to the bar. So, Sasha, what's your preference? White wine? Strawberry daiquiri. Rum punch? And I won't take no for an answer this time.'

'Okay. A white wine please with lots of soda water as it's pretty early to start drinking.'

'Nonsense, you're on holiday. It's allowed.'

Sasha felt a little intimidated by Geoff's strong features and devilish good looks. His dark brown eyes were almost hypnotizing her as she looked into them as he pulled up a seat and sat down across from her.

'First time in the Caribbean?' said Geoff.

'No. I've been a couple of times before, but it's my first time going through the Panama Canal. I'm really looking forward to it.'

'Me too. Apparently this ship will only just make it, another few inches and it would have been too wide to pass.'

'Oh, really,' Sasha replied not knowing what else to say.

'It's an early start though. I think the first set of locks is at six thirty. I hope you're a morning person.'

'Not really,' Sasha answered honestly. 'But I'll make an exception tomorrow. It wouldn't be right coming all the way here and sleeping through the transit of the canal. Mind you, I say that now, but it all depends on how late we are tonight.'

'That's true. The entertainment on board is fantastic, but there's never enough time to do and see everything. At least, that's how I feel, anyway. Sorry, you said 'we'. Are you travelling with friends, or your husband?'

'Here we are,' said Tom, returning from the bar. 'One white wine for madam with lots of soda, and one bottle of Carib for you.'

'Thanks, Tom.' Sasha and Geoff laughed, while Tom was completely unaware he was treating Sasha as if he was serving her at the dinner table.

'What?' Tom shot Geoff a confrontational look. 'It's only polite. Sasha's a guest onboard.'

'And what am I?' said Geoff.

'Just Geoff, I guess, wherever you are.'

'Charming,' said Geoff, throwing back his head. 'Well cheers, everyone. Here's to a great cruise!'

As it approached six o'clock, Sasha suggested heading back to the ship. Tom insisted that he and Geoff accompany her. After all, they were all going to the same place. Once onboard, Sasha thanked the guys for their company, and for the drinks, and headed back towards her cabin. Geoff walked Tom back to his cabin, as far as he could anyway without going below passenger decks. As Tom opened the door, which read 'CREW ONLY', with a grin he turned to his friend.

'You like her, don't you?' he said.

Geoff playfully hit Tom on the shoulder.

'Shut up, I do not,' he replied, running his fingers through his hair.

'She's travelling on her own, you know?'

'Really, Tom? And why would I be interested in knowing that?'

'No reason. Just making conversation. She's nice though, don't you think?'

'Yes, Tom, she's nice. But I don't think your girlfriend will be over the moon to hear you say that.'

'I didn't mean for me, you idiot. I meant for you.'

'See you later, Tom,' Geoff smiled, patting his friend on the back. 'Much later, if you keep this up.'

'Just give it some thought!' Tom shouted back, even though the door was now closed.

Back in her cabin, Sasha puzzled over the relationship between Tom and Geoff. Geoff had given away very little about himself, but Sasha had a strong inclination he was single. He was also incredibly attractive, and charming. Surely there was a story there somewhere.

As Geoff opened the door to his cabin, he heard the phone ringing. He hadn't realized the time, and he had forgotten all about his plans to go on an evening tour of Panama City with his friends, Rick and Chris.

'I'll meet you at the gangway in twenty minutes,' he'd said.

The day had been nice and relaxing. All he wanted to do now was make a cup of coffee and sit out on the balcony; he was in no rush to get ready to go ashore again. But Geoff wasn't the sort to let anybody down. If he made an arrangement with someone, he would stick to it. Anyway, it might be fun, he thought, as he abandoned the thought of coffee and made his way towards the shower.

The three of them met at the gangway as arranged, but there was no sign of the tour gathering. There were plenty of people going ashore, but no one seemed to be in charge of the organized trip they had bought tickets for two days earlier.

'Where are the tickets, Rick?' Christina asked, searching through her purse.

'I've got them here. It says seven fifteen departure.'

'Hold this and I'll go and find out what's going on.'

Chris handed Rick her bag, and walked up to reception, while Geoff popped off the ship to ask if the bus had left.

'Right. Well, it seems that the tour has been cancelled,' said Chris. 'The tour's manager didn't inform us as our names weren't on the list. Although it doesn't make any difference. We wouldn't have got on if it was running. Apparently it was full.'

'Why was it cancelled?' said Geoff.

'Something to do with the shore side guide. The tour's manager is not very impressed, as you can imagine.'

'I see. Well we might as well go on our own if you're still up for it?' Rick suggested. 'Casco Viejo is the place to be, apparently. That's where we were going first on the tour. I'm sure there is a church or some building of interest there; anyway it's meant to be worth a visit. There are also a couple of restaurants mentioned in the port guide. Maybe we could get a bite to eat in one of them later, if you fancy something different.'

'It will certainly be different, that's for sure. What sort of food do they eat here anyway?' Geoff asked.

'Your guess is as good as mine,' said Christina.

Rick and Chris strolled ahead while Geoff lingered behind taking photographs capturing the eeriness of the unfamiliar surroundings in every picture. Various groups of Panamanians hung out together, and the subdued streetlights added to the thrill of the unusual setting. The atmosphere was exciting. It was tranquil and captivating.

A few minutes later, however, Geoff's heartbeat quickened when he looked up to see a young Panamanian male approach Christina from behind. The figure was small, dark, and nervous. He was clad in loose fitting casual clothes. Something glinted in his hand. Something clearly dangerous.

'Chris!' Geoff yelled. 'Watch out! That man's got a knife!'

Rick spun around, startled. He saw the knife first, and then saw the figure. Instantly, he knew what was wanted here.

'Whoahh!' he said. 'Stay cool everyone. Just give him the bag, Chris.'

His voice was cool and calm, but insistent.

Christina stiffened. She clutched the bag closer. Tighter. 'No way. It's my new Gucci.'

'Chris,' Geoff yelled, running to catch them up. 'Just do it! Hand it over!'

'Yeah, bitch!' said the guy with the knife. He jabbed with the weapon and looked like he knew how to use it. 'Give me the bag or I'll cut it out of your hand.'

The robber made a move. It was fast. It was slick. A second later, the bag fell open on the ground, and Christina's purse, phone, camera and make-up spilled all over the street in front of her.

'Shit!' she said, stunned. 'I can't believe this. Rick, do something!'

'Just leave it, Chris. Let's get out of here it's clearly not safe,' he replied as he took her by the hand, urging her to walk away. He gave a soft, ironic laugh. 'I think I know now why they recommend you go on a tour here.'

'You're not kidding,' said Geoff. 'Come on; let's get back to the ship. We're going to have to report this to someone.'

They hurried away hardly daring to look back. The figure with the knife began scooping up the possessions as if it was the most natural thing in the world for him, which it probably was.

'Chris,' said Rick as they walked. 'Are you okay?

'No, I'm bloody-well not. I've just been mugged by a guy young enough to be my nephew. Jesus. Look at me. I'm shaking like a drug addict.'

'I'm really sorry, but there's nothing you can do in these situations, especially when someone's got a knife. Just think yourself lucky you weren't wearing your engagement ring.'

'Shush, Rick,' said Christina, conscious of the fact that Geoff didn't yet know they were engaged. She wanted to keep it that way for the time being.

'Oops.' Rick reddened. 'I forgot. But we have to tell him sometime, Chris.'

She considered that as she looked back down the street. The robber was already vanishing into the shadows together with her bag and all its contents. 'Well now's certainly not the bloody time.'

'I think we were lucky there wasn't a gang of them. We could have lost everything. At least we've still got our wallets,' said Geoff.

'I know, and don't worry Chris; I'll get you a new bag in Acapulco.'

'And a new phone, camera, purse, makeup,' said Chris.

Geoff flashed some teeth. 'All that too.'

Rick put his arm around her to comfort her as they made their way back to the ship. 'I'm really sorry, Chris.'

'Me too,' said Geoff. 'Now we need to explain what happened to your ID pass.'

The security officer was very understanding. He escorted them to his office where they each gave a detailed account of what happened ashore.

'I'm sorry you had to go through such a traumatic experience,' he said. 'Scary place at night. But all things considered, it could have been a lot worse.'

'Yeah, we were lucky,' said Rick.

'Listen, I'm sure you could all do with something to eat. Tell you what, do you know Zen the Japanese restaurant on Promenade deck?'

Chris nodded.

'Well let me finish up here, and I'll meet you there in ten or fifteen minutes, dinner is on me.'

'Thanks, John, but you don't have to do that,' said Geoff.

'Not at all. I was going there myself anyway. The sushi really is fantastic, see you all shortly.' John insisted.

* * *

Sasha ran herself a bath and poured herself a large glass of Robert Mondavi Cabernet Sauvignon. She wasn't a huge fan of red wine, but had sampled this particular one at dinner the other night and decided it would be nice to order a bottle to have in her cabin. However, it would have been a whole lot nicer if she had someone to share it with, but for now the wine was destined to be enjoyed by her alone.

As she lowered her sun-kissed body into the bubbles, book in one hand and glass of wine in the other, the phone rang.

Typical.

Unsure what to put down first, and more importantly where to set the glass of wine that was now incredibly slippery from the steam, she decided the bathroom unit was the safest option. Leaning forward out of the bath, she overstretched and lost her balance sending the wine soaring out of the glass and all over the bathroom mirror, the walls, and the ceiling. Even the toilet took a hit.

The only saving grace was the glass that was still somehow firmly in her hand.

Horrified by what had happened, she gasped at the mess. The bathroom looked like a scene from Silence of the Lambs. Even her book was lying face down in the bath.

Then the phone stopped ringing. She gazed at it, irritated, her eyes shrinking.

'Bloody hell!' Why is nothing ever straightforward? All I wanted to do was enjoy a nice long bath. Why is that too much to ask?

She was pretty sure the call she had missed was of no importance.

Half an hour later, after cleaning up the evidence of what looked like a bathroom massacre, she decided it would be a lot safer to do one thing at a time. After cleaning the wine off the toilet seat, she doubted she would ever look at a glass of red again. Presently, she lay back in the bath with one of her less interesting, but dry, books and began to relax, but now she was having trouble concentrating. All she could think about was how much she had enjoyed her afternoon with Tom and Geoff, and she couldn't help but continue to wonder what the connection was between them. They couldn't be brothers. Tom was South African and Geoff was from London. They must just be friends, she decided.

As it approached a quarter past eight, and the once hot water had turned lukewarm, she wrapped a fluffy white towel around her body and contemplated what to do with her evening. Just as she started drying her hair, there came a knock at the cabin door. For a moment, she hoped it was Geoff calling to ask if she would like to meet him one evening for a drink. Ideally this evening. But the fantasy was short-lived, as she reminded herself. He already had company this cruise, didn't he? It was her who was the sad individual who was travelling alone.

She recalled that there was a meeting every morning for passengers travelling unaccompanied. It was hosted by one of the entertainments officers. Sasha had passed through the group one morning as they sat making small talk over a cup of coffee in

Café Zero. The group consisted of twelve men and ten ladies, all in their eighties and nineties, most of whom looked like this could be their last cruise – or so Sasha thought as she passed by, grateful she was only travelling alone and not dying alone, which was what she had predicted for some of those poor souls. She opened the cabin door and Lucy came bouncing in.

'What are you doing? It's the Captain's VIP party in thirty minutes. Why aren't you ready?'

'What?' Sasha looked at her friend in amazement. 'Why would I be going to the captain's party?'

'Don't tell me you haven't opened your invite?'

Sasha had no idea what Lucy was talking about.

'It's his private party, and we have all been invited. So come on you silly girl. Now what are you wearing?'

Lucy scanned the room and, as predicted, sitting on the dressing table still in its envelope was Sasha's personal invitation to the party. Joe had obviously left it there for her thinking she couldn't miss it.

'Oh, Lucy, to be honest, I think I might just have an early night.'

'You'll do nothing of the sort. You're coming to the party with Richard and me. Then we're taking you out to dinner. We've booked a table for three in Jasmines, and I won't take no for an answer.'

'Well, in that case,' said Sasha. 'I suppose I'd better find something to wear.'

'Where were you earlier, anyway? I tried ringing the cabin but there was no answer.'

'That was you?' Sasha looked at her, grimacing. 'Seriously, don't ask!'

* * *

'William and I have been invited to the Captain's VIP party,' Edna had announced a few nights earlier when she had everyone's attention at the dinner table.

'So have we,' Megan said, determined to knock the wind from the old woman's sails.

'Hmm, that can't be right,' Edna said. 'This is only your first cruise. How can you be invited to such an exclusive event?'

'Edna...' said William, patiently.

'There must be some sort of mistake.'

'Obviously we were invited by mistake too,' Richard added mischievously, causing Edna to choke on her iced water.

'In that case, Sasha is probably invited by mistake as well,' Kris remarked, enjoying every second of making the old woman squirm in her chair.

'You must all be invited through association with me and William,' Edna remarked, quite unprepared to back down and acknowledge they had all been invited for a reason she couldn't explain. 'We're Gold Class cruisers you know.'

Sasha had been present throughout the conversation, but quite often lately she switched off when Mrs Cockburn had something to say and had missed the fact that she too had been invited to the party.

If it hadn't been for Lucy popping round unexpectedly, Sasha would still be none the wiser.

The eighty guests had been handpicked by the captain and were invited to attend an exclusive pre-dinner cocktail party in Bubbles champagne bar. The guests were offered a selection of drinks and mouth-watering canapés while enjoying the company of the captain and the ship's senior officers.

The guests at Sasha's table were still completely unaware they were invited through association with Richard and Lucy and not William and Edna Cockburn – as she would have had them believe.

Richard and Lucy had neglected to tell the table that Richard was the son of Lord Clinton, and as such had a personal fortune of £12 million. This was his and Lucy's 44th Cruise; not their third as they had told the table on the first night they were onboard. They were also personal friends of the captain and his wife Sally, and were on the VIP list. That's why they were invited, along with their dinner companions, to the captain's exclusive party.

Richards's status allowed him and Lucy to have the most luxurious lifestyle. The couple owned a four bedroom apartment in London's Knightsbridge, a beautiful country manor hotel in the Lake District, and two properties on the French Riviera; one in the old town of Nice, and one on the beautiful hillside of Villefranche overlooking the port. They also had a fifty-foot luxury yacht, which they berthed in Monte Carlo.

Although their personal fortune was more than that of all the passengers on A, B and C Deck put together, Richard and Lucy were the most down to earth and easy going couple imaginable. Always extremely careful in company not to name-drop or talk about money, there were inevitably the odd occasions when they would have to catch themselves on, especially after a couple of gin and tonics when excitably describing a holiday or a party they had attended.

The couple absolutely adored cruising and meeting new people, but always kept their status private, appreciating people taking them for who they were, not what they have, or how much they were worth.

'Is it the captain's birthday today?' Katie asked.

'Not that I know of, sweetheart. Why do you ask?' Penny replied, intrigued by what the four-year-old meant.

'So why is he having a party if it's not his birthday?'

'Oh, I see. You lost me there for a second, Katie.'

'It's a cocktail party like the chocolate party you went to in The Play House, remember? Except without chocolate. At least I'd imagine so, anyway.'

Josh was in Penny's bathroom busy putting gel in his hair. Danny had made him and Katie go next door to get ready as he feared he wouldn't have enough time to get showered himself if Josh got in the bathroom first. He put his head round the door, and looked at Penny as if she was mad.

'How could she forget about the chocolate party? The chocolate almost killed her, remember?'

'I had to stay in hospital all night, I was very, very sick,' Katie added.

'Of course you were, honey. But you're all better now aren't you?' Penny replied, nodding and smiling.

'Yeah, I'm okay now.'

Since that night, Katie hadn't so much as looked at anything sweet. She had convinced herself she might die if she ate things that were bad for her, especially chocolate. Danny was struggling to make her understand that it was an accident, and it wouldn't happen again, so long as she checked with him or Penny before she ate anything new. Now he was worried he had a food-paranoid four-year-old on his hands.

Most parents were trying to stop their children eating too much junk food, but Danny had the opposite problem. He was worried Katie would give herself an eating disorder if she continued to analyse everything that went in her mouth. Unfortunately for Josh, Katie had taken to looking after his diet as well as her own.

'Boys can be careless, especially when they are hungry,' she had told her father. 'Someone needs to take control of Josh's diet, and it's lucky for him I'm here to do it.'

Apart from the worry about Katie's excruciating food analysis, Danny was also getting a little fed up with meal times. Josh would order something to eat, and Katie would have to decide if he was allowed it or not. Generally hungry and tired by the end of the day, Josh wasn't in the mood to put up with his little sister's new and very annoying habit, which almost without doubt would lead to tears.

'Tell her to stop it, dad,' Josh would protest. 'I'm starving! I just want to eat my dinner in peace.'

'That's enough Katie,' Danny would say. 'Leave your brother to enjoy his dinner.'

'Don't let him eat it, dad,' Katie would say. 'Pizza's not healthy food. He might die.'

On putting his foot down, and telling Katie she was once again going too far, it would lead to more tears and tantrums.

Uncertain how to resolve the problem, Danny had asked Penny for some advice. Surely this wasn't a common mealtime dilemma? Nevertheless, at the Harper dinner table, it was becoming one.

* * *

Edna had given William firm instructions to be ready early. She wanted to be the first person the captain met as he stood at the door to welcome his guests to the party. Doing his best, as normal, William had hurried along to the champagne bar, but the couple had been beaten to the post by a handful of passengers. Oh, goodness, Edna in a queue. My worst nightmare, William had thought to himself.

As they approached the captain, William held out his hand to meet Alex, but without warning Edna opened her handbag and pulled out her old tatty Polaroid camera. Fully aware she was holding up everyone behind her, she thrust the camera into Williams's hand and moved towards the captain putting her arm firmly around his waist.

'You don't mind, do you? Smile,' she said.

'Well actually...' Alex paused, astounded by the woman's blatant rudeness. 'We have the ship's photographer here to take professional quality pictures of the guests.'

'I'm sure you do, captain, and at great expense to the passengers, no doubt.'

Aware that William was affronted by his wife's behaviour, Alex smiled obligingly for the camera just to get the 'old dear' out the way so he could carry on welcoming the rest of his guests. Once again, tremendously embarrassed by his wife's manners, William walked briskly towards the bar.

'A gin and tonic, please,' he requested from the steward. And then, in a lower voice, 'Better make it a bloody large one.'

'Good evening everyone. And what's your name, young lady?' Alex said, looking down at Katie as she stood in line waiting to meet him.

'Katie Mary Harper.'

'And how are you enjoying your cruise, Katie Mary Harper?'

'Very well, thank you. And happy birthday, captain.'

'Birthday? Oh, it's not my–' Alex paused. 'Oh. Right well... umm, never mind. Thank you, I guess.'

Alex gazed at Danny and Penny for an explanation. Sniggering, Josh approached the captain.

'She thinks it's your birthday because you're having a party.'

'Oh, I see.' Alex laughed. 'Well please come in and help yourself to a drink. My waiting staff will be more than happy to serve you. And young man, I don't suppose you would care for a visit to the bridge tomorrow afternoon?'

'Wow! Really?' Josh's face lit up. 'I would really love to, captain, sir.'

'Well if you let me have your cabin number, I'll send you an official invitation. Your family can join you, of course. I can't say for certain what time, but it will be approximately 2.00pm during the approach to the Miraflores locks. Okay with you?'

'Fantastic!'

Hardly able to contain his excitement, Josh walked into the room looking as if he had just won the lottery.

* * *

'What do you prefer, Kris? The trouser suit? Or my little black dress?'

'Seriously, Megan, either is fine. The dress code is casual, remember?'

'Yes, I know. But it's not every week we get invited to the Captain's VIP party. I need to make sure I get it right. I bet Sasha and Lucy will be looking ever so glamorous, as usual. Christ, Sasha could wear a bin liner and pull it off as the latest Versace number.'

'Sure, Megan. But you are so much more attractive. I mean, look at your figure. Sasha is too skinny. She doesn't have the same curves as you.'

'You mean she's not fat like me?'

'No, Meg, I never said that.'

'For God's sake, Kris, I was already feeling bloated. Now I feel like a beached whale.'

'Don't be silly.' Kris smiled indulgently and brought his hands together. 'Right, enough of that. It's decision time. And if you don't start getting ready soon, it will all be academic. The party will be over before we get there.'

'Fine. The black dress it is, but don't rush me, Kris, otherwise I won't feel comfortable.'

'Do you want a glass of wine while you're getting ready? It'll put you in the mood.'

'Good idea,' Megan replied, while Kris poured them both a glass wishing he had offered earlier.

* * *

'There's Kris and Megan,' Lucy announced, waving to the couple as they entered the room.

'We thought you weren't coming,' Richard remarked, looking at Kris for an explanation as to why they were so late.

'We couldn't decide what to wear,' Kris replied, rolling his eyes towards Megan.

'Oh right,' Richard said, capturing the look of horror on Megan's face.

'Oh, God!' she replied, looking at Sasha who was wearing the same dress as her, only three sizes smaller. 'This is so embarrassing!'

'Don't worry about it, Megan,' said Sasha. 'Our accessories are so different, no one will notice.'

'Yeah, right,' Megan said under her breath.

Lucy, who was in a completely different outfit, thought the whole thing was hilarious. Catching Richard and Kris's eyes, they had a private chuckle to themselves.

'Look,' Lucy indicated towards the bar, 'there's Ed and Will. Should we go over and say hello?'

'Maybe, but not straight away,' the men replied in unison.

'Oh, I don't know. From here, she looks like butter wouldn't melt,' Lucy joked.

'Yeah, it's only once she's reeled you in that there's no escape from her blatant rudeness and insulting comments.'

'Poor William,' Sasha added, looking sympathetically at the old man who was now on his third gin and tonic. 'I really do feel for him.'

'I know what you mean,' Kris added, agreeing with Sasha, and getting an 'if looks could kill' stare from Megan.

What the hell is he agreeing for, she thought to herself. As if I don't know.

'Kris and I aren't going down to dinner tonight,' Megan announced. 'We're having a romantic meal in Jasmines, aren't we darling?'

'Apparently so,' Kris agreed, smiling at his partner.

'How funny,' said Lucy. 'We're going there too. Maybe we could get a table together?'

'Maybe Kris and Megan would like a bit of privacy, darling?' Richard said.

'Nonsense,' Kris remarked, before Megan could even open her mouth. 'We'd love the company, wouldn't we, Meg?'

'Absolutely fantastic,' Megan replied, shooting daggers at Kris at every opportunity.

'That's settled, then.' said Richard. 'I'll make a quick call and change the table to a five.'

'I'll come with you,' Kris said, leaving the girls to it.

'So where can I get one of those dresses?' Lucy asked, feeling the odd one out.

'Coast,' Sasha and Megan replied at the same time.

Charlie and Mike were one of the last couples to arrive. They couldn't figure out why they had been sent an invitation to the captain's private party, and weren't sure whether to go or not in case it had been mistake.

A few days earlier in the shopping arcade, Sally and Mike had met. Sally was looking to buy some new jewellery, while Mike had been shopping for a wedding present for Charlie. They had approached the same display unit at the same time, and were interested in the same Cartier watch. The shop assistant had informed them it was the last one in stock, and so, recognizing this, Mike backed off immediately leaving Sally to pursue the purchase. Moments later, the pair had bumped into each other again in another part of the shop. Having not found anything he liked, Mike was exasperated, and Sally, realizing this, had offered him assistance.

Mike had gone on to explain that he and Charlie were getting married onboard, and Sally was pleased he had asked for her help. After two and a half hours browsing the display cabinets, Sally convinced Mike the Cartier watch was by far the best purchase in the shop. Thrilled that she hadn't bought it herself, the pair rushed over to see if it was still available. A few thousand pounds later, Mike and Sally had left the shop. Mike had been so grateful for Sally's help he offered to buy her a coffee. Sally had told Alex all about her afternoon, and Alex had insisted on inviting the couple to his party.

'After all, I'll be marrying them in a few days,' he had told his wife.

Now Mike had to pretend he didn't know Sally, otherwise Charlie would obviously start asking questions.

Having not thought about the fact that Mike's fiancée would be confused by the captain's wife's obvious familiarity, Sally made her way over to the couple.

'Hi, Mike. Nice to see you again.' She smiled at the couple. 'And you must be Mike's fiancée?'

'Yes, I'm Charlie.' Looking puzzled, Charlie glanced at Mike for some sort of hint as to who the lady was who knew his name.

Wishing the captain would make a speech, or the string quartet would increase its volume, Mike just stood there looking uncomfortable.

All of a sudden, realizing that she had put Mike in an awkward position, Sally introduced herself as the captain's wife and quickly nodded to Alex to come and join them for a drink.

Appearing by his wife's side within minutes, Alex chatted away to the couple, making small talk about the cruise before being interrupted by the hotel director.

'Excuse me, sir.'

'Yes, James. Great party isn't it?'

'Yes, sir. Everyone certainly seems to be enjoying themselves.'

'The young lady standing by the bar in the red dress. Do you know her at all?'

'No, I can't say I do, James. Why? Is there a problem?'

'I'm not sure, sir. It's just that she turned up without an invitation, and when Kelly, the entertainments assistant asked her about it, she said you invited her personally. I can't say for sure, but I think she came in the back entrance.

'Now that you mention it, I don't recall meeting her on the door. But that doesn't mean anything. My memory has been terrible lately. I don't think we have a problem anymore. She has just left, but I think you should alert security if she starts acting strangely.'

'Very well, sir. I'll instruct them to keep an eye out.'

'Bizarre,' Alex said. 'Some people will do anything for a free glass of champagne. Now, if you will excuse us, my wife and I have some mingling to do. Nice to meet you both.'

'So how do you know the captain's wife, Mike?' Charlie asked, as soon as Alex and Sally left.

He knew the question was coming but wasn't willing to admit the truth and ruin the surprise.

'I met her the other night when I was out searching the deck for my fiancée,' he lied, knowing fine well that Charlie didn't want to discuss the events of that evening again for as long as she lived.

Flashing her fiancée a brave smile, she said, 'Ooh, I see...'

Chapter 8

Transit Panama Canal 0600 — 1600

Reaching out from underneath the duvet, Alex groped around in the dark for the phone. Lifting the receiver as quickly as possible, in the hope of not waking his wife, he sat up in bed and spoke in a near whisper.

'Captain.'

'Morning, sir. It's Daniel, third officer. It's 04.15 and we're clear for standby below. I've spoken to the pilots and they've confirmed boarding for 6.00am. As expected, we're going to be number three in the convoy. The weather conditions are good. The visibility is a little more than six miles, and there's a light wind from the northeast, approximately fifteen knots'

'Thanks, Daniel. I'll be up shortly.'

Alex hung up and stretched as he reluctantly pushed back the duvet and climbed slowly out of bed. Today wasn't like any of the others. Today, he reminded himself, it wasn't even close. No, today he had to take a 109,000 tonne, two hundred and eighty metre long, thirty metre wide cruise ship through the Panama Canal. Slightly apprehensive about the day ahead, Alex padded to the shower where he mentally prepared himself for his biggest challenge yet.

Once dressed, he kissed his wife gently on the forehead, and made his way into his office.

Logging onto his computer, Alex saw that his 'inbox' was far from empty, and it had only just gone a quarter to five in the morning. Scanning for anything important, he opened and replied to a couple of enquiries before deciding everything else could wait.

Arriving on the bridge a few minutes later, he was greeted by Naeem, one of the Pakistani seamen. Naeem handed him a steaming cup of coffee.

Alex took a sip. 'Mm. Thanks. Just the way I like it.'

'Excuse me, sir,' said the third officer. 'The pilot has confirmed port side for boarding at five knots.'

'Thanks, Daniel.'

'Immigration and clearance officials will be boarding with them, and the hotel department has been informed and will be on standby.'

'That's it then,' Alex confirmed as he finished his coffee.

By six o'clock, most of the passengers were up and about lining the decks of Ocean Magic and eagerly waiting for the ship to approach the Gatun Locks. Many were on their private balconies, while others preferred to be out on the open decks mingling with the other passengers and capturing the many different views of the locks. Once the pilot was onboard, the ship moved expertly into position, and everyone looked on in wonder.

Gatun was the first set of Locks through the Panama Canal performing the biggest lift of all three sets raising the ship twenty-six metres in total. Each lock was approximately three hundred metres long and thirty-three metres in width. Everyone watched the mules; the tiny electric locomotives that guided the ships through the lock chambers as they ran along side pulling the ship at an incline as they went. Ten locomotives were used to assist Ocean Magic through the canal due to the sheer size of the mighty vessel.

At approximately twenty past eight, Ocean Magic cleared Gatun, and there was a loud cheer for Alex as he ventured on towards San Pablo Cut.

That's one down two more to go, Alex told himself, pleased at how well it had gone.

On completing the first set of locks, Sasha decided it was a good opportunity to get showered and dressed. She had received an invitation from Richard and Lucy to join them for a champagne breakfast at ten o'clock in their cabin. Richard and Lucy enjoyed a large suite at the aft end of Deck 9 and, as a way of marking the occasion, were having a select few round for smoked salmon bagels and Danish pastries.

Sasha arrived fashionably late, and was welcomed by the hosts, Kris and Megan, and two other couples who had suites on either side of Richard and Lucy's cabin. Sasha immediately recognized the waiter. Richard had requested Tom's expert service for the morning's festivities. Sasha was excited by this, seeing it as an opportunity to find out more about the mysterious Geoff.

Tom greeted Sasha and paid her the same amount of attention as everyone else, but as keen as he was to set his friend up with her, he resisted the opportunity to meddle. As the ship approached the Pedro Miguel Locks, just after 1.00pm, the champagne was flowing steadily. Kris plugged his MP3 player into the stereo and chose some appropriate music to keep everyone in the party spirit. Minutes later, the butler arrived with the most amazing selection of tapas for the group to enjoy as they continued on route towards Miraflores, the third and final set of locks. There was no expense spared. Richard and Lucy really knew how to throw a party.

Tom discarded the third empty bottle of bubbly and, as instructed by Richard, continued to offer a selection of additional beverages to the guests – not that anyone needed any more to drink, least of all Kris and Richard who were now doing their impression of Rose and Jack in *Titanic* as *My Heart Will Go On* was turned up to full volume and blared out of the cabin onto the balcony.

Kris had been assigned the part of Rose, and had no difficulty performing the role. He looked like he was enjoying it, which was more of a worry. More worrying still was that he had disappeared for five minutes before the performance and had come back with a curly red wig to add more authenticity to his five minutes of fame.

The day had been wonderful, but Sasha feared the glass of champagne she had drunk had gone straight to her head. She decided to save herself for the evening, and thanked Richard and Lucy for their hospitality before saying her farewells. Leaving the cabin, she walked forward towards the mid ship staircase where she spotted Geoff leaning against the bulkhead next to one of the lifts. He had his back turned to her, and was chatting to a very attractive looking girl. She was tall and slim and looked about twenty-five, or, at a push, maybe twenty-six. She was wearing a black Burberry bikini with matching sarong, and had a pair of large dark sunglasses propped on her head and sweeping her long blonde hair back off her face – also Burberry, Sasha predicted from afar.

Geoff was wearing a pair of green combat shorts and a light grey t-shirt with a surfing logo splashed on the back. A professional looking camera was slung over his right shoulder. As Sasha approached, Geoff moved towards the girl and kissed her on the lips. He then gave her a huge hug, lifting her off her feet. They both looked remarkably pleased with themselves.

Sasha's heart sank quicker than the anchor of the ship. He must have met her during the cruise. Yes, he was probably just being polite yesterday at the beach, humouring her because she was on her own. Now, seriously regretting every mouthful of the champagne she had enjoyed at Richard and Lucy's, she worried in case she slurred her words or said something stupid in front of Geoff and his girlfriend.

As she approached the couple, she lost her nerve, and quickly turned back in the opposite direction.

But it was too late. Geoff noticed her leaving and called out, 'Sasha? Is that you?'

Unsure of how to handle this, she stopped, drew breath, and considered the options. Pretend she hadn't heard? Ignore him? Or just run? Finally, steeling herself, she turned again and walked towards them, all smiles.

Geoff's eyes lit up. 'Hi.'

'Yes,' she said. 'Hi.'

As she approached, he looked genuinely pleased to see her. In fact, he was even friendlier than he had been the day before. He didn't introduce his friend, but talked excitedly about the locks and how much he was enjoying himself.

Her heart racing, Sasha listened politely for a few minutes aware of the fact that she probably looked as uncomfortable as she felt. Finally, latching onto a pause, she quickly checked her watch.

'Gosh. Is that the time? I think I'm supposed to be somewhere.'

'Oh?' said Geoff. 'Where?'

Sasha pondered that, but her mind was suddenly blank. 'Just… you know, somewhere. *Else.*'

'Oh.' Geoff frowned. 'Well okay. See you later maybe?'

'Yes. Later. Great.'

'Or maybe you'd like to join us for a coffee?'

Finding the invitation a little strange, Sasha was surprised his new girlfriend didn't protest or at least raise an eyebrow.

'No but thanks. I've been invited to a cabin party with some friends, and I'm running late, so I really must get going.'

Well it wasn't *technically* a lie. She had indeed been invited to a cabin party. And she had also just left it, but Geoff didn't need to know the details.

Sasha decided to take the long way back to her cabin, wandering past the shops instead of waiting for the lift with Geoff and his bikini-clad friend. As she walked away, confused, troubled – and more than a little jealous – she realized Geoff would never have been interested in her. Judging by the sort of girls he went for, he was clearly out of her league.

Watching Ocean Magic Transit the Panama Canal was all very exciting, even if it was the first or second time one had experienced it, but this was Sally's *fourth* time through. Having been out on the balcony for the first set of locks (more for support and admiration for Alex than anything else), she decided he was so busy anyway he wouldn't notice if she slipped off for a bit to check her emails. She had been onboard a little over a week, and was beginning to miss her friends and family, so decided she would give them an update on how the cruise was going and all the exciting ports she and Alex had visited since she had been away.

Alex's offer for her to stay onboard for another cruise was really playing on her mind. *If he was having an affair, why would he want her to stay?* She was completely baffled by the situation, and time was running out. She needed to decide in the next couple of days. Alex was pressing her for a decision for the numbers of passengers onboard, and there was a flight to change. There was also the fact she would have to take another two weeks off work. Not that it really mattered at this time of year. No one else would be on holiday. It was just another thing nagging at her to deal with.

The Cyber Café was empty. Everyone else was making the most of the sunshine, and, of course, busy watching Ocean Magic squeeze through the canal.

One hundred and twenty two unread emails. Good God! I've only been away a few days. And look who's suddenly Mrs Popular. Junk, junk, junk, more junk... and, well, maybe not that one. Hmm, not sure who that is. Better keep that one too. Oh good, one from mum...

She opened the email which read; *Hi, darling. I hope you're having a wonderful time with that adorable husband of yours. We are all missing you, of course, but no need to hurry home. Everything here is fine. Your father is looking after your house for you, and little Jaffa's well. Its just wonderful looking after him!*

Jaffa. Oh I miss that little puppy... she thought to herself, remembering how upset she was when having to say her goodbyes to him. His lovable little face said; *I'll miss you too* while he settled into his bed in his holiday home.

The email went on; *Weather terrible. Three feet of snow. Better off staying where you are. If I had the chance, I know where I'd rather be. Anyway, okay and bye for now. Your father sends his love, and he says to tell Alex not to bend it and try not to park it like he does that sports car of his. He's seen him just abandon it in the street like a kid's bike! He's joking of course!*

Of course, Sally thought, but there was some degree of truth in it. Alex's parking was the worst she'd seen.

Lots of love, Mum, Dad and little Jaffa. XXX.

That was nice, but I'll reply later, Sally decided, continuing to work through the emails and deleting all the junk.

Right, that's better, now who was that other email from? Puzzled by the email address, and no subject matter, she clicked on the message and opened the page. *Oh not again*, she cursed as she sat upright in her chair. *Who was doing this?* Without a second thought, Sally knew there was only one person she could trust to talk to, so she quickly made her way to the nearest phone and dialled her friend's cabin number.

'Joyce? Oh good, you're there. Look, any chance you could come down to the Cyber Cafe? I need your help with something.'

'Are you kidding? I've only been through the Panama eight times. I don't want to miss a thing! Give me five minutes and I'll be down.'

'You don't need to dress up. There's no one here.'

'But a lady must always look her best, Sally. You know that you're the captain's bit of fluff, remember?'

'Well that's the thing you see, I'm not sure I am.'

'Understood, and over and out. Give me two minutes and I'll be there.'

Sally sat staring blankly at the computer screen, still pondering the photo. A moment later, one of the waitresses came in to offer her a coffee.

'No, thanks,' she replied, and without hesitation, 'do you have anything stronger?'

'Yes, sure. I'll just call a bar steward.'

'No, it's okay. I'm kidding,' Sally answered while the girl walked off, looking rather nonplussed by the conversation.

Soon after, Joyce came bounding into the room looking like she had been sitting waiting for a phone call or any excuse to get out of the cabin.

'So what is it?' she said.

Sally pointed grimly at the screen.

Joyce edged forward and saw the photo for herself, her eyebrows rising by the second.

'Jesus! Another one! Sally, this is serious. You need to tell Alex.'

'I *can't* tell Alex, can I? If it wasn't about him, then yes, it's no problem. But it's *all* about him. It's all there, Joyce. My God, it has to be true.'

Trying her best to control her emotions, but clearly upset by the latest of piece of evidence against her husband, Sally covered her face with her hands and began sobbing.

Putting her arm around her friend's shoulder, Joyce realized the seriousness of the situation. But she still wouldn't allow herself to believe there was any truth to the allegation against Alex. Well, at least she couldn't let Sally think for a second that the thought might have crossed her mind.

'Come on, Sally. You're stronger than this. I mean, a poxy photo of Alex and some girl. So what? It doesn't prove a thing. In fact, wasn't there a company event last month where three of our ships met up in St Thomas? It was probably taken there. *Bingo!* Yes, it was. Look, there's Tommy Hilfiger. Remember? We had lunch in a restaurant right next to it. It was this time last year. Come on, you must remember.'

'I do remember, and it does look like it, but Alex didn't mention the fact that he went ashore. In fact, when I'm not here he rarely sets foot on dry land, and he always tells me when he does.'

Joyce shrugged. 'Well maybe he just forgot.'

'Maybe, but it's really not making any sense, and he does look to be enjoying himself. Look they're both drinking beer and – oh, did I mention he has his arm around her?' Sally added sarcastically before bursting into tears for the second time.

'*Ask* him about it,' Joyce replied. 'If he denies going ashore, then you'll know he's hiding something. I'm sure it's completely innocent.'

'Well I'm not so sure I'll ask him. But if I did, I'm pretty certain I know what he will say.'

'Come on, Sal. Whatever happened to innocent-until-proven-guilty? Like I said, he's a good-looking guy. He's bound to attract the ladies.'

'But what if it is true? What if he *is* having an affair? What will I do then?'

'Sally, you need to keep this in perspective. Yes, worst-case scenario, it might be true. But if it is, and I know its not, well, we'll cross that bridge when we come to it.'

'It's all right for you. Martin would never dream of cheating on you.'

'Now that's not true, Sally. He might not be as good-looking as Alex, but you can still never be one hundred percent sure.'

Sally sighed and nodded slowly. 'Right, so what do I do now?'

'Well, first of all ignore the email. You don't want her, whoever the bitch is, to think you even care. Then we take ourselves to Flutes for a sneaky glass of Bollinger.'

'Flutes? The champagne bar? I hardly think that's appropriate. What are we celebrating? The fact that my husband has gone off with another woman?'

'Oh, for goodness sake Sally! You need to lighten up a little. Come on, it's my shout.'

'Okay. But wouldn't it be better if I replied? She might get in touch again and let something slip.'

Joyce considered that.

'You might be right,' she said. 'Okay. Just type something along the lines of; *Are you completely insane, emailing me a picture of yourself with my husband? Because now I know what you look like.*'

'Seriously, Joyce. I need your help here.'

'Okay, okay. What about; *I don't believe you for a second. But if what you're saying is true, why don't you make yourself known to me? Then I'll consider leaving my husband.*' Joyce paused for thought, and then added, 'Hey, I don't want to freak you out or anything crazy, Sal, but how did this person get your private email address, anyway?'

'I don't know. I guess the same way she found out my date of birth.'

'Yeah, I think it's safe to say the woman has got a screw loose. She's obviously determined to cause trouble between the two of you. But that's enough for now. Log off and let's go and give the staff in Flutes something to do.'

* * *

'It's here! My invite from the captain!'

Ripping open the envelope addressed to Master Joshua Harper and Family, Josh's little face lit up again like a beacon.

You are invited to visit the bridge on deck 14 forward today at 2.30pm for the transit of the Panama Canal Access through deck 14 forward starboard door.

Penny couldn't decide who was more excited about the bridge visit; Josh or Danny. All morning, Danny had been hanging out round the cabin, not wanting to do anything in case he missed this fantastic opportunity. But more importantly he was waiting for the official invite. Josh, who was going on the bridge visit, official invite or not, couldn't have paid more attention to his appearance if he was about to meet the Queen. The pair were hilarious to watch, choosing their best shorts, shirts and shoes.

'You have to make an effort,' Danny had insisted. 'The captain won't be impressed if we turn up looking like we've just forced ourselves off a sun lounger to visit him.'

Katie, not fully understanding what was going on, knew only that she had to look smart and be polite if spoken to. Penny was of much the same opinion.

But finally it was time. Danny and Josh followed closely as Penny and Katie left the cabin and walked promptly towards the front of the ship before getting the lift to Deck 14. They arrived at 2.30pm exactly, and were greeted at the 'CREW ONLY' door by Matt, the head of the security team, who lead them through to the bridge where Alex had made himself personally available to welcome his guests.

He introduced them to one or two of his officers, and gave them the grand tour. Josh couldn't believe his eyes when he saw the sheer size of the bridge. For the nine- year-old, the vast amount of equipment was quite overwhelming.

Alex had arranged for the ship's photographer to be there to take photos of Josh and Katie in the driving seat and wearing his cap. Thinking it would be funny; Josh placed the cap on Penny's head and insisted she posed for a photograph. Danny, who was about to tell Josh off for misbehaving, did a double take. As she unintentionally posed beneath the air conditioning vent with her long blonde hair gently blowing, he was impressed at how sexy she looked.

Wow!

After photographs, they all stood on the port bridge wing looking through the enormous window watching the ship arrive at the Miraflores Lock. Katie squealed with delight as she gazed down and realized the only thing between her and the lock was a pane of glass. A very secure pane of glass, perhaps, but nevertheless just glass. Penny was less impressed as she looked down to see what all the fuss was about. The view was vertiginous and made her recoil slightly.

'Oh, sorry. I probably should have warned you,' said Alex, having momentarily forgotten how daunting it was to be so high.

Just as the ship entered the lock, two stewards appeared with a glass of champagne for Penny and Danny. They also brought a selection of soft drinks and a small tray of chocolates for Josh and Katie. Katie almost had a fit when Alex offered her the plate, looking up at him as if he was trying to poison her. She remembered, however, that she had to be polite, and she flashed a smile before saying, 'No thank you, captain. I won't if you don't mind.'

'Hmm. A child – sorry, a young *lady* – who doesn't like chocolate. That's a first.'

'It's not that I don't *like* chocolate,' she replied, a little tartly. 'It's the chocolates that don't like *me*.'

'Oh. I see. Well, I'm sorry about that. Chocolate should like everyone.'

Alex looked up hoping someone could make sense of the conversation he was having with the child.

Josh, who was finding this all too amusing, came forward and said,

'Katie has an allergy to nuts. She only found out a few days ago when she ate some chocolate at the chocolate party. So now she won't eat anything sweet at all.'

'Right,' said Alex. 'I see. Well I'm not surprised. That would be enough to put me off chocolate too.'

'I wish *I* had an allergy to chocolate,' said Penny. 'That would save me a few hours in the gym every week.'

'I know what you mean. It's just not worth it,' said Danny, never having visited a gym in his life.

Alex had gone to such an effort to make the experience special for them; Josh felt that he had actually just met the Queen.

Katie, on the other hand, simply couldn't understand why the captain was trying to put her back in hospital.

Once the ship was clear of traffic and on its way back out to sea, Alex joined Danny and Penny with another coffee. They chatted for a while before Katie handed him a card to thank him for the visit.

Alex had enjoyed the experience as much as his guests. It was Josh and Katie's innocence that had prompted him to ask them along for a visit. He and Sally weren't fortunate enough to have children of their own, so whenever they got the opportunity, they very much enjoyed spoiling other people's kids.

After the visit, Danny decided to carry on the celebrations. He booked a table in Le Beaujolais, the French restaurant in the shopping arcade. They enjoyed a wonderful meal whilst talking endlessly about the bridge visit and how generous the captain was. By eight o'clock, Katie was fighting to stay awake, and eventually began to fall asleep at the table. She and Josh had had enough excitement for one day, and were well and truly ready for bed.

* * *

All things considered, it had been a very eventful day. Sasha had fallen asleep on the balcony trying to erase the memory of Geoff and the gorgeous blonde, when there came a knock on the door that made her jump. Startled, she eased herself off her deckchair and walked towards the door and opened it. But there was no one there. After looking up and down the corridor, she turned and noticed an envelope in her mailbox. Troubled, she opened it straight away and read the very brief text; *Sasha please call home as soon as possible.*

Unsure who it was she was meant to be calling, she panicked for a moment hoping that nothing terrible had happened to her mum. She sat on her bed and took a few deep breaths before picking up the in cabin phone.

'Kyle, it's Sasha. What's wrong? I got a message to call home. Is everyone alright?'

'Sort of,' Kyle replied. 'It's Ben. We had a phone call from his brother to say he's fallen ill and been taken to hospital. He was expecting you to be here. When we told him we thought you were on a cruise with Ben, he hung up. What happened, Sasha? Why is Ben not with you?'

'It's a long story, Kyle, but basically we fell out at the airport and he decided not to come with me.'

'What? That's crazy!'

'Well not exactly. We had already missed our flight, so we had to buy another two tickets. Ben refused and left the airport, but I stayed. Anyway, enough about that. What's happened to Ben? Why is he in hospital?'

'I don't know. All I understood from his brother was that he took ill last night and he was taken to hospital. We've tried calling several times, but no one will give us any information. His parents won't speak to us either. Mum called round last night, but they wouldn't answer the door. Man, mum is going to freak when she finds out you went on your own.'

'Yeah, well she must know by now.'

'Yeah, she suspects something, but you know what she's like. Anyway, this is Nathan's number. I got it from the caller ID last night, but I'm not sure how he will be with you. He sounded pretty pissed off when he discovered you went on the cruise on your own. Have you got a pen?'

'Yes, go ahead.'

'Okay, it's 07955 555599.'

'Thanks, Kyle. Can you email me if you get any further information about Ben? My mobile doesn't work out here, and I have no other means for you to get in touch.'

'Sure. Alright, take care Sasha, and happy cruising.'

'Yeah, right.'

Unsure of what to do next, and realizing that pacing endlessly round the cabin was getting her nowhere, she reluctantly decided that she had to swallow her pride and call Ben's brother. After all, she owed Ben that much. Picking up the receiver, she carefully dialled his number and began the dreaded conversation.

'Nathan? It's Sasha. What happened? Is Ben alright?'

'You mean, apart from being abandoned by his fiancée who left him to go on a cruise on her own, and the stroke he had last night?' Nathan replied. 'Yeah, he's fine. He's on top of the world.'

'Nathan, don't be like that. You don't know the facts.'

'You mean the lies?'

'No, I don't. Just tell me what happened.'

'For the record, I don't think you deserve to know. But on the off chance I can make you feel guilty for what you've done...' He paused. '... Ben called me on my mobile to say he wasn't feeling well, but by the time I got to him he was passed out on the floor. The doctors don't know what caused it but I've got a fair idea.'

'Nathan, that's not fair. What happened is between Ben, and me and if you must know *he* left *me* at the airport, not the other way around. Where is he now? Can I call and speak to him?'

'I don't think so, Sasha. I think you've caused enough damage, don't you? Anyway he's wired up to all sorts of machines so he's not fit to talk.'

'Look, Nathan, I'm in port the day after tomorrow. I'll get a flight arranged straight away.'

'No. Look, Sasha, Ben has made it quite clear he doesn't want to see you. Not now, not *ever*.'

'That's not true. You said yourself he can't talk.'

'You're missing the point, Sasha. I know my brother better than anyone else. He's not interested in your pathetic excuses. Don't waste your money, sweetheart. You won't be allowed near him. I'll make damn sure of that!'

Chapter 9

At Sea

The conversation with Nathan had been a difficult one. There had been no reasoning with him. He had made up his mind that Ben was to be left alone to recover. Nobody was getting near him, regardless of what Ben himself actually wanted. Although, the way things had been lately, and especially with what Ben had said in his last email, Nathan probably had a point. It was for the best.

Apart from anything else, Puntarenus and Puerto Quetzal were the only two ports left to visit before the ship berthed in Acapulco for an overnight stay before she flew home as planned. Realistically, neither was going to be an easy option to get a last minute flight home from. She would leave as soon as possible if she had to but Acapulco really was the only sensible choice, and that was still five or six days away.

With nothing to be gained, there really was no decision to make. Providing there was a way to find out if Ben was going to be okay, she would stay. Going home early would cause only more pain and heartache, and the way things were looking, she wasn't going to be allowed to see her ex-fiancé anyway. Ben's family would make damn sure of that.

It had been a terribly restless night. No matter how bad things were with her and Ben, she couldn't help but worry about him. Ben was normally so fit and healthy; she didn't know anyone who took as much care of their body as him. Fortunately, the time difference was working in her favour. If she gave it another hour or so, she could phone her friend, Claire, who was a senior nurse at St David's hospital. She was almost certain that that was where

Ben would be, and there was also an extremely good chance he might even be under her care.

Browsing through the ship's daily newsletter, Sasha noticed there was a yoga class starting in twenty minutes in the aerobics studio next to the gym. This seemed like a good opportunity to help calm herself down. It would also pass a couple of hours before Claire started her shift.

Still feeling as if her head was going to explode, she reasoned that it was a sound idea. Yoga wasn't exactly the sort of class that couples would go to together, so she wouldn't feel out of place either.

However, the idea of setting foot inside a gym petrified her. She had been gifted with a slim toned body, and never had to work at keeping it that way, so she had never seen the point in building up a sweat on those funny looking machines. *God only knows how you even got them to work*, she thought to herself.

Searching in her wardrobe for something suitable to wear, Sasha pulled out a pair of khaki combat trousers and a fitted vest top. That should do the trick. Thankfully, she didn't need a pair of trainers for yoga, which was actually just as well she thought as she searched for her second flip flop. She collected a bottle of water from the fridge, and arrived at the studio just as the instructor was introducing himself. *Ben the fitness instructor? What are the chances?* Sasha thought. *And just as I'm trying not to think about him.*

Ben was at least six feet tall. He had short spikey blonde hair, a dark tan, an extremely fit and toned body, and a concave stomach. Sasha, like every other woman in the room, couldn't help but admire his perfect physique. She could see he was talking, but couldn't hear a word he said.

'Hey, Sasha!' a voice interrupted her thoughts.

Oh no, he's noticed me eyeing him up. How embarrassing, he's going to say something in front of the class. Quick look away!

' Sasha, behind you.'

She turned to find Geoff standing there.

'Oh, hi!' she said, unsure of which way to look.

He was wearing a pair of black Nike tracksuit bottoms with a matching black vest top. He looked almost as good as Ben, and was definitely more toned than Sasha had remembered.

'I haven't seen you in here before,' he said.

'No, you wouldn't have. This is a first for me. I'm not really sure what I'm doing here.'

'Nonsense.'

Gosh, that smile! Sasha remembered being drawn to it the first time they met on the beach.

The class soon began and finished at eleven fifteen. The group had clearly been enjoying themselves, so Ben had carried it over an extra quarter of an hour. Picking up her bottle of water, she thanked Geoff for his helpful tips. He had talked her through practically the whole class.

Remembering the phone call she had to make, she headed for the door. But before she got very far, Ben stopped her in her tracks.

'Hi, there,' he said. 'Thanks for coming to the class. It's always nice to see a new face.'

'Sure. It was fun. You're obviously very popular.'

'It's a busy cruise with plenty of younger passengers, which is always good. I prefer to keep busy. Oh, don't forget to fill out an entry card for the prize draw. There are lots of great things to be won.'

'Thanks.' Sasha smiled, taking a card from Ben.

'Your name and cabin number will do.'

Patiently, waiting his turn to talk to Sasha, Geoff hovered by the door. Sensing that the conversation – or more like a chat up attempt – was over, he made his way over to Sasha.

'Hey, what's that?' he said, looking at the card Sasha was holding. She studied it at eye level. 'It's for a prize draw or something.'

'Geoff Harrison, cabin D453,' she wrote.

'I think that was intended for you, Sasha.'

'Wait here and I'll get you another one.'

'No need,' Sasha said. 'I'm possibly the unluckiest person alive, I haven't won anything before.'

'Hey, how did you know my sir name? And more importantly, my cabin number?' Geoff said, suddenly confused by Sasha's knowledge.

'Geoff Harrison, Cabin D453,' she repeated. 'It says it right there on your cruise card.'

'Right. I'd better be more careful with this.'

He gestured to the card he was wearing on a Nike band round his neck. 'I don't want all the pretty girls onboard making a note of my cabin number. I have enough trouble sleeping as it is!'

'I don't think you need to worry about that.'

'Oh, really? Why not?'

'Well, take me for example. I've forgotten it already.'

'Your loss,' Geoff said, smiling as they left the studio together.

Not knowing what to do with that comment, Sasha pretended he hadn't said anything. Feeling the awkwardness of the silence, Geoff put his arm across the lift door to stop Sasha disappearing. If he let her go this time, what were the chances of them bumping into each other again before the end of the cruise? She knew *his* cabin number, but he still didn't know *hers*.

'So what are your plans for the rest of the day?' he said.

'Nothing much. I'll probably find a quiet spot out on deck and get stuck into my book, I'd imagine.'

It should be dry by now, she thought, mindful of the bathroom incident the other evening.

'So you're free for lunch then?'

Unable to stop herself, Sasha blushed a little at Geoff's offer. 'It's just that I was wondering if you would like to join me?' he said.

Sasha considered that.

'Sure,' she replied after a few seconds, shrugging. 'Why not?'

'Great.'

Confirming the arrangements, she was free to go back to her cabin to have a shower and change her clothes. When she was alone again, she was slightly puzzled by what had just happened. Geoff must be intending to take his girlfriend along. *He couldn't possibly just leave her and go out for lunch with me. Could he?* She wondered.

With a spring in her step, and feeling rather pleased with herself, she began dressing. Regardless of whether he was bringing his girlfriend, Geoff had asked her to lunch. It was nice to be asked.

As usual, she arrived ten minutes late. There was no sense in appearing too keen. Geoff was sitting at a table in Mariners Seafood restaurant in the shopping arcade. As she approached the table in the far corner of the restaurant, Geoff rose from his seat, pushed past the waiter and pulled out the chair for her.

Wow, she thought, *this is a first.*

'Can I get you both something to drink?' said the waiter.

'Please,' replied Sasha, smiling at Geoff. 'I'll have a sparkling mineral water.'

'A coke for me please. No ice.'

'Certainly,' the waiter replied with a glimmer in his eye, obviously sensing this was the first time the couple had met for lunch.

Sipping her water, and making small talk, Sasha waited patiently for Geoff's friend to arrive. But she failed to show.

Presently, the waiter returned and asked if they were ready to order. Geoff agreed and invited Sasha to choose.

Realizing that it was going to be just the two of them, Sasha glanced at the menu and ordered the first thing on the list.

'The grilled seafood platter sounds lovely. I'll have that please.'

'And for you, sir?'

'I'll have the salted sea bass.'

Geoff looking pleased with himself, watched the wine steward appear with an ice bucket, followed by a bottle of white rioja.

'I knew you liked white wine. I hope this one is okay.'

'Yes. Wonderful.'

Taking another sip of her water, she relaxed a little more. Still confused and certainly intrigued by what she had seen a day or so ago, she decided to put it to the back of her mind; for now anyway. It wouldn't be right to interrogate Geoff about the beautiful blonde she saw him kissing while transiting the Panama Canal. It must have just been a one-night stand, she decided.

Lunch was quite a success. The conversation didn't stop for a second. Geoff chatted away about the cruise. How wonderful the ship was, and what a fantastic time he was having. He talked about Curacao where he went diving before spending the afternoon snorkelling with his friends, Rick and Chris. The pair chatted non-stop, but somehow managed not to give away too much about themselves.

Sasha learned that Geoff was from Crawley, only an hour and a half from where she lived – or *used* to live as things may well turn out. He was in the fire service, and seemed to have a lot of very nice friends and family. Sasha briefly talked about her own family and her career, which seemed to impress him.

'So maybe we'll see each other in the gym from now on?' said Geoff, knowing fine well that wasn't going to happen.

'I'm not so sure about that. This morning was more of a one-off for me.'

'But you enjoyed it, didn't you?'

'Yes, I suppose I did.'

It had just gone three o'clock when the waiter approached with the bill. Geoff insisted on paying, and for the first time since they met there was a brief silence, as neither knew how to end the lunch.

'Thanks,' she said at last. 'It was a lovely meal, and the company wasn't too bad either.'

'My pleasure.' Geoff laughed. 'Same here. Well, enjoy your afternoon. I guess that I'll see you around the ship.' Deeply regretting not asking Sasha for her cabin number he called after her. 'Sasha!'

She looked round, eyebrows up. 'Yes.'

'Thanks again for your company. I had a really nice time.'

Pleased by the added comment, Sasha waved back, and then continued back along Promenade deck leaving Geoff to kick himself for being such a coward.

Bringing herself quickly back down to earth, she decided to make the call and find out what was happening with Ben. They had officially broken off their engagement, as far as they were both concerned, but she still felt she owed him her friendship.

Unfortunately, the situation was real, and the call had to be made. Scrolling down her phone book she found Claire's direct number at St David's and punched in the number on the satellite phone in her cabin.

'Good afternoon. St David's Royal Infirmary. You're through to Claire Morrison. How can I help you?'

'Hello, Claire. It's Sasha. How are you?'

'Sasha! I'm great thanks. Nice to hear from you.'

'Claire, it's not actually a social call. I need a favour and was wondering if you can help me out.'

'Sure, Sasha. Anything at all. What is it?'

'Well...' Taking a deep breath, Sasha began. 'This may come as a bit of a shock, but Ben and I are going through a difficult time.'

'Oh, Sasha. I'm sorry to hear that. Are you okay?'

'No not really. The problem is that I'm out of the country at the minute, and Ben has fallen ill at home; as far as I'm aware he had a stroke. But because his family is aware of the problems between us, they won't let me see or even talk to him and I just need to know if he's alright.'

'Okay. Where do you think he is?'

'Well, I actually thought he was at St David's, but obviously he's not, or you would have been aware of it.'

'He might be here, Sash, but I've been on holiday for two weeks and am just back today. I'm in the middle of a handover at the minute, but if you can call me back later I'll have had a chance to catch up with the patients and I'll let you know if he's here. Do you want me to give him a message from you if he is?'

'No, I don't think that's a good idea. His brother doesn't want me to have any contact with him, at least until he's better.'

'What ward is he in?'

'I don't know.'

'No problem. I'll check with the desk. If you could call me back at six o'clock, I should have some news for you by then.'

'Thanks, Claire. I really appreciate this. Speak to you later.'

* * *

'Go, Josh. Win, win. Faster, faster. Yeah!' Katie squealed with excitement as Josh sprinted his way to the end of the pool. Peeling his goggles from his face and throwing them on the side of the pool as if to say *that's how it's done*, he looked to his dad for praise.

'Only the breast stroke and the backstroke left, son.'

'Don't worry, dad, I was the fastest in the heats yesterday.'

'I have no doubt you were, Josh, well done.'

'Yeah, well done, Josh.' Giving her the thumbs up, Josh winked at Katie, quickly making sure his mates hadn't seen him being affectionate with his little sister.

'He's very good.'

An attractive looking strawberry-blonde haired woman appeared from nowhere and complimented Danny on Josh's efforts.

'Well he's keen, I'll give him that,' replied Danny.

The woman smiled. 'Hi, I'm Nicole. I'm James's mum.'

'Oh right, yes. The boys have become quite friendly this cruise, and from what I can see they are both very competitive. I hope it doesn't end in tears.'

'Me too. The Club is fantastic for them. They seem to really enjoy themselves. The only problem is that I never see James. I originally booked the cruise thinking it would do us both good, a bit of mother and son bonding. Maybe get to the bottom of some of the things that are bothering him about losing his father.'

'You're travelling alone then?' said Danny.

'Might as well be, seeing as I never see him.'

'I know exactly what you mean. To think I paid the nanny to come along and look after my two. There really was no need.'

'Their mother's not here then?'

'Better not be. That would be all we need, her turning up with her new husband in tow.'

'Oh, I'm sorry I didn't mean to...'

'No. That's okay. It was a while ago now, and I'm over it. But I'm not sure the kids are in the same place as me, though.'

'Yes. I see.'

'Is James in the next race?'

'Yes. He's warming up over there. You would think it was the Olympics the way he carries on, really.'

'Here we go, daddy. Come on Josh!' Katie shouted, pulling at Danny's shirt.

Everyone was silent, carefully watching as the whistle was sounded and the seven boys dived into the pool. Two of the boys weren't very strong swimmers, and struggled to keep up, while the three in the middle were swimming stroke for stroke. Already halfway up the pool, Josh and James battled it out for first place, the two boys catching a glimpse of each other as they looked quickly to the side to see the other's position.

Josh was taking no chances and quickly ramped up his speed as if starting his engine, and he left James for dust. As James touched the wall, and finished the race, Josh was waiting for his friend. The two boys, showing great sportsmanship, reached across the ropes and hugged each other and congratulated one another on their performance.

At that moment, Penny appeared at Danny's side.

'Hi, Penny,' Katie called out.

'How's the champ?' Penny asked, keen to know how Josh was getting on.

'He's won three already,' Katie answered excitedly. 'He's really very fast.'

'Brilliant! Only one more to go then.'

Sensing the woman who was talking so enthusiastically to Danny was more interested in him than watching her son's race, Penny thought it would be best to give them a bit of space.

'How would you like to go up to Deck 14?' she asked Katie. 'We'll get a better view from there.'

'Yeah. Great. Bye, daddy!'

'Bye, darling. See you in a minute,' said Danny, patting her on the head.

'So what do you do with yourself in the evening?' Danny asked Nicole. 'It must be quite difficult going out on your own all the time.'

'Well, it's not ideal, to be honest. But I'm making the most of it.'

'So you don't want me to take you for a drink tomorrow night, say, about eight? Once I get the kids organized, that is.'

'Oh, I'd love that. Some adult company would be nice for a change.'

'I hear the Jazz Cafe is great for pre-dinner drinks.'

'The Jazz Cafe it is then. See you tomorrow eight o'clock.'

'Can't wait.'

Nicole smiled as she watched Danny climb the steps to Deck 14 to join Katie and Penny for Josh's last race.

'Congratulations, Josh,' said Danny. 'All that training is certainly paying off. You were *amazing* out there, kid.'

'I know, dad. Some of the boys are two or three years older than me, but I showed them.'

'You certainly did. Come on, let's all go and get an ice cream and celebrate.'

Josh and Danny walked behind, while Penny and Katie skipped on ahead discussing what sort of ice cream they were going to order.

'That reminds me, Josh,' said Danny. 'Is there something you've forgotten to tell me?'

'Like what?'

Josh had been hoping the subject of the flowers would never raise its ugly head, but he knew full well that was where this conversation was heading. He also knew that telling his father the truth would get him a much lighter sentence than if he was found to be lying, but no matter how much he tried, he couldn't bring himself to tell his dad that there was a girl onboard who had... well, sent him overboard.

Danny was trying his best not to show his bemusement whilst thoroughly enjoying the opportunity to watch Josh squirm like an eel caught in a net.

'Let me see.' Danny rubbed his chin and gazed up at the clear blue sky. 'Your trip to the florist maybe...'

'Oh that!' Josh sighed. 'Yes, I bought some flowers for Katie to make her better.'

'Did you really? Well that's funny, because I never saw them. Did Katie like them?' But before Josh could answer, Danny continued, 'It's just that when I questioned the charge on my account, the girl from reception told me they were delivered to someone called Miss Carly Richardson. What's even more bizarre, Josh, is that it was the day before Katie fell ill.'

'Oh.' Josh's face said it all. He was well and truly done for. He thought back to the last time he told a lie to his father. The punishment was a week without television, but that was for a much lesser crime. Danny's reasoning for punishment was based partly on the crime itself, but much more relevant was the idea of being man enough to admit that Josh had done wrong.

'I'm really sorry, dad. Look, I sent them to a girl from my club. She was sick and I wanted to cheer her up.'

'That's more like it, Josh, but did you have to spend thirty-five pounds on the bouquet?'

'I didn't know how much they cost until the man had finished sorting them.'

'Well, I'm tempted to ground you from The Club, Josh, or move you down to the lower age group. That was the arrangement wasn't it?'

'Oh, no. Please, dad! I couldn't stand it. Everyone will laugh at me.'

Danny frowned and considered that.

'Well, I'm feeling in a good mood this afternoon, and since you did so well in the swimming gala today, I'm going to let you off with a warning.'

'Great!'

'Not so fast, young man. I will also be docking half the money from your holiday spending money.'

'Thanks, dad, and I *am* very sorry.'

'Apology accepted, and maybe you could just *ask* in the future. You don't need to be so secretive all the time.'

'Okay. I will, dad. I promise.'

Danny watched as Penny settled Josh and Katie for the night. Josh was exhausted from all the swimming earlier, and Katie had had too many late nights. When they both struggled to eat anything much at kid's tea, Danny had put his foot down and insisted on an early night.

'It's not fair that I have to go to bed at the same time as Katie. I'm a lot older than her.'

'Well think of it as doing me a favour, Josh. You owe me one, remember? I'll also go as far as to top up your spending money again if you babysit for me tonight.'

'Deal! How much do I get?'

'That depends on how quickly you both go to sleep.'

'Aw.'

Josh knew he was on thin ice, so he decided to back off immediately.

'Penny's a funny name,' said Katie. 'Is it a real proper name?'

'Is it your *full* name?' Josh joined in. 'My name's really Joshua, but people call me Josh for short.'

'I'm not sure I want to tell you my full name. It sounds even funnier than Penny.'

'Go on tell us,' Josh said. 'You *have* to now.'

Penny smiled. 'Okay, but you both have to promise not to laugh.'

'Promise,' the children said in unison.

'My full name is Penelope. Okay?'

'Pheneoply?' Katie giggled into her blanket. 'That's not your name.'

'*Penelope*, not *Phenepoly*, stupid. You know, like Penelope *Cruz*.'

'Who's Pheneoply Cruz?'

'She was married to Tom Cruise.'

'Who's Tom Cruise?' said Katie.

She was so confused now that she had forgotten how the conversation had even started.

'Okay, you two. Settle down,' said Danny. 'It's after eight. You don't want Pheneoply to miss the show, now do you?'

Josh and Katie laughed aloud while Danny and Penny left, closing the door behind them.

'I really like Pheneoply, Josh,' said Katie. 'She's really nice.'

'So do I. Now go to sleep, stupid.'

'So what are you doing about getting something to eat?' Danny asked Penny as they made their way to the lift.

'Oh, I'm still full from all that ice cream earlier. I'll probably get a slice of pizza or something later on after the show.'

'Alright, well have a nice night and we'll see you tomorrow. Don't forget I've set up the 'in cabin listening' so the kids will be fine. You can relax for a change and enjoy an official night off.'

'Thanks,' Penny replied, walking off in the direction of the show lounge.

Was Danny hinting about getting something to eat with him? She wondered. *No, surely not when he had a date lined up with James's mum.*

The two-tier theatre was full-to-capacity, and the atmosphere in the room was electric. Unfortunately, Penny was too late to get a seat towards the back half of the room. There were, however, odd seats here and there. But as the show had already started, she felt uncomfortable about making her way down the steps and having to excuse herself past a row of about twenty people just to sit down. So she decided it would be best to stand at the back. There was always the chance someone would leave early and she would get a seat.

The stage was alive with colours and music. The very talented theatre company energetically sang and danced their way from one side of the set to the other. They performed a medley of music from the musicals *Phantom Of The Opera*, *The Lion King* and *Cats*, among others.

Penny's favourite performance was *Rent*. That was probably because she had watched the musical on Broadway a couple of years earlier when she worked as an au pair for a British family named Kensington who had, for employment-related reasons, relocated to New York.

Overjoyed by the offer to work for the Kensington's, Penny had convinced her parents that she should leave college and pursue a career as a nanny. She had never been particularly academic anyway, and she was keen to start earning a living as soon as possible. Along with this job in particular, she would be living in another country; gaining much more life experience than any of her college friends. She thought that that was a fair trade.

It's your life, Penny. Only you can decide what's best for you, she remembered her father saying those words when she showed him the offer of employment. *It's actually not bad money, and they're offering her the chance of further education. I think she's landed on her feet here,* he had said to his wife.

I know, his wife had agreed. *It's just that we'll all miss you terribly, Penny. But if it's what you want, I won't stand in your way.*

The job had started out perfectly. It couldn't, in fact, have been better. Steven Kensington was an executive director for a successful film company. His wife, Linda, didn't work. She spent her days either in the beauty salon, shopping in Manhattan, or doing lunch with her friends – and more often than not doing all three. The couple had a beautiful baby daughter called Monica who was the sole reason for Penny's employment.

The house was like something out of a Hollywood film set with seven bedrooms, four bathrooms, two day rooms, one lounge, one large dining room, two studies, a gym and a twenty by eight metre swimming pool with a Jacuzzi. There was also a sauna and steam room attached to the gym.

As for the kitchen, she had only ever been in it once when, shortly after accepting the job, she had received the grand tour. The Kensington's had their own cook, a middle aged woman called Suzy, and a very charming butler named Robert. Penny had been so excited to be offered the position; everything had seemed so wonderful in the beginning.

On arrival in New York, she was given her own apartment, just a couple of blocks from the Kensington's, and a brand new top-of-the-range Audi TT to drive around in at her leisure.

Linda Kensington, however, was not the easiest of people to get along with. At every opportunity, she treated Penny with very little respect. In fact, it bordered on contempt. From the beginning, it was made blatantly obvious where she stood. Their relationship was purely business, and at no point during her time with them was it ever considered to be anything more than that.

Steven Kensington, on the other hand, was quite the opposite of his wife. Constantly giving Penny the impression he was a lot more approachable than Linda, he made sure that should she ever need anything at all, he would make it happen. And everything was going well until one evening when Steven's casual manner became a little too familiar.

Linda Kensington had gone to one of her ladies dinners at the Waldorf Hotel. As usual, Penny had been looking after Monica, and Linda had asked her to stay on until Steven returned home from work. By seven o'clock Penny was starting to worry where he had got to, but without wishing to call and disturb him, she decided to settle Monica for the night and relaxed in front of the TV in the main day room until one or the other parent returned.

'Ah, Penny, sorry I'm late,' Steven Kensington said when he finally arrived. I got held up with a client. You know how it is sometimes. You're all set to walk out the door, and then from out of the blue you end up on a conference call for the next two hours.'

'No problem, Mr Kensington. Monica is tucked up in bed. She's been asleep for the last two and a half hours, so you don't need to worry about her. Mrs Kensington said to tell you she would be back by eleven thirty. Midnight at the latest.'

'Nonsense,' he replied. 'Chance would be a fine thing,' he continued in his clipped London accent. 'You know what those women are like when they get chatting…'

Penny had smiled at that remark, but didn't comment, not wishing to be disrespectful.

'So it's just you and me then?' he said, bringing his hands together.

'Well not exactly. I really must be off. I've got a lot on tomorrow.'

'Oh? Well all the more reason to relax a little now. Come on, have a seat. I'd like to get to know the woman who is looking after my little girl, and you can call me Steven. I thought we could have a glass of wine and a bit of a chat. You're not really in *that* great a rush are you?'

Not knowing what to say next to free herself from the situation, she was feeling increasingly uncomfortable.

'I'll tell you what,' he said, 'I'll get Suzy to rustle us up something to eat. That way you don't have to worry about cooking dinner when you get home.'

'No really, that's not necessary.' Penny panicked at the thought, imagining Linda walking in to find her drinking wine and having dinner with her husband.

'Nonsense. How do you fancy spaghetti carbonara? It's Suzy's specialty.'

Not wishing to turn her boss down anymore, Penny replied, 'Okay then. That would be lovely.'

'Great. That's settled then.' And he left the room to deal with that.

Ten minutes later he returned with a bottle of wine, two glasses and a corkscrew. The wine was a classic full-bodied and lightly spiced Thorntree.

'I've given Robert the night off,' he said, casually. 'Thought he could do with a break. Suzy's also calling it a night after she's brought the dinner in. And what Linda doesn't know won't hurt her, now will it?'

Taking a large sip of wine, Penny was suddenly all too aware that she would shortly be left in this huge house alone having dinner with Mr Steven Kensington, her employer. A flood of unease overcame her.

Soon, Suzy arrived with a tray.

'There we go, Mr Kensington, Miss Penny,' Suzy nodded at her as she placed two large bowls of pasta and a side salad on the table. It looked and smelt delicious. 'If there's nothing else, I'll be off now.'

'Thanks, Suzy. Have a nice evening,' said Steven Kensington.

Before Penny had tried the pasta, she had finished her glass of wine. The plan was to finish the wine, and eat the pasta as quickly as possible, and get herself out of this awkward situation as soon as decency and good manners allowed. Unfortunately, before she could say no, Steven had topped up her glass to the brim.

'I thought you would like this wine. Looks like I was right. It's one of my favourites as well, from my South African collection.'

'It's... er, lovely.'

'So, tell me something about yourself. Do you have a boyfriend?'

'No, I don't, and there's really not too much to tell.'

'What rubbish. A beautiful young woman like you. I'm sure you've got *some* tales you want to share.'

Reluctantly, she chatted for a while, and then it was time to make a move. Yawning and stretching for effect, she turned and said, 'Oh you'll have to excuse me, Mr Kensington. I'm feeling really tired all of a sudden. I think I'm going to head home now.'

Steven had grinned across at her and reached for the wine bottle. 'Another glass and some more pasta and you'll feel good as new, I promise.'

Things were getting more uncomfortable by the minute, and Penny was now feeling extremely uneasy.

'You know, I really am going to have to take off, but thanks for dinner.' Standing suddenly, she snatched her bag from the coffee table, but before she could get to the door, Steven Kensington had grabbed a hold of her arm.

'I don't think so. A gorgeous young thing like you all alone in my lounge? You're not going anywhere, do you understand?'

The look on Penny's face showed sheer terror as he moved closer to her forcing himself up against her, his hands groping frantically over her pink Ralf Lauren blouse. With one hand he ripped it open, then tore her skirt at the seam. Penny's heart was racing as he threw her down on the sofa and climbed on top of her.

Unzipping himself, Penny cried out. His weight was too much for her to shift. He was going to rape her, and there was nothing she could do to stop him.

The trauma of the assault was short lived however as the lounge door burst open and Linda Kensington appeared and stood there staring at them both. Her jaw unhinged as she witnessed her husband and her nanny lying half naked on the sofa.

'Steven! What the hell are you doing?'

'It's not what it looks like, Linda. It's the... the little slut you hired. She got me drunk, ripped her clothes off and pulled me on top of her. She basically begged me to have sex with her. I was just about free of her when you came in. Oh, thank God you're here! This is terrible,' he wept.

'You little bitch,' said Mrs Kensington. 'You better get out of here this second, you hear me? Now get moving before I call the police and have you arrested.'

Grabbing for any clothing she could find, Penny ran out of the house as quick as she possibly could. Leaving the car in the drive, she ran straight back to her apartment where she threw her belongings into a suitcase and ordered a taxi to the airport. She got the next available flight home. The experience had been extremely traumatic, and had taken Penny months of counselling to get over. Her love of children was the only reason she had built up the courage and accepted the job with Danny. Now, with all that behind her, she was delighted she had been blessed with such a nice family.

* * *

'Are you okay, Sally? You look to be miles away. Is there something bothering you?' Alex asked, quickly bringing his wife back into the real world.

'No, nothing at all. I was just thinking about Jaffa. I was wondering how he's getting on at mum and dad's.'

'He's probably put on a few pounds, knowing your father. He'll be feeding him a steak dinner every night.'

'They do tend to spoil him, but he's just so adorable. When he looks at you with those big brown eyes, you can't say no to him.'

'Yes, but when he looks like a giant inflatable puppy, then putting him on a diet is going to seem cruel. He'll probably sulk and get doggy depression. A cup of tea, sweetheart?'

'Mm, yes. Please.'

'Listen, I hate to pressure you...'

Oh great, Sally thought, knowing fine well what was coming next.

'But have you given any more thought to next cruise? It's just that I really have to get the paperwork into the office and ensure we don't exceed the requirement for passenger numbers.'

'Yes, the souls on board. Well you can add one more soul. I'm going to stay, if that's okay?'

'Yes. Of course it's okay, silly. I want you here with me all the time, but I won't push my luck. Another cruise is just fantastic.'

Oh, God, what have I let myself in for? Sally wondered. *I'm going to end up like the doctor's wife, I just know it.*

'Cheers then. Here's to the next cruise.'

Sally held out her mug to meet Alex's.

'Cheers. Here's to the Caribbean Delight. I think that's what the cruise is called. I really should look it up and find out where we are going.'

So here goes, Sally took another sip of tea and a couple of deep breaths before she popped the big question.

'So, Joyce was telling me about the big event in St Thomas last month, you know. When three of our ships were in together. She said something about a huge party ashore.'

'Yes, there was a company barbecue on the beach. We made sure that all the crew and officers got a few hours off so they could get something to eat and have a couple of drinks, soft drinks of course. It was a great day. A huge success all round.'

'Good. Sounds like you enjoyed yourself,' Sally replied with as much enthusiasm as she could muster.

'Oh, no. I didn't go. The junior captain had his wife on for the cruise so I let him go ashore for the day. It seemed only fair.'

'You stayed *onboard* then?'

'Well yes, like I said, Tim had his wife on. She only travels with him once or twice a year, and I wasn't going to go ashore on my own. You know what I'm like. I just don't see the point in it. It's never the same without you, sweetheart. Anyway, by the sound of it, they thoroughly enjoyed themselves.'

'Oh, good. That's *great* news, really it is. Can you excuse me a second? I said I'd call Joyce. It totally slipped my mind.'

'Okay, but be quick. We have to order room service shortly and make the most of our night in together.'

'Can you order for me? Actually, I'm not very hungry all of a sudden, so just something light. A sandwich or a salad would do fine. I'm just going to use the phone in the bedroom if that's okay. Won't be a second.'

'Suit yourself, but I'm having the Ocean Magic double cheeseburger with extra fries and onion rings. You'll regret ordering a salad when you see it.'

'Joyce, it's Sally. You won't believe it.'

'What, the Paragon has run out of your favourite Clinique lipstick? And you had to settle for a lighter shade of Chanel?'

'No. For heaven's sake, Joyce, this is serious.'

'Yes, of course, sorry. Sally, what is it?'

'He denied even *going* ashore. And that means it's true. The photograph is proof. Alex is having an *affair*.'

'Jesus, Sally. Is that what he said? Lying bastard. I'll divorce him if you don't. What did you say?'

' I'm not very hungry. I'll just have a sandwich.'

'Seriously, Sal. You're thinking about food at a time like this?'

'Of course I'm not; I don't want him to overhear the conversation. We were meant to be having a romantic night in. You know, room service and a bottle of wine. Now I'm locked in the bedroom talking to you. What should I do?'

'Well, firstly, I'd go out there and pour yourself a glass of wine. You might need it if he suspects you know something.'

'Joyce, I'm this close to hanging up...'

'Okay, I'm sorry. I'm just shocked that's all. I never thought he had it in him.'

'Bizarrely, neither did I, but it looks like we were both wrong.'

'Hang on a second, Sal. Maybe we're jumping the gun. Just... just don't do anything irrational. We both need to sleep on this. I'll meet up with you the day after tomorrow. We need to talk this through. Have you had anymore emails?'

'No, nothing. I'm checking every five minutes.'

'Okay, good. Look, try and stay calm. I'm still not convinced this is for real. Try and have a good night and I'll call you with a plan, I promise. But I can't make tomorrow. It's our anniversary and I need time to think.'

'Okay. Happy anniversary.'

'Thanks, and Sally, I mean it. Don't do anything crazy...'

Chapter 10

Puntarenas 07:00 Arrival 19:00 Departure

'Sat on a long thin peninsular just north of Panama in the Gulf of Nicaragua is the tiny country of Costa Rica. Famous for its impressive variety of beaches national parks, rainforests etc., it really is an experience to treasure, just a few hours here and you will leave feeling fresh and invigorated.' *Interesting*, Sally thought as she turned the page of her copy of *Your Guide to Costa Rica* that she had picked up at the airport on her way to Ocean Magic. *Where was it Alex said we were going? Oh yes, Los Pajaros. I'm sure that's what he said. Yes, here it is.* 'Los Pajaros, a petite but sultry island off the bay of Nicaragua. View the golden sandy beaches and deep green waters of this picturesque island after a mere two-hour boat trip from Puntarenas...' she read.

Two-hour boat trip? Well that's not going to happen. Where is he anyway? She thought, *we were meant to be ashore by now.* Pouring herself another cup of green tea, Sally debated whether to pack the new Pentax 8-megapixel camera that her parents had given her the day she had dropped Jasper off for his two week holiday in the Cotswolds. Sally's father had won the camera in a raffle a couple of weeks earlier and had decided (after three hours of not making head nor tail of the instruction manual) that he and Sally's mother would instead be far better off keeping hold of their 1970-something Polaroid, and decided it would be a nice gesture to donate the new camera to Sally.

'Technology nowadays is far too complicated for an old couple like us,' he had told his wife.

He had, however, managed to charge one of the two batteries that came with it, and had taken a photo of Jasper to remind Sally of her little Prince while she was away.

If we are going on a boat trip, Alex's slightly less sophisticated Nikon model might be a better idea, she decided, then checked it had a memory card before popping it in her beach bag. She collected two beach towels and a pair of swimming shorts for Alex in case he felt like taking a dip while ashore, and then the phone rang and interrupted her thoughts.

Lifting the receiver on the first ring, she presumed it was Alex checking to see if she was nearly ready. He normally called at fifteen-minute intervals to check if Sally was going to change her clothes again. Then he would finish work, and get changed himself, usually in two minutes flat, pulling the first thing that came to hand from the wardrobe and throwing it on. Sally wasn't sure why he kept doing it. It was a very rare occasion that he had actually selected attire that Sally would be happy with, which only ever resulted in her insisting he get changed, and thereby inevitably delaying them going ashore.

Holding the receiver close to her ear, Sally realized there was no caller ID displayed on the screen. 'Hello Alex? Is that you?'

The line was silent as she waited for his usual cheeky, 'I told you never to answer my phone' joke, a line he once heard Richard Gere say to Julia Roberts in 'Pretty Woman' and thought was hilarious.

'Hello, Alex? 'Sally repeated, but with no reply, she hung up.

Three or four minutes later, just as she had finished packing, the phone rang again. Sally quickly realized it wasn't Alex when she heard a woman's voice on the line.

'Hello? Is that Sally?' the woman asked, speaking in an unrecognizable accent.

'Yes. Speaking. Sorry, who am I talking to?' Sally asked, a little confused by who might be calling her. The only female who ever called her onboard was Joyce.

'My name is not important. I trust you received my card and my email?'

Oh, God. No! Not again!

Her heart was racing and her palms were sweating as she gripped the receiver tight enough to turn her knuckles white. Not knowing what to say, she froze on the spot. *Where was Joyce when she needed her most?*

After a few seconds that felt like hours she spoke, her voice quavering with anticipation.

'Yes, I did receive them, and they were a sick joke. Who are you, and what exactly are you hoping to achieve by all of this?'

'Oh, I can assure you, Sally, this is no joke. I presume you asked Alex about his little rendezvous ashore?'

'That's none of your damn business!' said Sally before slamming down the receiver.

Since the nightmare had begun, she had done everything possible to put the dreadful thought of Alex with another women out of her mind. Sure, there was something strange about him denying being ashore last month in St Thomas. But he was a busy man. It might have slipped his mind. Although this had made no sense to her, Sally had decided that every time it got the better of her, she would pick up a book, go for a walk, or do anything just to drive the notion from her head. She had watched her husband's moves closely, and was convinced Joyce had been right all along. He was in love with her; every bit as much as he was when he asked her to marry him. There was no indication that anything was wrong, and he wasn't hiding anything from her. She was sure of it.

But the card, the email, and now a phone call? Sally thought about all this as she remembered to brush her teeth. *Someone is determined to cause problems between us, maybe now it was time to let Alex know what was going on.*

Barely over the last call, she jumped as the phone rang again. Dropping her toothbrush in the sink, her mouth still tingling from the fresh mint toothpaste, she approached the phone with caution and picked up the receiver.

'Who is this?'

'Hello to you too!' a voice replied. 'It's your husband. Alex. Who did you think it was, darling?' There was a long pause before Alex continued, 'Sally? Are you ok?'

'Yes, sorry Alex,' Sally replied, sighing with relief. 'There was a wrong number earlier. I thought someone was messing about, that's all. Kids or something,' she added quickly, realizing she had been rather abrupt.

'Oh. Well, I was ringing to let you know that I'm running a little late. I'll be along in twenty minutes, or half an hour at the most. Will you be ready by then?'

'Yes, that's fine. I'm running a bit late anyway, so take your time. There's no rush at all,' Sally insisted, lying through her teeth in the hope that she had enough time to calm herself down before Alex returned to the cabin.

'Sorry about this. But something has cropped up. I'll explain when I see you. I'll be as quick as I can.'

Returning to the bathroom, Sally finished cleaning her teeth. Momentarily believing she was having a nightmare, she splashed several handfuls of ice-cold water on her face. Realizing quickly she was continuously living the nightmare, she returned to the day room and poured herself a third cup of tea.

Herbal tea was good for calming the nerves. She was sure she had read that somewhere. Taking a few deep breaths, and thinking a little more clearly, she decided once again not to tell Alex about what had happened. He had enough on his plate with work. He really didn't need this to deal with as well.

Returning to his cabin at eleven thirty, Alex put his arms round his wife's waist. Pulling her body close to his, he kissed her softly on the neck and signalled towards the bedroom.

Horrified by his advances, Sally released herself from his grasp and subtly suggested there wasn't time, as she desperately wanted to go on the boat trip to Los Pajaros. With his ego slightly dented by nothing less than blatant rejection, Alex also felt terrible he had let Sally down. Handing him a pair of beige linen shorts and a light blue Hugo Boss shirt, Sally smiled at her husband and promised to make it up to him later.

'I'm so sorry the hearing took a lot longer than planned. I ended up sacking three crewmembers. It was meant to be one quick meeting, but the investigation opened up a whole can of worms. Unfortunately, now I think it's too late to take the trip. Sorry, honey.'

'Oh. Well it's okay really. I was coming to that conclusion myself. By the time we get there, we will have to turn around and come straight back. It's not worth it,' Sally agreed, not in the least bit upset.

'How about we go for a nice lunch somewhere instead?'

'Yes, that's fine. At least that way we still get to go ashore and see the place.'

Finally collecting his ship pass, wallet and sunglasses, Alex announced he was ready to set off. He had been unreasonably excited about the boat trip to Los Pajaros, but there quite honestly wasn't time. He would have to postpone it.

Although she was there in body, she was not there in mind, and Sally was finding the simplest of things a challenge. Try as she might, she couldn't get the events of the last week out of her head.

He is having an affair, I'm sure of it. He's not having an affair, he wouldn't dream of it. He could quite easily be seeing someone behind my back. He would never do that to me, would he? She had asked herself these questions over and over again.

'I really am very sorry I ruined our trip ashore together, Sally. I hope I can make it up to you. Is there anywhere special you fancy having lunch? I was thinking either Captain Moreno's, or La Leda's. Both are said to be very good, but really it's up to you, sweetheart.'

He awaited a reply. But she was silent.

'Sally? You there?'

She jerked her head round. 'What? Oh, sorry. Yes. What did you say?'

'Sally, are you feeling alright?'

'Yes, yes I'm fine really.'

Realizing that Alex knew fine well she wasn't okay, Sally had to pretend for the time being that she was just side-tracked by the hustle and bustle of the town. It was a lovely day, and by lunchtime the temperature was in the high thirties. Joining hands, the couple walked around the plaza admiring the church, and surveying the local market, while they squeezed passed visitors and locals, all standing around chatting in large groups and people watching, no one was in any hurry.

Thinking his wife was probably just in need of some nice food, and maybe even a glass of wine, Alex made the decision for them to try Capitan Moreno's restaurant in the port. The menu was mainly seafood along with a selection of international cuisine. The port agent had recommended it to Alex that morning, which usually meant it would be well worth a visit.

Chatting away enthusiastically over the vast menu selection, Sally began to relax once again in her husband's company. Excited to be away from the ship for the time being, Alex was determined to enjoy himself. He very rarely, if ever, went ashore when he was away on his own, and not stepping off the ship in a three or four-month trip wasn't uncommon. He was making quite an effort this cruise, for Sally's sake. He was also still trying desperately to encourage her to come away more often, like she used to when they were first married.

As the waiter approached the couple with their drinks order, Alex decided now was a good time to surprise Sally with his latest idea.

'So, I've been thinking...' he began, grinning at Sally as if he was up to something.

'What about exactly?'

'Well, how do you fancy a week in Barbados before we go home? I wanted to surprise you, but thought it was only fair to ask. In case you were desperate to get back, that is. I thought we could stay at the Coral Mist Hotel. Remember? The really nice one in St Laurence Gap.'

The waiter put down the drinks and left wordlessly.

'Sounds great,' Sally agreed. 'I'd love to.'

Surprised at his wife for agreeing without hesitation, Alex leaned across the table and kissed her on the lips. 'That was easier than I thought. I'll book the hotel tomorrow before you change your mind.'

'Okay. Fine.'

A few minutes later, the waiter reappeared to take their lunch order; Sally threw back the rest of her wine and immediately asked for another.

'Thirsty, Sally?' said Alex. 'I'd better have another lemonade in that case.' He gestured to the waiter. 'Make it a large wine this time, and lots of ice in the lemonade please.'

'Certainly, sir. And are you ready to order something to eat?'

'A few more minutes, I think,' Alex replied, looking at Sally to see if she was nearly ready.

Realizing she wasn't, he picked up his lemonade and toasted. 'Here's to Barbados, honey. This is going to be amazing. I can hardly wait.'

As Sally reservedly joined in, negative thoughts were once more getting the better of her. Alex was far too excited to even notice. He might as well have been ashore for lunch on his own, she decided.

In between hammering his grilled crab into bite-sized pieces, Alex chatted enthusiastically about the ports they were going to visit on the next cruise and where he and Sally should go ashore. The junior captain also had his wife and daughter onboard, so Alex wanted to make sure he had the first say with regards to port days ashore, as either the captain or junior captain had to remain onboard while the other was off the ship.

Listening intently to her husband, and agreeing that Antigua and Grenada were the main ports of call she wanted to go ashore in, Sally felt the strangest sensation. It was as if she was being watched. She looked up suddenly, to see a group of ship's crew laughing and joking at the bar. They were enjoying a selection of virgin cocktails and some bar snacks that the manager had thrown in to keep them happy.

At a table to the left of the bar was an elderly couple browsing the lunch menu while sipping some iced tea, and at the far right hand side of the bar was a table of four. Two couples, not necessarily passengers from the ship, were enjoying a leisurely lunch together. Next to them, a woman sat alone at a table for two. She was reading a book through her large dark sunglasses, which appeared a little strange considering she was inside. Sally continued picking at her salad, nodding and answering Alex in all the right places. At the same time, she was watching the woman who was quite clearly pretending to be engrossed in her novel when in fact the only thing she was engrossed in was Alex.

She hadn't even noticed that she had attracted Sally's attention.

The woman was about five feet six inches tall, although it was difficult to be precise as she was sitting down. She was slim, with shoulder length light brown hair and a fair complexion. She was wearing a knee-length beige skirt with a short-sleeved white blouse. It was difficult to pinpoint how old she was, but she was definitely no more than forty-five.

'I wonder what we should get up to in Barbados,' Alex said. 'Any ideas, Sal? I'd love to do some diving this time if I get the chance. I miss it you know. It's not the same now that I have a responsible job to do. I remember when I was a cadet, I used to play all day and work all night. Those were the days. You just never seemed to get tired.'

Was this the woman? Sally wondered. *The woman who sent the card and emailed the photo. The woman who called the cabin this morning, who is claiming my husband is having an affair. Whoever she is, she is involved one way or another, that's for certain.*

'Sally? Are you still with me? You seem to be miles away,' Alex asked as he turned his body in the direction of the table where Sally's eyes had been fixed for the last five or maybe even ten minutes.

Sally froze, waiting for Alex's reaction. *Did he know her? Will he be shocked to see her? Will he pretend he doesn't recognize her? God, I hope he doesn't introduce us.* Swiftly picking up her glass and downing a large mouthful of wine, Sally looked up to see a very puzzled expression on Alex's face. Glancing round, she saw that the woman was gone.

'Sorry, darling. I was just thinking what I would do with myself next cruise, that's all. I'm really excited to be staying.'

'Me too,' Alex smiled 'More than you know.'

* * *

'Come on, Megan! We're not going to have time for a drink before dinner if you don't hurry up.'

173

Appearing from the bathroom, wrapped in her bathrobe, Megan was towel drying her hair at a pace far too slow for Kris to be witnessing. He had been impatiently pacing the cabin for the last twenty minutes already showered, shaved, dressed and ready to go out.

'Stop it, Kris; you're making me feel uneasy. I don't like being rushed, especially when I'm on holiday. It's all I do all day, every day when I'm at home. Rush to get ready for work, rush to get to work, rush to finish my work, rush to get home. It's just rush, rush, rush, all day long. Well not when I'm on holiday, so no more rushing. That's what I say.'

'No problem, Megan. Enough said,' Kris said as he walked towards the cabin door. 'I'll be in the Jazz Cafe when you're ready. I'll have a drink waiting for you. No rush, babes. In your own time.'

'Oh, Kris...' Megan groaned, as he closed the cabin door.

It was five past eight, and the Jazz Cafe was full. There were large groups of passengers, couples and the occasional child seated throughout the room. The main bar had fourteen stools equally spaced along it. Kris decided the best spot was beside the good-looking girl perched on the stool right at the end towards the port side door.

'It's busy tonight. Is there something special going on in here?' Kris asked the girl as he took a seat.

The young girl blushed as she turned to face him. 'I'm sorry, were you talking to me?'

A little taken aback by the sheer beauty of the blonde haired, blue-eyed stunner he had just engaged in conversation, Kris nodded and smiled, but no words came out.

'No, the band is just really popular,' the girl said. 'They almost need a bigger venue to accommodate everyone. They're the only reason I'm here. I don't normally come to the bar alone.'

'So where's your husband? Is he ill or something? Sorry, that's none of my business.'

'It's okay, really. I don't have a husband.'

'Boyfriend then?'

'No, I don't have one of those either.'

'*Girl* friend?' Kris raised his eyebrows to suggest he knew he had gone too far.

'No! Definitely no girlfriend!' The girl laughed, giving Kris a 'what are you trying to say?' look.

'I meant like a friend. As in someone you came on holiday with?' He frowned apologetically. 'Sorry, I hope you don't think I'm being too forward.'

'Not at all. I came onboard to work. I'm a private nanny, looking after two children, but the kid's club on here is so good they prefer to be there most of the time.'

'Are you sure that's the only reason they don't want to hang out with you?' Kris grinned. 'I'm Kris, and you are?'

'It's Penny. Nice to meet you. And very charming. Meet a guy in a bar, and within five minutes he's blatantly insulting you,' Penny joked back.

'Sorry, Penny, but deep down you must know the truth. I am just kidding, of course. Can I buy you a drink to make up for my bad manners?'

'Well I suppose that's the least you can do. So yes, I'll have a glass of wine white please.'

Kris raised a hand. The bar steward appeared.

'Yes, sir. What can I get you?'

'A glass of Sancerre if you have it. Better make it a large one. And a gin and tonic with lime. No ice thanks.'

Just after eight o'clock, Danny entered the room and looked around to see if he could spot Nicole. Immediately noticing Penny at the bar chatting enthusiastically to a rather good-looking, tall, dark haired man, Danny looked surprised. She's kept this a secret, Danny thought to himself as he watched from the far side of the lounge. There's definitely some chemistry there. Appearing just in time to stop Danny going over to introduce himself, Nicole gave Danny a peck on the cheek and suggested they head for the table at the back of the room that had just become free.

* * *

'Isn't that Kris over there talking to that blonde at the bar?' Richard asked Lucy as he signed for their drinks and accepted a receipt from one of the bar staff.

'God, you're right. Where's Megan?' Lucy looked puzzled. 'They look pretty friendly, Richard.'

'I know what you mean. Don't make it obvious you've seen him. Here, I'll carry the drinks. Let's take that table in the corner over there. It's facing away from the bar.' Richard signalled to the only free table in the room.

'I hope he's not up to no good.'

'Don't worry, Lucy. I'm sure there's a reasonable explanation. He must know her from somewhere.'

'It doesn't make sense,' Lucy continued. 'I'm sure I've seen her with her husband and two kids. They usually sunbathe in the same place, next to the family pool. She's been teaching her little girl to swim.'

'I'm sure her husband will be here in a minute. We mustn't jump to conclusions.'

Twenty minutes later, when neither Megan nor the girl's husband had appeared, Richard and Lucy ordered another round of drinks and tried to ignore what appeared to be an overly friendly conversation between Kris and another woman.

'Don't look now Richard, but that's him.' Lucy signalled with her eyes towards the stage.

'That's who?' said Richard, confused by what was coming next.

'The girl that's with Kris. That's her husband. He's with another woman.'

'It can't be, Megan. How can she be out with Kris, and her husband be out with someone else? I thought you said they have children?'

'I'm telling you, Richard. It's him, and look he's got his hand on her thigh.'

Slowly coming to the same conclusion, Richard and Lucy exchanged glances.

'You don't think they are... you know?' said Lucy.

'Yes, I do know, and I really don't want to even think about it.' Richard squirmed as a cold shiver moved down his spine.

'But how did they all meet? Do you think they arranged it before they came away? Maybe over the Internet or something?'

176

'I really don't know, Lucy, and to be perfectly honest I'm not sure I want to. But I do have to say it's making me feel a little uneasy. We've spent so much time with Kris and Megan this holiday, I really thought we knew them.'

'Just because Megan's not here, it doesn't mean she's up to the same thing. We should give her the benefit of the doubt.'

'Yeah, I think you're right, Lucy. I also think I'd better stop drinking. I can't believe what I'm seeing.'

Finishing his drink, and placing his glass back on the bar, Kris turned to Penny.

'It's been really nice to meet you Penny, but I have to go and find my friends before dinner. Maybe I'll see you around?'

'Yeah. Nice to meet you too, Kris, and thanks for the drink,' Penny replied, looking pleased with herself.

As luck would have it, and just in the nick of time, Kris walked out the port side exit as Megan walked in the starboard entrance door. She looked round for Kris, then spotted Richard and Lucy towards the back of the room.

'Don't look now, Richard,' Lucy squealed.

'What? Where? Lucy, I really wish you would stop saying that. I don't know how much more of this I can take.' Richard let out a loud sigh, while looking round frantically.

'It's Megan, and she's walking this way. She's just come in with William. My, this is getting more interesting by the minute,' Lucy giggled.

'Lucy, don't. That's disgusting.'

As Megan and William approached the table, the couple tried their best to compose themselves. The swift kick on the shin from his wife more than composed Richard. More like completely sobered him up.

'Hi. Have either of you seen my mischievous other half? He said he would be here,' said Megan.

Still slightly flustered by what was going on around him, Richard spoke first.

'No, sorry, but we haven't. Not today. Have we Lucy?'

'Not that I recall,' said Lucy, taking a large sip of her cocktail and thinking that would somehow make her look more relaxed.

'Oh, well, I'd better go back to the cabin and wait for him. One of the problems with these ships is they're too big. We keep losing each other. I think I need to buy him a pager.'

'You'll need more than a pager to keep track of that one,' Lucy muttered under her breath as Megan walked towards the door.

William was clearly in the same predicament as Megan, leaving the room just after her to look for Edna.

'William and Megan,' Richard continued joking a short time later, having more fun than he'd had in ages. 'There's life in the old fox yet.'

Half an hour later, when William appeared for the second time that evening, Richard took pity on the old man and offered to help look for his wife. The couple had had a few cross words, and Edna had stormed out of the cabin. A few minutes later, the pair found her wandering around the Promenade deck humming away to herself as if she didn't have a care in the world.

'My work here is done,' Richard told Lucy as he returned to the table 'Now, how about getting something to eat? Do you fancy Chinese? I was thinking that a table in the Red Panda might be nice, I don't think I could face anyone in the restaurant tonight.'

'Good idea,' Lucy agreed. 'I'm starving'

* * *

'Right, I see,' Sasha nodded while tapping her fingers on the dressing table. 'So there really is no point in coming home?' she asked Claire.

'Well I just don't see what can be achieved by you cutting your holiday short. The family have left strict instructions that you and your family are not permitted to visit Ben day or night.'

'Charming,' Sasha mumbled into the phone. 'So it's not as serious as Nathan made out, am I right? God, I can't believe that guy.'

'No, it's serious enough, Sasha. But he's not wired up to anything. He's just resting. I think the shock was the worst bit. It's not the sort of thing you expect to happen to someone of Ben's age.'

'Where are you anyway?' said Claire, realizing that she had no idea where her friend was holidaying.

'I'm in the Caribbean on a cruise. Remember I told you about it a while ago?'

'Oh, yes. I do remember. But I thought you and Ben were going away together, that's all.'

'We *were* meant to be, but that's where the whole thing went wrong between us. We fell out at the airport, Ben went home, and I came on the cruise.'

'Bloody hell, Sash. That's brave isn't it?'

'Probably more stupid than brave,' Sasha replied. 'Although I was having quite a nice time until I heard about Ben. Now I'm worried sick.'

'Well if it makes you feel any better, there's nothing you can do. If you come home early and insist on seeing him, it will only make things worse. In fact, the truth is, you will end up being asked by security to leave the hospital. Mind you, if you and Ben are still engaged, then they will have to let you see him.' Waiting for her friend to say something to that, Claire added, 'you *are* still engaged aren't you, Sasha?'

'No, not exactly. Ben called it off just after I left.'

'Jesus, Sasha, are you alright? I hate to think of you so far away and on your own.'

'I'm fine. It's been quite eventful on here, and I've met some nice people who have helped take my mind off of what I'm coming back to in a few days time.'

'I'm sure you have met some nice people. Hmmm, anything else you want to tell me?' Claire said, hopeful of some gossip. 'All those good-looking officers. What I'd give to be young, free and single touring the Caribbean on a luxury cruise liner. Better make the most if it while you can. It's cold, wet and depressing back here; which pretty much reflects the choice of talent available. All the good-looking ones are married.'

Laughing at her friends attempt to cheer her up, Sasha added, 'I must admit the talent on here isn't so bad now that I think about it. In fact you would have a blast.'

'Okay, that's enough. If it's not bad enough that my holiday is over for another year, I'm now getting this rubbed in my face. Do us both a favour, Sasha, and don't come home without the best looking one onboard.'

'I can't promise anything, but I'll do my best,' Sasha agreed. 'And seriously, Claire, I really appreciate what you have done for me. I'll give you a call when I get back and we can catch up properly. Okay?'

'Absolutely,' Claire agreed. 'Enjoy the rest of your trip, and I mean that.'

'Okay. Bye for now.'

Hanging up the phone, Sasha had no doubt in her mind that her friend was right. What possible good could come from booking an early flight home? Apart from anything else, booking additional last minute flights was what had caused the problem in the first place. There were only four days left before she would be returning to London as planned, and goodness only knew when she would be in the position to cruise again. If Ben was as determined not to see her again, and it certainly seemed that way at the minute, then the priority from now on would be to find somewhere to live, not swanning off to the travel agents to book her next holiday. After this, holidays were going to be pretty much a thing of the past.

* * *

'Good evening, room service. May I assist you?' A young man's voice asked as he answered the phone.

'I certainly hope so,' a middle aged woman replied in a seductive voice. 'I'd like to order a bottle of your finest champagne, Dom Perignon preferably, or the next best thing. Also, some beluga caviar for two. Do you think you can manage that?' The woman's tone was sarcastic.

'Of course, madam. And where would you like the order delivered to?'

'The captain's cabin, and as quick as you like.' The woman was smirking as the final phase of the plan was beginning to take shape.

'And to what account would you like the order charged, madam?'

'The captain's, of course,' the woman replied, even more sarcastically than before.

'I'm sorry, madam. But I will need an account number in order to process the transaction.'

'Silly me. It slipped my mind. Can you just send it up and I'll sort out the small matter of an account number once I have surprised my husband. It's our anniversary you see, and I don't want to spoil the surprise by asking for his account details.'

There was silence for a few seconds.

Then, 'Well, this is not normal protocol, madam. But as it's for the captain, I'm sure we can make an exception. We can follow up the payment tomorrow. Your order will be with you shortly.'

'How very kind,' she muttered, then hung up the phone and added, '... and how very stupid.'

* * *

Leaving the dinner table after another enjoyable evening, Alex and Sally made their way back to the captain's suite.

'Dinner has been a success once again,' Sally beamed, as she took hold of Alex's hand. 'We've really struck gold with the company we've had, and one thing's for sure, they really do know how to enjoy themselves.'

'I know what you mean, Sally. It makes such a difference if you get nice company. I always dread the first night you go down to dinner. You never know who you are going to be dining with all cruise, although generally the captain's table works out okay. Having said that, do you remember the dinner table we had on the Ocean Delight, a couple of years ago? That was without a doubt our worst table ever.'

'Remember! I still have nightmares about it,' Sally said laughing. 'I couldn't believe it was happening.'

Sally recalled that horrible evening. Arriving on time at the dinner table, Sally and Alex had waited patiently for their dining companions to join them.

'I think we've been stood up,' Alex had joked as all the other tables around about them enjoyed pleasant conversation as they worked their way through their starter soups and even their main courses.

'I think we should order,' Sally had suggested. 'This is embarrassing. Can we at least have a glass of wine?'

'Just a little longer,' Alex had insisted. 'It's rude to pour the wine before we at least introduce ourselves.'

'It's rude to be forty minutes late for dinner,' Sally protested. 'But okay, five more minutes and then I'm ordering. People are leaving already, for heaven's sake.'

'Calm down, Sally. Look, this must be them,' Alex had signalled. He stood quickly to welcome his table quests.

'I hope not,' Sally had replied, with a look of horror on her face. 'Maybe they haven't seen us. Should we just leave?'

'Too late,' Alex replied. 'We've been spotted. 'Oh my, I don't believe this is happening Sally.'

'No way,' said one of the approaching guests. A twenty stone Welshman. 'Check this out, love. We're on the captain's table. Bloody hell, what are the chances of that happening? You would think we've won the lottery, wouldn't ya love, ehhehh,' he continued prodding his wife in the ribs with his elbow.

'You *would* think we've won the lottery,' the stick thin, shaven head, tattooed woman replied. 'That's bloody hilarious, Tommy. We *did* win the bloody lottery, and that's why we're here remember?'

Along with the pair were their two young children, and their equally repulsive friends.

With almost the entire restaurant watching, Alex had felt obliged to go through with the dinner.

'A glass of wine, madam?' the waiter asked Tommy's wife.

'God, no. What you trying to do, man? Poison me or something? Get me a pint of lager, for Christ's sake.'

'Please,' Tommy added. 'We're on the 'captain's table. Remember your manners, love...'

'Better make that *four* pints' the wife of the second couple requested, 'unless you two want a pint an' all,' she asked, looking at Alex and Sally.

'No, thank you,' Alex had replied. Feeling sick at the thought.

'Hey, sit down for, Christ's sake, kid,' Tommy shouted at the little boy. Grabbing him by the arm and forcefully assisting him to his seat.

'Are you all ready to order?' the waiter asked politely as he approached the table.

'Yeah. Can I have a burger and chips?' Tommy's wife asked.

'No, I'm afraid not madam,' the waiter replied holding back a snigger. 'This menu is specifically designed by our head chef. There is a special of the day, and it's salmon provencal with new baby potatoes and an assortment of garden vegetables.'

'Salmon? That's fish, ain't it?' Tommy asked with a horrified look.

'Yes, sir. That's correct.' The waiter looked at the captain, wondering if he was going to react.

Exchanging glances, and reading each other's mind, Alex and Sally stood up and excused themselves from the table.

'I'm terribly sorry, but I've just remembered that I have some urgent work to attend to,' had been the only excuse Alex could come up with. Moving as quickly as possible in her long formal evening gown and high heels, Sally led the way out of the restaurant and back to the cabin.

'If it's okay with you, I think we'll be changing tables,' had been Alex's first words once he was over the shock and able to speak.

'Are you sure, honey? They seemed so nice,' Sally had teased.

'They were sent home the next day, remember?' Alex reminded Sally.

'That's right. One of them got drunk and there was a domestic or something, I recall. I knew the minute I set eyes on them they wouldn't last the cruise.'

'After you, sweetheart.' Alex opened to door to his office and gestured to his wife to go ahead. 'I was thinking we could have a couple of hours to ourselves now that dinner is out the way. Maybe a little TV and a cup of tea before we call it a night. It's a sea day tomorrow, so I won't have to be too early to bed tonight.'

'Sounds perfect,' Sally replied. 'I'm just going to get changed, then I'll have a look to see if there is anything on worth watching.'

'Don't worry if there's not,' Alex replied. 'I'm sure we can think of something else to do if there's nothing on TV.'

Realizing what was on her husband's mind, Sally's heart started to beat a little faster. For days now she had managed to talk her way out of every situation that had the potential to lead to her and Alex being intimate. The rollercoaster ride of emotions she had experienced had been unbearable, but this had to end soon. If nothing else, Alex was going to become suspicious.

'Really? Like what?' Sally asked, on the off chance Alex was talking about something completely different.

'I'll leave that up to your imagination,' he replied. 'I just want to check my emails, and then I'll be in. I'll be five minutes at the most.'

Thought so, Sally confirmed.

Walking through the curtain that separated Alex's office from his day room, Sally kicked off her heels and froze in her tracks.

'What the hell!'

Concerned by his wife's outburst, Alex jumped up from his desk and pulled back the curtain into his day room.

'What is it Sally? Are you... Oh my God!' Alex stopped in his tracks. 'What the hell are *you* doing here? And how did you get into my cabin?'

There was a naked forty-something year old woman sitting cross-legged on his sofa in front of him. His heartbeat escalating from a normal relaxed seventy beats per minute to what felt like seven hundred. Inside he was yelling. *Heart attack imminent! Quick someone call the doctor!*

Taking a deep breath, in what felt like the first in ten minutes, Alex turned to Sally, 'Fetch me a bathrobe, sweetheart. Then I'm going to find out exactly what's going on.'

Removing her own robe from the back of the bathroom door, Sally suddenly put two and two together. *The birthday card, the email, the phone call, the women in the restaurant.* It was all beginning to make sense. There was only one question that remained. *If this was the woman behind it all, why didn't she look like the girl in the photo?* Returning to the day room, Sally handed the robe to Alex.

'Put down the champagne and get this on now. You're a disgrace, do you know that, Samantha.'

Samantha? Sally looked at Alex, the expression saying it all.

'I can explain,' Alex continued taking hold of his wife's hand. 'But first I need to call security.'

'I'll be there right away, sir,' John replied after Alex gave him a brief insight into the situation.

'This ought to be good,' Samantha smirked, as she slowly wrapped the robe around her slender frame, before taking another sip of champagne.

'She's my ex-wife,' Alex began, looking as shameful as ever.

'Ex-wife!' Sally edged away from Alex; her face as white as the bathrobe that Alex's ex-wife was now wearing.

'It's a long story,' Alex continued 'Please hear me out.'

'I bet it is.'

'Longer than he thinks,' Samantha said, grinning even harder and clearly dying to hear what Alex was going to say.

'We were young, and I was very, very foolish,' said Alex. 'We had too much to drink one night when we were on holiday in Las Vegas. One thing led to another, and… well I'm sure you can guess the rest.'

'You got drunk and decided it was a good idea to get married? Am I right? Please feel free to fill me in on the minor details.'

'Yes, we thought it was one of those fake chapels. It wasn't until we sobered up the next day we realized it was for real. We returned home the following day, and I went straight to my solicitor and got the marriage annulled. So technically she's not my ex-wife. I never told you, Sally, because I was so embarrassed by what I had done. I just never thought it would come back to haunt me, not after so many years, but I guess I was wrong'

'He's telling the truth, Sally, I'm not his ex-wife,' Samantha confirmed. 'But I am the mother of his child,' she added, now with an even more smug expression on her face.

'She's lying, Sally. Don't listen to her. She's out of her mind. I mean look at the woman for heaven's sake. She's entered my cabin unauthorized, ordered champagne on my account, not to mention stripped naked in my day room. She's clearly insane.'

'Show him, Sally,' Samantha continued. 'Go on. Show him the photo of his daughter. I know you will have printed it off by now.'

'What is she talking about, Sally,' Alex asked, terrified by what might be coming next.

'None of this is my fault, Alex,' Sally pleaded before entering the bedroom and opening the bottom drawer of her bedside cabinet. Holding the photo she had believed was of Alex and some girl he was having an affair with, Sally looked more closely at the girl. She had studied it for hours, not denying the young woman the beauty she possessed, but now she was looking at it in a whole different light. Those midnight blue eyes, and those perfect white teeth enhanced by a warm and loving smile. Her hair colour was a close match to Alex's, and her ears and nose practically identical.

The mystery girl was Alex's daughter.

Handing her husband the photo, Alex stared at the girl, a million and one questions buzzing around in his head. But first and foremost, how did Sally get hold of the photo?

'I suppose you're wondering how Sally came across the picture?' Samantha asked, as if reading his mind.

'I'll explain everything later,' Sally reassured Alex, 'as soon as we get rid of her. All you need to know for now is I didn't know she was your daughter.'

'It's amazing what you can do on the computer nowadays,' Samantha added for good measure. 'Photoworkshop.com. It's amazing.'

Entering the captain's suite with two female security officers at his side, John approached the woman on the sofa.

'I hope you've enjoyed your cruise, madam, because it's definitely your last,' John informed the woman. 'Unfortunately, we are at sea tomorrow. Otherwise you would be disembarked from the vessel straight away. You will, however, be on the first flight home from Puerto Quetzal, and that's a promise. This way please.' John signalled for the two officers to escort the woman out of the captain's suite.

'Well, that wasn't exactly what I had in mind for a relaxing evening,' Alex smiled sympathetically at his wife. 'I think we need to talk.'

'Champagne?' Sally asked, collecting two glasses from the drinks cabinet.

'Might as well. I did pay for it, after all,' Alex replied.

Chapter 11

At Sea

'William?'

'Yes, dear?' the old man called from the bathroom while wrapping a towel around his waist.

'I've looked out your best shirt, the blue one with the white collar. You know the one I bought you for Christmas?'

'Thanks, Edna,' William replied, not wishing to upset his wife.

'You never know who might be at our table for lunch. Apparently there are only fifty Gold Club passengers aboard this cruise. We might even get to sit with the captain. You never know.'

'Which trousers should I wear?' William asked as he opened the bathroom door.

'Your blue cords. I bought the shirt to go with them. You know that.'

'Of course you did. Silly old me.'

'Come along, dear. We don't want to be late,' Edna announced as William hurriedly fastened his tie.

It's not happened in the last fifty or so years we've been together, so it's highly unlikely to happen today, William thought to himself, almost joking.

He began searching for a comb. 'Just a minute, Edna. I still need to fix my hair.'

Presently he was ready and they left the cabin. Closing the door behind her, Edna turned to her husband with a stern expression on her face.

'Now, only a small sherry before lunch. Remember, William? It's too early in the day for anything more. I mean, we really shouldn't be drinking at *all* at this time of day.'

Great.

The free bar before lunch was the only thing William had actually been looking forward to, and a small sherry was the last thing he was thinking of ordering. A couple of gin and tonics were more what he had in mind.

'Look, William,' Edna screeched into her husband's ear. 'That's our table over there, table eight.' Stopping in her tracks, she searched in her handbag for the invitation. Reading it aloud for confirmation, she nodded. 'Yes. That's it. And look who we will be dining with. It's the captain. Can you believe it?'

'I bet *he* can't,' William said. *The poor man doesn't know what he's in for.*

'But where is his wife? She would normally attend these sorts of functions,' Edna went on as they made their way across the restaurant. 'I remember the last time we were here. The table next to ours had the captain sitting with them, and his wife was there. I'm sure of it.'

I recall the cruise, William thought to himself. The entire time, Edna had sat staring at the table opposite blatantly ignoring the company on her own table which were actually quite good fun. Added to that, he had been able to top up his wine as much as he cared while Edna was busy eavesdropping on another conversation.

'It's not the captain, Edna. It's the hotel director. The captain and his wife have a table over there to the right. Number five, I think it is.'

Edna looked where William was indicating.

'Yes, you're right. Oh well, we'll just have to make do with the hotel officer, I suppose. Unless...' Edna eyes lit up as she began plotting.

'It's definitely the hotel director not officer,' said William, 'and you can put that thought out of your mind. We are not going to request that we move tables, and if you don't mind, there will be no more comments like that. It's the height of rudeness to talk that way.'

'Welcome to the Gold Club lunch,' James announced as he stood up from the table and welcomed the elderly couple.

'I'm James, the hotel director. You must be Mr and Mrs Cockburn?'

Edna smiled. 'We are indeed.'

She loved being made a fuss of, especially by someone in authority.

'This is Mr and Mrs Johnston, Mr and Mrs Gordon, Mr Murray, and Ms Walker.'

'Very pleased to meet you all.' Edna smiled as she took the lead as usual.

'This is the Gordon's', the Johnston's', Mr Murray's and Ms Walker's eleventh, twelfth and thirteenth cruise, respectfully,' James informed the Cockburn's as the wine steward hovered by the table waiting patiently for their drinks order.

Ignoring the young man, Edna turned to the group. 'How lovely for you all. This is our eighteenth cruise, isn't it William? Well, I say eighteenth, but it's the nineteenth really if you consider that our last cruise was three weeks long.'

Wondering if anyone would notice if he slipped under the table and crawled out the door, William decided it was probably a safer option to order himself a glass of wine and relax into a pleasant state, hopefully allowing him to quite happily ignore his wife and her bear faced arrogance.

The Gold Club lunch, hosted by the captain and his senior officers, was the one place where passengers like Edna Cockburn felt it not only necessary, but absolutely essential, to brag about how many cruises she and William had been on, but hoping, above all, not to meet anyone who had cruised more than themselves.

On the odd occasion when this would happen, Edna generally had a well rehearsed reply such as; 'Well obviously you've cruised more, being that bit older than ourselves...', which on one occasion led to Edna Cockburn being escorted out of a cocktail party after upsetting a female passenger.

Unfortunately for her today, she was sitting on a table with people who had no interest whatsoever in discussing how many cruises they had been on. They were simply there to enjoy some nice food, a little bit too much wine and socialize with the other Gold Club passengers.

Lunch was a set menu of five courses, so there was no need to wait for orders to be taken. With minimum interruption from Edna, the group chatted away while enjoying a starter of mushroom risotto, while James signalled to Oliver, the drinks waiter, to make his way round the table with another bottle of Pouilly Fume.

Everyone except Edna accepted a glass, so William felt it was only polite that he joined in. James had ordered two bottles of white and one bottle of red wine for the table of nine, so there was more than enough to go round. The look on Edna's face, however, would have suggested William had just downed three shots of vodka at the table. Ignoring his wife, William carried on his conversation with Ralph and Tina Gordon who undoubtedly were having the time of their lives.

Unable to hide what she was thinking, Edna stared across the table at the Johnston's. They were a young couple in their mid-thirties. Edna estimated that if they kept cruising at this rate, by the time they were her age, they would have been on at least fifty cruises. Confirming this, her nose had well and truly been put out of joint.

While the cheese board was being offered round the tables, the captain made a brief speech thanking everyone for attending the lunch and their continuous loyalty to the company, many of whom returned year after year.

'And now for the bit everyone has been waiting for,' he announced. 'The draw to win a bottle of champagne.'

Everyone watched in silence as the captain handed the box of cards to his wife, and asked her to choose one.

'The winner of the bottle of Bollinger is... Mr William Cockburn!' With a prompt nudge from Edna, William stood a little quicker than he would have done without the unnecessary assistance of his wife. A little shocked by the announcement, and confirming that the two glasses of wine he had enjoyed with lunch were having an effect, William steadied himself as he walked towards the captain and his wife. Finally reaching the couple, Sally handed over the bottle and congratulated the old man by giving him a kiss on the cheek.

'Well done, William!'

Edna continued to cheer long after everyone else. With a smug look on her face, she flashed the table a coy smile. After the lunch, some of the passengers stayed behind chatting among themselves. Even though William was in his element, being congratulated by several individuals from the other tables, Edna decided it was time to head back to the cabin for a lie down. After all, she and William weren't used to eating such a big lunch. So she decided an hour's nap was in order whether William needed one or not.

'I don't like to sound ungrateful, Edna, but you know that neither of us like champagne all that much, and it would be a shame to just leave it behind.'

'What are you thinking, dear?' Edna said.

'Well, I was thinking that if you wouldn't mind terribly, we could pass by Sasha's cabin and give it to her. I recall her saying how much she loves champagne, and you never know, she might have met someone she could share it with by now.'

'That's a *lovely* idea William. Yes, let's pop past now,' Edna agreed rather easily, and much to William's surprise.

They hurried on their new errand to the appropriate deck, both with a slight spring in their step.

'I hope she's in,' William commented as he knocked on Sasha's door. 'I don't really want to take it down to the restaurant tonight, as it wouldn't be right to give it to her in front of the others.'

There was the sound of a door lock being undone, and then Sasha appeared. The Cockburn's smiled and presented the bottle and explained why they were there.

'For me?' said Sasha. 'Really? Are you sure?'

'Absolutely dear, it would be our pleasure,' Edna said, making Sasha believe the gesture was all her idea.

'Well, if you insist,' Sasha replied, accepting the bottle of Bollinger from William. 'I'm not sure I've got much to celebrate at the minute, but by the end of the cruise, I'll do my best to find a good reason to open it, I promise.'

William smiled. 'That's the spirit.'

'Would you like to come in?' said Sasha. 'I can make some tea if you like.'

'No thank you, dear,' William replied. 'We'd better get back for a quick nap. We've just been for the biggest lunch you can imagine, and I think I need an hour to sleep it off, if you don't mind.'

'You need to sleep off the *wine* more like,' said Edna. 'I told him a small sherry would be okay, but no, he wouldn't be told.'

'*Two* glasses, Edna. That's all I had,' said William. 'The Gordon's had near enough a bottle each.'

'Sounds like it was a fun lunch,' Sasha said, winking at William.

'It really *was*, Sasha. You would have loved it. The food was amazing, and the wine ...' William winked back at Sasha, '...well, that's another story.'

Shaking her head, Edna took William by the arm. 'Come on, let's get you into bed.'

'Sounds like an offer I can't turn down.' William sniggered. 'But really, Edna, you shouldn't proposition me in front of people like that.'

'Come on, silly. I think a strong black coffee is in order. Bye, Sasha. See you later.'

Edna waved as she led William along the corridor and back to the cabin.

* * *

'Kris, I think I'm going to stay here for a bit. I really don't feel very well,' said Megan. Sitting down on the sofa next to her, Kris put his hand on his partner's knee.

'Why? What's wrong, babe? You look okay to me.'

'Well, I'm not. I've had a migraine threatening all day, and it's just got a whole lot worse.'

'I'm sorry, Meg. Why didn't you say?'

'I'm fine. I just need a couple of hours in bed. You go ahead. I'll join you when I'm feeling better.'

'I really shouldn't leave you when you feel like this, Megan. Just tell me what I can do to help.'

'Nothing, Kris, really. I just need to be left alone in a dark room. If you stay, you'll need the lights on. Please, just go.'

Kris frowned.

'Okay,' he said at length. 'But I'll be back in a couple of hours to check on you. I'll take a walk or see if the golf simulator is free or something.'

'Fine.'

Collecting his cruise card, he blew his partner a kiss and closed the door quietly behind him. Megan's migraine had come as an unexpected bonus. He had been trying to figure out a way to see Penny again, although that wasn't going to be easy. The ship was so big; you generally don't see the same person twice during a cruise. Wondering where she was most likely to be, Kris walked out onto Deck 14 and looked around. Then he glanced down onto the deck below, and as if it was meant to be, Penny was in the family pool giving Katie her seventh swimming lesson of the cruise.

Approaching them slowly, Kris watched for a moment as Katie for the first time took off her armbands.

'All you have to do is hold onto the float,' he heard Penny say. 'I'll support your tummy, and I promise you won't go under the water.'

'Okay,' Katie replied, a little apprehensively. 'Just don't let go of me in case I drown.'

Laughing at Katie's innocence, Kris stood back not wishing to interrupt the big event.

'Just keep your head up, Katie. That's it, and keep kicking.'

'I *am* kicking!' she yelled, catching a mouthful of water.

'Good girl, we're nearly there. That's it, a little bit more. Well done, Katie, that was excellent work!'

'I made it!' Katie squealed with excitement before letting go of the float and catching a second mouthful of water.

Lifting her up, Penny added, 'But you mustn't forget you're not wearing armbands. And it's just a thought, but you might want to think about leaving some water in the swimming pool for everyone else.'

'Mmm hmmm,' Katie coughed. 'I mustn't forget I'm not wearing armbands.'

'So you're not just any sort of nanny,' said Kris, looking down at Penny. 'You're also a swimming coach, and a pretty good one from what I've seen.'

Penny looked up, surprised to see him there.

'Oh,' she said, colouring a little, 'it's nothing really.'

'She's brilliant,' Katie piped up, determined not to let the praise pass unnoticed.

'Maybe you could teach *me* to swim?' said Kris.

'You mean you *can't?*'

Kris shrugged and coloured a little too. 'No, and I'm a little ashamed about it.'

'Sorry. It's just that—' She stopped herself before she embarrassed Kris even further. *Well, you look so fit,* was what she was about to say.

Looking suitably discomfited, Kris decided to change the subject.

Realizing Katie had been sitting patiently waiting for Penny to wrap her towel around her, Penny climbed out of the pool.

'Sorry, sweetheart. I nearly forgot all about you.'

'It's okay,' a shivering Katie replied.

Taking this as a sign that the lesson was over, Kris decided to make his move.

'So what time do you finish work?' he asked, a hopeful glint in his eye.

Penny looked at Katie before replying. 'I think we're pretty much done here. What do you think?'

'Yeah. We're done,' Katie replied, looking very much worn out and in need of something to eat.

'I'm off until tomorrow lunchtime,' Penny said to Kris. 'Well, that's the plan at the minute, but things can change. You know how it is.'

'So I'd better not waste any more time in asking you to join me for a coffee then.'

'That would be lovely. When did you have in mind?'

'As soon as you're showered. I thought we could go to the Cabana bar on Deck 15. It's lovely up there at this time of day.

With a couple of iced lattes I thought, we could watch the sun go down.'

Realizing she was the only one standing in the way of Penny and this man, who Penny seemed to quite like, Katie got herself showered and dressed in no time.

'That was very quick,' Penny said.

'I can be sometimes.' Katie grinned, 'When I'm hungry.'

Penny wasn't sure about telling Danny about her coffee date with Kris, but realized that if she didn't, Katie surely would. Danny, who was not in the least bit shocked, had to hold himself back from asking too many questions. He also had to pretend he was pleased for her.

'Two iced lattes coming right up.'

Tom, who knew Kris from the dinner table, seemed rather confused by the couple as they sat outside on the aft end of Deck 15 sipping their drinks and making small talk. Fortunately for Kris, Tom had been at sea long enough to know that one should never question a couple when they appeared out of place, no matter how well you knew them. Kris had always been the least friendly person on the dinner table. Now Tom knew why. The look of shock on Kris's face said it all when he peered over the bar and ordered the drinks. Now all Tom had to do was keep his mouth shut and not slip up while serving at the dinner table.

'Another coffee, sir?' Tom said as he passed by collecting glasses from another table.

'Yes, the same again please,' Kris, replied.

Penny, who wasn't used to drinking so much caffeine, agreed on the proviso it was her last. The combination of being in the pool all afternoon, and the baking hot sunshine, had made her a little dehydrated she was also beginning to feel slightly dizzy. Tom served the second order, and informed the couple he had to close the bar and that any additional drinks should be purchased from the Sun Downer bar on Deck 14, mid ships.

As the sun set in front of them, the last couple left the bar. Kris, sipping his latte as slowly as possible, waited patiently for Tom to leave. Finally alone, Kris moved his chair closer to Penny's, and without any warning he turned to face her. Knowing what was coming, Penny's heart started to race. Kris pressed his lips against hers, slowly rubbing his hand up and down her thigh. Penny was shocked at how exciting it felt. A little stunned by what was happening, she didn't make any attempt to stop him. She was actually more than happy to let him continue.

'So how did it go?' Danny asked, dying to find out what happened between Penny and the mystery man who had invited her to join him for coffee.

'Really well, actually,' Penny replied, grinning from ear to ear and unable to contain how she felt.

'You sound a little surprised,' Danny said.

'No, not really. It was fun, we just... you know, chatted non-stop.'

'So where did he take you?'

'Just to the Cabana bar on Deck 15. It's a fantastic setting for watching the sun go down.'

'Are you going to see him again?' said Danny, doing his best to make it appear like everyday conversation, but failing miserably.

'Yes, I think so. I gave him my cabin number, and he said he'd call to arrange dinner.'

Damn, Danny thought as he walked towards the fridge in search of a bottle of beer.

* * *

'How are you feeling Megan?' said Kris when he returned to the cabin.

'A little better, thanks, but I'm not sure I'm up to going out tonight. I'm sorry; I'm just so tired. You don't mind do you, Kris?'

'That's fine, Meg, I'll order room service and we can stay in and watch a movie.'

'Are you sure, Kris? I don't want to ruin your night too. You should join everyone else for dinner really.'

'Don't be silly. I'd rather be here with you, Megan.' Kris put his arm around her and kissed her on the cheek. Relieved, Megan had hoped that was what he would say. She didn't want him to go to dinner without her, especially if Sasha was there. She really didn't trust her to stay away from Kris.

Megan hadn't touched her room service and was dozing off for a third time. Kris knew it was now or never if he was going to get the chance to see Penny again. As he lay beside Megan, stroking her hair and comforting her, he couldn't think of anything else but the kiss he had shared with Penny that afternoon. Without thinking too much about his actions, he left the cabin and wandered down the corridor, pulling from his jeans pocket the piece of paper with Penny's cabin number written on it. He thought about calling first, then decided against it. It risked Penny refusing to see him again so soon. Therefore, he reasoned, it would be better to go straight to her cabin. That way, when face-to-face, he felt sure he could convince her to let him in.

Opening her cabin door, Penny's eyes lit up. 'Kris, what a surprise. I was just thinking about you.'

'Really? All good thoughts, I hope?' Kris smiled. 'I just had to see you again. Can I come in?'

'Of course. I was just watching a movie, but it's not up to—'

But before Penny could finish what she was saying, Kris had wrapped his arms around her. Pressing his body against hers, he kissed her passionately before pushing her back into the cabin and guiding her across the room and laying her down on the bed. Penny hadn't expected such a forward move, but found it impossible to resist his advances.

The connection between them was strong and sexual, but Penny was determined not to let anything happen too soon. Unbuttoning her jeans while he took off his belt, Kris continued to kiss her passionately.

'Wait, Kris,' Penny said. 'I think we should slow down a little.'

'Sorry, I just find you so irresistible. I want you right now.'

Slowing down a little didn't mean for a second that Kris was keeping his hands to himself. Finding it impossible to resist his toned and tanned physique against hers, or his gorgeous lips against her mouth, Penny surrendered to his charms...

'Wow, Penny,' said Kris, some time later. 'That was amazing.'

'Yeah,' Penny replied, quite shocked she had allowed herself to go so far.

'So when can I see you again?' Kris asked, buttoning up his jeans almost as quickly as he had taken them off.

'I'm not sure. How about I call you?' Penny replied, surprised that Kris was leaving so soon.

Panicking at the thought of Megan answering the phone if he gave his number, Kris arranged to come past the pool sometime. They could make plans later. Kissing her goodnight, he hurried back to the cabin praying that Megan would still be asleep. But it was too late; Penny had already memorized Kris's cabin number as his cruise card fell from his jeans pocket in his hurry to undress.

* * *

The idea of having a joint stag and hen party was probably the best decision, or so Mike concluded as he searched in the drawer for his tie. The attire for the evening was informal thereby adding a little sophistication to the evening. Considering there were only six guys and six girls attending, separate parties just wouldn't have worked.

It was only ten minutes to six, and Charlie was enjoying a long relaxing bath before her last night of fun – as Laura had reminded her possibly one too many times in the last twenty four hours.

Already dressed, Mike was well and truly up for a big night out. He was getting married the day after tomorrow and he just couldn't wait.

Meeting in the Sports bar at 7.00pm as arranged, the night took off in tremendous style.

'Just order whatever you want,' Mike announced as the couples arrived one by one. 'It's all on me,'

A couple of cocktails later, the group went from the Sports bar to Bubbles champagne bar where, in an hour and a half, they worked their way through three bottles of Veuve Clicquot. They then made their way to The Grill Room where they had reserved a table for twelve at the back of the restaurant. They wanted to be out of the way of the other passengers to enable them to have as much fun as they wanted. Moreover, they would also be able to get away with a little more noise than was generally acceptable.

The hotel staff had done them proud, presenting them with the most fantastic selection of steaks, which they chose individually from a large silver tray. For those who fancied a little extra, there was a huge tank full of lobster clawing their way around the rocks until their fate was decided by one of the hungry passengers. The menu choice was vast, but generally anyone who booked a table in the Grill Room chose to have one of their legendary steaks, and quite often the 'surf and turf'.

To begin with, Charlie had arranged to have three trays of mixed starters laid on the table to allow the group to sample the different dishes. The choice was excellent, from hot entrees to an array of salads.

Mike had laid on three bottles of Australian Sauvignon Blanc and three bottles of South African Cabernet Sauvignon wine which he and Charlie had agreed would be far too much for twelve people, but Mike wanted to do things properly and made sure that for tonight, money was no object. Judging by the rate the group had got through the champagne, Mike was beginning to think he might have got it wrong after all.

After dinner, it was on to The Cellar bar where the girls separated from their male company for the first time all night.

'You guys should go and have a brandy and smoke cigars, or whatever it is guys do without us women,' Laura insisted, giggling. 'We girls are going to the nightclub where you can pick us up later – if you're *lucky*, that is.'

With absolutely no intention whatsoever of having anything else to drink, let alone start smoking, Mike decided to leave everyone else to it. At just after eleven o'clock, he made his way back to his cabin. He wasn't a huge fan of stag parties, and he had only just met the guys who were involved in organizing his. It was clear Charlie was having a good time. In fact, she was thoroughly enjoying herself, so he decided not to interrupt her evening and gave her a kiss goodbye. Shortly after arriving back in his cabin, there was a knock on the door. Rushing to hang up his trousers before answering it, he presumed Charlie had lost her key. As he stood there with nothing on but his boxer shorts, he was confronted with Laura, Charlie's least favourite friend. When she saw Mike in his undressed state, she wasted no time and jammed her bright red Jimmy Choo shoe in the doorjamb stopping him from closing it.

'What the hell are you doing Laura?' said Mike. 'And where is Charlie? Is she okay?'

'Oh, she's fine Mike. It's you I'm worried about.'

'What are you talking about? I'm fine. Now can you please move your foot?'

'Oh, Mikey, I'm just having a bit of fun. It's your stag night darling, so lighten up. I didn't want you to miss your last opportunity as a single man, so I was thinking...'

'Yeah, so was I. So get your bloody foot out of the door because I'm not interested. Charlie was right about you. You're just a little tart.'

Laura recoiled a little, but smiled and came right back.

'If you miss this golden opportunity to have one last fling, you're more stupid than I thought. Charlie is going to tie you down for the rest of your life, you do realize that?'

'Whatever you say, psycho,' said Mike, trying to close the door on her. 'Now get lost!'

'You really mean it?'

'Yes. I bloody well do.'

Laura raised a perfectly shaped eyebrow.

'Your loss, Mikey boy. I hope Charlie's as strong willed as you. You should see the guys who are queuing up to get a bit of her since I announced it was free kisses for everyone – and believe me; some guys are getting more than that. See you later, big boy. But if you change your mind, you know where I am.'

Laura smirked before finally removing her foot from the door and making her way back to the nightclub furious about what had just happened.

Slamming the door behind her, Mike couldn't believe she could have been so stupid and, more to the point, so dam full of herself.

Still lying awake at 2.00am, he waited patiently for Charlie to come back to the cabin, but decided it best all round not to mention the incident with Laura. The idea of having a proper wedding with guests was all Charlie needed to go ahead with marrying him, and nothing was going to affect their big day now, especially not a silly little tart like Laura, or so he told himself before closing his eyes.

* * *

It was half past three in the morning. Penny was finding it difficult to get to sleep when her phone rang. She answered it immediately, thinking something was wrong with one of the children.

'Good morning, madam. It's Lucas from the Sports Bar. I'm terribly sorry to bother you at this hour, but I have a rather under-the-influence Mr Harper here who is refusing to leave the bar. I was due to close at two o'clock, but I'm afraid he's not making it very easy for me. I believe you are travelling together?'

Penny suppressed a yawn. 'Yes, that's correct. We are. Just give me five minutes and I'll be down.'

Reaching for her faded blue jeans and the white t-shirt she had been wearing earlier when out playing football with Josh and Katie, she fumbled by the bed for a pair of shoes. But every one she picked up wasn't part of a pair. Finally finding her flip-flops, she quickly put them on and looked in on Josh and Katie to make sure they were asleep.

The baby listening service wasn't going to be much good if Danny wasn't in any fit state to use it, but at least Josh had had the sense to put his sister back to bed once she got up to use the loo as she did every night at about midnight. If someone didn't physically carry her back to bed, she would only get as far as the sofa, and would curl up on it.

The kids were fast asleep, but Danny was in no fit state to be anywhere near them. *This is what I'm here for*, Penny realized all of a sudden as she walked into the bar. *I'm here to look after the big kid.*

'Penny! Hows are you?' said Danny, clearly seriously rat-faced. 'Come and haves a drink withs me.'

'Thanks, Danny, but how about we go back to my cabin and have one there instead?'

'Oh my!' Danny's face lit up. 'That's a bit fordward isn't it?' Danny replied.

It was a struggle, but between her and Lucas, the pair managed to help Danny out of his chair.

'Thanks.'

Lucas smiled at Penny. 'Will you be okay, madam?'

'Of course, we'lls be fine,' said Danny, his eyes puffy and unfocussed.

'Yes, we'll be just fine,' Penny, said.

It was nearly four o'clock before she got Danny back to her cabin. She did well to get him onto the sofa where she placed a blanket over him and a bottle of water beside him and crept next door to sleep with the kids. She didn't want to leave Danny alone, but she had no option. She didn't want the kids see him like this, and she couldn't let them sleep alone. But most of all, she couldn't sleep in the same room as her boss. That would just be wrong, no matter what the circumstances.

The next morning, Penny collected a change of clothes and took them next door for Danny, so by the time he walked in, Josh and Katie would presume he had been up for a while and she was just there to look after them as normal.

'Thanks,' Danny acknowledged as he reached out to Penny who was holding a mug of strong black coffee and waving a box of painkillers in front of him.

'No problem,' she replied. 'Sugar?'

He smiled as he reached out to take the coffee and tablets. 'Just call me, Danny.'

Chapter 12

'Was that the door?' Kris asked Megan as he towel dried his hair after a long, hot shower.

'I think so.' Megan turned down the Bose stereo system. 'I'll get it, darling. You pour the wine.'

She padded across the cabin, turned the door handle and eased it open a few inches. She found herself looking at a beautiful young woman who looked remarkably like... yes, like Sienna Miller, actually.

'Yes? Can I help you?'

'Oh, I'm terribly sorry to disturb you,' said Penny, the air-cooling instantly. 'I must have the wrong cabin. I was looking for someone called Kris.'

'Kris?'

'Yes, that's right. Do you know him?'

Opening the door all the way to allow the young women to see into the cabin, Megan stood aside and smiled. 'Yes I do, actually. He's right here.'

With a bottle of wine in one hand, and two glasses in the other, Kris stood practically naked with only a towel wrapped around his waist, his bronzed physique on display once again. Sensing the tension, Penny's brain suddenly registered what was happening.

The complete bastard! Was the first thing that sprung to mind. *Deceitful pig* was the next, followed by *downright utter womanizer.* Kris, the man she had found herself thinking about constantly – and, more to the point, falling in love with – clearly had another, and more immediate personal commitment.

'What's going on Kris?' Megan face lost colour. She fixed her hands firmly on her hips and stood motionless. 'Who is she?'

Kris licked a tongue across his lips. 'This is... well, it's Penny.'

With no additional information forthcoming, Megan turned and glared at the stunning young blonde.

'Well, Penny?' she asked as calmly as she could. 'How do you know my partner?'

I don't really. I've just been seeing him off and on over the last few days. Oh yes, and then we slept together last night.

The words were on the tip of her tongue, but instead she said, 'Sorry, there seems to be some sort of misunderstanding. I was looking for Kris to thank him for helping me get into my cabin last night. My key got jammed in the lock, and he very kindly got it back out for me.'

Megan, unsure of whether to believe the story or not, felt her blood pressure increasing to boiling point as she watched the young woman hover uncomfortably at the cabin door.

'Hmm,' Megan pondered, not believing a word of it. Guilt was written all over the pair of them. 'Well, if that's all?' Megan added, bringing the brief meeting to an end.

'Yes, that's all. Thanks again, Kris. Thanks a *lot*.' Shooting him a look that suggested they had better not meet alone, or she was likely to throw him overboard, Penny left the cabin and tearfully made her way back down the corridor.

Before Megan could close the cabin door, Kris had opened the bottle of wine and had already downed a quick mouthful. *Thank goodness for screw tops*, he thought to himself. Holding out a glass filled almost to the brim, he handed it to Megan and smiled to suggest she really had nothing to worry about. Inside, however, his stomach was doing somersaults.

Could she see right through him?

'You never told me you helped anyone get into their cabin, Kris,' said Megan, determined to find out the truth.

'Didn't I?'

'No, and it's not exactly the sort of thing that slips your mind.'

'Well it was nothing really. It was last night, when you had a migraine. Remember?'

'No. As you never mentioned it, I don't. Anyway, I thought you stayed in with me all night?'

Realizing his mistake as the words fell loosely from his mouth, he reached for the bottle of wine and topped up his glass. *We're going to need to order another at this rate*, he thought to himself.

'Actually, I did, Meg. But you were half asleep. You obviously just don't remember. Anyway, I really don't see what the big deal is. I went out for some fresh air, and a girl stopped and asked me to help her out.'

'Really?'

'Yes, really. For Christ's sake, Meg, what are you suggesting I should have done? Would you have preferred it if I'd turned round and said, 'Well that's your problem, sweetheart? My partner might get suspicious if I help you. After all, I don't know this isn't a plan to get me into your cabin. Maybe you're looking to seduce me'. Is that what you'd prefer?'

'Don't be ridiculous, Kris!'

'No, Megan. There's only one person being ridiculous here, and that's you. Now, are you going to let it go, or are you going to make my entire evening a misery?'

'Okay. I'm sorry,' Megan replied, half-heartedly.

Kris gazed at her for a few seconds, his lips tightly drawn.

'Okay,' he said presently. 'Apology accepted. Now, let's get back to more important business, shall we?' He removed his towel. 'Now where were we before we got so rudely interrupted?'

* * *

'Hey, what's the matter?' Danny asked Penny as he entered her cabin.

He had got into the habit of knocking once, and walking into Penny's room as she always left the door unlocked in case the kids needed her urgently. But maybe today he should have waited for a response.

'Nothing,' Penny replied, wiping away a tear as she sat up in bed. Her novel lay open next to her, but she was finding it too difficult to concentrate on the words. Collecting two cans of soda from the fridge, Danny handed one to Penny and sat down on the sofa next to her bed.

'You can talk to me as a friend, you know? I'm not just your boss. Anytime, honestly. I'm quite a good listener.'

Penny forced a smile. 'Thanks, but it's nothing really.'

'Are you sure? If it's something to do with the guy you've been seeing, if he's hurt you in some way, I'll go and have a word with him.'

'No, please don't. I'm okay. It's nothing to do with him, really.' Penny didn't like lying, but she couldn't afford for Danny to go storming off after Kris. His wife or girlfriend, whoever she is, would become even more suspicious causing all sorts of problems.

'So if you won't tell me what's wrong, you have to allow me to take you to dinner to cheer you up. What do you say? It's your call. Any restaurant of your choosing.' Leaning forward, Danny reached out his hand and turned the corners of Penny's lips up with his fingers. 'That's better. I knew that dinner with the gorgeous, sophisticated, and not to mention extremely charming Danny Harper would bring a smile to that pretty face. Anyway, after all the support you've given the kids and me, I owe you. So where are we going? No, you don't have to decide straight away, you've got half an hour to decide. Then I'll need to make a reservation – unless you fancy the Mexican restaurant. You don't always need to book to go there.'

Penny forced another smile. 'Mexican sounds fine thanks, Danny.'

'But you won't thank me tomorrow when you're nursing the biggest hangover you've ever had. The margaritas in Nachos are loaded. They have a menu of 101 different flavours to choose from, and I know exactly what you're having. So let's make it a proper date, huh? I'll pick you up here at eight. If you like, we can go to Bubbles first and get a glass of champagne?'

'Perfect. See you at eight.'

'Hey, Josh, my mum reckons your dad is loaded,' James announced out of the blue. 'She said that if she keeps going out with him, he'd probably ask her to marry him.'

'What?' Josh looked at his friend with disgust. 'She actually *said* that?'

'Yeah, she did.' James replied, with a pleased expression on his face. 'That would mean we would be like proper brothers.'

'My dad doesn't need to marry anyone. He's happy with Katie, and me and we have Penny to look after us. She's like a real mum.'

'But think about it,' James continued, completely unaware of how much he was upsetting Josh. 'It would be really cool.'

'No, it wouldn't, you idiot! Your mum's just after my dad's money, can't you see that? Tell her to forget it, okay?' Josh replied, now at the top of his voice.

'Hey, boys! Boys! What's all the shouting about?' said Gill, the youth leader.

'Nothing, Miss,' they both replied, echoing each other.

'Well, keep the noise *down* or you'll disturb the younger kids next door.'

'Yeah, Josh. Calm down,' James said, continuing to annoy his friend.

'*You* calm down, you idiot,' Josh replied, before pushing back his chair and storming out of The Club. 'I'm out of here.'

* * *

Going out for dinner was the last thing on Penny's mind as she stood in the shower wishing the warm water would wash away the memories of her horrific earlier confrontation with Kris. The mere fact he thought he could get away with it made her stomach churn inside. In fact, it hadn't really stopped churning since the minute she came face to face with Kris's partner. But it could have been worse, she reassured herself. She could have been the one being cheated on. Although, technically she was, she decided to ignore the fact. There was no doubt in her mind, however, that she was not the first girl Kris had cheated with, and she most certainly wouldn't be the last.

The whole operation must have been very carefully planned for him to carry out an affair while his partner was onboard. I can't believe I fell for his lies, and to think I actually slept with him. What a completely selfish pig. He'll get what's coming to him. Men like that always do, Penny thought as she stepped out of the shower.

Next door, Danny was doing some contemplating of his own. He knew it was over between Penny and the mystery guy she had been seeing. At least, he was as certain as he could be. Penny wasn't the sort of girl to shed a tear over nothing. She was single again. She had to be. The only problem now was that he wasn't exactly unattached. Nicole hadn't quite grasped the whole one-night-stand thing.

Blue shirt with white stripes, or the slightly dressier black one? Danny pondered this question as he stared into his wardrobe for the best part of ten minutes before he decided on neither and opted for his new dark grey Ted Baker shirt instead. He hadn't worn it yet, so it was probably the better option.

'You're back early,' Danny said, turning to Josh as he entered the cabin looking rather deflated.

'Am I?' Josh replied as he picked up his handheld Nintendo and sat on the end of his bed. 'I hadn't noticed.'

'Is everything okay, son?'

'Yeah, I'm fine.' Josh helped himself to a handful of the sweets Danny had bought from the shop onboard in the hope of tempting Katie. She was still in her health-food-or-no-food phase after the chocolate incident, and Danny was getting seriously worried about her.

'So what's on in The Club tonight?' Danny asked, hoping for a more enthusiastic response.

'I'm not sure. I was wondering, could I come out with you tonight?

I don't feel like going to The Club.'

'Oh, Josh. Tonight's not great for me. How about tomorrow? We can bring Katie along and make a night of it. Just family.'

'Yeah, okay,' Josh, agreed, appearing not bothered in the slightest.

'Here,' Danny said, handing Josh a menu. 'Order yourself some room service if you like. Harry Potter is on at eight, and no wild parties while I'm out. And—' Danny patted Josh on the shoulder, '—I know how many beers are in the fridge.'

'Thanks, dad. Where are you going anyway?'

'I'm taking Penny out for a meal to thank her for all her hard work.'

Looking up from the menu, dazzled by the vast amount of choice of room service, Josh nodded with approval.

'And then you should take her for a drink. That would be a nice thing to do.'

'Really, Josh? Your matchmaking skills exceed you.'

'I know,' he replied with a fake grin on his face. 'Right, I think I'm going to order a cheeseburger with curly fries. Yep, decision made.' Josh closed the menu.

'Are you sure you're all right, Josh? You know, if you want to come with us, I'm sure Penny won't mind,' Danny said, feeling bad at letting his son down like this.

Josh was about to reply when the phone rang. Danny let it ring twice as he gazed at his son, then picked up the receiver. He listened for a moment and said, 'Just a second.'

Danny handed the receiver to Josh. 'It's for you. It's James.'

'Tell him I'm not here,' Josh whispered.

Putting his hand across the receiver, Danny looked disapprovingly at Josh. 'Okay. This once, but I'm not going to get in the habit of lying for you,' Danny whispered back. And into the mouthpiece, 'James, I'll get him to call you back. But it might be tomorrow as we're on our way out.'

'Thanks.' Josh smiled. 'You'd better go, dad. Harry Potter is starting, and I need to order my burger. Have a nice time with Penny, and don't be too late.' He winked, knowing very well that he was being cheeky.

* * *

Soaking her increasingly tanned body in a warm bubble bath, Sasha considered what to wear to the Tropical deck party that evening. The deck party was one of the highlights of the cruise, she recalled, topping up the bath water before lying back and covering her entire body in bubbles. She and Ben hadn't missed a single one in all the years they had cruised together. The party was a great excuse to dress as outrageously as you liked; the men in the loudest Caribbean shirts they could find, and the ladies in their bright summer dresses complete with a lei around their neck.

Armed with a rum punch, or the cocktail of the day, they would party the night away with the extremely energetic entertainments team. Sasha had bought a sexy little red number from Jaspers before she came away. Thinking well ahead, she had decided to cover the possibility that she might not find anything more suitable in any of the ports they visited. So far, she had been right. It really hadn't been a shopping cruise, or at least it wouldn't be, not until they reached Acapulco. Having been there once before, she had huge plans for the last port of call.

Stepping out of the bath, she heard the phone ring in the next room. Grabbing the nearest towel, she wrapped it around her body and unlocked the bathroom door. But as she made a dash for the phone, pausing only for a second to curse out loud after stubbing her toe on a chair, it stopped ringing.

'Damn it, every time.' She cursed again. *I wonder who that was.* The only problem with the phones on the ship was that you couldn't just dial 1471 and find out who had called. It was probably Mrs Cockburn again, she decided. In that case, it was just as well she missed it. Edna Cockburn had somehow got into the habit of ringing Sasha every second or third day, just to make sure she was okay. At least, that's what she would say when she called. Sasha couldn't decide if she was actually making an effort to be nice, or calling as a constant reminder that she was on her own.

After drying her hair and carefully applying her makeup, Sasha was almost ready to get dressed. Confirming that the little red dress was the best option open to her, she collected it from the wardrobe and matched it with some strappy red sandals and a little red clutch bag.

Catching a glimpse of herself in the mirror, she noticed the dress was a little loose. It didn't hug her body like it had done when she tried it on for the first time just over a month ago. Losing weight on a cruise was almost unheard of. In fact it was well known amongst the regular cruisers that each passenger would gain up to seven pounds during a two-week cruise. Knowing fine well there was only one reason for her sudden weight loss, she decided not to dwell on it. Instead, she would make it work to her advantage.

Closing the cabin door behind her, she heard the phone ring again. Typical, she thought, searching in her bag for the key. Moving as quickly as possible in her new heels, her big toe still throbbing, she reached for the receiver.

'Hello,' she answered in an exasperated voice thinking that at this rate, the evening would be over before she even left the cabin.

'Hi, it's Geoff. Sorry to bother you, Sasha. You sound a little flustered there.'

'No. That's alright. I was just on my way out, that's all.'

'Oh, I see.' There was a long pause before Geoff spoke again. 'Look, I was wondering what your plans are for tonight? But I guess I'm a little late in asking. You've obviously already made some.'

'No, not really,' Sasha said, her face lighting up on hearing Geoff's voice. 'I was just going down to dinner,' *and maybe onto the deck party.* But on the off chance Geoff was going to suggest something else, she decided not to say that.

'Would you like to have drink with me later?' he asked, biting his lip in anticipation of Sasha's answer.

'Absolutely.' Sasha beamed, grateful that the conversation wasn't face to face. 'That sounds nice.'

Her tone was calm.

'Great. Shall we say nine-thirty in the Sports Bar? We can always go on to the deck party after that, if it looks good.'

'Perfect. I'll see you then.' Sasha eyes danced with excitement.

Everyone in the restaurant had made an effort to fit into the theme of the night. Some tables had probably taken it a bit far, such as the guests wearing their beachwear to dinner, but so long as there were no swimsuits on view the restaurant manager didn't seem to mind too much. Richard and Kris were there wearing their equally awful Caribbean shirts. Richard's was blue and yellow with a slight hint of black, while Kris was sporting an orange, green and white shirt, which was particularly unpleasant to look at.

Lucy and Megan had obviously discussed what they were wearing to the party, as they looked fantastic in their little white dresses; Lucy's slightly longer, falling just below the knee. The Cockburn's had decided that wearing a lei around their neck was tropical enough to be included in the night's festivities. William had taken it upon himself to organise the wine for dinner. He had ordered it through the wine line earlier that evening. It had taken the wine waiter a little longer than normal to confirm the order, due to William's lack of knowledge of the wine's on offer, but with Edna's unwelcome assistance, he had got there in the end.

Kris and Richard were very impressed by the old man's kind gesture, as they had taken turns buying the wine until now – although Sasha had offered on several occasions, but the men wouldn't allow it.

'You'll have to excuse me.' Sasha smiled at her friends, before thanking William and Edna for the wine.

'And where do you think you're off to?' Lucy asked, clearly intrigued.

'Got something to tell us have you, Sasha?' Kris said, winking at Richard. 'A hot date, perhaps?'

Feeling slightly uneasy at the sudden interrogation by her dining companions, Sasha wondered if she should sit back down at the table and explain herself. Standing her ground instead, she turned to her friends and smiled.

'No, no hot date, I'm afraid. I'm just going back to my cabin to get changed. I'll see you all at the deck party a bit later.'

'You look great, Sasha,' Lucy insisted. 'You shouldn't get changed.'

'Yeah, Sasha, that dress is smoking,' Kris added, scoring himself a sharp kick on the ankle from Megan.

Leaving the restaurant while it was still full always made Sasha feel particularly self-conscious. Feeling the same eyes on her as she passed by night after night, she knew they were all thinking the same as Edna Cockburn had so politely voiced on the first night of the cruise. *There she goes again, on her own. How terribly sad, isn't it?* She could practically hear the words out loud. But tonight was different. She felt consumed with confidence, and for the first time during the cruise she even looked the particular individuals in the eyes as she walked calmly past with her head held high.

'My, my,' one old woman said. 'There's a transformation if ever I've seen one.'

'You really shouldn't stare, it's very impolite,' the woman's husband had scorned.

They should meet the Cockburn's, Sasha had thought to herself, laughing inside.

Sasha had no intention whatsoever of going to the deck party now, not after Lucy and Kris had almost blown her cover at dinner. If the group were to see her with Geoff, it would be a complete disaster. From day one of the cruise, Megan had made such a fuss about setting her up with someone. Getting spotted with anyone would be right up her street.

It was only nine-fifteen, so there was more than enough time to nip back to the cabin and freshen up before what appeared to be a date with Geoff. After fixing her hair, and quickly reapplying her lipstick, she sprayed a little more perfume on her neck and was finally ready. Arriving just after nine-forty, Geoff was already sitting at the bar waiting for her.

'What time do you call this?' he asked, holding up his watch, a serious expression on his face.

'I know, I'm sorry. I couldn't get away from dinner,' Sasha replied, not knowing how to take Geoff.

'I'm kidding, Sasha. You look *great*, by the way.'

Sasha smiled, accepting the compliment. 'Thanks.'

'Now, more importantly, what would you like to drink?' Geoff handed over the drinks menu while signalling for the bar steward to come over and take the order.

'A glass of red wine would be lovely, thanks,' Sasha said but just a small one please.

After talking her through the various wines on offer, the steward recommended the South African Pinotage.

'I love red wine, but I can never remember which one is which.' Sasha smiled at Geoff, holding up her glass. 'Anyway, cheers.'

Their glasses met with a pronounced 'chink'.

'I agree,' said Geoff. 'I've got a terrible memory for wine. There are too many good ones to remember. In fact, they're pretty much all great.'

Hm, Sasha thought, *this is the perfect opportunity to ask Geoff along to the wine tasting session in Puerto Quetzal tomorrow.* But no matter how much she tried, she was unable to muster up the courage to ask him. So she decided to leave it. *He might think I'm being too forward,* she decided. This was only the second time he had officially asked her out, and she wasn't ready to be blatantly rejected by a man she was beginning to quite like.

Not yet anyway.

'So, I was thinking, since you were late for drinks tonight...' Geoff grinned, his teeth looking whiter than ever against his tanned face.

'Yes?' Sasha asked, an intrigued glint in her eye and wondering what was coming next.

'I think it's only fair that you should take me to lunch tomorrow,' Geoff said.

'I was literally only five minutes late,' Sasha flirtatiously protested.

'*Ten* minutes, actually.'

'Okay, *ten* minutes. Anyway, I really don't think being ten little minutes late deserves such a harsh sentence.'

'Oh really? You don't? Well, if you're not prepared to accept your punishment, how do I know that you won't be ten minutes late next time?' Geoff asked, now flirting back.

The next time, Sasha thought, slightly taken aback, *things are looking up.*

'You don't,' she replied. 'That's the beauty of being a woman. It's quite acceptable to keep a man waiting, but it's not acceptable for a man to keep a woman waiting.' She smiled to indicate that she was joking. 'But since you asked so nicely, I do know of a nice little restaurant I could take you to.'

Lucy had mentioned that Jasmines did a special lunch menu on a sea day. Maybe she could book a table there.

'How about we meet at the Wave Pool bar around one?' she said.

Geoff took another sip of his wine. 'It's a date.'

'Same again?' the steward asked, appearing by their side and smiling attentively.

'Sorry I can't.' Geoff looked at Sasha. 'I've just remembered I have to go. My friends Rick and Chris are in the casino. They've asked me along for a flutter, so I said I'd pop in. Unless...' Geoff paused. 'Maybe you'd like to join us? You're more than welcome. In fact, you'll get on great with Chris.'

'Thanks, but I'll have to pass.' Trying not to sound pathetic, she added, 'I said I would go up to the deck party and meet some people. Maybe another time though?'

'No problem. Listen, Sasha, do you mind if I don't finish that?' He put down his glass. 'I really am going to have to go.'

'No, that's fine. Honestly, enjoy your night,' Sasha replied, wondering what the sudden rush was to get away.

'Thanks; I'll see you tomorrow at one. Don't be late!' As he walked off, Geoff looked back at Sasha and winked.

The first half hour had gone really well, but suddenly Geoff was giving off mixed vibes. It was almost as if he had decided he had had enough of her company. Sasha's mind wandered away with her as she watched him rush off along the Promenade deck towards the casino. Although, maybe that wasn't entirely fair. He had invited her along to meet his friends. Finishing her wine, Sasha questioned why Geoff insisted she would get on great with his friend, Chris. Was he trying to set her up with him? Was that what all this was about?

Thinking about it a little too long, Sasha was now convinced that's what Geoff had meant. Was he going to set her up on a blind date tomorrow? *Surely not,* she thought, but none of it made any sense. Added to which, she still couldn't say for sure that Geoff wasn't seeing the girl she had seen him kiss on the day the ship went through the Panama Canal.

Deciding to give the deck party a miss for the second time that evening, Sasha thanked the bar staff and made her way back to her cabin. There would be so many people on deck she would never find Lucy and Megan anyway.

* * *

'Two fire margaritas, please,' Danny said as the waiter approached him in Nacho's.

'No, Danny. I couldn't possibly.' Penny shook her head until she felt dizzy.

'Sorry, wrong answer. You failed to finish the 'naughty but nice' margarita, and you didn't even try the 'atomic' one I ordered, so I figured you need something with a bit more of a kick to it.'

'But it's got chilli in it. How am I supposed to manage that?'

'The same way you managed to make that giant plate of chilli nachos disappear! Now come on, 1, 2, 3...'

'God, that's disgusting,' Penny screwed up her face as if she had just been forced to suck a lemon.

'Yes, but it was worth it to see the look on your face.' Danny held his stomach and laughed hysterically as Penny grabbed the jug of iced water and quickly topped up her glass. 'Seriously Penny, you don't have to drink it if you don't want to.' Danny moved the margarita away from her. 'Come on, let's finish up here and go to the party on deck.'

'Okay, but only if you promise I can choose my own drink water preferably.'

The deck party was in full swing, with over two thirds of the passengers crammed together on Deck 12 singing and dancing along to Brian Adams' *Summer of 69* .The less energetic, mainly older passengers, were spread evenly over Decks 14 and 15 getting a bird's eye view of the party in a slightly less confined environment. Ocean Magic was renowned for its hugely successful deck parties, which were mainly down to Andrew Henson, the entertainments director. He really knew how to give the passengers a good time.

Arriving at the party just after 11.00pm, Danny was determined to join in the fun.

'Come on. Let's show them how it's done. I love this song.' But before Penny could answer, Danny had swept her into his arms and was flinging her around the open deck like a rag doll. Thankfully, she narrowly missed an old lady who had most definitely had one too many cocktails of the day.

'You look great,' Danny said as he spun Penny round for a third time before an arm reached out and stopped her dead in her tracks.

'Kris, let go of me,' Penny protested.

'I can't. I need to talk to you. I need to explain what happened,' Kris insisted, pulling Penny towards him.

'I don't want to hear your lies,' Penny yelled back at him.

'Let go of her, and there won't be any trouble,' said Danny.

Freeing Penny from his grasp, Kris held up his hands. 'Alright mate, I just want to talk to her, to explain...'

'Look mate! The only thing you'll be explaining is a broken nose if you don't back off.'

'Fine. Your loss, Princess.'

Kris laughed and glared at Penny before walking off towards the bar.

'Are you okay?' Danny said, putting his arm around Penny's shoulder.

'I'm fine. Thanks for that.' She began sobbing quietly. 'He really is a jerk.'

'Come on, let's get out of here, and don't worry about him. He won't be bothering you again.' Danny smiled. 'Hey, I had a great night, didn't you? That idiot aside, I mean.'

Penny forced a smile. 'Yeah, it really was great.'

'It doesn't have to end yet. I thought we could go back to your cabin for coffee. Josh is asleep next door, otherwise I'd invite you in to mine.'

'Sure, coffee would be nice,' Penny agreed.

The night really had been fantastic. The pair had laughed and joked their way through dinner, and were possibly even flirting with each other on one or two occasions. But unfortunately, because of

Kris's untimely outburst, Danny felt it would be inappropriate to take things any further with Penny – for tonight anyway. Penny was also still under the impression Danny was seeing Nicole, and he really needed to clear that up as soon as possible.

'Here you are,' Penny said, holding out a mug of coffee once they were back in her cabin.

'Thanks,' Danny replied, setting it down on the sideboard.

'What are you looking so thoughtful about?' Penny asked, noticing that Danny seemed miles away. 'If you're tired, don't let me keep you.'

She sat cross-legged on the bed.

'I'm not tired. It's nothing really,' Danny replied casually. 'I'm just thinking what a great holiday this has been for the kids and me. I mean you've been working, so it's obviously a bit different for you.'

'Working? I wouldn't call it that. I'm having the time of my life. Josh and Katie have made things so easy for me.'

'Well, we can't have that. I might need to have a word and get them to play up a bit more.' Danny joked. 'Seriously, Penny. That's because they like you.' Taking a deep breath, he continued, 'and who could blame them? They've got great taste, if you ask me.' He reached out his arm and held Penny's hand in his. *Oh my God, he thought*, shaking slightly, *now is the perfect opportunity to make a move. Kiss her, you idiot, he told himself.*

The electricity between them was strong. He was certain Penny could feel it too. But the washing machine feeling in his stomach made him react opposite to his intentions. Getting swiftly off his chair, he moved towards the bar.

'Think I'll have a nightcap,' he said, holding out a miniature bottle of brandy. 'Want one?'

His feelings were so intense; he didn't know where to look.

'No thanks,' Penny replied, declining the offer.

It was approaching 2.00am, and Danny still had to collect Katie from the youth centre. Arriving minutes before the youth leaders were due to close for the night, Danny realized quickly he was the last one to pick up. Lisa, the girl on duty, had tidied away all the cots and beds but had been careful not to disturb Katie.

'Sorry I'm so late,' Danny said to the youth leader as soon as he entered the room. 'How has she been tonight?'

'She went out like a light at about seven-thirty just after you dropped her off.'

'Oh, good,' Danny replied, collecting Katie's things.

'How's your son, Josh?' Lisa asked, 'I heard there was a little bit of trouble in The Club earlier.'

'What kind of trouble?' Danny asked, concerned that Josh had been misbehaving.

'It was nothing serious,' Lisa reassured Danny, filling him in on the small disagreement the boys had had in The Club earlier that day.

'Josh, why are you not asleep?' Danny asked, as he crept into the cabin with Katie fast asleep in his arms.

'I just woke up when you came in,' Josh replied, rubbing his eyes.

'Well, while you're awake, is there something you want to tell me?' Danny asked.

'No, why?' Josh replied, rather sheepishly.

'Are you sure? If I find out you're keeping something from me, I'll be forced to keep you out of The Club.'

'I don't care, it's a stupid club anyway.'

'Josh, what happened today? Please talk to me, son.'

'I don't want to tell you.' Josh threw his duvet over his head as he started to sob. A moment later, however, he popped his head out from under the covers. 'Okay. If you must know, it's James. He told me his mum is only after your money, she wants to marry you and everything.'

'Is that all? Well of course she does. I'm a catch remember, who wouldn't want to marry me?' Danny joked in an attempt to make Josh feel better.

Josh looked up at his father in amazement. 'But I'm not going to let that happen,' he insisted, with a severe look on his face.

'Don't worry about James's mum, Josh. Come on, dry your tears. I saw straight through her out the minute I met her.'

'So you're not going to marry her?' Josh said, looking for confirmation from his father.

'No, Josh. Not now, not ever. But I think you might owe James an apology. He was very upset after you left, and then you wouldn't take his call. I think you need to go and see him tomorrow and make up. Now come on, it's very late, let's try and get some sleep.'

'Did you have a nice time with Penny?' Josh asked, hopeful of the reply.

'Yes. It was perfect.' Danny smiled. 'Goodnight Josh.'

Chapter 13

At Sea

The big day was at last here. Charlie had hardly slept a wink all night, and by seven o'clock she couldn't contain her excitement any longer. Welcoming the sound of the alarm clock, she bounced energetically out of bed.

Right, let's get this day under way, she told herself. Admiring her slim figure in the mirror, eight pounds was what she had managed to lose, which meant the wedding dress she loved so much was going to look *amazing*.

By this stage, everything had been pretty much been taken care of. Her nail appointment was booked for 9.30am. It was followed by her hair appointment at 10.15am. Make-up, she confirmed as she consulted the appointment card, was scheduled for 11.30am.

Maddy was booked in for the same time, so they could have a girly chat and sip a glass of buck fizz together while they were being pampered by the salon girls who were going to make them look their very best.

Mike was under strict instructions to be out of the cabin by nine o'clock at the latest. Charlie had arranged for him to get ready in Maddy's cabin, while Maddy got ready in hers.

The continental breakfast she had ordered the night before arrived at eight o'clock, and it looked wonderful. Unfortunately, Charlie could do justice only to the orange juice. The butterfly feeling in her stomach wouldn't permit her to eat anything solid. Mike, on the other hand, was clearly not nervous. He polished off a full fry-up before working his way through Charlie's croissant and petit pain basket.

Arriving at the salon on time, Charlie and Maddy were welcomed by two of the salon girls who were obviously keen to get started.

'Hi, this is Vanessa, and I'm Helen,' a chirpy, well turned out girl announced from behind the reception desk. 'We'll be looking after you this morning. So if you would like to come through and have a seat at the nail bar, we'll get started.'

'Good idea,' Maddy said. 'Then we'll have our hands free for that glass of buck fizz.'

Grinning at Charlie, she eagerly led the way into the salon.

Maddy's husband, Kim, had been so nice and easy going that Mike didn't feel at all awkward imposing on him. As instructed, he arrived at the cabin at nine o'clock. Although Mike had met Kim only during the cruise, Kim had very kindly agreed to fill the role of best man. He had, according to Charlie, been honoured to be asked, and so far he was playing the role perfectly. On the off chance Mike would need some Dutch courage before the big event, he had arranged for a selection of drinks to be delivered later that morning to the cabin.

By midday, Charlie and Maddy arrived back in the cabin. They were both extremely excited with the results of spending the morning in the salon. Maddy had convinced Charlie to invite all the girls round at midday so they could help them get dressed and assist with any last minute eventualities.

Once everyone had arrived, and when the big day was well underway, there was an unexpected knock on the door. Maddy raced to answer it in case it was Mike. She was unreasonably superstitious and couldn't have him seeing Charlie before the wedding. The fact that Charlie and Mike had spent the night together seemed to have slipped her mind, or for some reason didn't seem to count. Maddy squealed with excitement when she opened the door to a very attractive, extremely charming young butler who was holding a silver tray with a bottle of champagne, a beautiful selection of canapés and a gorgeous bouquet of flowers with a card which read; 'Enjoy yourselves, girls. Love, the boys xxxxx'.

Maddy was so excited she could hardly contain herself. She couldn't possibly have been more excited if it was *her* who was getting married.

An hour later, while the girls were enjoying their canapés and were halfway through the bottle of bubbly, Mike gave into resisting the Dutch courage, allowing Kim to pour him a generous measure of brandy along with a coffee. He hadn't needed it to calm his nerves, he told himself; he just thought he had better keep up with Charlie knowing the effect two glasses of champagne can have on his 'soon to be' wife.

'Okay, girls. Lets go,' Maddy announced, popping another smoked salmon roulade into her mouth while collecting her handbag. 'It's 1.45pm. We need to get out of here before Mike arrives to pick up Charlie. We don't want to spoil the wonderful moment when he sets eyes on her.' As Laura, laid back as ever, decided there was plenty of time to top up her make up, Maddy was beginning to lose patience. Knocking frantically on the bathroom door, Maddy yelled at her friend; 'Laura! Time's up! The boys will be there by now. And more importantly, so will the captain. Now seriously, hurry up!'

'Yep, coming,' Laura replied, casually making her way out of the cabin.

'And you won't be needing that,' Maddy said, taking a glass of champagne out of Laura's hand.

'Spoilsport,' Laura replied, making a face behind Maddy's back.

By 2.00pm, the guests were all in position. Maddy, Charlie's bridesmaid, and Kim, Mike's best man, were standing beside the beautiful floral archway next to the captain, while the other couples occupied the two rows of chairs which were beautifully decorated in white silk bows.

Covering her mouth with her hand, Maddy gasped as she watched Mike walk towards her, no Charlie in sight. Turning their heads to see what Maddy was looking so shocked about, Sarah, Joy and Kay looked equally stunned by what they were witnessing. Laura, on the other hand, had a huge smirk on her face.

'Oh my,' she giggled, then whispered to the couples next to her, 'Looks like there's not going to be a wedding after all.

It would appear that Charlie's done a runner or should I say jumped overboard.'

'Shut up, Laura!' said Kay. 'You really can be a little bitch sometimes.'

'Touchy, touchy,' Laura continued to torment her friend. 'You would think it was *you* who had been 'stood up' on your wedding day.'

'That's enough, both of you,' said Lee Sarah's husband. 'I'm sure there's a reasonable explanation for what's happened.'

'God, I knew I shouldn't have left her alone to wait for Mike,' Maddy whispered in her husband's ear.

'She'll be fine,' Kim said, squeezing Maddy's hand for support.

Finally approaching the captain, Mike took him aside and whispered something in his ear.

'Okay,' Alex replied, nodding.

The knock on the cabin door induced Charlie's fifth spasm of butterflies. *Here goes*, she thought as she cracked open the door.

Picking her up off the floor, her father smiled affectionately at his daughter.

'Come on, darling. There's no time for that fainting malarkey. We've got a wedding to get to.'

'But how?' Charlie asked, picking herself up off the floor and throwing her arms around her father.

Closing the cabin door behind them, he turned to his daughter and smiled. 'It's a long story. I'll explain all after the wedding, I promise. Now, I know I really shouldn't tell you this, but at the risk of the shock being too much and you fainting on me again there is one more surprise.'

'Mum?' Charlie asked, her eyes as bright and beautiful as the first time her father had ever seen them. 'Dad, is mum here too?'

'She is indeed, and it get's better.'

What could possibly be better than this? Charlie wondered.

'We aren't expecting it to be easy, but we are making a go of getting back together.'

'Seriously? This is the best wedding present I could possibly ask for.'

'Yeah, well, you've got your future husband to thank for all of it.'

Almost fainting herself, Maddy was the first to witness Charlie's mum join the group in order to watch the ceremony.

'It gets better,' Mike announced, winking at Maddy.

'This is unbelievable.' Maddy smiled, brushing away a tear as she watched her friend being escorted down the spiral staircase from Deck 14 to Deck 12.

Gosh, she is truly beautiful, Mike thought as he admired the stunning looking woman who was making her way towards him, the inexorable sunshine adding an amiable glow to the occasion.

As the wedding party expertly came together, the two thousand-plus passengers (who were previously relaxing by the various pools and bars) looked on in amazement as Charlie and Mike exchanged vows and were finally announced husband and wife.

'You may kiss the bride,' Alex concluded as everyone cheered.

* * *

Geoff grinned at Sasha as she approached the bar. 'You're on time. I'm impressed.'

'Don't be *too* impressed. Jasmines was fully booked, so we'll have to go somewhere else the buffet would probably be the best option, or the coffee shop next to the Cyber Café if you prefer it.'

'Or we can use the table *I* booked.' Geoff grinned again, taking a sip of the beer he had just ordered.

'You booked a table in Jasmines?' Sasha said. 'Why would you do that when you knew I was booking one?'

'Maybe because I knew you wouldn't manage that simple task. Looks like I was right. Cheers anyway.' He lifted his bottle. 'Can I buy you a drink?'

'Yes, I'd love one,' Sasha said, puzzled by what Geoff had done. She smiled at the girl behind the bar. 'A soda with lime, please.'

'I made the reservation for one-thirty, but they won't mind if we're a little late.'

'Fine.' Sasha raised her glass to meet Geoff's bottle of beer. 'Cheers.'

'Cheers. Here's to a nice lunch.' Geoff smiled, with a mischievous look in his eyes. 'So how was your morning Sasha? I mean, you must be pretty tired after spending two hours in the gym as usual. I really don't know how you do it.'

Although she would never admit it to him, Sasha was quite attracted to Geoff's cheeky schoolboy personality.

'You know how much I hate the gym,' she replied, giving him a gentle nudge on the shoulder.

'I know,' he smiled. 'But you enjoyed the yoga class the other day, didn't you?'

Only because you were there, she thought.

'Yes, it was okay,' she agreed.

'So, maybe I could one day give you some tips on using the equipment? I'll be gentle I promise.'

'Maybe,' Sasha said, knowing fine well there was more chance of her flying to the moon and back than stepping foot inside a fully equipped gymnasium.

'Right, we'd better go if we're going to make our reservation,' Geoff said, placing his empty beer bottle on the bar.

'Sure.' Sasha left her soda behind, and they departed.

'The food smells great. Do you know what you're having?'

'I'm not sure,' said Geoff. 'It's between the red duck curry, and the grilled fish with three chilli paste. What about you?' He sneaked a quick glance at Sasha while she tried hard to study the menu. *Gosh her eyes are so gorgeous*, he thought.

'Anything to drink, sir, madam?' said the approaching waiter.

'Just a beer for me, please. A Bud if you have one. And a white wine with soda.' He looked at Sasha. 'Is that OK?'

Sasha nodded at the waiter. 'Yes. Lovely.'

The conversation was soon flowing, and flowing well. Sasha asked about Geoff's friends. She found it a little strange that she hadn't seen them out together through the cruise, but Geoff gave very little away, too preoccupied as he was in trying to find out more about Sasha. Minutes later, he went straight in with the big question.

'I know you're single, Sasha, but what made you come on a cruise on your own?'

Sasha's face fell. She knew that at some point she was going to have to be honest with Geoff, so she decided to start at the beginning. She took a deep breath and explained that she was engaged to Ben and that they had not long broken up. It wasn't the whole truth, but it was a start. Geoff listened intently, not showing any emotion, and not commenting on, or challenging her story. The talk intensified, and it lasted for three hours – and they talked only about Sasha and what she had been through.

Geoff asked about her family, and she held nothing back. Explaining what had happened to her father and how the only thing she really had going for her now was her job. Geoff sympathised deeply, the look on his face saying how sorry he was to hear what she had to say.

After lunch, they parted ways. Sasha had booked an appointment in the spa to get a hot stone massage. Geoff thanked her for her company, and they arranged to meet later that evening for a coffee.

They all sat patiently waiting for Mr and Mrs Cockburn to join them, but as it approached a quarter to nine, they realized the elderly couple weren't going to show. Second sitting dinner started at 8.30pm, and the Cockburn's hadn't once been late during the cruise. In fact they had generally always been the first to arrive at the table.

Sasha scanned the menu and asked Lucy to order the fish for her before excusing herself from the table and leaving the restaurant. She took the lift to Deck 10, and walked promptly towards the Cockburn's cabin.

In a strange sort of way, the Cockburn's had looked out for her during the cruise, so she felt obliged to check everything was okay; the phone calls every other day, the random knock on the door when they were passing just to make sure she wasn't sitting in her cabin bored and alone. There had also been the kind gesture of lunch in St Lucia on the second day of the cruise, although at the time she hadn't realized how thoughtful it had been of them to invite her along, and of course the bottle of champagne the couple had so kindly donated to her the other afternoon.

Sasha knocked for a third time, listened, then turned to leave, presuming the couple were dining elsewhere. *They probably thought they had told someone*, she thought. *Then again, they aren't obliged to reveal their every move, are they?*

Seconds later, the door was partially opened by Mr Cockburn.

'Hello, dear,' he said in a weak voice; a voice very much unlike his usual chirpy manner.

'Sorry to bother you,' said Sasha, suddenly embarrassed and afraid William would think she was intruding. 'I just wanted to check if you were coming down for dinner, that's all. We didn't want to start without you.'

Mr Cockburn opened the door a little further this time, allowing Sasha to see two packed suitcases lying on top of the bed.

'Is everything okay?' she asked, now deeply concerned for the old man.

'I don't think we will be coming to dinner tonight, but thank you for calling past,' Mr Cockburn replied, now trying to shut the door again. But Sasha knew there was something wrong.

'William,' Sasha called, to fully get his attention. She hadn't called him by his first name since they had met. 'Look. If... well, if I can help at all with anything, please call me.' She scribbled down her cabin number in case he had forgotten it. Handing it to him with a sympathetic smile, she reluctantly left the cabin, knowing all she could do was offer her help and hope he would accept it if necessary.

Returning to the table to join the two couples for dinner, the men decided that the Cockburn's must have had some bad news from home. That's why they were packed and departing a day early. The girls agreed, and the Cockburn's didn't take up any more of their dinner conversation.

Lucy tapped Megan on the foot under the table and nodded her head in the direction of Tom, who was looking at Sasha with a glint in his eyes. Tom topped up Kris and Richard's red wine glasses before walking round to Sasha where he started a casual conversation about her day. When Tom left to fetch the wine account for Kris, Lucy went straight in, interrogating Sasha about Tom. Sasha blushed, discounting the suggestion that there was something going on between them.

When the drinks chit was signed, Lucy suggested they all got a table in Mandarin's, the show lounge. The theatre company were doing a special 'Rock and Roll' tribute, and Mandarin's was one of the smaller show lounges, so the numbers were limited to three hundred per sitting. They would have to get in early. Sasha tried to make her excuses, saying she needed an early night, but the girls were on to her straight away.

'You've got a date with Tom, haven't you?' said Lucy.

'Oh my God. I *knew* he liked you,' Megan added. 'How long have you been seeing him?'

'Don't be ridiculous,' said Sasha.

'Who is it then?' Lucy asked, unable to contain her excitement.

'It's a guy called Geoff, and he's really nice.'

'I knew it!' Kris joined in. Richard was busy talking about share options, but Kris found the girls' conversation a lot more interesting. 'You've kept that one quiet haven't you, you little player.'

'Well, it's very early days, and I don't want to jinx it,' Sasha said, looking rather bashful.

'So, when can we meet him?' said Richard, realizing that it was either this conversation, or a conversation with the salt and pepper mills.

'Tonight?' Lucy and Megan asked, echoing each other in giggly voices.

Excellent, Megan thought, relieved that Sasha was no longer a threat to her and Kris. He couldn't have her now, even if he wanted to. She was taken.

'Maybe we can all meet for lunch ashore in Acapulco or something?' said Sasha.

'Well I'll have to check my diary,' said Kris.

Flirt, Megan thought to herself. *He's probably jealous.*

'Okay, so now you all know about my private life, you'll have to excuse me. I have a coffee date,' Sasha announced as she left the table.

'Enjoy your night, Sasha,' Richard added sincerely as they all followed on, Lucy and Megan skipping along behind their men and gossiping about Sasha and her mystery man. They were elated by what they had just discovered.

'Hey, gorgeous!' Geoff said as he approached Sasha from behind.

Gorgeous? Thought Sasha. *Boy, someone's in a good mood tonight, but I can't believe he called me that.*

She was beaming inside. They had arranged to meet in the Sports bar away from the hustle and bustle of people coming and going from the shows. Geoff wore the usual ear-to-ear grin on his face. He looked really pleased to see Sasha. Leaning forward, he gave her a firm kiss on the cheek. A little taken aback at Geoff's behaviour, Sasha returned the smile and promptly asked Geoff what he would like to drink. The couple ordered two cappuccinos and had the waiter bring them over to a quiet table at the far side of the room.

'Good,' Geoff said as he sat. 'Now we can talk.'

'That sounds serious,' Sasha said, and they both laughed at her clever attempt to break the ice.

As it turned midnight, Geoff suggested he would walk Sasha back to her cabin. They had once again got on incredibly well together. The evening had been perfect, and there was definitely a spark of chemistry between them. Now that Geoff seemed more relaxed, there was a strong possibility they could be more than friends. Sasha walked slowly along the corridor, giving Geoff time to make the first move. She considered inviting him in for another coffee, but decided it would be too forward of her. Their night had been wonderful, and she didn't want to make Geoff feel awkward if he declined her offer.

It was pretty late anyway, she told herself.

Geoff wished Sasha goodnight, and went to kiss her on the cheek, but as he moved towards her he raised his hand slowly and placed it gently on the back of her head running his fingers through her hair. He then moved even closer towards her lips, and kissed her passionately for what felt like a couple of minutes. Sasha returned the affection by putting her hands around his back, holding him close. Once their lips parted, Geoff kissed her quickly on the cheek, flashed his normal gorgeous smile, and wished her a goodnight. Sasha had hoped it would go further. Geoff was an amazing kisser. She had been so close to pushing the door open and throwing him onto the bed. But that didn't happen, and soon after he was gone.

She watched him walk away, then shrugged and went into her cabin to sort herself out and get ready for bed. She stood for a moment behind the door, her back pressed against it, her eyes closed, her heart tripping softly.

Presently, she went into the bathroom and checked her face in the mirror. As she reached for her makeup remover from the cabinet, she heard her phone ring in the cabin. She threw the cotton wool in the sink, which was followed closely by the bottle of Clinique cleanser. She raced to the phone, her mind going wild. *At last he was ready to take things a step further*, she thought. But when she answered the phone, there was a long silence before she could hear someone crying.

'I didn't know who else to talk to,' said the voice of an old man. Mr Cockburn. In the excitement of her evening with Geoff, she had forgotten all about him.

'Do you want me to come round?' said Sasha.

'If it's not too much trouble,' Mr Cockburn answered, speaking in the same painfully quiet tone she had heard earlier that evening. Squeezing her feet back into her little strappy heels, she ran out the door and down the corridor.

When she arrived at the Cockburn's cabin, the door was open. Knocking gently, she cautiously entered where she found William sitting on the end of one of the single beds. The two suitcases beside him, packed and ready to go, like they had been earlier that evening.

'Where's *Mrs* Cockburn?' Sasha asked as William sat staring into space, his eyes full of tears.

'She's gone, Sasha,' he sobbed. There was a long, long pause. *Gone?* Sasha thought. *Gone where?*

'She died tonight at 5.30pm,' said William. They took her, the doctors took her to the ships mortuary he added sobbing a little more, she will be flown home tomorrow.

This was not what Sasha had expected. They had talked about this at dinner. Kris and Richard had told her the Cockburn's were going home early because someone else had probably taken ill, or at the very worst died. But not Mrs Cockburn. No one had anticipated that.

Moving towards the weary old man, Sasha sat down beside him and put her arm around his shoulder and held him close.

'I am so sorry, William, really I am,' she began. 'I don't know what to say.'

Spotting a bottle of twenty – year old Glen Morangie malt in the glass cabinet beside the TV, she realized that this must be Mr Cockburn's chosen tipple.

Collecting two glasses from the drinks unit, she poured a large measure into one and a splash into the other. She handed Mr Cockburn the decent measure, and sat and listened to his tragic story.

It had all been very sudden. Apparently Mrs Cockburn had complained about not feeling too well, and had gone for a lie down. Mr Cockburn had tucked her in, but when he went to wake her an hour later, he couldn't.

The pair talked until 4.00am when Mr Cockburn finally lay back on the bed and fell fast asleep. His glass still firmly held in his hand. Gently removing it, Sasha put it on the sideboard before covering the old man with a blanket she found in the wardrobe. Then quietly, she sneaked out the door back to her cabin for a couple of hours sleep. She planned to go and see off William on his early morning flight home. The poor man had been through a lot with his wife, but you could tell he was going to miss her terribly. They had been married fifty years. This cruise was marking their Golden Wedding anniversary and was a present from one of their sons. It certainly hadn't ended the way they had planned.

Chapter 14

Acapulco 07:00 Arrival Overnight

It was approaching half past six. The one and half hours of sleep that Sasha had managed to get only made her feel worse. She was edgy. Unfocussed. The news of Edna Cockburn had come as quite a shock. Less than two weeks ago she hadn't even known the old woman existed, and now she was lying in bed staring at the ceiling grieving for the old dear while the ship moved into position and was arriving in the last port of call, Acapulco.

That was the main problem with cruising, Sasha reflected. You joined the ship of your choice as an individual, embarking on a holiday of a lifetime, but no matter how much you try to keep yourself to yourself, undoubtedly you meet a bunch of people who influence you in one way or another and get under your skin.

William. She remembered him as she'd last seen him. The poor man was devastated by the loss of his wife, and she was the one he had chosen to call late last night when the reality of the situation had hit him. The hotel department had been fantastic and had made arrangements for him to fly home this morning, and she had promised to pop in before he left the ship at eight o'clock. She intended to keep that promise.

Having lain on the bed for a little longer than intended, Sasha showered quickly and threw on whatever came to hand before making her way back to Mr Cockburn's cabin. When she arrived, however, the door was wide open, the suitcases were gone and there was no sign of William.

'Hi. Can I help you?' said a voice.

Sasha jumped as the cabin steward came bursting out of the bathroom with a handful of used towels and a bin full of left over toiletries.

'Yes, I was looking for Mr Cockburn. William Cockburn. This is his cabin isn't it?'

The steward frowned and shook his head. 'I'm sorry, but I don't know. I'm servicing this cabin only for today. One of the passengers on Deck 11 has requested a move, so I've been asked to attend to it. That's all.'

'Well do you know if he got away okay?'

'I'm really not sure who you mean. There was no one here when I arrived. Sorry I can't help you more.'

'Okay, thanks anyway,' Sasha replied, leaving the cabin with a puzzled look on her face.

Later that morning, she decided to take advantage of her last day in the sun, and was lying by the pool just about to doze off when Geoff strolled past.

Sasha lifted her sunglasses and revealed her bloodshot eyes.

'You,' he said, gazing down, 'look terrible!'

'Thanks. Aren't you a charmer?'

'Sorry, I just meant you look like you didn't get much sleep.'

'I didn't.'

Crouching beside her and taking her hand in his, Geoff added, 'Hey sweetheart, what's the matter?'

Wiping away a tear, Sasha sat up in her lounger. She thought for a moment and composed herself.

'Remember I told you about Mrs Cockburn? The crazy old lady who drove me insane for most of the first week of the cruise?'

'Sure I do.'

'Well, then I saw the other side to her. The caring, good natured side.' She took a deep breath before continuing. 'Well, they didn't come down to dinner last night and nobody thought anything much about it. Then William called me last night, after you left. He told me that... well, that Mrs Cockburn died yesterday evening.'

'Oh, Sasha, that's terrible.' Now sitting beside her, and sensing her pain, Geoff put his arms around her and held her tight.

'I stayed with him most of the night, until he fell asleep, but when I went back first thing this morning he wasn't there, which is strange as his flight wasn't until 10.30am,' Sasha continued, trying not to let Geoff see how upset she really was.

Reassuring her that she had done her best, and that William would have really appreciated her help, Geoff smiled sympathetically.

'The problem is,' she continued, 'I'm not sure if he made it, if you know what I mean.'

'I'm sure he did, Sasha. He probably just wanted to get away from the ship as soon as he could.' Pausing for a moment, Geoff looked into Sasha's tearful eyes. 'So that's where you were when I called?'

'You called me last night?' Sasha's eyes lit up.

'Yes, and then I find out you were round another man's cabin until the small hours of the morning. How do you think that makes me feel?' Geoff flashed another one of his mischievous smiles, hoping to lighten the conversation. 'I'm not one of those guys you can pick up one minute and discard like a rag doll the next, you know?'

Sasha laughed for the first time in what felt like forever. His sense of humour had managed to take the edge off the unpleasant conversation.

'So what were you calling for?' she said.

'I'm afraid I can't tell you. Not now anyway. Not now I've found out you're seeing someone else.'

'It's okay,' Sasha said. 'He's going home today, so I'm available again.'

The gentle flirting was definitely helping Sasha get into a better frame of mind. The pair continued their conversation until Sasha heard the familiar shrieking and giggling of Lucy and Megan approaching. *Oh God,* she thought, *this is all I need right now.*

'Have you heard?' Sasha said, looking up at her friends.

'Heard what, Sash?' Megan asked eagerly, a big grin on her face. 'Come on, tell us. What's the big news?'

'About Mrs Cockburn?'

'No, why? What's she gone and done now? Invited herself to yours for a long weekend. Oh my, wouldn't that be funny?' Megan said, prodding Lucy in the ribs.

'She died last night,' said Sasha. 'That's why she wasn't at dinner.'

'Oh, that's terrible!' said Lucy. 'Poor William. I hope he's alright.'

'He's fine,' Sasha continued, now filling them in on the details, but Megan was completely uninterested and had already turned her attention to the man whose arms had, just moments earlier, been around Sasha.

'Geoff, this is Lucy,' Sasha said, introducing them.

'Hi. Pleased to meet you.'

Lucy acknowledged the drop-dead gorgeous man.

'And this is Megan.'

'Hi.' Geoff stood up and smiled at Sasha's friends. 'So, you're the lovely ladies that Tom told me he's been waiting on this cruise.'

'You know Tom?' Megan said.

'Yes, we're good friends.'

'Now that makes sense.'

Megan nodded towards Lucy and Sasha, but she had lost Geoff completely.

'Okay, well we'd better be off,' Lucy said. 'We're meeting the guys in reception. We're going ashore for lunch.' Hesitating, Lucy added, 'If you like, you're more than welcome to join us. Both of you,' she added.

'Thanks,' said Geoff, smiling at Lucy. 'That's very kind, but we're planning to go ashore tonight. That's still the plan, isn't it Sasha?'

He glanced at her realizing that she may well have changed her mind given the circumstances.

'Yes, if you don't mind,' she said. 'I think I'm just going to stay by the pool for now, then go ashore with Geoff later. But have a good time.'

'You too,' Megan replied, grinning at the couple.

Sitting back in their sun loungers, Geoff and Sasha watched Lucy and Megan wander off to get ready for lunch.

'They seem pretty nice,' said Geoff.

'Yes, they've been so good to me.' Sasha sighed. 'I'm really not sure what I would have done without them.'

Standing up from his lounger, Geoff said, 'There are Rick and Chris. Since I met *your* friends, it's only fair you should meet mine.'

Calling them over, Geoff said, 'Sasha, this is my best friend Rick and his fiancée, Christina. They got engaged at the beginning of the cruise, and sneakily, Chris didn't tell me. She waited until I noticed the ring on her finger, which wasn't until four or five days later.'

'It was the day of the Panama Canal,' Christina giggled. 'Which was like a week later, Geoff. He's not the sharpest tool in the box, Sasha, so don't expect him to notice when you've had your hair done or anything.'

'Oh, really? Well that's enough from you,' Geoff said, picking his best friend's fiancée up and holding her over the pool, threatening to throw her in.

'Rick, tell him to put me down!' Chris yelled.

'No, I don't think so. You got yourself into this.' Rick laughed aloud at the carry on. 'I'm afraid you'll have to get yourself out of it.'

'Okay, okay, I'm sorry.' Chris giggled, whilst trying to wriggle herself free.

'Sorry, I didn't hear you Chris.'

'I said I'm sorry!'

'That's more like it.' Geoff paused for a second, returning Chris to her feet.

'Nice to meet you, Sasha.' Rick smiled, taking his fiancé by the hand. 'Maybe we can all have dinner some time?'

'Sure.' Geoff agreed, waving his friends off.

'She's nice, Rick.' Chris said.

'I think so. She's the first since Molly. He must really like her.'

'So what are the plans for tonight, Sasha?'

Sasha said nothing.

'Is everything okay?'

'It is now,' she replied, relieved that now the mystery Panama girl made sense.

'What do you mean?' Geoff said, intrigued to know what Sasha was talking about.

But, still not willing to let Geoff know that she had been jealous when she had seen him and Christina together, she just laughed and said, 'Sorry. It was a bit of a shock. I thought you were on holiday with two of your mates.'

'I am,' Geoff replied with a confused look on his face. 'So are we going to go and get you into bed for an hour or so?'

'That's a bit forward isn't it?' Sasha replied, gathering her book and towel while flashing Geoff a cheeky smile before heading off to her cabin.

'See you at seven Sasha,' said Geoff. 'Hope you get some sleep, I'm off to the gym.'

Back in her cabin, Sasha collapsed on her bed. She was definitely feeling the effects of her late night with William, and lying in the sun all morning had only made her feel more tired. She knew she had to get some rest before her big night out in Acapulco. For her, this was to be the highlight of the cruise, but as much as she tried, she couldn't get to sleep. Constant thoughts off Geoff were running through her mind, making her feel restless. She had known Geoff for eight days now, and she was certain there was a connection between them. It had been there from the start, since the day they met through Tom at Coco's beach. But, apart from the odd drink here and the odd lunch there, he had kissed her only once.

It wasn't that there was any amazing rush for them to jump into bed together, but considering they were both going home tomorrow, it all seemed a little strange. He had introduced her to his best friends, so all the signs were there. There had even been a little flirting. But one kiss in eight days? What was wrong with him? No man had ever taken so long to make a more advanced move, Sasha thought – not that she would entertain pushy behaviour when it came down to it. But with Geoff, she wondered if anything would ever happen. Why wasn't he acting like a normal hot-blooded male? Or at the very least trying something on?

Mystery.

'Hey, Josh. Who are you asking to the farewell ball? We need to decide by 4.00pm so that they can do the table seating plans,' said James, adding, 'I'm asking Anna.'

'Yeah, like she'll go with you!' Josh laughed at his friend.

'Course she will, Josh. Can't you tell she fancies me?'

James grinned while strutting from one side of the room to the other

'No, she doesn't. She likes that older guy that's been hanging about.'

'Who, Nick? No, he's way too old for her. He's fourteen already. She's only eleven, so I'm pretty much sorted. I'm sure of it. What about you? Carly's nice, and I think she likes you.'

'Seriously, you think she would say yes if I asked her?'

'Definitely. She's well into you.'

'I don't know. What if she says no?'

'Well, at least you'll know. But if you don't ask soon, someone might beat you to it. Honestly, Josh, I saw her checking you out the day of the swimming gala.'

'Okay, but if you're kidding, I'm going to kill you.' Josh made a playful fist towards his friend. 'So, you first. If Anna says yes, I'll ask Carly.'

'Okay, brother. Watch and learn.'

'Mate, not brother,' said Josh.

After an hour and a half in the bathroom, and a heavy splash of his dad's aftershave, Josh had just about built up enough courage to ask Carly to The Club's farewell black & white ball. *Okay, here goes*, he thought to himself as he casually walked into The Club.

'Hi, Carly,' he said as he approached her.

'Oh, hi.'

She smiled. Josh smiled back and cleared his throat.

He said, 'I was wondering if you'd like to be my partner tonight? You know, to the farewell dinner?'

'I'd love to,' Carly said without hesitation.

'Really?' Josh's face lit up like a Christmas tree. He couldn't believe his luck.

'I mean I *would* love to,' Carly continued, 'but Kieran has already asked me. It's been arranged for ages.'

'Oh. That's okay,' Josh replied, now looking like the fairy that was about to fall off the Christmas tree. 'Just thought I'd... you know, ask.'

'Sorry.'

'Yeah.'

He smiled again and pushed his hands into his back pockets and nodded and wandered off.

'See? I told you,' said James when they were alone. 'It's not that she didn't *want* to go with you, Josh. It's just that you were too late in asking.'

'I *know* that, dummy. But what am I going to do now?'

'Nothing you can do. You'll just have to ask someone else.'

'Oh? Like who?' Josh asked, looking desperately round the room.

'Well what about sporty or bookworm?'

'Oh, forget it.' Josh screwed up his face and looked suitably disgusted by the suggestion. 'I'd rather not go than go with either of *them*.'

'You were the one who sent her flowers, weren't you? That day she was ill. You remember? At the beginning of the cruise.'

'Don't be stupid. Why would I do that, you idiot.'?

'Because you like her, don't you?' James continued, not giving up.

'No, I don't. The only reason I asked her is that we have to have a partner for the dinner table.'

'Yeah, right, Josh. Whatever you say.' James sniggered, not helping his friend's situation.

'What did Anna say?' said Josh.

'Picking her up at 7.30pm. Told you she likes me.'

Josh sighed. 'Great.'

* * *

The knock on the door at seven made Sasha's heart skip a beat. He was here, and right on schedule. But by the time she had eventually woken up this evening, she had only managed to shower and dress. She hadn't even got as far as doing her make up.

'Hi, you look great,' Geoff said as soon as she opened the door.

'Please come in. I'm afraid I'm running a little late.'

'In that case it's just as well I brought this...'

Producing a bottle of white wine from behind his back, Geoff gestured to the drinks cabinet for some glasses.

'Sure, help yourself,' Sasha said, impressed by the thoughtful gesture. 'I won't be long. I just need to finish my hair and throw on some make up.'

Geoff handed Sasha a glass of wine.

'Please take your time. We've got all night.'

'Thanks. Here's to what's been a great cruise.'

Raising his glass to meet hers, he added, '... and to a great friendship.'

Friendship? Sasha thought. *There we have it. He couldn't have made it plainer if he'd tried.*

The restaurant Geoff had booked was amazing. Casanova is one of, if not *the*, top restaurant in Acapulco. By the look of things, it was just as well he had booked ahead. There wasn't a spare table in sight.

With its fabulous views of Acapulco Bay, Geoff couldn't have picked a more romantic setting. *Shame it was only friendship on the cards, not romance,* Sasha reminded herself.

'What?' Geoff smiled at her as she took in the ambience of this elegant and sophisticated venue.

'You might have told me where we were going. I would have made more of an effort.'

Looking her in the eyes, Geoff raised his eyebrows. 'Were you ready tonight when you thought I was taking you somewhere less impressive?'

'Point taken,' Sasha admitted, with a smile. 'Well, thank you anyway. This place looks totally amazing.'

Geoff nodded and gazed at her.

Veal Scaloppini, and linguini pasta with clams, tomatoes and garlic were among many of the speciality dishes served at Casanova, and with only candles for lighting, the ambience couldn't have been more perfect.

After some small talk, Geoff said, 'Sasha, look, there's something I need to talk to you about.'

On hearing those familiar words, Sasha's heart immediately began to race. As calmly as possible she replied, 'Sure, Geoff, what's on your mind?'

With images of Ben getting down on one knee and producing the engagement ring she had locked in the safe onboard, she began to feel weak. *Oh, God, he's one of these; 'I-can't-sleep-with-you-until-I-marry-you sort of guys'.*

Yes, that's it. Now it all makes sense, Sasha confirmed. *Dear God, I've only known him a little over a week, this can't be for real.* Looking around her; the restaurant; the wine; the fact he called her last night after they parted ways; and being introduced to his best friends; the list went on and on.

'Sasha? Are you listening?' said Geoff, interrupting her thoughts. 'This is very important.'

'Yes, sorry, Geoff. You've got my full attention.' *So I leave with one fiancé and come back with another, two weeks later. No big deal, right?* Sasha thought to herself. *Oh, I knew I shouldn't have had that second glass of wine, I can't think straight.*

'I'm sorry to tell you but I'm not exactly in a position to start a new relationship,' Geoff began.

'What?'

'Not *just* yet,' Geoff continued.

'Okay.' Sasha giggled, dismissing his comment, but the look he gave her made her realize he was deadly serious.

Geoff looked suitably shameful. 'So I'm sorry if I've given you the wrong impression.'

Wrong impression!! No. What, seriously? How could you possibly have given me the wrong impression? It's normal to buy wine for girls you're not interested in and take them out to fancy – not to mention extremely expensive – restaurants like this.

'The thing is...' Geoff paused '... my fiancée...'

'Your fiancée! You've got a *fiancée*? You bastard!'

Sasha couldn't help herself, and before she knew it, she was out of her chair, out of the restaurant, in the street and hailing a cab. The street was busy. The lights of the neighbouring restaurants and bars lit the darkness in a soft electric haze. The air was thick with warmth.

Running after her, Geoff yelled, 'Sasha! Wait! Hear me out, for Christ's sake! *You see, maybe this is why I haven't dated since Molly. Women, seriously, why won't they just listen!*

'Save your lies, Geoff, I've heard enough,' she called back.

'No, you haven't. Let me finish, please?'

Geoff quickly closed the gap. He tried to take hold of Sasha's hands as she stood facing him, arms crossed, her eyes smoking but refusing to look directly at him. She finally, reluctantly, allowed Geoff to take a grip of her fingers. He squeezed gently.

'I was going to say,' he continued, a little breathlessly, 'that my fiancée died a few months ago, and I'm not sure I'm ready to move on just yet. Anyway, I like you Sasha. In fact I like you a lot, but this is extremely difficult for me. I don't expect you to understand, and I certainly don't expect you to wait for me but....'

'Oh,' Sasha mumbled, looking rather embarrassed as she took a step back in the street and leaned against a wall in a less confrontational pose. 'I see. I ... I thought that—'

'I know. That's okay. But it's not like that. Look, I'm sorry I haven't been completely honest with you from the start, but you have to understand that I didn't realize until the other night just how much I really liked you.'

Sasha forced a smile. Softened.

'I'm sorry too,' she said, 'for shouting at you and ... well running out the restaurant. The thing is I haven't been completely honest with you either.'

'Oh?' Geoff said, his eyebrows raised and eagerly waiting to hear what Sasha had to say.

'The thing is, I broke up with my own fiancé, Ben, only two weeks ago.'

'Really? Well, well. It seems we have both been a little sparing with the truth. Wouldn't you agree?'

'We were meant to be coming on holiday together. It's a long story, but we basically fell out and I decided to come anyway. On my own.'

'So, it *is* over? Right?' said Geoff.

'Yes, but...'

'But?'

'But *technically* we still live together.'

'Technically?'

'Yes. Technically.'

'And actually?'

'Yes. Actually. Technically... actually...'

'Oh, I see.' Looking puzzled, Geoff asked 'So if you still live with your fiancé, how do you ever propose to move on?'

'We broke up at the airport, before the cruise. It's so embarrassing, I didn't know how I was ever going to tell you.'

'You don't say?'

Sasha nodded her head.

'Well, I think it's pretty cool,' said Geoff.

'Pretty cool? How can breaking up with your fiancé before going on holiday possibly be pretty cool?' Sasha looked at him for some sort of reasoning.

'Well, first of all, it's a very brave thing for a beautiful young woman like you to do on her own.'

'Is it?'

'I think so. And secondly, it's his loss and my gain, right?' Geoff said as he leaned over and gave Sasha a kiss on the cheek.

'Right,' Sasha agreed, now more confused than ever.

Taking her by the hand, Geoff turned and smiled. 'So as for tonight, how about we start over. Let's take a walk and see if we can find somewhere else for a bite to eat. Somewhere without a table next to the door, so it's less easy for you to escape from me, perhaps? Then we could check out that nightclub that everyone is raving about. Paradise, I think it's called.'

Sasha nodded. Smiled. 'Sounds great. Lead the way.'

* * *

'Josh!'

'Yeah, dad?' Josh replied, coming out of the bathroom. He had done his hair regardless of not going to the farewell ball.

'There's someone here to see you.'

245

Josh edged forward. He peered cautiously around his father and was surprised to see what was, to him, the girl of his dreams standing at his cabin door.

'Carly? What are you doing here?'

'I'm sorry I turned you down,' Carly replied.

Embarrassed that his father might have overheard the words 'turned you down', Josh spoke more quickly. 'That's okay; I'm fine about it. Black and white dinners aren't really my thing anyway. So what happened to Kieran? Or whatever his name is?' he added as casually as he could.

Danny looked at them and wandered off.

'I decided to set him up with one of my friends so I could come and find you. I thought that maybe I could convince you to put on a shirt and bow tie and take me to dinner. We're on James and Anna's table. It will be fun but we must hurry.'

Overwhelmed that his evening could be turned around so quickly, Josh called out to the balcony. 'Dad can you look after Carly for a minute while I get ready? I won't be long.'

'Of course I will, Josh. It would be my pleasure. Please, Carly, have a seat.'

'Thank you, Mr Harper.'

Josh rushed away to sort himself out. Danny gave his full attention to Carly.

'So did you like the flowers?' he said without thinking.

'What? They were from *Josh?*' Carly asked, her eyes almost popping out of her head.

'Yes, but that's a secret between you and me, okay?'

'Sure, Mr Harper,' the pretty young girl agreed.

Danny laughed as he watched her pretty little face light up.

Josh and Carly left the cabin in plenty of time, Josh grinning like a Cheshire cat on the inside, but acting cool as a cucumber on the outside as he opened the door for what could possibly turn out to be his first girlfriend ever.

'Enjoy your night, kids,' Danny called after them.

'We will, dad. Don't wait up,' Josh replied, feeling like the man in the family.

Danny was so relieved to see Josh back to his old self that he didn't bother to remind him of his usual curfew. He was growing fast, almost too fast for Danny to understand. One thing was for sure; it will be a different story when it's Katie's turn to go to the farewell ball. *I'll have to lock her in the cabin*, he reminded himself.

Danny sat in the cabin on his own for the first time in days. He had originally planned to spend the night with Josh, which was before the girl of his dreams arrived and swept him off to the 10–13 year old's farewell ball. Katie was settled in the kids centre, as per every other evening, and now Danny was at a loose end. He knew what he wanted to do, but wasn't sure he had the same amount of courage as Carly in turning up at the door of the person you like and asking them out. Although, if a ten year old girl could do it, there was no reason why he couldn't, was there?

Penny had been made pretty much redundant during the cruise, with the kids never away from the kid's club for more than a couple of hours a day, and even that was a struggle to enforce. She had been fantastic support to Danny, and he was determined to keep her as their nanny for as long as possible. The only problem was, he hadn't planned to fall head over heels in love with her during the two weeks onboard. Now he couldn't decide how to handle his feelings.

He had tried hard to resist making a move on his children's nanny, but to ask her out properly was equally nerve wracking. If she knocked him back, he risked spoiling everything for the kids, and they had been through enough after their mother walking out on them months earlier. It was approaching nine o'clock and nearing the end of the cruise. If anything was going to happen, it had to happen soon before they were back home back in the old routine of work and school and travelling all over the place. Surely this was the perfect opportunity to do something?

While Danny lay on his bed contemplating what to do, the phone rang and disturbed his train of thought.

He picked up the receiver. 'Hello?'

'Sorry to disturb you, Danny,' said a voice; a very familiar voice, 'but I just called to say that if you want to go ashore in Acapulco, I'll stay onboard and look after the children.'

Oh God it's her, Danny thought. *That wasn't meant to happen.*

'That's very kind, Penny, but I'm not too bothered about going off.'

There was a pause.

Then, 'Okay. Well if you change your mind, I'll be in my cabin.'

'Thanks. I'll remember that.' He paused and swallowed quickly. 'So you're not actually doing anything tonight?'

'No, nothing in particular. I'm all packed for tomorrow. How about you?'

'Yeah, we're all packed and ready to go, too. Look, I was just wondering, Josh is off out and I don't need to collect Katie until 2.00am. Do you... you know, fancy getting a pizza or something?'

'Sounds great,' said Penny without hesitation. 'Yes. Just let me get changed quickly and I'll come round. Okay?'

'Yes. Great. I'll be waiting.'

Danny hung up and gazed at the phone. He wasn't sure where the courage came from, but he had done it now, so the rest was going to be easy. Twenty minutes later, Penny was standing at the door dressed in a pair of tight blue jeans and a white blouse, which showed off her golden tan perfectly.

'You look great,' Danny said. 'You really have got a fantastic colour.'

'Thanks. You're really dark too.'

Collecting two beers from the fridge, Danny handed one to Penny and, without thinking too much about what he was going to say, started chatting casually. Well, as casually as he could given the fact that he was alone with Penny in his cabin, and she looked unbelievably attractive.

'Sorry,' said Penny, holding out the beer, 'but I don't drink this.'

'No? Oh. Okay. All the more for me.'

Penny nodded and smiled.

He took the beer and put it back.

'By the way, I've had an idea,' he said. Taking a deep breath, Danny looked at this beauty that was now perched on the end of his bed. 'How do you fancy ordering pizza from room service, putting on some of Josh's terrible music and getting horribly drunk with the leftovers from the mini bar?'

'Sounds good to me,' Penny agreed immediately. 'I'll order the pizza, if you get me something nice to drink.'

Three slices of pizza, two Coronas, one wine cooler and a blue lagoon later, while Penny was on her second glass of red wine, Danny had built up the courage to let Penny know how he felt. As the music slowed down, they sat next to each other in a relaxed state. Danny reminded himself of Josh and Carly. If she hadn't had the courage to come round, Josh would still be sitting in the cabin watching TV instead of being out on his first ever date.

'Penny, I've got something to say to you.'

'Sure, Danny, what is it?' Penny asked, now sprawled across the bed looking sexier than ever. Danny's heartbeat quickened. The palms of his hands were sweaty. He took a deep breath and then said, 'I like you a lot, you know.' He paused, waiting for a reaction, but there wasn't one. 'I mean, I like you more than just as our *nanny*.'

Penny's face still gave nothing away, not for a second. She couldn't believe what she was hearing.

'Okay, let me put this to you a little planer. The thing is, I've been thinking and... well, I was wondering if you would consider us being... you know, together, like a couple?'

Penny couldn't let Danny suffer any longer. She could tell how nervous he was about asking her out. Without saying a word she leaned forward and kissed him on the lips.

'Is that a yes?' Danny said. He needed confirmation.

Penny smiled and put her hand on his thigh to support her while she moved in for another kiss. This time Danny put his hand on her waist and moved her effortlessly into the middle of the bed. Danny's body was pressed against Penny's in a way that nothing was ever going to separate them, their lips pressed hard against each other's. The pair were so engrossed in each other, they didn't hear the key in the lock. As the door opened, they both looked round to see Josh standing at the end of the bed with a huge grin on his face

'Yes! I *knew* it would happen,' he laughed. 'Where's Katie? I want to tell her the good news.'

'Not so fast, Josh. You weren't meant to see that,' Penny said, doing up the top button of her blouse. She didn't know where to look, but the excitement of what had just happened completely outweighed the embarrassment. Josh, not wanting to get in the way of his dad and Penny getting together, volunteered to go straight to bed and out of the way.

'Sorry about that,' Danny whispered into Penny's ear. 'I completely forgot the time.'

'No problem. He was bound to find out sooner or later.'

'But not like that.'

Penny smiled. 'No, I suppose not.'

They got up and went out into the corridor and closed the cabin door.

'So long as you are sure about us?' Danny said, as he held Penny in his arms.

'I've never been more certain about anything in my life.'

'Me too.' Danny grinned. 'I suppose I'd better go and collect Katie. It's early yet, but hey, it's been one hell of a night all round. Huh?'

Penny nodded. Smiled. Kissed him again.

✻ ✻ ✻

After aborting dinner at Casanova, Geoff spent half the night telling Sasha about Molly, and Sasha spent the other half talking about Ben. They talked themselves round in circles, and they knew their previous relationships were over. But there was no indication from either party that they were going to take theirs any further. At 4.00am, Geoff and Sasha climbed into a little white and blue VW Beetle taxi and requested to be taken back to Ocean Magic.

It was very late, but there was no sign whatsoever of the bars and clubs closing. But they had both had more than enough. Geoff gave Sasha a helping hand up the gangway and, with a look of disapproval from the security staff, he offered her cruise card to be swiped into the system indicating she was back onboard.

Geoff then gave Sasha a helping hand back to her cabin, where he removed her shoes and hair clip and tucked her into bed. She had had one busy day, what with poor old Mr Cockburn, and then finding out Geoff didn't actually intend to start a relationship, and tomorrow wasn't looking too bright either, having to go home and face Ben.

The following morning it was clear that their decision to get drunk together, and to forget their problems existed, was not as clever as it had seemed at the time. Geoff had practically packed, but the thought hadn't even crossed Sasha's mind. She woke to find her wardrobes all still full, and various random belongings scattered throughout the cabin. With only an hour to go until disembarkation, she called Geoff in the hope he would be slightly more organised than she was. As Geoff opened the door, Sasha had a strong black coffee waiting for him. The way he felt, it was almost appreciated as much as the wine he brought round the night before.

'That's us then. Let's go home,' Geoff announced as they finished up.

'Guess so,' Sasha agreed.

Two Alka – Seltzers, and an energy drink or three at the airport, and they were almost back to their normal selves. In their own ways, they had both tacitly decided not to show any sort of affection to one another from now on, but fully intended to stay in touch. Geoff hadn't intended to call things off completely with Sasha, but when he found out about Ben, he felt compelled to.

While Sasha wasn't exactly sure what Geoff's intentions were, she decided that he wasn't ready for another relationship. Unfortunately, this meant neither was prepared to try and keep things going for fear of being rejected.

Chapter 15

Gatwick

'Thank you for flying British Airways. Please remain seated with your seat belts securely fastened until the aircraft comes to a complete standstill. Do take care when opening the overhead lockers as some items my have shifted during the flight. From myself Russell Anderson and all the crew, have a safe onward journey. Thank you and good afternoon,' the captain concluded, as the plane taxied into position at Gatwick North Terminal.

Geoff sighed as he took his backpack out of the overhead locker. 'Well, that's us then.'

'Guess so,' Sasha agreed, rolling her eyes. 'Back to reality. Great.'

'Just a minute, Sasha. I'll get it for you,' said Geoff.

Realizing that she didn't have a hope in hell of recovering her hand luggage, Sasha took a step back.

'Thanks. I think I was lucky to get away with that at check in.'

'That's true, but you are female after all,' said Geoff, trying to lighten the atmosphere a little. Seriously, looking around, you would have thought the planeload of Ocean Magic passengers were about to engage in a year's community service.

Arriving at the baggage carousel, the tense downbeat atmosphere continued. Among the crowds of tanned but distressed looking passengers, Kris and Megan fought their way forward to collect their luggage.

'Leave it, Megan,' said Kris. 'Just stand by the trolley and I'll get the suitcases.'

Megan made her way back out of the chaos. 'Fine.'

'Sorry, Meg.'

Megan threw her suitcases onto another trolley. 'Sorry? Are you really, Kris?'

'Jesus, Megan. What's got into you?'

'You just don't get it, do you?'

'Get what, Megan? What the hell are you taking about? I was only trying to help. God! You've been in a foul temper for days. What is *up* with you'?

'What's up with me?' Megan looked Kris in the eye. 'Seriously, you don't believe for a second I bought your whole story about helping that girl Penny out with her cabin key, do you? I saw you at the deck party, Kris. I knew you were lying to me, and that night confirmed it. You're a lying bastard, and I want nothing more to do with you. It's over between us.' Sobbing uncontrollably, Megan started to walk away, then stopped suddenly she turned and added. 'You can make your own way from here. I'm taking the car, and don't expect I will have calmed down by the time I get home. I can't put it any planer. It's over between us, and I mean every word of it. Have a nice life, Kris.'

* * *

'I'll give you a ride home, Sasha, if you don't have any other plans. I first have to remember where I parked the car.'

'That would be great, thanks. But are you sure you don't mind?'

Loading both suitcases onto a trolley, Geoff turned and smiled. 'Not at all. I have a rough idea of where you live, but you'll have to keep me right.'

'Thanks, really. But I don't think it's such a good idea.'

'Why? Don't you know where you live?'

'No, it's not that.'

'Well *what* is it then?' Geoff asked, perplexed by Sasha's sudden change of heart.

Damn. He was hoping for one more kiss before they went their separate ways. But it looked like he'd have to do it here instead. Not ideal, but it was better than nothing.

Moving in for what he had planned as the kiss of his life, Sasha saw him coming and reached out her arm and pushed him away.

'What's wrong?' said Geoff.

Sasha discreetly jerked her head over to the right.

'The tall, dark haired guy over there,' she said. 'That's what's wrong. That's Ben.'

Trying not to show his feelings, Ben swallowed hard when he saw Sasha walking towards him with what could only be described as serious competition.

Stopping short of Sasha's fiancé, Geoff typed his phone number into her phone and kissed her gently on the cheek.

Scribbling her home phone number down as quickly as possible, Sasha pushed it into Geoff's jacket pocket.

Right, well now that the kiss he had spent the whole flight home thinking about was definitely not going to take place, Geoff off-loaded his suitcase, leaving Sasha with the trolley, and made his way out through arrivals.

Moving in body, but not in mind, Sasha reached Ben. The air between them was electric.

Trying desperately to pretend he hadn't noticed the tall, dark, extremely handsome man who had just exchanged phone numbers with his fiancé, Ben took Sasha in his arms and kissed her passionately on the lips. Finally, freeing herself from his grasp and taking a few steps back, Sasha looked Ben in the eyes.

'I didn't expect you to come and meet me.'

'Of course you did, honey. You didn't think I'd leave you to make your own way home, did you?'

Well, considering you left me to go on holiday alone, then making my own way home from the airport somehow doesn't feel particularly daunting...

'So how are you feeling?' Sasha asked, keen to know the details of Ben's medical condition. 'When did you get out of hospital?'

'I'm fine I got out a couple of days a go. And I've got some great news that I couldn't wait to tell you.'

'Great news, huh?'

'That's it. You'll want to hear this.'

Sasha considered that and breathed slowly and deeply.

'Look, Ben,' she said at length. 'I'm tired. I've just got off an eight-hour flight after a very late night out... in... no; I mean I didn't get in till late. Anyway, I just want to go home. So if you don't mind we can talk later.'

Ben brought his hands together and flashed his teeth. 'Excellent, that's exactly what I thought you'd say. So I hope you don't mind, but I've booked us a table at Luigi's. We can sit and discuss things over his gorgeous signature pasta. We'll have plenty of time for you to go home and freshen up before we go out. Then we've got lots to talk about.'

Oh great. A night out after two weeks of constant eating, drinking and partying was the last thing Sasha had in mind. A long hot bubble bath and an early night were much more what she had in mind. But the sooner she and Ben talked, the sooner they could go their separate ways. Although, seeing Ben again had caused some unexpected feelings to arise. He had definitely lost weight, and was looking incredible. His enthusiastic manner and new energy for life was also appealing to Sasha. This was a side of Ben she hadn't witnessed before.

It was worrying.

Entering the house for the first time in two weeks felt a little strange at first but after unpacking and reluctantly settling for a shower, in the hope of making herself feel a little more alive, Ben had selected some romantic music and uncorked a bottle of wine. *Oh what the hell,* she thought, accepting a glass. *What difference will one more glass of wine make after all I managed to put away during the cruise? No difference at all.*

Arriving at Luigi's also felt a little bit strange to Sasha, she and Ben had always arrived at the restaurant laughing or playfully flirting with one another, tonight the atmosphere couldn't have been more opposite.

'Well, well. It's been a while. And how are my favourite couple this evening?' said Luigi, greeting the pair as he always did.

'Very well, thanks,' Ben replied, looking around at the other tables, nearly all of them full.

Sasha merely smiled at her old friend and waited to be seated.

'Well you're in luck,' said Luigi. 'Your favourite table is free. I must have secretly known you were coming.' He glanced at Sasha. 'And someone's got a lovely tan, if I may say so. Been somewhere nice?'

'Yes.' Sasha smiled, accepting the chair Luigi pulled out for her. 'The Caribbean, actually.'

'Oh yes? Well it's alright for some, is it not, Mr Benjamin?' Luigi glanced at Sasha. 'That job of yours has you jet setting all over the place. It must be great to be paid to visit all those wonderful places.'

There was heavy emphasis on the word 'wonderful'.

Catching Ben's eyes that were screaming: *Oh God, please don't tell him it wasn't business he's bound to ask why I wasn't with you* Sasha looked up and said, 'Yes, I am very lucky.'

'There we are.' Now standing back from the table and admiring his romantic candle setting, Luigi signalled to one of the waitresses to bring two menus.

'What can I get you to drink then, Sasha?'

'Just some sparking water will be fine.'

'Nonsense,' said Ben. 'We'll have the usual. A bottle of Sancerre and some sparking water as well. Thanks Luigi.'

'My pleasure, Mr Benjamin. I'll be right back. Rose will be across in a moment to read you the specials. But if you ask me, the seafood linguini really is something *verrrrry* special indeed.'

When Luigi was gone, Ben and Sasha sat in silence for a moment forcing eye contact and smiling perfunctorily. In the background, Jamie Cullum was singing something vaguely familiar. The air was rich with the smells of cooked cheese, onions and bread. Sounds of laughter rang out from one of the corners. Someone was certainly having a good time.

'So, this is nice,' Ben said presently. 'I can't remember the last time we were here. It was so long ago.'

'Your birthday,' said Sasha.

'Really? Well, that was a long time ago. We must make more of an effort and dine out more.'

Sasha said nothing, and they sat in awkward silence again. A few minutes later Luigi returned.

'And here we are,' he said. 'One bottle of Sancerre. Now which of my favourite customers would like to taste it?'

'I'm sure it will be fine,' Sasha replied. 'You can just pour it, Luigi.'

Luigi gave her a hurt look, then shrugged and did as requested. He filled both glasses, left the bottle and backed away.

When he was gone, Ben said, 'That was a bit rude of you, Sasha.'

'You think so?'

'Yes. I do.'

She gazed at her wine glass and considered that, then nodded.

'Yes. You're right. I'm sorry. I guess I'm just a bit tired. I didn't get any sleep on the flight, and my body clock is a little out.'

Ben searched her face and smiled. He picked up his wine glass. 'That's okay. Cheers.'

'Cheers.' Sasha replied, raising her glass to meet Ben's.

After hearing the specials Sasha decided the seafood linguini sounded fine. It saved having to bother reading the menu, but Ben was a little more particular in choosing what he wanted for dinner and read the entire menu through twice anyway before settling for Luigi's choice.

'What?' he asked, sensing Sasha's discontent?

'Nothing. It's fine.' She sipped her wine, and decided that it was very good, which just made her feel even more guilty about her rudeness to Luigi. 'Now what is it you've got to tell me?'

Ben rested his elbows on the table and edged forward. 'Well, you know how I applied for the manager's position at Lawson's and Co?'

'Yes.'

'Well...'

'You got it?'

'No, not exactly.'

'What do you mean 'not exactly'? You either did or you didn't'

Ben smiled.

'Well, I went to all the interviews. There were three in the end. And guess what?'

'Ben, I'm too tired to play games.'

'Of course you are. And I'm sorry. What I'm trying to say is that I didn't get offered the manager's position. I was offered the *regional* manager's position.'

'Wow, that's great. Congratulations. I'm really happy for you, Ben.'

'But wait, it gets better. I'm on a salary increase of 25%, with annual share options worth a fortune. I also get a company car of my choice up to the value of £45,000, and BUPA healthcare for my family and me. Seriously, the list just goes on and on.'

Sasha sipped more wine and considered all that. 'That's great, Ben. I'm delighted for you. Really.'

'So, I was thinking, to make up for me being a complete jerk over missing the flight, how about we take a holiday together before I start my new job?'

'A holiday?'

'Yes. It's what normal people do normally.'

Shuffling uncomfortably in her chair, Sasha looked across the table at her ex fiancé.

'Ben, aren't you forgetting something?'

'Yeah, yeah I know, the wedding. Listen, one thing at a time, honey. I was thinking we could plan it for the spring.'

'No, Ben. I meant us. We're not even engaged, remember? Now you're talking about big pay raises, expensive cars and a wedding. I just don't think I'm ready for all this.'

'Is that right?'

'Yes, Ben. That's right.'

'Well that's just the bloody problem with you, isn't it?'

'Excuse me?'

'I'm sorry my big promotion is a problem for you time-wise. I'll tell them to hold onto the job for me, shall I? I mean, what suits you, Sasha? Three or maybe four months time. Will you be ready then? No probably not!' Pausing the conversation while their dinner was brought to the table, Ben thanked Rose while Sasha forced a smile.

'It's not that, Ben. It's just that I've spent the last two weeks away trying to sort my life out, and... well, get over you.'

'I know! And it looks like you managed quite well, if you ask me.'

'And what's that supposed to mean?'

'You know *exactly* what I'm talking about.'

'No, I don't actually. I don't have a clue. If you're talking about Geoff—

Ben's eyes narrowed.

'—We're just friends. We met on the cruise, and we hung out on the odd occasion. I also met a lot of other people *and* I didn't sleep with any of *them* either, if that's what you're getting at.'

'Did I say that?'

'You didn't have to.'

'Look, Sasha. All I'm trying to do is make up for leaving you at the airport—and just for the record, I thought it was a very brave move going on a cruise on your own. Quite frankly, I couldn't have done it.'

'Well it wasn't easy,' Sasha said, blushing slightly as she recalled all the good memories.

'I'm sure it wasn't. Do you want to talk about it?'

'No, not right now, thanks.' Twirling another mouthful of linguini round on her fork, Sasha realized all she had been doing was playing with her food, while Ben hadn't even touched his. 'Look Ben, this is no good.'

At that moment, Luigi approached the table and caught the tail end of the conversation.

'No good?' he said, picking up the threads. 'You're calling my speciality seafood linguini no good? Seriously, you have no appreciation for quality food.'

'No honestly, Luigi. Your linguini is *great*, perfect in fact.'

'How would you know? You have not even tried it.'

'I have, honestly. And it's lovely,' Sasha admitted, looking suitably embarrassed. 'I'm just not very hungry, that's all.'

'And what about you?' Luigi asked, throwing Ben an explain yourself please look.

'Sorry, Luigi, we just got carried away in conversation, that's all.'

'Ah, how wonderful. Young love. You can't eat, you can't sleep, it's beautiful. I tell you what, I'll make you a Luigi special pizza to take home, then you can enjoy it later.' Winking enthusiastically at Ben, he added, '... you know, once you've had the chance to work up an appetite.'

Luigi walked away looking pleased with himself. Shaking her head, Sasha poured them both a second glass of wine.

'He never changes, does he?'

'No, but to be honest I was probably more in the mood for pizza anyway,' said Ben.

'Me too,' Sasha added, smiling back at him.

* * *

Home sweet home, Geoff thought to himself as he turned the key in the lock.

Discarding his suitcase immediately after he opened the door, he turned on the lights. The walls, the floor, the ceiling and the furniture gazed back at him. He absolutely detested the feeling of walking into an empty, quiet, apartment and had stopped off at Starbucks for a couple of hours before he braved the inevitable. Desperate for some background noise, he reached for the TV remote control. In doing so, he knocked over the pile of mail that was waiting for him.

Ms Molly Charleston.

Ms M Charleston.

Molly Charleston.

God, why won't they stop sending her mail! She's dead for Christ's sake. She's not going to need any new shoes from Jimmy Choo, or a new credit card for that matter – unless there's a corner store just opened up on the other side. Man, some people can be so insensitive...

Opening the fridge door, he banged his head against it several times before locating his last bottle of beer. What the hell, he thought. Finally giving in, and throwing himself down on his large leather sofa, he sat back and began to relax.

Sasha. She could have been my second chance at love, but I guess I well and truly blew that. She's probably back with Ben by now, engaged to be married once again. She was so nice. God, I'm such a damn fool for letting her go, I should have been more honest with her.

His mobile phone interrupted his thoughts. Racing to the breakfast bar, Geoff found his mobile under the pile of mail.

'Sasha?'

'Nope, not since last time I checked,' said a voice. A male voice.

'Very funny, Rick,' said Geoff, his face colouring. 'What's up?'

'Nothing, really. I just thought I'd give you a ring and make sure you got home okay.'

'Yeah, I'm home alright.'

'What's wrong, man? You sound really off.'

'Do I?'

'Yes.'

'Well it's nothing really. Nothing important, that is.'

What did it matter anyway? Rick had already sensed something was wrong.

'When a man says it not important, it's probably important. So what's going on?'

There was a long pause. Then Geoff said, 'Well, you didn't know this, and don't tell Chris whatever you do. Okay?'

'I won't. What is it?'

'Sasha is e-n-g-a-g-e-d.'

There was another silence as Rick decoded that.

'Engaged?' he said at last.

'Uh huh?'

'As in to-be-married?'

'Is there another kind?'

'Oh. Great.'

'Well, she *was* engaged.'

'Was?'

'Or maybe is.'

'Is? Or was? Which is it?'

'I honestly don't know for sure. But she wasn't when we met.'

'Man, she doesn't waste any time. We've only just got home. She could be hitched with three kids by now. Grand kids even.'

'Rick, this is serious.'

'I know. Sorry. So run this by me again. It must be the jet lag or something. I'm finding it really difficult to keep up.'

'She was meant to be going on the cruise with her fiancé, Ben, but they fell out at the airport before they left. Ben – that's his name – abandoned her, and she booked another flight and went on the cruise regardless.'

'I see.'

'So she and I meet and get on great, but then there's the whole Molly thing.'

'Molly. Right. We can come back to that one.'

'Yeah. So we meet, and she's great. And we hit it off, big style. I like her, and she likes me. Meanwhile, Ben breaks off the engagement – although I think that might have happened before we met.' Geoff thought back to the conversation when Sasha had opened up to him. 'Yeah, it did. Definitely. I remember her telling me it was early on in the cruise.'

'Okay. The clouds of confusion are dissolving. But how is this guy a problem now?'

'He turned up at the airport.'

'Oh.'

'Yeah. Exactly. And fully intending to get Sasha back.'

'Did he punch you?'

'No.'

'Did you punch him?'

'Are you going to take this seriously?'

'I'm trying. But there's a joke in there somewhere.'

Geoff said nothing.

'So what are you going to do?' said Rick.

'Well, what *can* I do? I've got her number, but I can't possibly call her house. What if *he* answers?'

Rick made a clucking noise on the line.

'No, you're right about that. Did you give her your number?'

'Yes. I typed it into her phone.'

'Right. Well, sorry mate, but the only thing you can do is wait for her call.'

'That's your best advice?'

'That's it. But I'll work on it some more.'

Geoff nodded and frowned. 'Yep. I guess you're right. I'll wait.'

'Just don't hold your breath,' said Rick, hanging up.

'Do you want the last slice of pizza?' Ben asked, hoping the answer would be no.

'No, thanks. You go ahead,' Sasha replied.

'Are you sure? We can share it if you like?'

'I'm certain. Really, please carry on,' Sasha insisted wishing he would stop being so nice.

'Okay.' He stuffed the last slice of pizza into his mouth like he hadn't seen food in months. Then he said, 'Our conversation earlier didn't get off to the best start, did it?'

Sasha shook her head dolefully.

'So can we talk things through? Clear the air a bit?'

'I think we really need to. But maybe we'll wait till you finished eating.' Sasha remembered a lunch she had enjoyed with Geoff. He had used a knife and fork to eat his pizza, not his fingers. That was a lot more appealing, and the contrast was stark.

Ben took the hint and munched away and swallowed and looked satisfied.

'Okay. Finished,' he announced, speaking as if he was a five-year-old kid looking for permission to leave the table. 'Right, well, I've been thinking that—'

He stopped speaking suddenly and got up from the sofa. He walked over to the sideboard and opened the top drawer and collected an envelope. Walking back towards Sasha he handed it to her and urged her to open it.

'When I was ill, it gave me a real shock. It made me realize that life is too short to not be with the one you love. So I know I said we should wait until the spring to get married, but now I realize that I don't want to. Look, Sasha, I want to marry you as soon as possible, so I hope you don't mind but I've taken the liberty of booking the Hilton for our reception. I've booked the church too. Granted I had to pull a favour or two, but my parents helped out and it's all sorted, so what do you think?'

'What do I think?' Sasha gazed at him, her jaw unhinging. He looked as excited as she'd ever seen him. Discarding the envelope with the wedding brochure for the Hilton 'Are you serious?'

'Of *course* I'm serious. Why do you think I went to all this trouble?'

'Well I'm terribly sorry you did, Ben. But you can't just spring a wedding on someone like this. When *is* the big day by the way? Did it even cross your mind I might be out of the country with work?'

'Oh. I take it from your tone, you're not too pleased?'

Sasha said nothing.

'Well for the record, I checked with your work and they said it would be fine.'

'They did, did they?'

'Yes, they did.'

'Look, Ben. This is all too much. You have to stop. You have to at least slow down.'

'Slow down? Sasha, if we slow down anymore we'll be *eighty* before we get married, and even then I'm not sure you would go through with it.'

'That's not fair.'

'Fair? Who said anything about fair? The truth is, I love you, Sasha. I've *always* loved you, but I'm not going to hang around my whole life waiting for you to decide if you want to marry me or not. I'm sorry for what happened two weeks ago at the airport. I've apologised for that already, and I'll apologise for it every day of my life if you'll lower your barriers and consider marrying me.' He made a face. 'There, that's it. That's all I have to say on the matter. It's yes, or no, as simple as that. I'll give you until the morning to decide, and then we'll take things from there. So goodnight. I'll be in the spare room.'

Ben gazed at her a moment longer, then stormed out and slammed the sitting room door.

Chapter 16

That's it then, Sasha confirmed, as she sealed and labelled the last box. Looking around the living room for the final time, she surveyed the brand new Philips home entertainment system that she and Ben had agreed to buy each other for Christmas, the Bang and Olufsen stereo, and the dark brown leather three-piece suite. There was no doubt about it; Ben had certainly ended up better off.

One by one she moved several bags and boxes into the hallway ready for the taxi driver to load into the car when he arrived. With two hours to spare, and nothing to do but hang around waiting for the inevitable, Sasha decided she might as well bring the taxi forward and get things moving. The decision to leave had been made, and there was no turning back.

'Sorry love, we can't,' the receptionist at the taxi station informed her. 'We're chock-a-block today, I'm afraid. But it won't be long now, love. The driver will be with you in just under two hours.'

Two hours?

'Fine,' Sasha agreed reluctantly. 'Two o'clock, and he mustn't be a second late.'

She hung up and gazed at the phone until she heard a familiar thud in the hallway. The twelve o'clock post. The postman was always late on a Saturday. *Guess I better see if there's anything for me*, Sasha thought to herself. Picking up the pile of mail, she sieved her way through it. *Electricity bill? Nope not my concern any more. Sorry, Ben, but this one's for you. Telephone bill? House insurance? My my, Ben. It's not your lucky day, is it?*

265

She looked at the next letter.

Ms S Carter?

This one was for her, though at first glance the handwriting on the envelope looked a little like her father's. Opening the envelope, her face lit up for the first time in days. Inside was a card, and on the front of that card was a picture of Ocean Magic tied up alongside in Barbados. The ship looked clean and new and elegant. A hotel for cruising the seas in splendour and comfort.

Wondering who the card could be from, she opened it quickly and read the very fine print:

Dear Sasha,

Thank you for being there for me when I desperately needed someone to talk to. I'm sorry I left without saying goodbye. There was a mix up with the flights and I ended up going early, so I'm sorry I missed you. I requested your address through Tom, the wine guy. I knew if anyone could get it for me, Tom could. I hope you don't mind me doing so.

Take good care of yourself

Love William.

William, Sasha thought. *What a thoughtful thing to do.* Wiping a tear from her eye, she smiled. *I'm so glad he's OK.*

Hearing a key in the lock, Sasha knew it was Ben. He had been out all morning allowing her space and time to pack. During the last week, things had been quite uncomfortable. They had only just managed to stay in the same house together and act civilly towards one another.

Ben was finding the break-up unbearable. He wasn't eating properly, and certainly wasn't sleeping. But he had tried everything he could think of to get Sasha back -with the exception of getting down on his hands and knees and begging.

Upon entering the living room, he shook his head in despair. 'You're really going then? You're really leaving me?' There were tears in his eyes.

'No, Ben. It's not like that. Come on, you know as well as I do that we've just grown apart.'

'No, Sasha. I don't know that. That's what you keep telling me. But I don't believe it's the case.'

'Ben, we've been through this,' Sasha said, barely keeping control of her emotions.

'Have we?'

'Yes. You know we have.'

'Do you want to know what I really think?' Ben said, a quaver in his voice.

'Okay. What do you *really* think the problem is between us?'

'It's Geoff. That guy you met on the cruise. If it wasn't for him, you would have come back to me and we would be getting married,' Ben said, unable to look Sasha in the eye.

'Nonsense! That's ridiculous.'

'Is it though, Sasha? Is it really all *that* ridiculous? Because it's not to me. It makes perfect sense.'

Not knowing where to look, and wishing the taxi could have come earlier as she had requested, Sasha turned to Ben and took his hand. She smiled thinly as she searched for the right words.

'Don't do this, Ben. Let's not fall out and ruin all the good times we've had together. Please, we will always be friends.'

'Just friends?'

'Yes. Just friends. But *good* friends.'

'Fine,' Ben agreed reluctantly, wiping away another tear.

She held his hand a moment longer, then released it and got up and made her way to the bathroom. She was now also beginning to well up.

As she left the room, Ben immediately noticed her bag lying open on the sideboard. He zoomed in on it, his eyebrows arching.

What was his name again? He asked himself. *That bloke? Yes, Geoff, as if I need reminding...*

He got up and sidled over to the bag, delved inside and grabbed the phone and unlocked it. Immediately he began scrolling through the contacts menu.

Alex, Angela, Claire, Caroline, Elle, Fiona, Geoff. Excellent. Got ya! Ben smiled to himself and began searching for the details. On hearing the toilet flush, he didn't have time to delete the whole of Geoff's number. It would also have been too obvious. Instead he decided to delete only the middle digit before locking the phone and placing it back in Sasha's bag.

Two seconds later, Sasha re-entered the room.

'Think that's your taxi just pulled up,' said Ben. 'I'll give you a hand with your stuff.'

'Thank you.' Sasha acknowledged the kind gesture, and flashed Ben a smile.

As the last bag was placed in the back of the taxi, Sasha could hear the house phone ring out. But it was Ben's phone now. She didn't have the right to answer it anymore. In future, people would have to reach her on her mobile – well, at least until she got herself settled. Then she could install her own landline.

Reaching into the fridge for a cold beer, the first of many that Ben had planned to drink that afternoon, the phone rang for a second time. Lifting the receiver, Ben waited for someone to speak. *I knew she couldn't go through with it, I knew she would come crawling back,* he thought to himself, laughing inside.

'Hello, can I speak to Sasha please?' a voice asked. A male voice.

'Who is this?' said Ben.

'My name's Geoff. I met Sasha on a cruise a couple of weeks ago and I just thought I'd call for a chat, that's all.'

'Well you're too late, mate. Sasha doesn't live here anymore,' Ben, wrenching on the inside but sounding as confident as ever, replied.

'Do you have another number I can reach her on?' said the voice on the line. 'Her mobile perhaps?'

'If I did, do you really think I would give it to you?'

There was a pause. Then; 'Fine. Thanks for you help.'

Not even slightly fazed by Ben's arrogance, Geoff hung up. All he could do now was wait for Sasha to call him.

Her new home was quite different. There was only so much you could get last minute, and this really was a last minute arrangement. Sasha had taken a rental on a small apartment on the east side of Hammersmith; a relatively safe area, that had taken priority over a nicer apartment in Knightsbridge, for example. If money was no object, Knightsbridge was her ideal location. But deep down she knew that the timing wasn't right, and now simply was not the time to make a rash decision.

The entrance hall was dark. Three of the four lights on the stairwell were out. As she opened the door, she could tell immediately that the last occupant had been a smoker. The small entrance hall led into the living area. Surprisingly, it was reasonably well decorated with an open plan living-kitchen-dining area. That was probably the cause of the food smell lingering from the previous occupant's cooking, but to Sasha it was all fairly superficial. Nothing that a few scented candles, and a bag or two of pot-pourri, wouldn't sort out.

The bedroom was small, but cosy, with a small adjacent bathroom. At least it was presentable enough, if not cleaned to the standard she was used to. Next, was a small coved area of wall with a perfectly sized desk that looked ideal as a separate study. This was the selling point of the apartment. Sasha could picture herself working away, late at night, finishing articles to meet the usually pressing deadlines. Her job was extremely challenging, although she cherished the satisfaction of yet another one of her articles being published. As it approached 4.00pm, she decided to abandon the unpacking until the following day and picked up the phone to call Geoff. All week she had been intending to get around to it.

A little nervous at the thought of speaking to him again, she took a deep breath and pressed the call button. A second or two later the tone that rang out was short and sharp, followed by a woman in a high- pitched voice saying: *The number you have dialled has not been recognised please try again.*

After trying for the third time, Sasha realized that the number Geoff had given her was not his mobile number. With that, Sasha compared the number to hers, and quickly realized that Geoff's saved number was one digit short. Feeling a strong sense of disappointment, followed by a feeling of being cheated, she slammed the phone on the table. *Geoff must have given me the wrong number on purpose; he must have only been after a holiday fling after all. Then, when he realized we lived so close to one another, he bottled out and gave me a wrong number. What a bastard. To think I actually really liked that guy.*

Answering her phone on the fifth ring, and praying it wasn't Ben begging her to come home, Sasha waited for the caller to speak. It couldn't be Geoff, could it? Sasha hoped for a brief second, before remembering she hadn't given him her mobile number.

'Sasha? It's your Mother.'

Oh great. This is all I need.

'Sasha, I can't believe you've been home for over a week and you haven't called.'

'The phone works in both directions, mum.'

'Sasha, what's wrong with you? For heaven's sake. I've just called the house, and Ben tells me you've left him. The poor man is distraught. Tell me this is some kind of joke?'

'It's no joke, mum. We've split up.'

'Split up! How *can* you have split up? You're engaged to be *married*, for heaven's sake.'

Sasha said nothing. She merely closed her eyes and began a slow mental count.

'You see,' continued her mother. 'That's exactly the problem with young couples today. They give up too easily. Marriage takes commitment.'

'Spare me the lecture, mum. There's not going to be a wedding.'

'You won't get many chances like this, Sasha. Ben is a one-off. If you blow your chances with him, you'll end up on your own. You're *thirty-one* for goodness sake.'

'I know.'

'Do you want to end up a spinster?'

'Yes, mum. Right now, that is *exactly* what I'd like.' Wishing she hadn't answered the phone, Sasha pressed the phone against her ear and began wandering round her new home looking in the cupboards and checking that the fridge was turned on.

'Where are you staying anyway? Ben mentioned something about a flat or something?'

'It's an apartment, mum, and it's quite nice.'

Even as she said those words, she was cringing as she opened the fridge door and saw that it needed a serious scrub out before anything could go near it.

'Well, there was no need for you to get a place of your own. I have more than enough room for you to stay here.'

'I'm only renting and, like you said, I am thirty-one. I don't really think that moving back in with my mum would be appropriate.'

There was silence on the line for a few seconds.

'So, when can I see you?' said her mother. 'Give me your new address and I'll come over with a casserole. I'm quite sure you haven't eaten.'

'No, I'm okay, thanks. One of my friends is coming over. We'll get a take-away, or we'll pop out for something a bit later. Look, if you want, I'll meet you for coffee tomorrow. But I've got a lot to do now, so let's make it eleven o'clock at Nico's coffee house. Okay?'

'Fine, I'll see you tomorrow – and you better not be too skinny, otherwise I'm moving in with you to look after you. Understand?'

'Yes, I understand.' Sasha rolled her eyes. 'See you tomorrow then.'

'Oh, Sasha, that friend of yours who's coming over. It's not Geoff by any chance, is it?'

Sasha shook her head at the cheek of her mother, and said nothing in reply.

Mrs Carter continued. 'Yes that's right, Ben has told me everything.'

Sasha hung up.

Thinking she had had enough for one day, but realizing the boxes weren't going to sort out themselves, she moved them into the appropriate rooms and started unpacking.

By 11.00pm, the apartment was looking a little more homely. It still needed a deep clean, but that could wait until tomorrow, or so Sasha told herself as she climbed into bed.

Horizon Fitness Centre, on Jacob's Street. Sitting bolt upright in bed, it was 2.30am, and it had just come to her. Horizon Fitness was the gym Geoff used every day before work. She wasn't familiar with it, but was certain this was her breakthrough to get in touch with him. It seemed like such a stab in the dark, but there was no way she was going to sit back and accept he had conned her with a fake phone number. She would at the very least track him down and confront him. Maybe just maybe it wasn't intentional at all they were both a bit flustered at the airport and he was in a hurry to type in his number, there was still hope Sasha told herself.

It was late, and Geoff knew it was a bad idea to ask his local for a 'lock in' for him and his mates. But what the hell? *Either that, or I go home to an empty apartment and sit and watch whatever rubbish happens to be on the TV.* It had been a long week and, as time went on, he was trying desperately to convince himself that things between him and Sasha had been good while they had lasted onboard Ocean Magic. But as a couple, they were obviously not meant to be. She had his number, but she hadn't called. Therefore she was clearly not interested in him anymore, not even as a friend. Out of sight, out of mind, Geoff told himself day in, day out, but not for him.

Every day that passed, his feelings became stronger. The yearning he was feeling for this woman he barely knew was becoming unbearable. With her mind-blowing figure, gorgeous features, and those piercing green-blue eyes which made the tropical Caribbean look cloudy, she was not that easy to forget.

Back at work, the lads had laughed and joked about Geoff having had the time of his life with several 'hot' females lining the decks in their skimpy bikinis.

'Well, you must have been up to something, Geoff,' said one of the guys at the fire service where Geoff worked. 'You look burned out, mate. Get it? Burned out?'

'That's hilarious,' Geoff had replied, having heard the joke countless times.

'So come on. Tell us. Did you meet a rich old widow who swept you off your feet? Or wasn't there even a spark of romance?' one of the other lads joked.

'But never mind. It'll be worth it when she leaves you everything she owns in her will,' said another.

'Or did she simply meet an old flame?' said a voice to his right.

Geoff spun round. 'Shut up, you idiot!'

'*Ooooh.* I see we had a sense of humour transplant whilst getting a facial in the spa,' were the last words spoken before Geoff pushed one of his work colleagues up against the wall and threatened to shut him up personally.

He gazed at his friend for five or ten seconds, then slowly took his hands away, an expression of contrition on his face.

'Sorry.'

It had been a tough week all round. Now a little worse for wear, he backed away and ordered another pint of Stella.

'Cheer up, Geoff.' His old friend Brad sat down at the bar stool next to him. 'You look like you've got the weight of the world on your shoulders. Hey, I know what will cheer you up.'

Looking at Brad, as if to say don't even think about it, Brad called over to Naomi Waterman. 'Hey, Nom's, have you met Geoff? He's available.'

'No, I don't believe I have,' Naomi replied, making her way across the room in her skin-tight red dress and black stilettos. Her breasts were so much on display; she might as well not having been wearing the dress.

'*You bastard,*' Geoff said under his breath, smiling as Naomi approached.

'You'll thank me later,' Brad said, as he left the couple alone.

'So you're the fireman?' Naomi began.

'Yes, and what is it you do?' Geoff asked, thinking pole dancer, stripper, or something worse perhaps.

'I'm a waitress,' Naomi replied. Her tone was flirtatious.

Thought so, Geoff mused, *although not in any regular coffee house establishment, I shouldn't think.*

'I work at Harvey Nichols, in the wine bar on the top floor.'

Seriously, Geoff thought. *That can't be for real.*

'Oh great,' he replied. 'It's nice up there. Good selection of cocktails,' he continued, not knowing what else to say.

'So what does a girl have to do around here to be bought a drink? A lap dance perhaps?'

Ah, I knew it, Geoff thought, laughing to himself.

'Sorry, how rude of me. What can I get you?'

Naomi ran her fingers up and down Geoff's thigh. 'I'll have 'Sex on the Beach'.'

His eyes narrowed.

'No, just kidding, lover. A glass of wine will be fine, thanks.'

Geoff gently removed Naomi's hand and placed it on the bar. 'Red or white?'

She planted a kiss on Geoff's left cheek. 'You choose darling. I'm easy.'

'Okay. Red it is.'

'So what do you want to do after this?' said Naomi.

'I think bed would be in order, don't you?'

'Hmm. Your place or mine, honey?' Naomi whispered into Geoff's ear.

'I meant to *sleep*, and on my own. It's late. In fact it's nearly four.'

'Spoil sport.' Taking his pint glass out of his hand, Naomi moved in between Geoff's legs and kissed him passionately on the lips. 'You don't mean that.'

'That's a bit forward,' Geoff said, reaching for his beer.

'Not as forward as this,' Naomi replied.

She put his beer glass on the counter, pushed it out of reach, then took him by the hand and lead him out into the car park. He resisted a little at first, then slowly took his foot from the brake.

A gleaming Mercedes was parked twenty yards away. She found a key fob and popped the doors as they approached. The courtesy light winked on.

'Jump in,' she said. 'We'll go to my place.'

Geoff hesitated, then slid into the passenger seat and watched as Naomi slipped in behind the wheel.

'Better start your engine,' he said, buckling up.

Chapter 17

It was the smell of freshly baked pancakes that awoke Geoff the following morning.

Oh shit. Where the hell am I? Were the first thoughts that came to mind. *And who the hell was I with?* Were the thoughts that followed seconds later.

Reaching for his clothes, Geoff dived back under the covers as a rather undressed looking Naomi entered the bedroom with a breakfast tray for two.

'I'm not hungry,' were the only words Geoff could force out.

'Nonsense,' said Naomi. 'After last night, you must have worked up an appetite.'

'Last night?'

Naomi nodded and smiled.

'Look, about that...' Geoff began, '... I was really, really drunk. I'm not this kind of guy. Normally, that is.'

'And what kind of guy is that?'

'You know what I mean.'

'No. Maybe I don't. Why don't you tell me?'

'Okay. The kind that goes around picking up random women and sleeping with them. You have to believe me. It's just not me.'

'Yes, yes, sweetheart. I believe you, really I do.' Naomi smirked and patted Geoff's hand. 'That's what they *all* say.'

'No, now that's unfair, I don't. Seriously, you have to believe me.'

'So how was it for you, Geoffrey?'

'I don't know. I don't remember, do I?'

'Don't you?'

'No.'

Naomi burst out laughing. She was clearly enjoying every second of watching this gorgeous hunk squirm like an eel in her bed.

'What? Tell me?' said Geoff. 'What is it? What's so goddamned funny?'

'Your face, that's what. Look, Geoff, we *didn't* sleep together last night. By the time we got home, I knew you were in no fit state for anything of the sort. I offered you the spare room, but you insisted you wanted to sleep in the double bed. So I took the spare room.'

Geoff rolled his eyes and breathed a sigh of relief.

'Oh, thank God.' He looked up sharply. 'Sorry, I didn't mean it like that. I just couldn't remember anything, that's all.'

'And you can let go of the duvet now. You still have your boxers on. I helped you out of your shirt and jeans only to make you more comfortable. I had no other intentions, believe me.'

Geoff gazed at her for a moment, then nodded meekly.

'Thanks,' he said, accepting a mug of strong black coffee whilst hinting with his eyes that maybe Naomi should think about covering herself up at little.

Naomi laughed. 'I know. I only did that to scare you.'

Well it worked, Geoff thought to himself. *Damn, I'm going to kill Brad when I see him.*

* * *

Arriving at Horizons Fitness Suite at 10.00am, Sasha took a deep breath and entered the terrifying building. There were people everywhere panting and sweating. It was so abnormal. Masochistic. Why would anyone do that to themselves?

Short of a conversation asking her to take out a gym membership, she got very little information from the incredibly fit – not to mention rather attractive – blonde haired guy behind the sales desk.

'Now this may seem a little strange,' she said, launching into it, 'but I've come here to get the phone number of one of your members. Or an address. Either is fine.'

The good-looking blonde behind the desk smiled back at her. He had a nametag on his t-shirt that read: ANDY.

'Sorry,' he said, 'but that information is confidential.'

'Confidential?'

'DP.'

'D-what?'

'Data Protection.'

'Oh. Well his name is Geoff ...' Sasha persisted.

It was obvious from the blonde's reaction that he knew Geoff, maybe even on a personal level, but for confidentiality reasons he maintained that he couldn't release any details of his customers.

He smiled. 'Like I said. Data Protection.'

'But no one would know.'

'*I'd* know.'

'I wouldn't tell anyone.'

'Same here. And that's why I can't tell you.'

Sasha gazed at him for a full ten seconds. He was as immovable as the Rock of Gibraltar, and almost as tall. It was clear that she'd get a better response from an answerphone.

'Okay,' she finally replied, opening the door. 'Thanks for your help.'

'You're welcome. And let me know if you'd like a membership form sent out. You're in great shape, but we could all lose a few extra—'

But that was all she heard. The door was closed and she was gone.

Walking back towards her car, Sasha continued racking her brains for any other information Geoff may have given her while they were away. She leaned against the door and closed her eyes and concentrated. Seconds later there was a noise beside her. Movement. Someone running. The fit young blonde guy was hurrying in her direction.

'Why are you so keen to track Geoff down?' he said.

'What?'

'I mean, if he wanted you to know where he lived, he would have told you, or at least given you his mobile number.'

'Oh.'

Pulling her phone from her bag, she showed it to the guy named Andy. He studied the display.

'The thing is,' she said, 'the number is missing one digit.'

'You don't think that maybe he did that on purpose?'

'I don't know. It wasn't like that, he left in a rush. That's why the number is wrong. And anyway, he could have punched in any old number. But he punched in his own. He just left one number out, that's all.'

'He left in a rush? Really? And why do you think that was?'

'Look, you obviously know him. So can you help me or not?'

The blonde guy gazed at her and nodded.

'Yes, I can help you. Hold on, I'll give him a call and ask him if he wants you to have his number. Would that do?'

'Yes.'

'Right.'

Overcome with excitement, Sasha's feelings were quickly replaced with a nervous churning in the pit of her stomach. All of a sudden she didn't know what to say. On the one hand, she was still mad at Geoff for giving her the wrong phone number and not calling her. Maybe he'd had second thoughts, and now she was about to make a huge fool of herself in front of a complete stranger. But on the other hand, she didn't care if Geoff didn't want to see her. At least, she needed to hear it from him. She would accept that.

Andy took out his own phone and from memory keyed in a number. There was a pause, and then they connected. Andy gazed at Sasha and said what he had to say to Geoff.

'Yes, I know her,' Geoff replied. His voice was audible to Sasha, but tinny. 'How does she know you?'

'She doesn't,' said Andy. 'She came into the gym hoping to get your number, so I offered to call you in case she was a lunatic stalker or something. She does have that look about her.' He smiled at Sasha to show that he was joking. 'I've told you before Geoff, you can never be too careful.'

Giving Andy a friendly knock on the shoulder, Sasha's face broke out into a grin, this was looking very hopeful.

'Do you want to talk to her then?' said Andy, thinking about Cilla Black on *Blind Date*. 'Or should I just give her your number?'

'I'll have a word now,' said Geoff. 'If you don't mind. I need to apologise for something.'

'This all sounds a bit suspect,' Andy said before handing the phone to Sasha.

Sasha smiled and put the instrument to her ear.

'Hello? Can you hear me, Geoff?'

'Hi. Yes. It's good to hear your voice.' Geoff sounded genuinely excited to be talking to her. 'How have you been?'

'I've been okay, thanks. And you?'

Geoff told her how much he had missed her and said that he *had* called, but her ex fiancé wouldn't give out her mobile number. Sasha leaned back on the car and made herself comfortable. Ten minutes later, Andy was beginning to look bored.

'Look, Sasha is it?' he said, shoehorning in on the conversation. 'This is all very nice, but I have to get back to work. Any chance I can have my phone before the Second Coming?'

Sasha looked up at him and remembered that he was there. She nodded.

'Geoff, look, I have to go. Andy needs his phone back before the world comes to an end. I know your number now, so I can call you later. Okay?'

'No, Sasha. Give Andy his phone back and wait right there. I'm on my way home, so I'll come past and see you.'

'I'll be waiting.'

Geoff turned to Naomi. 'Change of plan.'

'What's that darling? Change of plan? Or change of heart? You do want me after all, don't you? Hang on and I'll pull over at the next hotel.'

'Not exactly what I had in mind,' Geoff replied. This woman really was wild. 'I need to go to the Horizon Gym on Jacob's Street. It's not far from here.'

'You want to go to the gym after last night? Oh honey, I really don't think that is wise. You need a nice meal and an early night. That's what I think anyway.'

'I'm meeting someone there,' said Geoff.

'A woman?' Naomi asked, raising an eyebrow.

'Yes. It is actually.'

This should be fun, Naomi thought to herself. I wonder what kind of woman Geoff would be attracted to. Even as the thought entered her head, they turned the final corner. Ahead was Sasha. Watching his face light up as if he was a kid on Christmas morning, Naomi guessed exactly what kind of woman floated his boat.

Geoff climbed out of the car and ushered Naomi out of sight. Sasha caught only a glimpse of the twenty something's long blonde hair and definitely 'surgically enhanced' breasts popping out over her bright green camisole vest top.

Not one to miss an opportunity, Naomi circled the car park at ten miles per hour, then lowered the passenger window before blowing Geoff a kiss and thanking him for his company last night.

'It's not what it seems,' Geoff protested.

'It seems fairly obvious to me what she meant. Who is she?'

So all this 'I'm not ready to move on', 'I'm still not over my ex fiancée' was a complete and utter load of bullshit, Sasha thought to herself. One minute she was on cloud nine, the next she felt like she had been knocked over by a bus—or a Mercedes convertible, as luck would have it.

'Sasha, look at me.' Geoff said. 'I don't know who she is, honestly.'

'Well, you know, Geoff. You really shouldn't hitchhike. It's not safe.'

'Listen, sweetheart. I'll explain everything later, I promise. There's no point in us starting a relationship off on the wrong foot. You can trust me, okay?'

Watching his friend from the reception window, Andy cringed. Man, I would not want to be Geoff right now, two hot women on the go at once, can't figure why one dropped him off to meet the other though, never mind enough excitement for one day better get back to work.

'So what do you say, Sasha? Are we going to give things a go?'

'It depends what you have to tell me about what you got up to last night?'

'And I will.' Geoff promised while beating himself up inside for accepting a lift from Naomi, *Seriously why did I not get a cab then she'd be none the wiser.*

'Look, I have to go right now. I'm meeting my mum for coffee and – believe me – the mood she is in over my break up with Ben, unless you want the coffee thrown over you, you had better stay clear, for now at least.'

'Say no more,' Geoff replied, wondering what he would do with his afternoon.

'Listen, it seems we are living even closer to each other now than we were. If you are free tonight, you could come over. I'll cook us dinner, say around seven o'clock?'

'Sounds great, but you have to promise to give me the right address.'

'See you at seven!' Geoff replied, kissing Sasha on the cheek.

Desperate to go in for the real thing, he thought he had better wait until last night's story was out of the way. Only then would he truly know if Sasha wanted to be with him.

'You're on time.' Geoff smiled, as he opened his apartment door his stomach doing summersaults, which was nothing, compared to how Sasha was feeling. 'I'm impressed.'

'Of course.' Sasha handed over a bottle of red wine her hand shaking slightly with nerves. 'Mmmm, something smells good.'

'Well, I hope you *are* hungry. We're having Beef Bourguignon with glazed vegetables and pont-neuve potatoes.'

'Very nice' Sasha said, accepting a glass of wine. A little calmer now, why she didn't feel this way earlier when she had set eyes on Geoff for the first time again in ages was beyond her.

'But, first we need to talk.' Geoff led Sasha into the lounge and turned down the stereo to be sure of getting her full attention.

She sat and made herself comfortable and gazed at him.

'Well,' said Geoff, 'first things first.'

'Yes.'

'About last night.'

Sasha pressed her lips together momentarily.

'Look, Geoff. It doesn't matter,' she said. 'We weren't together. You were a free agent. You don't have to explain anything to me. Really.'

'Well, that's very kind, but Sasha I need to you to know nothing happened. I promise you.'

'And I believe you.'

'Okay. Well, that was easier than I thought it would be. Are you sure you don't want to ask me what happened, only I might be a little vague with some of the details, but I promise you we didn't sleep together.' Unable to stop himself rambling on, Geoff continued speaking. 'She made me believe we had, but it wasn't true. She came clean this morning. We even slept in separate rooms. There, that's it all out in the open.'

Taking a deep breath, Geoff stood up from the leather sofa and announced. 'Now for something a little more exciting.'

Sasha watched as he walked over to his sideboard, and collected an envelope. Handing it to Sasha he said, 'Go on. Open it.'

'Are you sure?' Sasha asked, placing her wine glass on the coffee table.

'Yes.'

She opened the envelope and read for a moment, then looked up.

'That's wonderful Geoff,' she said. 'I can't believe it. I'm so pleased for you.'

'I know.' Geoff's face lit up. Topping up Sasha's wine glass, he asked, 'so, how about it? You were the one who put my name into the prize draw that day in the gym, so I think it's only fair you join me on the cruise of your choice.'

'Well, it's certainly something to think about. Cheers.' She added. 'Have you ever been to Italy?'

Lightning Source UK Ltd.
Milton Keynes UK
UKOW02f1258070115

244093UK00003B/56/P